REDEEMING JUSTICE

Justice Brothers
Book 3

Suzanne Halliday

Edited by www.editing4indies.com
Book Cover Design by www.ashbeedesigns.com
Formatting By Champagne Formats

ISBN-13:978-1500442668
ISBN-10: 1500442666

Other Books by Suzanne Halliday

BROKEN JUSTICE
FIXING JUSTICE

Dedication

I am blessed to have been raised in a home where reading and the love of books surrounded me. It fed my imagination and nourished my soul in ways that I'm only now beginning to understand. Everyone read, even my dad, but the greatest influence came from the quirky women in my family.

To my unique and hilarious grandmother who used to bring us stacks of magazines after she'd read them. And that was before recycling was a trend!

To my mother who read everything she could get her hands on and who gladly took me to the library at the drop of a hat. I still have an ancient copy of *The Prince and the Pauper* held together with masking tape – the corners well worn from my youthful fingers devouring every page. It reminds me of her and the way she encouraged me to read, read, read.

I miss both those irreplaceable women more than words can convey.

Thankfully ~ the tradition continues
To my fabulous, wonderful, unique and totally bad-ass daughter without whom absolutely none of this would have happened.
~You Are My Sunshine~

And finally, I dedicate this book to my readers with love; I appreciate and thank you for allowing the Justice Brothers to be a part of your lives.

Prologue

"MAJOR, YOU REALLY DON'T have to do this," the quietly efficient Army nurse told him with a look of exhaustion etched on her face. They'd been together most of the day as he endured the endless rounds of tests and excruciating physical therapy necessary to repair his shattered body. Feeling a little bit like Humpty Dumpty, Major Alex Marquez wondered if all the military doctors and a slew of skilled therapists could ever truly put him back together again.

Even though the military casualty office had handled the death notifications for the men and women under his command after the suicide bombing that had come perilously close to claiming his life, Alex was driven by unseen emotional forces to contact each and every family member or next of kin for the list of names he kept in a notebook next to his hospital bed.

So much more than a duty, it was an ethical obligation that defined the man he was. Every one of those names represented a human being, a person who at the time of their death had been Alex's responsibility. In his mind, it was his unequivocal duty to speak one last time for and about the good people who had given the ultimate sacrifice in a fucked-up war that didn't seem like it was ever going to end.

"Actually, yes I do Blake. As their commanding officer, it's the only thing left that I can do for them." He eyed the nurse through the heavy pain medication that made his brain fuzzier than he was comfortable with. When she nodded silently and stepped back to let him struggle with the pen and paper she'd brought, he knew she'd seen the determination in his gaze and probably the torment too. She was military through and through, and he didn't doubt for a nanosecond that she misunderstood what he was getting at.

From practically the moment he'd regained consciousness after the blast that had flattened his command post, Alex had focused on those who hadn't survived. Instead of concentrating on his own nearly fatal injuries and the long road of healing and convalescence ahead of him, he'd obsessed over the list of deceased. Reading and re-reading it over and over until he could recite each person's name by rote, the command officer in his conscience struggled to deal with the senseless loss of life.

His commitment to the men and women who lived and died by his side was without compromise. Bloodshed, death, and acts of true heroism and selflessness played out in his mind each time he closed his eyes. The public didn't know what war was like on a day-to-day, minute-by-minute basis. But the troops on the ground understood all about living with the dust, heat, and unrelenting fear. Afghanistan was nothing short of hell on Earth and as long as he lived, Alex was never going to escape the repercussions of his time there.

"Has the mail come in today, Blake?" he asked with a labored sigh. Letters from home and the half-assed correspondence he looked forward to from members of his former squad were the only bright spots in his days. He hated the hospital atmosphere, hated the constant reminder that his Special Forces days were effectively over now that he was held together by pins and skin grafts. If not for the love of his parents and sisters, he might have succumbed to the unrelenting emotional trauma that went hand-in-hand with almost being blown to bits.

It was his buddies from the Justice Squad though who really made the difference. Bonded forever through an initiation of fire and blood, Alex held tight to their friendship. Before he'd been promoted to a command position, he'd been just another Special Forces hotshot. Fighting, eating, sleeping, and surviving together created a strong family-like bond that kept them all sane in an otherwise chaotic existence. Together with Cameron and Draegyn, he'd held himself together through a shitload of fuckery that would probably haunt him forever. They were like the Three Musketeers – inseparable and very much living all for one and one for all.

When he got out of this medical nightmare, whenever that proved to be, Alex had decided that come hell or high water, the three of them would be together again. He had a huge spread of land in the Arizona desert where they could escape the fucking war and build a new life. Thanks to the military, they each had skills and talents that were unmatched and would be in high demand in the world of private security and counterintelligence. Might as well put what they'd learned to good use once they were all back in the civilian world.

Nurse Blake gave him something that was supposed to look like a smile. She wasn't an idiot. No one who had to deal with the wounded coming back from the war zones was. She knew damn well that he relied on those letters to keep him sane almost more than he needed the endless parade of doctors and specialists who jigsaw puzzled his body back together.

"Rest assured Major, I will make sure you get your mail before the hour is out. You okay while I go check?"

Alex nodded even though the fucking morphine they pumped into him made the motion more of a wobble. "Thanks Blake. If you weren't a butt kicking Army nurse who could crack my skull with one hand, I'd kiss your ugly ass."

She laughed and patted him on the shoulder. "Said like a butt fucking ugly Special Forces shithead. Hold that thought and I'll see what I can do."

THERE WAS NO DOUBT about it. Meghan O'Brien loved sunshine. When the story of her life was written, surely there would be a notation about her love hate affair with the sun. Being a fair complexioned Irish beauty meant she'd learned to be clever about protecting her skin. Tilting her head skyward, Meghan felt a mass of auburn curls tumble down her back the same second the blazing sun lit up her face. Both sensations were delicious and made her sigh. As she stood there absorbing the invigorating energy, she closed her eyes and concentrated on her other senses.

Pressed up against the side of an SUV, her butt was warmed from the heat of the desert Southwest radiating off the vehicle. It was an oddly pleasant feeling that helped alleviate some of the tension in her back from long hours spent behind the wheel.

There were muffled voices from the people in the roadside rest area where she'd stopped for a break. Kids laughing. Parents yelling. *The usual*, she chuckled. There was even the low bark of a big dog and the dull rumble of an idling motorcycle.

She clutched a very cold bottle of water in one hand, while the other rested on the door handle. Her inner teacher's voice fed fast facts into her thoughts making Meghan grin. *Vitamin D is primarily synthesized in skin exposure to UV light and is essential to healthy skin.* The grin became a laugh. Some things won't ever change.

Where a year ago she'd known exactly what she wanted to do and how she wanted to live her life, today she was in a curious limbo. At the age of twenty-eight, her résumé was a study in perfection. Bachelor's degree in Education followed by a Master's in Kinesiology. Every job known to mankind in those two fields; camp counselor, fitness trainer, motivational coach, gym teacher, licensed massage therapist—she was a respected member of the Belmont Circle School District faculty where she'd been assistant athletic director. Not bad for being a girl in a man's field.

She was also loud and proud, a true Irish Daughter of Boston and was more than capable of taking care of herself. Having three brothers taught Meghan how to navigate the world of men. She was competitive by nature and didn't cry when she lost. With a straightforward, take no shit attitude, her students liked her, and the parents and her fellow faculty members respected her. Life had been damn good. She had no complaints and while the idea of finding a guy she could put her faith in, someone she could trust, was a shining ideal, she was content living alone as a successful professional.

And then it happened. One day, one very *ordinary* day, she'd been nesting at home, cartons of takeout food on the table as she hunkered down with her Kindle to catch up on some reading when the phone rang and her entire life changed.

Meghan, along with five colleagues from her school, had pooled their money and purchased lottery tickets that had incredibly won them a mega jackpot. That phone call had done more than change the direction of her life. With the staggering amount of money she suddenly had, the mortgages on her parents' and brothers' homes got paid off and a sizeable trust fund established for her nieces and nephews, ensuring that each of them would have the money for college when that time came.

With the job market being such a tough place for educators, Meghan reluctantly stepped down from her position so someone else could have the chance to chase their dreams. She didn't want to stop working, but others immediately started showing signs of jealousy and disdain for her and her fellow jackpot winners. Hanging onto a job when she didn't need the income was only inviting judgment.

The midday heat starting to make her clothes feel heavy and uncomfortable got Meghan moving into the driver's seat of her shiny, new SUV on a reluctant sigh. As much as she enjoyed basking for a few minutes in the relentless Southwest sun, it didn't take long for her to throw in the towel once the heat took over. Starting the engine she flipped the A/C to low and took a long, slow pull off the bottle of chilled water, settling comfortably into the plush seat. The car had been her first big purchase. She'd felt giddy at the freedom of having unlimited options and went a little crazy when it came to all the bells and whistles.

All that stuff, from the navigation system to the satellite radio and heated seats, had come in handy though. On a whim, she'd packed up her apartment, put everything she owned in storage, and headed off on a cross-country road trip. *Because she could.* That was three months ago.

In that time she'd traveled from Boston to Seattle then down the California coast, stopping at every giant wind chime or world's largest whatever along the way. Putting her teacher skills to creative good use, she'd been taking thousands of pictures either with her phone or the fancy digital camera she loved, designing digital scrapbooks with a running commentary of her adventures.

While in California, her mother had flown to join Meghan for a weeklong spa retreat and a sweet mother-daughter bonding experience. Maggie O'Brien was everything Meghan hoped she'd be one day; smart, loving, fiercely devoted to her family, and possessing a wicked streak a mile wide. They knocked back a couple of bottles of Jameson Irish Whiskey during their ten days together laughing like schoolgirls, and at night she would sit at her mother's knee like she had as a child, listening to her mom's calming voice as she smoothed Meghan's curls.

After California, it was time to get back on the road, which was what brought her to this rest stop along old Route 66. This portion of her American adventure had been the most fun she'd had. The rich history turned her on. The desert Southwest was so incredibly beautiful that she pulled over constantly to take pictures.

Tonight she'd be in Flagstaff, where she planned to stay for a few days. After that it was a slight detour south toward Sedona and a visit she'd been thinking about for a very long time. More than five years in the making, she would at long last be meeting face to face with a man she barely knew who had been uncommonly kind to her during a dark time. Knowing that his kindness came during a difficult period in his own life, she'd always hoped to share her enormous gratitude in person. Now that the opportunity was upon her, Meghan was excited and a bit apprehensive too.

It had felt so forward and pushy to tap out an email that basically said - *Hey, I'm in town and inviting myself over to your place for a visit* – but that was what she'd done. *Well,* she thought as her SUV pulled onto the highway, *the deed was done.* Now the stage was set for whatever came of her impulsive desire to settle an emotional debt that only meant something to her.

ALEXANDER VALLEJA-MARQUEZ WAS FIT to be tied. Depending on which hat he was wearing at any given time, whether Spanish Don of inherited nobility or retired Special Forces Commander or senior partner in a prestigious security agency, or friend, he was a handful at the best of times. When he had an itch up his butt though, he was a fucking nightmare to deal with. And he knew it. But frankly, knowing didn't slow his roll for a second.

The agency's summer calendar was fully booked for the season making the Marquez Villa and surrounding Justice Agency compound a bustling mini-town of activity. It was their busiest time of year and with both his partners slightly distracted by personal matters, Alex had assumed a bigger role in overseeing day-to-day agency operations.

As out of sorts as he was, that didn't stop Alex from a moment of happiness recalling the unexpected chain of events that found two of the three Justice brothers married and with babies on the way. As if Cameron's life-changing romance with his ponytailed wife wasn't mind-boggling enough, the approaching birth of their first child had blown everyone's mind. And then there was Draegyn who was also a married man with a baby on the way. Never in a million years had he thought any of them would be the happily ever after sort.

Snorting in disbelief for the thousandth time, Alex left the dimly lit tech cave where he spent the majority of his time and made his way to the tiled walk leading to the pool. Zeus, his constant companion and the only female to speak of in his life, trotted along amiably at his feet. At least the dog seemed to like him.

He was heading for the pool to work off an excess of nervous energy that was tying him up in knots. With the non-stop agency activity to keep him busy you'd think he wouldn't have time for wandering thoughts, but pretty much the only thing he could think about for the past couple of days had been an email from someone he'd known briefly during his special ops days. Back when he ordered people into danger, then was the one to tell families about their son or daughter's brave sacrifice.

That last awful day of his command not only ended his military career, it was when the families of more than a dozen soldiers and civilians he was responsible for had gotten bad or devastating news. Even though Alex had been one of the severely wounded, he hadn't shirked his responsibility as the commanding officer in charge to write personally to each family. It was the least he could do, and while it did nothing to ease the black mark left on his soul from that day, it did serve as a reminder of his own humanity, something that came perilously close to being lost in the months before and for a long time afterward.

One of those he wrote to was the fiancée of a young soldier who hadn't stood a chance when the bomb went off. He'd been surprised when she replied, sending a long heartfelt letter about her fiancé and how much he loved every minute of his time in the service and respected his C.O. At the time, Alex was struggling through months of endless surgeries, physical therapy, plus mental and physical anguish that were stripping his soul. Her letters had been the start of a brief pen pal exchange. By the following year when he was stateside again and starting to build a life outside the military, they'd remained Christmas card pals but nothing else. Until she emailed him out of the blue and said she'd be in the Sedona area soon and could she come by for a visit.

Could she come by for a visit? Alex had been flabbergasted. It wasn't every day that a ghost from the past came a-knocking. Even though they'd never met, she still reminded him of an awful time. Then he remembered how friendly and sweet she'd been during his long convalescence – sending long chatty letters full of everyday details that helped take his mind off the pain and his weary spirit.

She'd intrigued him with her straightforward outlook, refusing to wallow in self-pity for her loss. He liked that. She wasn't a crybaby. For reasons he didn't want to mull over, he sent her a holiday card every year that she always reciprocated. It was an unusual friendship without detail or substance.

And that was part of the problem. The idea of finally meeting her was rattling his cage. What did you say to someone whose future was destroyed by his decisions and actions?

Kicking his pants off and reefing his t-shirt over his head in one smooth motion, Alex dropped it on the deck and dove smoothly into the deep end of an enormous lap pool. A dozen slow, measured laps later he felt a little better.

Deciding it was no big deal to entertain someone from the past, he tried to calm his nerves by concentrating on what the visit should entail. He'd talk to his housekeeper, Carmen, and tell her to expect company. He wouldn't have to do much more than that. Carmen would take care of everything – it was what she did best.

Alex relaxed and let the water take him away. They agreed she'd text once in Sedona so he could give her detailed directions to the Villa. There wasn't anything else to do now except wait for her to contact him. The slow burn of excitement in his groin unsettled Alex more than it should. It was just a visit. This was a courtesy call, nothing more. Why did he feel so anxious?

MEGHAN WAS PRACTICALLY JUMPING out of her skin she was so nervous. It was unlike her. Nothing really rattled her cage. She had her brothers to thank for that. She couldn't even count the number of times she'd been a victim of one of their pranks until she learned the fine art of sibling retribution. The three of them would think twice nowadays about tangling with her. Paybacks were a bitch and something she was extremely good at. She giggled at the thought.

This nervousness had everything to do with the man she was driving to meet. Major Alex Marquez, age thirty-six, former Special Forces commander who now operated an exclusive security agency based near Sedona. He had been her fiancé's commanding officer. When David had been killed in a bombing attack on his base in some God-forsaken corner of Afghanistan, she'd received a beautiful letter from the Major.

Now, here it was five years later, an entire lifetime removed from those awful days, and she was on her way to finally meet the man who touched her emotions during a confusing time. She'd Googled him of course, hoping to find a picture but he seemed to be something of a recluse. The only shot she found was one of him in full battle gear on a soldier's blog. She might not know what he actually looked like but she knew he had been deeply respected by his men.

As she drove along following the detailed directions in her navigation system, a surge of anxiety ripped through her. What the hell was she doing? Was she out of her friggin' mind? It suddenly seemed awfully pushy and forward to just announce she was showing up on some strange man's doorstep.

Okay. So he wasn't some random stranger but that didn't mean she knew him well enough to sashay her ass into his home for God only knows what reason. *Oh shit*, she thought. What if he was married? Had a family? *Damn!* She hadn't considered any of that before now. Meghan winced, the soft sound cutting through the silence in the car. Was she about to make a huge fool of herself?

Well, it didn't matter. This was about her putting the past to rest once and for all. Somehow, meeting Major Marquez and personally thanking him for the thoughtful letters he'd sent had come to symbolize the closure she needed. Losing David had been dreadful. Many people had shared her pain. He was a beautiful human being who shouldn't have been blown to bits in some Afghani shithole. But there were other things, deeply personal things that she, as his fiancée, needed to get over.

The universe had given her this amazing opportunity to redefine her life and she wasn't going to squander the gift. But before she could determine a direction, the past had to be dealt with. She didn't want to drag unnecessary emotional baggage along on her journey.

Being from Boston, something she found thrillingly surreal during her time in the Southwest was how one moment she was driving along a highway with other cars, and the next she was on a long stretch of flatland with only the occasional vehicle going by. She liked how it felt though, this driving along, the satellite radio thumping out classic rock as she sang, sunroof open, speeding down a deserted highway—gave new meaning to the expression Zen driving.

When she came to where the navigation system said she should turn, Meghan stopped the car and turned the music off. It was absolutely open and desolate and so breathtakingly evocative of the desert Southwest that she had to snap a few pictures.

The road she was to take had a wide Spanish-style arch and a length of fencing down either side of the turn off. She saw an inconspicuous keypad at the entrance and wondered whether she should announce her arrival until she caught sight of a small red light indicating a sensor of some sort. Maybe a scanner. She was, after all, heading into a security zone. They would know she was coming long before she got to the end of the drive.

From the turn off it took several minutes to reach the main drive-way to the Villa, another long drive that stretched on for minutes. *Well, this is interesting*, she thought. Talk about being off the beaten path.

When the Villa de Valleja-Marquez came into view, she was speechless. The main portion of the house, an enormous Spanish influenced structure, looked like it had weathered a century in the hot Arizona sun. It was every romantic thing you could envision of a sprawling colonial hacienda, from its Moorish arches and distinctive Spanish tiled roof to the vine covered trellises. She gasped in delight, pressing her hand above the swell of her breasts at the charming beauty.

The wide driveway was littered with half a dozen vehicles. Trucks, golf carts, at least one motorbike, a Lamborghini, and a sleek and sexy Mercedes that made Meghan drool a little bit. Pulling into the middle of the jumbled parking, she marked the tree-lined walkway that led to the front of the massive house and pulled herself together. This was it. Once she crossed Major Marquez off her list, it would be smooth sailing from here on out.

ALEX HEARD THE DOOR chime as he made his way from the deep recesses of the main house into the open living area, having perfectly gaged the length of time it would take her to drive up to the house once the gate surveillance announced an approaching vehicle.

He thought of an old childhood poem from *Alice in Wonderland*. *The time has come,* the Walrus said, *To talk of many things,* and smirked.

He was thinking what he really needed was an attitude adjustment as he swung the massive wood door open to greet his visitor.

Attitude adjustment delivered with a vengeance, he thought seconds later when his gaze encountered the most beautiful woman he'd ever laid eyes on standing at his doorstep. Meghan O'Brien was nothing short of breathtaking. Tall and curvy with long auburn curls and a sweet as sin mouth, she had the body of a 1950's Hollywood goddess with bountiful breasts, a tiny waist, and provocative hips. There wasn't anything about that first impression which didn't melt Alex's brain into his socks or get his manhood sitting up and taking notice.

"Major?" the red-haired beauty asked. She had the same half-assed look of shock on her face that matched his. Apparently he wasn't what she was expecting either. Sporting a beard in progress and a riot of messy, disheveled hair, Alex belatedly realized he probably looked like a bear just waking from his winter nap. So much for first impressions.

Quickly recovering his manners he offered her a warm smile, grabbing hold of the hand she offered to pull her into the cool interior of the house.

"Miss O'Brien, welcome to my home."

Alex was instantly captivated. She had beautifully arched eyebrows and sexy, cat-like green eyes above a pert nose with a mouth that made him stop and look twice. Her full bottom lip curved in a sexy pout with a well-defined cupid's bow on top. He had to stop from reaching out to touch her face to see if the pale skin felt as soft and luscious as it looked. He couldn't believe he was reacting like a hormonal teenage boy meeting a beautiful girl for the first time but he couldn't help it. She was that drop-dead fucking gorgeous.

"Please call me Alex," he murmured at the same moment her delightful sexy scent reached his nose. Inhaling sharply, he pictured open spaces with the fresh scent of vanilla and blackberry in the air. He was sure her skin would taste sweet, maybe even melt a little bit under his tongue.

Wait a minute, his mind barked. *What the fuck are you doing?* The woman was here on a social call not a date. *Grow up and mind your manners son*, he could hear his father tell him with that sardonic inflection that made every comment an inside joke between the two of them.

Don't get caught drooling over a woman, he told him once. *Gives her the upper hand.*

She smiled at him as he drew her into the large entryway with her cheeks flushing a gorgeous pink. When her face lit up she looked like an angel.

"Alex." She said his name with a soft purr. His dick instantly got hard. "No formalities! Please call me Meghan."

He was still holding her hand, and since she wasn't making any effort to disengage, he hung on, covering their joined fingers with his other hand. The odd gesture was bold and intimate.

"It's a pleasure to meet you at last, Meghan." She grinned when he said her name.

"Welcome to the Villa," he graciously declared. "It's been in my family since the eighteen hundreds, and I don't mind telling you that keeping a historic building up-to-date with modern features is a never ending challenge."

Laughing, she shook her head in understanding. "Oh, believe me, I know what that's like. My folks live in a turn of the century building, and my dad is forever grumbling about every little thing."

She looked around and gasped when the full impact of the great entryway to the mansion house opened to her view. Plaster columns supported the huge open space with a second floor balcony running the entire length of the house. An exquisite wrought iron railing framed the wide steps leading to the upper floors. A double row of windows on the front wall suggested a second story but on the inside the entire entryway was open to the height of the second floor ceiling. Moorish arches anchored either end of the magnificent entryway; it was a breathtaking space. Alex was unapologetically proud of the beautiful house. Seeing it through Meghan's excited eyes was exhilarating.

"This house is so…" She was at a loss for words.

He shrugged like it was no big deal. "Hey, it's home, y'know?"

She laughed and gave him an unexpected elbow to the ribs. "Don't be so humble, Major. Your home could easily be the feature spread in *House Beautiful* magazine." She eyed him humorlessly. "And I suspect you know that."

Alex couldn't help the delighted laugh he barked. *Yeah,* he knew the Villa was impressive. But it was kind of cool to hear someone else say so. What was also way cool was how readily his emotions responded to his unusual houseguest.

She caught sight of the vintage baby grand tucked in an alcove under the staircase and quickly hurried over to it. Touching the wood she asked, "Do you play?"

Another shrug. "Sometimes." He ran his hand along the curved edge of the mahogany piece that had been in his family for a hundred years and told her, "Mostly it's for show." Something about how her eyes shone and the way she caressed the instrument made him pause. "What about you? Do you play the piano?"

Her green eyes twinkled with merriment when she answered. "Yep! Miss Dalton's Piano School for Young Ladies. Took lessons until I was in high school."

She had one of those happy smiles that could light up a room. Alex was suddenly very, very glad Meghan O'Brien had come to visit.

As she turned slowly, taking in every angle of the grand Spanish villa, he checked her out as well. Alex's primitive side tightened as he appreciated her striking figure. Wearing a short wrap dress with a fluttery hem, the simple style accentuated her tiny waist and curvy hips. When she swung away and he saw her backside for the first time, the generous bounty of her ass caught him off guard. Choking back a groan, Alex didn't know whether to curse or thank whatever power in the universe put such a tempting sight within arm's reach.

He loved bare skin, especially legs, and she didn't disappoint. Hers were long and well-toned. He glimpsed painted toes on feet slid into a pair of kitten heel sandals. Judging by the way she moved and held herself, he suspected Pilates. Or maybe dance. A riot of rich auburn curls rolled across her shoulders standing in stark contrast to her pale complexion.

Far and away though it was her breasts that melted his brain. Men lost their shit over boobs like the ones he was leering at. Each sexy globe was a hearty handful plus some. He didn't doubt they were real. There was something natural and enticing about the way they swayed and shifted with her movements. In her pretty dress, the bouncing tits, tiny waist, and seductive hips were an invitation to a good case of thundering lust.

"Alex," she murmured, cutting through his intense perusal earning her his attention. The green in her eyes was disarming up close. He smiled. "Would you mind if I took some pictures while I'm here? It's sort of a hobby," she told him. "Your home is just so beautiful. I'd like to remember the moment."

He was bemused by the request but nodded graciously in permission. "Let's head onto the patio." Stepping into her personal space, Alex gently guided her by the elbow toward the back of the house. Being so close, he smelled the vanilla and blackberry again and remembered thinking that she'd taste sweet. The fingers of the hand against her elbow drifted up her arm teasing the soft skin he found. It was just a quick touch but enough to fire up his libido in a very big way.

"Holy crap!" he heard her gasp as their route took them through the enormous custom kitchen. "How many people do you feed with a kitchen this big?" she laughed. Her fingers drifted across the beautiful granite countertops the same way they had touched the piano. She was a sensualist. The realization sent shockwaves racing along his spine.

Tearing his eyes from her face, Alex looked around as if seeing the space for the first time. "It *is* kind of over-the-top, huh?" He smirked and shook his head. "Know that saying, *Go Big or Go Home*? Well, my designer came from that school of thought. There's a separate cookhouse and dining room for the compound. This bad boy," he gestured with his chin, "is a rich man's indulgence. Besides, I believe the kitchen is the heart of the home. It's where families gather. I wanted something that made a statement."

Meghan snorted out a hearty laugh. "Well, statement received. Loud and clear!"

Stepping with her through a tiled archway onto an outdoor patio, his guest gasped again and came to a halt. Next to his tech cave and pool, this was Alex's favorite spot. The interior patio had a massive stone fireplace along one wall while the rest of the space was dotted with windows into the various rooms of the Villa. Comfortable seating areas with large padded loungers were clustered here and there under an enormous pergola. In the middle hung a sweeping fan that kept the air moving on the hot summer day. Everything about the outdoor room screamed of his ancestral roots. It was Spanish influenced grace and comfort at its best.

He felt a surge of satisfaction that she was visibly moved by his home. Large earthenware pots and stoneware bowls planted with an abundance of greenery and colorful blooms gave the space a special vibe. Dark terracotta curved Spanish tiles on the roof mirrored those on single story sections of the hacienda while the ground was covered with beautiful stone slabs. Olive trees flanked the ornate, carved fireplace surround while all around the space were lanterns of every size and shape holding massive candles.

"This is unbelievably beautiful, Alex," she told him as a dreamy look softened her expression. "I love the Southwest." Walking ahead of him she took a few steps then turned back, genuine delight shining from her green eyes. "It's so different from Boston. Worlds apart."

She was still beaming when Alex detected a sound coming from inside the house. "I think my housekeeper is about to make an appearance," he told her with a wry grin. Shooing Meghan along under the pergola cover to shade her from the midday sun, he got her seated comfortably at an enormous wood table a second before the woman who ran his home came onto the patio.

"Hola, M*eee*ster Alex," the older woman trilled in accented English as she approached them holding a tray laden with glasses and a pitcher of something icy cold.

Plopping it onto the big table the woman fixed him with a smug grin as she eyed up his guest. At that second Alex realized his visit with a woman, a fucking *beautiful* woman, would be the talk of the compound in supersonic time.

"Thanks," he muttered feeling quickly out-of-sorts. He didn't relish having his personal life discussed. Drae and Cam would be in his face within a nanosecond if they discovered just who his visitor actually was. He was sure learning he was entertaining the fiancée of a dead soldier they all had known would open the floodgates.

Unfailingly polite when he needed to be, Alex knew his mother would be proud at how fast he recovered his manners.

"Meghan O'Brien, this is my housekeeper, Carmen."

Meghan smiled and put out her hand in greeting.

"Carmen, this is the guest I told you about, Miss O'Brien." Carmen took Meghan's hand and greeted her effusively.

"Welcome, welcome M*eee*z O'Brien! I hope you like lemonade from scratch," she told his guest as she went to pour them a glass.

"There is mint from our garden as well, if you'd like to add some to your glass."

Alex felt peeved as the two women began debating the many uses of organic mint as they fell into conversation like they were old friends. He had to admit Carmen's lemonade was, in fact, to die for, but that didn't stop him from wanting his housekeeper gone so he could have all of Meghan's attention again. Jesus. When did he turn into such a pussy?

"Oh God, yes!" He heard her laugh in a throaty chuckle that set his nerves on edge. "In Boston, it's all about the sweet tea. My mom makes gallons of the stuff in the summer."

"Maybe you can show me how to make a big batch?" Carmen asked. "The crew at the compound would love it. I can pass the recipe on to Ria, who does all the cooking around here."

Oh, for fuck's sake, he groaned inwardly. Really? Zero to exchanging recipes in less than five minutes? He would never understand women and how their minds worked. When Carmen turned her attention back to him he caught the smug grin again and made a lame attempt to stare her down. She knew him too well.

"I'll let you two have your visit. Let me know if you need anything. Ria will be here soon with lunch. Nice try, M*eee*ster Alex," she whispered so only he would hear, touching his arm as she turned from them.

Alex lowered into a chair alongside his guest and watched her as she sipped the tall glass of lemonade. His eyes took in a thousand tiny details. The way condensation on the outside of the ice-filled glass dripped onto the table. How her lips opened as she lifted the drink to her mouth. When she brushed a mass of curls over her shoulder, he spied simple pearl earrings and noted her nails were painted with a soft shade of polish. She wore no rings but had a delicate gold chain around her wrist with a small heart-shaped charm. The pretty necklace she wore, another delicate chain hung with a tiny half-moon, was just long enough to kiss the top of her cleavage. And speaking of cleavage. Holy God, hers really was magnificent.

MEGHAN WASN'T SURE WHERE to look. Her senses were inundated with so much input that she was having a hard time keeping up. The beauty and charm of the Spanish hacienda had affected her deeply. It was old worldly elegant and homey at the same time. A little like the Major himself. She'd expected a curmudgeon of a man, some caricature of how she supposed a commanding officer should look; not a sexy, slightly patrician Don of an old Spanish family. Why had she envisioned someone all buttoned up tight with a military buzz cut in the first place?

He was nothing like she expected. *Nothing.* First of all, the man was friggin' huge—like football player huge. *No one should have a chest that broad*, she thought. It invited all sorts of thoughts like how wonderful it must feel to snuggle into it. *Oh good lord*, she silently groaned.

And secondly, this was no boy she was looking at. The thought made tingling sparks of awareness shoot along her nerve endings. Used to younger guys, they all seemed like men-in-waiting compared to him.

Dressed in a button-down shirt with the sleeves rolled back that stretched perfectly across his shoulders and molded to his massive chest, it disappeared into a pair of charcoal grey trousers that made his trim waist, flat stomach, and muscled thighs gloriously obvious.

As if a body that would make a supermodel swoon wasn't enough, he had a face that horny teenage girls dreamed of. Rugged looking and hot as hell, Alex Marquez had brown eyes sparkling with a devilish glint of wickedness in a face covered with a beard that wasn't sure if it was a week without shaving or actual facial hair that was there to stay. The hair on his head was longish and adorably messy, like he'd just run his hands through it a moment before he opened the door. She wanted to lean into his massive body and run her fingers through his tousled hair. *Uh oh.*

Ordinarily, it pissed her off when guys stared at her breasts. She'd developed a mocking leer for those who had the gall to ogle her public-ly. But there was something spine tingling about the Major's bold gaze that made her panties damp. He certainly wasn't making any effort to hide his appreciation of her ample bosom. Shockingly, Meghan felt her nipples harden as she fought back a telltale groan.

Luckily, the lemonade his housekeeper made was super yummy and just what her parched throat and idle hands needed. After a couple of good slugs of the icy treat, she put her glass down and tried to pull her wayward thoughts back in line. She was here to check off an item of closure on her to-do list, not get all moony-eyed and giggly over a hot guy.

"Thanks again for agreeing to see me, Alex." Crap. Could she sound any lamer? She was a teacher, goddammit! Nothing scared her, not a gym full of teenage testosterone or a Latin Hercules. *Get your act together*, she chided silently. *Stop acting like a twit.*

The devilish twinkle in his eyes wrecked her brain when he smiled. "It's been a long time coming, wouldn't you say?"

Did he just ask if she took a long time coming? Wait. No, that was not at all what he said. Oh my God. She was losing it. Meghan sat back in the chair and crossed her legs earning her bare limbs an appreciative glance from the man who was scattering her thoughts.

And then the dynamic shifted. The reminder of how they knew each other and the long years between their initial contact and this beautiful sunny day settled around them. Meghan could feel the anguish rolling off him the minute he remembered. She didn't feel the torment quite like she used to. But then again, she hadn't been there that day when a bomb-carrying civilian had killed so many and sent others, Alex included, to the hospital. That was why she was here. Time to put things in perspective and finally leave the past where it belonged—the past.

She hadn't planned what to say, preferring to let the moment unfold as it was meant to. All she hoped to bring was the authenticity of her feelings.

"Your letter saved me, y'know. Really. It did," she added when she saw his jaw clench and the twinkle disappear from his eyes. "David's parents were distraught, and I didn't know what to do to ease their suffering. You see, he was an only child. Not only was he not coming home but the family they prayed he'd have waiting for him would never be. I think that was the hardest part for them. They already treated me like a daughter. Knowing all their hopes and dreams were crushed tore me up."

"What about you?" he asked somberly. "What about your hopes and dreams? Losing the man you were going to marry must have been devastating."

She saw vulnerability and something else she couldn't identify flash across his expression. How could she explain that all was not how it seemed? Should she even tell him that part? Lifting her shoulders in an awkward half-shrug, she sighed, watching the clouds drift slowly by overhead.

"I was so young and despite the engagement, we hadn't started planning a future together. David proposed on the spur of the moment while he was home on a leave. Who knows how the future would have unfolded if things were different."

She hoped her voice didn't give too much away. Even after all these years she struggled to keep the spirit of David's memory intact. Honoring his sacrifice was more important than her feelings. There would be no closure for her on that score.

"I still have it—the first letter you sent." He seemed shocked to hear that from her. Didn't he know how important the words he shared with her were?

"That makes you uncomfortable. I'm sorry," she added quietly.

It was his turn to down a healthy guzzle of lemonade. When he was finished and set his glass down, he looked at her. "Writing those letters was damn hard. I can't imagine why you'd keep something like that."

By force of habit, Meghan reached for the tiny crescent moon dangling from the chain around her neck. Absently sliding it on the chain as her thoughts reached into the past, she remembered that autumn day, months after David's military funeral, when a big white envelope had arrived, postmarked from Germany with the letter his commanding officer had personally written.

She wasn't surprised to learn of the high regard in which her young fiancé was held. The boy she knew all her life had grown into an honorable man who took serving their country seriously. To this day she didn't really know what he did when he was off playing with the Special Forces. David had one of those high level clearances that suggested he was more involved with gathering intelligence than being boots on the ground.

Meghan had wept over that letter. Hearing praise of his bravery and courage and David's devotion to the canines he worked with had gone a long way to calming her heart.

"I kept it because what you wrote were things I needed to hear. Not just then, but for a long time after. So…thank you."

He didn't say anything for long moments. When he did respond, she was surprised by what he said.

"I have your letters too."

She turned wide, surprised eyes on him, shocked to hear that what she'd written during his long months of rehab had been any more than something to distract him from his injured body.

"Why?" she asked dumbfounded. "They were so—" She searched for the right word to describe what she knew were the inane ramblings of an overworked grad student. "God. I don't know. So, dumb and boring!"

He chuckled and some of the building tension eased off. "Well, I'll give you that!" he teased. "But dumb and boring was just what I needed."

She nodded, understanding what he meant. He'd kept her up-to-date on his condition with blunt assessments of his progress or lack thereof. Meghan knew all about the endless round of surgeries that pieced him back together and the exhausting, painful physical therapy that had followed. They'd written to each other for months, and then briefly for a time after he'd been moved back to the states.

She didn't know what he was thinking, but it was probably the same as her. Learning that she'd had as much an impact on him that he'd had on her was quite a surprise. Everything got quiet again after that.

Carmen chose the perfect moment, right before the silence got uncomfortable, to reappear on the patio pushing a cart laden with dishes and an impressive bouquet of fresh flowers stuffed in an oversized mason jar.

"Lunch has arrived," she chortled with glee as she eyed them upon her approach. "I hope everyone's hungry," she said with a good-natured huff. "Ria got crazy with the fruit again."

Crazy was an understatement, Meghan thought when Carmen plunked an enormous stoneware platter on the table overflowing with every fruit imaginable. The presentation was impressive. Mounds of strawberries and slices of kiwi were piled high alongside melon slices, bananas, apples, berries of every color, orange sections, and loads of pineapple spears. A second platter was piled with small sandwiches and assorted tapas that also looked beyond delicious.

"I hope you like it," Carmen offered as she set out plates and utensils for their use.

"Are you kidding?" Meghan laughed. "I love it! Especially the part where someone else prepared and put it ready-to-eat on a platter. Does *not* get any better than this!" The two women roared with laughter.

She sat side-by-side with the Major for the next hour, picking away at her lunch, chatting amiably about everything and nothing. With each moment that passed, she found herself wishing the visit wouldn't have to end. Alex Marquez was not only one seriously good-looking guy; he had a quick mind and a pleasant sense of humor. Meghan couldn't remember ever being so instantly drawn to another person as she was to him. The realization put a fluttery feeling in her belly that extended deeper into that place inside which was wholly female and undeniably turned on.

Eventually he asked how long she'd be touring the area and what her plans were.

"Here's the thing," she told him with a grin. "I'm not on any kind of a schedule, which I know sounds odd, but that's the way it is."

He seemed intrigued by her answer and asked for clarification. *Ah. Time to 'fess up. This should be fun.*

She sat up straight and pushed her hair over her shoulders. "Okay. Reader's Digest version in the interest of time. You already know I'm a teacher. A gym teacher at that!" she chuckled. "Hold the lesbian jokes, please."

He nearly choked to death when she made the statement. Judging by the quick leer her boobs got she highly doubted he fancied for even a second that she played for the home team.

"Loved my career. Loved the school I taught at. Loved everything about it. Then one day last year, me and five colleagues hit a mega lottery jackpot."

His stupefied expression was funny and exactly how she felt when she first learned of the lottery windfall.

"I certainly never wanted to quit teaching, but with the job market so brutal for educators, it was the only thing I could do. Even though working is about way more than the salary, I couldn't hog a coveted position when I didn't need the money."

He nodded. Not working or putting her skills to good use was something she still hadn't come to terms with. It was true what they said about money not making happiness. Sure, life got comfortable and secure but the rest was still an open book with many pages left to fill.

"In April, I started off on an epic road trip that I wouldn't have missed for the world. This is an amazing country. Watching it go by under my wheels rather than from the window of an airplane has been amazing. Anyway, made it to the Pacific then traveled down the coast to L.A. My mom flew out for a ladies' spa retreat that was to die for! And now here I am, traipsing around the desert, checking out every world's largest tin foil ball and award winning tamale I can find!"

"So you're....*what*? Wandering aimlessly?"

"You could say that, I suppose. The teacher in me treats every day like an extended field trip. Thank God for the internet. I'm learning so much. Besides the Grand Canyon of course, I hope to stick around

Sedona long enough for the annual Cowboy Festival."

"You mean the one at the end of July?" he asked. "I remember from when I was a kid. Loads of gun slinging fun."

She blushed and studied her feet. If only he knew. Cowboys were a special passion from her childhood. Having brothers meant there was always some kind of boy fun happening. She'd spent many a fantasy filled afternoons joining in, pretending to be Annie Oakley or a fierce pioneer woman. In her mind, a man in jeans with a cowboy hat was all kinds of sexy. Especially if there was a horse involved. *Squee!*

"So, I take it this means you plan on staying for a while?"

"Well, there's no reason to run off so I guess the simple answer to that is yes."

Alex watched his next words form in a speech bubble that surprised him as much as it did her. "I'd be more than happy to be your guide, Meghan. You could stay at the Villa. It's a busy time so there's tons of stuff going on right here, plus all the things to see and do around Sedona."

He wasn't at all sure what made him say it except that he was enjoying her company. More than he could remember enjoying anyone else's. It was an odd place to be. He knew her. But then again, not really. Maybe that was why he put it out there. He wanted to get to know her—a whole lot better.

When the thought popped in his head, so did the thousand reasons why he shouldn't be thinking shit like that. Especially not about her. *Fuck.* What did it say about him that he couldn't keep his dick under control around a woman who had every right to hate his guts? After all, if it weren't for him, she'd probably be married now with a kid, a dog, and a mini-van parked in the driveway.

Still, she was just so damn beautiful. He knew caution was in order but a raging case of desire was driving him at the moment, complicating the shit out of things.

She was squirming in her seat, making the hem on her dress creep further up her thighs. Pretending that a fully loaded question wasn't hovering in the air, Alex watched her fuss with the mass of curls falling around her shoulders as she chewed on her bottom lip and looked everywhere but at him. In his mind's eye, he grabbed her around the waist to pull her decadent backside onto his lap. He bet she'd fit perfectly against him.

"Major," she squeaked then corrected herself when he frowned. "I mean, Alex. *Really.* I don't know what to say. You're so sweet to ask me to stay but I don't think that's what you had in mind when I invited myself to lunch."

Well, that was certainly true but once the door opened and he saw her standing there, all sense flew out the window. "Honestly Meghan. I didn't have much of anything in mind. Meeting you was enough and now that I have, well…" he shrugged.

"I want to say yes. I mean, look at this place! Who wouldn't want to stay? But I can't ask you to drop everything and be my tour guide. Are you just being nice? I don't understand."

Alex learned a lot about her just then. She spoke her mind and didn't beat around the bush. She was also completely unaware of her effect on him.

"I'd like it if you'd stay for a while." That was all he said. Frankly, he didn't understand either.

"Alex," she growled.

"Meghan," he answered right back. "C'mon. It'll be fun. Think of it like summer camp for grown-ups! Do you ride?" he asked. "We've got horses and electric carts and ATVs and even Segways. You haven't really lived until you experience a campfire cookout, and I can hook you up with one of those knock-your-socks-off helicopter tours of the Grand Canyon."

"Aaargh!" she growled even louder this time. "You're making it impossible to say no."

"Well good! It's settled then." He turned toward the house and yelled for Carmen who appeared before her name completely left his mouth. He shook his head knowing she'd probably been eavesdropping on the entire conversation. The housekeeper's look of complete innocence struck him as mildly funny.

Getting her back for earlier he murmured so only she could hear, "Nice try, lady." She grinned at him and chuckled.

"Uh, Carmen," he boomed so there'd be no mistaking that he was taking control of the situation. "Miss O'Brien will be staying with us for a while."

"Alex!" Meghan cut in.

He stopped any further words with a look. This was one battle he was going to win.

Carmen tried not to look surprised but failed miserably when she asked if she should open up the Casita where friends and family normally stayed, only to hear him instruct her to put Meghan in a guest room in the family quarters. Near his room.

And just like that he'd arranged for Meghan's luggage to be brought from her car into the main house while she sat there slack jawed as he started issuing orders like the commanding officer he once was.

CARMEN SCURRIED INTO THE house to do her boss's bidding, feeling rather pleased that he was doing something so uncharacteristic. He liked his solitude and his privacy. Not only was it unusual for him to invite anyone to stay over, it was twice as unusual for a guest to stay in the main house and not down at the Casita.

The minute she made it into the kitchen she found Lacey and Tori dropping off a stack of paint chips for Alex to look at. The wives of his two Justice brothers had convinced him that the offices and conference rooms needed some sprucing up and since he couldn't say no to either woman, they were taking full advantage of the situation.

"Hola Carmen," Lacey trilled sweetly. "Cómo estás?"

Carmen hugged both women and gave each of their tummies a little pat. At nearly seven months pregnant, Lacey Cameron glowed the way every happily expecting mother-to-be should. Not to be outdone though was Tori St. John. For being such a tiny thing, she was carrying her pregnancy like a champ but not without some difficulties. A few months behind Lacey, soon there would be two babies in the Justice brothers' family, and no one could have been more delighted by the prospect than Carmen.

Tori noticed that Alex wasn't alone on the patio and asked what was up. Carmen grinned like a schoolgirl when she announced, "He's got a guest. A *woman*." The emphasis she placed on the word *woman* got the pregnant ladies dashing for the archway leading to the patio so they could check out what was going on.

"Holy shit!" Tori giggled, peeking from behind a large antique pantry next to the doorway. "Quick, Lacey! Look. I think he's smiling."

"Ehrmygawd!" Lacey laughed aloud. "Who is she?"

Both sets of eyes turned on Carmen expecting an explanation of the situation.

"Well, I'm not sure where she comes from but I do know her visit rattled the M*eee*ster's cage. She's been here for a while. They had lunch together and talked. Next thing I know, he's telling me she's staying."

"Really?" Lacey asked. "Is she going to be in the Casita? I loved that little house," she added dreamily as an afterthought.

"Actually, no," Carmen replied.

"No?" the ladies chimed in unison.

"What does that mean exactly?" Tori questioned. She'd been working as Alex's assistant for months and anything outside his normal mode was going to pique her curiosity.

"What that means ladies is this. Alexander Valleja-Marquez just instructed me to put her in a guest room in the hacienda. So what do you think about them oranges?"

"It's apples, and I think flabbergasted covers it nicely, thanks," Lacey mumbled looking at Tori with a sly smile. Suddenly, both women had a burning need to run home and see what their husbands were up to. Carmen laughed knowing the earful the other two Justice brothers were about to get. Poor Alex.

With Cam and Drae joyfully married and babies on the way, only Alex was still clinging to the ridiculous notion that he didn't deserve to be happy. Carmen would never understand why any of them felt that way but she knew enough about their Special Forces experience to accept that dark shadows from the past sometimes made it hard to see the light.

MEGHAN WAS ASTONISHED HOW quickly and easi-ly Alex had maneuvered her into staying at the Villa. Truth was, she hadn't been all that difficult to convince. At some point during their time on the patio she'd started feeling more than just a little bit drawn to the handsome man with the mussed hair and broad shoulders.

She didn't have a type, the way most women did. Maybe it was because she came from a family dominated by men that she had simple tastes when it came to the opposite sex. Alex Marquez hit so many high marks she didn't know where to start.

He was large which was a plus. As a healthy Irish girl with more curves than straight edges, she felt like a hippo next to men of average height who wore skinny suits and looked like they got the occasion-al facial. His athletic build turned her on, plain and simple. He was also well-mannered and didn't take himself all that seriously. More big pluses in the win column.

And then there was the subtle undercurrent coming off him that made her think all kinds of wicked thoughts. He was what the girls referred to as a dominant. She could feel it in her bones. It wasn't overt—more like an aura of control that really got to her. She bet he was the type of man who would simply say, *get in my bed,* and a woman would eagerly crawl on hands and knees to comply.

The room she'd been given was tucked behind the master suite in a section of the hacienda that retained its original rustic colonial character and was so far beyond charming that it needed its own descriptive word. When he'd walked her through the enormous house and up the wide stairway to the second floor, Alex had kept a light hand on her, just above the swell of her backside. The gesture made her senses tingle.

As a card carrying *Ball Busting Boston Bitch,* she would be the last woman to get weak kneed over some big muscles and aristocratic manners. Right? Suddenly she didn't know. He made her feel ridiculously female and that was saying a lot. Despite being a curvy girl and a gym teacher to boot, Meghan had always been über feminine, the result of being the only girl in a large family dominated by men. As a little girl, most of her silly whims had been indulged. All outward appearances suggested she was a girly-girl. But it was that *BBBB* upbringing that made feeling small and female all the more surprising.

"What do you think?" she heard him ask softly. They were standing across from the bed where Meghan was peering out a window aware that when she leaned forward, her derrière would be making a statement. A big one.

What did she think? Wow. That was a loaded question. Think about what? How friggin' good he smelled? Or maybe how she felt about the romantic room with beams across the ceiling, a corner fireplace surrounded by ancient stone, and a platform bed draped with rich-hued linens? Better yet—what did she think of her well-laid plans to finally find some closure on the David chapter of her life? The Major exuded a fierce masculinity that made her forget why she was there in the first place. *What in the hell was she doing*?

Turning to look at him, she wasn't in the least surprised to find him admiring her ass. And he didn't flinch or pretend that wasn't exactly what he'd been doing. It felt like a challenge in some way. *Oh my God! Why was the thought so exciting?*

Coughing to clear away the sudden constriction in her throat,

Meghan smiled unsteadily. "It's so cool," she gushed like a teenager. *Oh for crap's sake,* she screamed in her head. *Really?*

"Um, it's really something is what I meant to say." Okay, good. That sounded better. Maybe she could actually pull off pretending his presence didn't turn her into a giggly twit.

"The door to the bath is behind the fireplace in that corner." He nodded toward it with his head. "I know it's small, but I thought you might like the rustic feel."

"Are you kidding?" she joked. "You call this small? I think my childhood bedroom would fit in the closet! It's perfect, Alex. Really. Thank you again for opening your home to me. I'm touched."

He smiled at her, and she saw the wicked glint come back into his eyes. Unless she was losing it, he was attracted to her. But she knew without question that he wouldn't act on it. No. There was an ocean of water between where they were now and the end of that particular bridge, but it was reassuring to know she wasn't alone in the unexpected attraction.

"My guys will bring in the stuff you need from your car. If you want to get anything else, let me know. I don't want you trying to lug anything up here."

He looked around and seemed a bit uncomfortable like he didn't know what to say or do. God, he was so adorable. She knew what he was feeling and wondered how she should respond.

Yep. This was certainly an interesting position to find herself in. When the day started, she had plans to settle an old debt with an afternoon visit that would let her close a chapter in her life once and for all. Period. End of story. She expected to wake up tomorrow and be ready to charge ahead.

What she hadn't expected was to not even get through the afternoon before life started throwing shit her way. And by throwing shit her way she meant putting one gorgeous hunk of a man in her line of sight. Unfortunately, she was her own worst enemy when it came to being careful—another by-product of keeping up with her brothers. Besides, *careful* didn't seem to feel quite right in this situation. There was nothing common sensible or careful about what she was feeling.

"Thanks again," she told him as she leaned in to press a kiss on his cheek. It probably wasn't necessary to lay a hand on his chest for balance, but she did it anyway. The heat coming off him was incredible. She bet he'd work up quite a sweat in bed—something she wouldn't mind licking off his body. *Yum.*

When she touched her lips to his face he grabbed her other hand, holding it firm at her side. He was either going to push her away and put some distance between them or he was holding her in place. A flood of heated moisture drenched her core when he held still, keeping her hand upon his chest and her body close to his for long seconds after the kiss ended. She swore he could hear her heart thumping—that was how loud it seemed in her head.

Before releasing her, he turned his face into her curls and breathed deep. She held her breath at the intimacy of the action.

"I'm very glad you're here Meghan O'Brien."

When she pulled back and looked at him, they were close enough to touch. She sensed his reluctance when he ran a trembling finger across her bottom lip. Disappointed that he hadn't kissed her, Meghan thrilled when he dropped a quick smooch on her nose, squeezed the hand he still held, and told her in a husky voice, "Very glad."

THE MINUTE ALEX LEFT his unexpected houseguest to get settled in, he headed for the tech cave where he could pretend to be busy while working out his thoughts about what was happening. There was no denying he was wildly attracted to the Irish beauty. Hell. When she bent over to look out the window he had to hold himself back from stepping up to rub his growing erection against her magnificent ass.

But he also knew that acting on the lusty feelings she evoked was just not going to happen. Not in this lifetime, anyway. He didn't do relationships. Even if once upon a time he'd envisioned finding a wife and starting a family, those days were long gone. Gone and buried many times over in the stench-filled, putrid remains of that mother-fucking war. It would take all of this and possibly many more lifetimes to atone for the part he played during that time. Redemption was not certain, was in fact highly in doubt. Some things were just so fucked up that trying to make any sense was a waste of time.

There was no good use in pretending that Meghan O'Brien wasn't just about the most gorgeously sexy and desirable woman he'd known in his entire lifetime. He'd been without a woman for a while, but he knew without question his response to her wasn't a case of simple horniness. It didn't mean that he had to act on that desire though. Wanting to sink his dick into the fiancée of one of his dead soldiers was a step so far beyond what his conscience could take that it wasn't funny. She was seriously off-limits. There was no fucking way he could handle anything less. He might be a bastard, but he wasn't that messed up.

Dammit. A drink was what he needed. Maybe a bunch of 'em. Anesthetizing his brain was a priority if he hoped to avoid taking a long, slow trudge down memory lane. Somehow though he doubted he'd be lucky enough to keep all that shit at bay while she stayed at the Villa. *Fuck.* Even right this second he was blocking the visual memory of her fiancé, the guy his old squad nicknamed The Kid. It wouldn't help to resurrect that particular ghost. Besides, there were plenty more where that one came from.

A little while later his trusted assistant Tori, who was also conveniently the wife of one of his Justice Brother partners, wandered into the tech cave.

"Hey Boss," she hollered across the room. "Did you see the paint chips Lacey and I brought you or did you ignore them?"

Alex eyed her as she scooted around stacks of hi-tech equipment making her way to his cluttered corner. Watching the little whirlwind, he had to admit that there was no mystery why Drae had fallen so hard and so fast for the feisty little woman. She was a piece of work, this one. Even though the two of them snarked at each other from time to time, her unabashed love for Draegyn St. John was apparent to everyone. His friend was one lucky son of a bitch.

Helping her into a chair, Alex smiled down at her. "How's the bump today?" Seeing her little round tummy restored his faith in humanity.

Tori giggled and rubbed a hand all over her protruding belly. "She's rocking and rolling today. Takes after her daddy. Restless energy."

He barked out a laugh. "I hope if it is a *she* that the precocious pink princess drives her daddy batshit crazy. Serves the old fucker right." They both laughed.

"*So*. Anything new with you?"

Alex wasn't stupid. He knew a neat segue to another subject when he heard one. The innocent tone in Tori's voice told him the gossip train had already left the station and made at least one stop. He wondered how long it would take before Drae came knocking too.

"Tori St. John – you would *so* flunk Private Investigator 101," he told her with a wry shake of his head.

"For real?" She laughed. "Aw, come on!" Their laughter filled the air. "How 'bout this instead? So. Alex. Who's the woman in your guest room? That any better?"

That was why he liked her. She had a take no prisoners approach to life. He hoped Drae knew to watch himself around her. She'd incinerate his ass if he were ever stupid enough to step out of line.

"I plead the fifth," he joked.

"Don't be mean to a pregnant woman," she teased while making a pouty face.

"What is it you want to know, woman?" he barked in mock annoyance.

Tori laughed in his face. "For Christ's sake Alex. Two simple questions! *Who* is the woman, and *why* is she in a guest room and not the Casita? There! Was that direct enough for you?"

"I'm going to have to speak to your husband about that smart mouth of yours," he grumbled.

She snorted in amusement. "Good luck with that! Now answer the damn questions or I'll get Lacey up here too, and we'll tag team you till we get answers."

"Fuck," Alex groaned. "I *knew* letting women in the compound was a mistake."

Patting her tummy for emphasis she stuck her tongue out and sneered, "Too late for that, don't you think?"

It was an old joke that never failed to get a laugh. The three of them—him, Draegyn, and Cameron—had been living in bachelor heaven until ten months ago when Lacey came on the scene followed shortly thereafter by Tori. In a neatly precise one-two punch, each woman had taken down one of the lone wolves of the Justice Squad. Only Alex was left now.

Sighing, he grabbed a rolling stool and pulled Tori's legs into his lap. "Your feet are awfully swollen little lady. Didn't the doctor tell you to slow down a bit and spend more time off your feet?" He slipped her flip-flops off and began rubbing her soles.

Tori sighed and grumbled, "I'm going to be huge in another five months!"

It pained him to hear her distress. She was going to be a wonderful mother, but her pregnancy wasn't going to be an easy one. He knew Drae agonized over her condition. After all, she was just a tiny little thing, and her growing belly was starting to look completely out of proportion to her small frame. She was going to need all of them to get through the months ahead.

They sat there like the oldest of friends as he rubbed her swollen feet and she caressed her baby bump. He was happy for Drae—and Cam too. They both found incredible women to stand by them. He sometimes wished that his future held something similar, until he remembered why it couldn't.

In the bluntest of terms, the burdens he carried from his time with the Special Forces didn't play nice with the everyday world. How exactly did one explain the nightmares and the bloody dreams reliving moments of hell and agony? How did you justify a botched nighttime raid or the collateral damage it caused? How did you tell a young woman that her fiancé didn't come home because of a crazed suicide bomber?

"You do know a foot massage isn't going to distract me, right?"

Alex switched gears, from deep introspection to lighthearted in a heartbeat. "It was worth a try, wasn't it?" He grinned.

"Out with it or I swear…Lacey…speed dial!"

"I surrender," Alex chuckled. "Her name is Meghan. She's a teacher from Boston. As for why she's not in the Casita, well…..she just isn't."

Tori sat forward and planted a huge smacking kiss on his lips obviously in approval. "I love you Alex Marquez!" she trilled. Sliding off the chair, she slid her feet back into the flip flops and headed for the door. Apparently, now that she had her information, she was done with him.

Waving over her shoulder she told him, "I'll have Carmen set enough plates for a family dinner." And with that she was gone.

"Fuck my life," he groaned as his eyes squeezed shut. A family dinner? *Shit.* How the hell was he going to explain who Meghan was and why she was here to Cam and Drae?

THE DINING ROOM WAS full of lively conversation and about a dozen people when Meghan made her way downstairs. Carmen had been in and out of her room multiple times throughout the afternoon, making sure she had everything she needed. When the housekeeper let her know that Family Justice would be gathering for dinner, she suspected she was about to be put on display.

Luckily the Hispanic housekeeper was also a fountain of information, which gave Meghan a grasp on the immediate cast of characters. There were Alex's two partners, Cameron and Draegyn, and their wives, Lacey and Victoria. In addition to Carmen there was the cook Ria, plus her husband Ben who was some sort of property manager. Betty, the woman who ran the business end of things, would also be there. Then there was Gustavo who took care of the horses and all the riding vehicles. Meghan got the impression Carmen had a soft spot for Gus. There was also Brody Jensen, the guy who trained the agency's guard dogs.

She also now knew that Brody was in residence all summer until the winter holidays, that Carmen lived nearby in town, that Cam and Drae lived on the property in their own houses, and that Betty had an apartment above the business center. Ria and Ben had renovated the old stable master's house where they lived year round. One big happy family that Meghan was now in the middle of.

The second she started down the steps, Alex appeared at the bottom to escort her in to the dining room. She was glad she'd changed into something less casual the minute she saw his eyes light up. Wearing a 1950's style dress with a halter top, cinched waist, and full skirt, she skipped down the steps and pulled up at his eye level.

"Major, you look dashing," she told him as her eyes took in the crisp white shirt and black trousers he wore. He'd made some kind of effort with his hair but it was so out of control it was hard to tell. The beard, however, stayed. She'd never kissed anyone with facial hair before. *Wait*. What? Had her thoughts actually gone there? Good Lord.

He smiled into her eyes for a brief second before slapping a neutral expression on his face. "C'mon Meghan. Come and meet the family. You look fantastic, by the way." She stumbled slightly at the sound of lusty appreciation in his voice but managed a quick recovery. When he put his arm out for her to slip her hand into, she almost died. Everything about his demeanor screamed *gentleman*.

"Everyone," he rumbled as soon as they got close to the gathering of people. "This is Meghan O'Brien. She's visiting from Boston." Short, sweet, and to the point.

To Meghan he said, "I'd make them all wear name tags but I suspect the teacher in you knows all about remembering who's who."

He took her around the room after that, introducing her to everyone. They were an uncommonly friendly bunch that clearly had a bond with and affection for each other. Especially for Alex who came off as the Big Daddy of the group. Meghan was deeply conscious of the emotional tie they all shared.

She'd have to have been blind not to notice a bit of eyeball hockey going on between Alex, Draegyn, and Cameron. It was interesting to watch—rather like a conversation that only they could hear. Meghan knew who they were of course; David had spoken of them all. Especially Cameron. She wondered if Alex had told them yet how he knew her. Until she got some indication that he had, she wasn't going to bring any of that up.

Dinner was off the charts good, as was the company. Hearing that she planned on doing some exploring while she was around, everyone chimed in with suggestions and told her what to definitely avoid. Gus even offered to give her a few riding lessons so she could take one of the horses out. Meghan couldn't believe it. Maybe she was finally going to live out her cowgirl fantasy. The thought made her giddy.

After dinner, everyone headed to the patio ablaze with the warm light of a dozen candles. Even though it was July, a small fire crackled in the fireplace since the evenings took on a chill in the desert once the sun went down. It was such a warm and friendly gathering that Meghan felt she'd known them forever instead of having just met that day.

Alex let her wander off to chat with others and didn't try to dominate her attention, but he did keep his eyes on her. She knew this because every time she glanced in his direction, she was aware of his gaze locked on her like a tractor beam. It was….well, it was disconcerting and thrilling at the same time.

Eventually, people started drifting away until just Cam and Drae remained along with their wives. This was the inner core of Family Justice. The brothers. Meghan had an easy time remembering David's words. He'd written so often of the three men and their fellowship. It certainly was an odd quirk of fate that found her here with all of them.

"Meghan," Tori said. "Alex says you're a teacher. What do you teach?"

"I would be the gym teacher!" She laughed at their startled expressions.

"Well shit," Cam snorted. "I'd have actually gone to class if my teacher looked anything like you!"

Lacey elbowed him and pretended to look peeved. "Oh great!" she dead-panned. "Hot for teacher much?"

Meghan grinned when Cam swatted his pregnant wife on the butt then kissed her soundly.

Drae moved closer to the fireplace and sat down with Tori on his lap. They looked adorably cute, his hand resting on her bump while she sat with her arms around his neck.

"I thought about teaching as a career," Tori told them. "But honestly, with my temper, I'd rip some kid's head off for being obnoxious on day two." Her frankness got a chuckle from everyone.

"It's not all that bad," Meghan assured them. "It's tough being a kid these days. They grow up way too fast. But teaching isn't all I do." Alex looked up when she made that pronouncement.

"When I'm not trying to get our nation's youth up off the damn couch and away from their portable technology, I do motivational work with athletes. Fitness training and stuff like that."

"For real?" Alex asked.

She chuckled. "Yeah. Why so surprised? Not a girl's job?"

"Oh, fuck no! That's not it at all. I'm intrigued."

She had his full attention so she fleshed out all that she did. "Well, in addition to my teaching certification, I also have an advanced degree in Kinesiology. You'd be surprised the demand for my services and not just for athletes. How the body moves in space goes well beyond sports and recreation. A lot of big corporations are heavily invested in wellness programs for their employees. Now that I'm not teaching in a school, I've been thinking about doing some freelance work in that field. Last year I earned my certification in massage so, if nothing else, I can always put my talents to good use in a rehab center."

"Before you go and do anything like that, let us know," Draegyn told her. "We've been talking about getting a trainer to help with the agency programs. I'd be interested in hearing your opinions on how best to make that happen."

"Sure. I'd be happy to share my expertise. With the ladies too!" Turning her attention to Lacey and Tori she asked, "What kind of exercise are you Mommy's-in-Waiting doing?"

"Yoga," Lacey told her with a grin. "It helps a lot."

"My exercise?" Tori snorted. "It's called lugging this bump around on my tiny frame. I want to try some yoga but Lacey's coach is booked solid."

"Well, this is your lucky day. I'd be happy to get you started on an easy routine that you both can do right through the end of your pregnancy."

Looking at Lacey she asked, "May I?" with her hands open asking for permission to touch her big belly. "I can probably tell you what position the baby's in."

"Really?" Lacey asked, her eyes shining with delight. "Well, then get over here and tell me what junior is up to."

Meghan laughed as she pulled Lacey upright and told her to stand with her back against her husband's chest.

"Junior, huh? Do you know it's a boy, then?"

Cam interjected, "No, we don't—because my wife wants it to be a surprise." He kissed the side of her face good naturedly as Lacey settled against him.

Meghan rubbed her hands together and then began gently running them over the pregnant belly. She mapped out the position of the fetus then asked Lacey if she wanted to touch her baby's head.

"Oh my God. Are you serious? You can tell that?"

"I have the magic touch and yes, I'm serious. *Here.* Give me your hand." Meghan took the woman's trembling fingers and placed them on her belly at the top of the baby's head. "Head," was all she said. Moving Lacey's fingers lower, she pushed them into a cupped position and pressed against her belly. "Butt," she informed the astonished pregnant woman.

Just like that something smacked against Lacey's belly on the other side making her flinch. "Oooh. He likes having his tushy rubbed," she joked. "I suppose that was a foot kicking me in the ribs."

"Dad," Meghan asked. "Wanna try?"

Cam's astonished expression was all kinds of cute. He looked shell-shocked, the way all pregnant fathers do, but he reached out with his hand and let her press his fingers against his baby's head. "Wow," was all he said as his wife turned her face into his neck.

Glancing away from the loving interplay between the expecting parents, she found Alex looking at her with an unreadable expression.

Catching Tori's eye she told her, I'll show you some yoga basics tomorrow if you're up to it. Will help with those swollen feet."

Drae chimed in at the mention of the swollen feet. "Is yoga okay with your doctor, honey?" he asked his wife tenderly.

Tori snuggled into his chest and rumbled, "Mmm hmm."

Drae laughed and gave her a big hug. "And that my friends is how the wife reminds her husband that it's time for bed."

It wasn't long after that before it was just her and Alex, alone again, on the patio.

WATCHING HIS BROTHERS BUNDLE their pregnant wives off to head for home, Alex felt emptiness in the area of his heart that was becoming all too familiar. He wasn't jealous of what they had as much as he was envious. How had those two managed to get so damn lucky?

"They're good people," he heard Meghan say. "David talked about you guys. I think he had a bad case of hero worship for Cam. Would they remember him?" she asked quietly.

He went and sat next to her on the wide sofa and reached for one of her hands. He wasn't sure why he did; maybe he wanted to comfort her although it was more likely that he just needed to touch her. She had the softest hands imaginable. He wondered how her velvet touch would feel on his skin—how could he not?

"Yes, Meghan. They'd remember him."

"You didn't tell them who I am, did you?"

"No," he answered quickly. "But I will."

"I hope having me here doesn't make them uncomfortable."

"No. They're not like that. They really liked David. He was one of them, if you know what I mean. Cam and Drae will want to take care of you once I tell them. There's a reason why so many Vets have worked here in the compound. We look after our own."

She nodded and changed the subject, gently pulling her hand from his. "Your leg is bothering you, isn't it? I can tell so don't bother with denials."

She shocked him with her dead on assessment. His leg was fucking killing him.

"Let me guess," she went on. "You don't bother with anti-inflammatory meds and prefer to tough it out. Am I right?"

He nodded with a self-deprecating smirk. "I fucking hate drugs." The half roll of his shoulder said this was a familiar defense. "Or maybe it's….I hate fucking drugs."

"Hmmm," she said. "Understood and duly noted. But you do know there are other things you can do to take the edge off, right?"

"I swim and that helps a lot but when it aches like it does tonight, well….," he waved his tumbler of scotch in her direction.

"Do you have a Jacuzzi?" she asked.

"Uh. Yeah. Of course."

She smirked at him. "Ever get *in* it?"

"Not so much," he replied.

"Well Major, your treatment plan should include liberal use of water therapy to keep the muscles from seizing up. That's what's causing your discomfort. The way you stand tells me a lot."

He chuckled and swallowed the end of his drink. "Woman, are you for real? Gym teacher, coach, trainer? Is there anything you can't do?"

"Well I can't ride a damn horse but Gus says he can help with that! But don't change the subject. Jacuzzi. Warm water. Your ass in that water. Was there anything about that you didn't understand?"

"Are you disrespecting my awesome ass, Miss O'Brien?"

"I most certainly am not, Major." She had a sly smile plastered on her face.

The whiskey was making his hard edges melt. He'd consider crawling into the hot tub if she did too. The idea of seeing her delicious body in a bathing suit fired up his brain and made the decision for him. "I will consider the Jacuzzi if you'll join me."

"Deal!" she squealed with delight.

"You wanna go grab a suit or are you the au naturel type?"

She burst out laughing at his audacious suggestion. "I've got three brothers. There's no skinny-dipping going on, sir! Not unless you want your ass kicked by a couple of Boston's finest; two firemen and an EMT. Feeling lucky?"

He was grinning at her. She was fun to flirt with. "Oh, fuck no! I've got too much respect for first responders to be dumb enough to tangle with any of 'em. Especially not over a naked sister in my hot tub. Go grab a suit and meet me back here, okay?"

She got up and dashed for the house telling him she'd be back in a hurry. Well, this was certainly turning out to be an interesting evening.

ALEX WANTED A FUCKING medal for minding his damn manners and for keeping his hands away from Meghan as they sat in the tiled hot tub next to the pool. His reaction to her in a bathing suit had almost turned embarrassing. When she appeared in a white halter styled one piece he didn't know what was worse, her magnificent tits or the curvaceous masterpiece that was her hips and ass. Both were wreaking havoc on his sex drive.

All but diving into the hot tub to hide his growing hard-on, he went to help her over the side and thought he'd been zapped when she put in her hand in his. Relaxing was no longer an option. Not while his cock danced in the warm, swirling water, and she looked like some pale skinned goddess in the moonlight. Maybe this wasn't such a good idea after all.

She'd put her curls up in a clip so they wouldn't get wet and all Alex could do was stare at her neck like he'd never seen one before. How he kept from sinking his teeth into her skin and sucking on the exposed flesh was a complete mystery. He wondered if she knew what she was doing to him.

"This is nice," she sighed with her head against the rest at her back. "Is it helping with the stiffness?"

Oh, for fuck's sake. She was referring to his leg but the only stiffness he could concentrate on was the one that wanted to be buried inside her.

When he didn't answer, her head came up and she looked at him with a worried frown. "Is everything alright, Alex?"

There were a bunch of options open to him at that moment. He could pretend everything was just dandy. Or he could claim his leg needed some attention. He could even fake a miraculous recovery, but he doubted she'd be fooled. Not after what he knew about her impressive qualifications. He settled on an option that wiped all the other ones clear off the slate.

Pulling her onto his lap in one smooth motion, he wrapped her in his arms and pinned her to the spot with a look. To her credit, she didn't shy away from the heat he knew was blazing in his eyes.

"I've wanted to do this since the moment you walked through my door."

He heard her small whimper as his mouth closed in. There was a warning bell going off in his head but the tsunami of desire swamping his senses muffled the sound.

Meghan couldn't move. And she could barely breathe. Being dragged onto the lap of a very aroused and incredibly sexy male instantly shut her brain down. *Shit.* It had practically taken an act of God to peel her eyes off Alex's athletic body when they dropped their towels and got in the hot tub. Seeing him in a pair of indecently tiny swim trunks, she hadn't missed the patchwork of scars and distressed skin running the length of his torso and one leg. The unexpected impulse to kiss each old wound shook her up, big time. *What the hell?*

Ten hours ago, give or take a few, she'd knocked on his door thinking she would zoom in, get the closure she hoped for, and zoom right back out. She had in no way anticipated sticking around as a guest, or drooling all over him in a hot tub.

She felt his hand move to the back of her head, his fingers speared into her hair spreading wide against her skull as his lips got closer and closer to hers. *Holy shitballz.* He'd wanted to kiss her since the moment she walked through his door? Really? *Oh my fucking God.* She might have been embarrassed by the moan of want that escaped her throat if not for the searing look of male satisfaction on his face.

His lips were soft, confident. Nibbling her bottom lip as he angled her head just so, she shuddered when his tongue licked the seam of her mouth. This was not going to be an ordinary kiss.

The sound of the churning water filled the air, broken only by her groaning, "Ahhhh," when his mouth closed over hers.

Wow. There was no way she'd ever been kissed like this before. He was so manly about everything he did, including devouring her mouth. Until that moment, she'd only known the kisses of boys if what he was doing to her was any indication of how a grown man went about things. It was like a movie kiss. Hot. Deep. Perfect. And that beard. *Oh my God*, it felt as good against her skin as she imagined. He seriously had no right to be this friggin' hot.

Alex's fingers dug into her flesh when she wiggled on his lap, turning into him to plaster herself against his chest. With an arm around his neck, her fingers clutched at his hair. Messing it up a bit more wasn't going to be a tragedy so she let her greedy hands loose, spearing trembling fingers into the shaggy mane, pressing against his skull.

The rumbling in his chest told her he liked what she was doing to him. After drawing back just long enough to give each of them some air he plunged onto her lips with a ferocity that set off pulsing waves of arousal inside her. God, he tasted so good. The hint of Scotch whisky on his breath invaded her senses. When his tongue slid against hers, she sucked on it and swirled hers inside his mouth. His earthy groan had her folding like a house of cards in a windstorm.

There was something about his hand on her head and the way he held her *just so*, that turned Meghan on like nothing she'd ever experienced before. Just about the time their kissing started to veer into animalistic territory, he wrenched his lips off hers so suddenly that a thin ribbon of saliva kept them connected for another heartbeat.

Abso-fucking-lutely, the last thing she expected was his pained growl as he pushed her away and put a good amount of space between them. When her butt slammed onto the seat again she was startled and confused. Had she done something wrong? Maybe been too aggressive? After all, she'd had her fingers so tight in his hair he probably had a bald spot now.

"Get out of here before we do something we shouldn't," he ground out in an angry voice.

Half of her hair was falling down from having his hand gripping the curly mane. She missed the power of his touch against her head. What in the hell was happening?

"I don't understand. You started it," she choked out.

"Yeah, I did. And I'm stopping it too."

"Why?" Her voice sounded anguished and forlorn.

"You shouldn't be here. None of this should be happening."

Meghan tried to wrap her mind around what he was saying but surging hormones and blank confusion was making that impossible. Trying to fix her hair with badly shaking hands, she felt panic seep into her senses. She wasn't the type to fall so willingly into the arms of someone she barely knew. To make it worse, he clearly wasn't having any of it. But he *did* start it, right?

Embarrassed beyond belief, she floated to the side of the tub and swung over the side. Coming to her feet on the stone tiles, she quickly snatched up a towel and wrapped it around her trembling body. If she didn't think she'd end up flat on her face, Meghan would have run at full speed away from the mortifying scene. At twenty-eight, she was hardly a girl, but the only thought rattling in her skull was that girls shouldn't play with grown men. She was way, way, *way* out of her league. And the hard, closed off expression on his face wasn't helping things.

Then the echo of his words, *"None of this should be happening,"* screamed in her mind. Before fleeing she chanced a look at his scowling face and asked breathlessly, "Why? Why was kissing me so wrong?" She needed to understand. Her self-confidence was hanging by a thread.

"Because if it wasn't for me, you'd be happily married by now; living the future you and David planned."

Wait. *What?* Married to David? Well, that actually wasn't how their engagement was going to pan out but that was a drama for another day. And besides, there was a dark undercurrent to what he'd said. *If it wasn't for him?* Dammit. She was missing something important, she was sure of it.

"Alex," she murmured, "I wasn't really going to marry David."

He cut her off before she could continue. "Doesn't matter. Fact is, he's not here because his commander let him down—him and a whole bunch of others. Don't look back, Meghan. I'm not worth it. Just get your ass out of here before I forget myself and make things worse."

She didn't know what exactly triggered his reaction, and she definitely didn't understand why he thought he was responsible for her fiancé's death but she knew an emotional brick wall when she saw one. Or when she slammed into it at Mach two.

Walking away was proving more difficult than she thought. Embarrassed? *Yes.* Mortified? *Yes.* Confused? *Hell yes.* Had she read the situation so wrong? Her heart clutched when she glanced at him and found him staring at her with an expression of utter desolation. He looked…well, he looked like he didn't have a friend in the world and yet she knew that not to be true. Good people who obviously cared for and held him in high regard surrounded him. What in holy hell had happened in his life that left him so wounded in spirit? His injuries were one thing, but whatever happened in his soul had left deeper and much uglier scars.

Mentally pulling her big girl panties on, Meghan reached deep for some confidence. When she found it, she fixed him with a look that suggested he listen to what she had to say. "We may have just met Alex, but I feel like we've known each other forever. I wanted you to kiss me."

His dark expression suggested he really didn't want to hear that. Tough. Things might be somewhat awkward right this moment but he hadn't seemed all that reluctant when his hand was tangled in her hair and his tongue was exploring the deepest recesses of her mouth. Pushing aside her embarrassment she told him, "I don't know what just happened here but you are *so* worth it."

Clutching the towel, she shivered in the cool night air, put her head down, and fled. He was clearly uncomfortable, she was freaking out, and nothing more would come of trying to figure out what was actually happening tonight.

Alex watched her go while an unfamiliar ache invaded his chest and his stomach turned to one big knot. He'd kissed his fair share of women but none of that mattered the second his lips took hers. Not all kisses were created equal and the one he and Meghan just shared brought that point home with alarming precision.

At first he'd been surprised by her obvious lack of experience. Probably been wasting her time with twenty-something dickheads who didn't appreciate that kissing was all about the build-up. He remembered being young and stupid, thinking with his cock—focusing on the end and not the journey.

She got up to speed quick though, giving him access to her mouth, tongue, and lips with a fervor that sent all the blood in his head racing with alarming speed to his groin. He thought he'd died and found heaven when those voluptuous curves shimmied on his lap in the swirling water while her hand clutched at his hair. Her passions ran deep. *For the right man.* And no matter what he was feeling, that man couldn't be him.

Seeing her all but run back to the Villa gutted him. She was embarrassed. Who could blame her? One minute he was devouring her mouth while she surrendered to him with a sweet vulnerability that fired up his passions, and the next he was a snarling, growling asshole. Yeah. He'd handled that with the finesse of a cranky three-year-old.

He didn't know where the fucking thought came from but the moment he remembered who he was, who she was, and what had brought her here, nothing could stop a cascading waterfall of icy memories. He'd killed her fiancé. Okay, maybe that wasn't the best way of putting it, but it was how he felt. There would never be enough time or denial to overshadow what were the undisputed facts of the situation.

David Anderson was a soldier under his command, and he and a shitload of others had been killed or injured on his watch. There was not a snowball's chance in hell of Alex ever atoning for what he felt had been his failures as commander.

Not only did he not have the right to be lusting after a dead man's fiancée, the burden of guilt he carried from those days made that lust feel immoral. He was a fucking pig for coming on to her. Didn't matter that she met him halfway and returned his desire kiss for kiss, lick for lick, and nibble for nibble. She didn't know what he knew. Didn't know her future had been wiped out by his failure to stave off that last horrific bombing. But he knew it and that was enough.

Plus, there was also the matter of his need for unconditional control. There was something about having power that was an absolute for Alex. While he sneered at the term dominant, it was an apt description of him. For him though, the mastery and control couldn't be taken or forced. He needed it to be given, freely. He wasn't a fool. Alex realized that the trust required in giving so much of one's self was the thing he desired most. Maybe that was what he needed to heal his soul—trust and control. He doubted someone as inexperienced as Meghan would understand the fierce desires fueling his lustful appetite.

Dragging himself from the bubbling hot tub with leaden feet, Alex toweled off, then set the timer for the lights and jets before he headed back inside. Looks like his original plan to drink the discomfort away was back on the agenda. Only now he'd be drowning his inappropriate desire for the sexy teacher at the same time.

Making his way wet and barefoot to the study, he shut the door firmly behind him and immediately peeled off the damp bathing suit leaving it in a pile on the floor. With the towel wrapped around his hips he made it to the wet bar in record time, pouring a tumbler of Glenfiddich that he easily tossed back like water, making his eyes water and throat burn. Fine with him. He didn't care at that moment if the Scotch burned a fucking hole in his stomach. The goal was to obliterate the memories dragging him into the shadows, make the sharp ache in his leg go away and turn off the current of desire for a woman he couldn't have before all three consumed him.

He must have tied on one hell of a drunk because that was where they found him the next morning when Cam and Drae came to grill him about the surprising guest he had stashed in the main house.

"WHAT DO YOU MAKE of this?" Cam asked Drae as the two of them surveyed the scene they found in the study. They'd come to talk to Alex about whatever the hell it was that was going on.

Seasoned surveillance experts, they didn't need to look very hard to see a shit-ton of evidence that created a pretty interesting picture of how Alex's night had ended.

Both noted the swim trunks inside the door and the towel that at one time covered his nakedness bunched in a ball and now stuffed down next to his passed out body sprawled in a recliner.

A big tumbler, one made more for water than sipping expensive whiskey, sat on the side table next to him while an empty Glenfiddich bottle lay on the floor.

"Jesus fucking Christ," Drae muttered. "Looks like Papa Bear had a bad night." Cam snorted in agreement.

"Told ya," Cam snarked. "He was too quiet at dinner. I *knew* something was up. Lacey did too."

"Yeah, I know. Victoria talked my fucking ear off after we got

home. I swear to God, being pregnant has made her some sort of em-
path. She picks up on everything. Even the little shit. She said Alex
watched Meghan all through dinner and not in that eye fuck kind of
a way. There's something else going on here. And now *this* bullshit."
Drae was less than pleased.

"Fucking, eh," Cam bit out. "What the hell do we do now?"

"Well let's start by getting him cleaned up and some coffee down
his throat. You go wrestle up a pot of that black sludge he likes while I
destroy the evidence and try to wake him up."

Cam wandered away muttering, "Great fucking way to start a day."

Sighing, Drae cleared away the tumbler and empty bottle, picked
the swim trunks up off the floor, and cracked open the shutters to let in
a bit of light but not too much. He was no stranger to a whiskey hangover. Alex wouldn't appreciate the glare of a sunny day.

He also knew better than to try and rouse him with a touch. Good
way to get his arm ripped off so he gave the recliner a good kick with
his booted foot to see if that got a reaction. Alex groaned but that was
it. Fuck, fuck, *fuck*.

He kicked the chair again and barked out Alex's name. A deep,
menacing growl split the air as his old friend started to come around.
Drae had the good sense to back off a few paces; not knowing what to
expect once Alex came to. Prepared for a blind rage, he was mildly surprised when first one blood shot eye and then the other slowly cracked
open and instead of fury he saw something else, an unguarded expression that was deeply unsettling. Drae knew that fucking look—knew
what a disturbance in the force looked and sounded like.

"Brother, you look like shit," he told Alex quietly. The bloodshot
eyes slowly focused, chasing away the unguarded expression Drae had
just seen.

Seeing Alex reach up and cover his eyes with a hand that was more
than a little shaky made Drae wonder just how much of that bottle he'd
had to drink. Judging by the evidence right in front of him the answer
was probably, a *lot*.

The door to the study opened briefly then shut again as Cam carried in a tray with a carafe of coffee plus a couple of mugs and dropped
it on the wet bar.

"Anything?" he asked.

"Yeah. He's on his way back," Drae answered with a look he hoped Cam would pick up on. They'd been through a lot, the three of them, and Cam's quick nod meant he understood Drae's unspoken signal that shit was off the hook.

Pouring them each a cup of steaming coffee, Cam walked one over to Alex and put it on the table next to his chair.

"Dude. Coffee," was all he needed to say to pry Alex's hand from his covered eyes as his gaze searched for the mug. When he sat forward the recliner returned to chair position and he leaned his head into his hands with his elbows resting on his knees. It took him a good minute or two before he was able to reach for the mug with a steadier hand. Drae and Cam calmly drank theirs and waited.

They knew he was back to the land of the living when his hand scraped back and forth against his skull making his mess of hair all the worse. After a few minutes Drae asked, "Better?" Alex nodded but they both knew his head was probably pounding like a motherfucker.

"Where are your clothes, man? Gotta get you dressed. We don't need to see Mr. Winky, bro," Cam snickered good-naturedly. Guy talk was generally a safe bet. They didn't want an unruly, hung over Alex on their hands.

Having it pointed out that he was butt ass naked, Alex grimaced and fell back into the chair as if it was too much to even sit up. *Well, this was going just great*, Drae thought.

Eventually, Alex managed to haul his uncooperative body from the chair and to standing on his unsteady feet. Naked and scowling at the other two he staggered awkwardly to the half bath at the back of the study where he shut the door behind him. Drae was going to let him have a few minutes to get his shit together, but if he didn't reappear in a timely fashion they would probably have attempted to offer some bathroom assistance. Part of the Bro-Code.

Inside the bathroom, Alex thought his brain was going to explode. Or maybe it already had and what he was feeling was the aftermath. In any case he felt like fucking shit. Luckily he found a pair of sweats hanging on the back of the door that he barely managed to slip on without falling on his ass. His stomach rumbled and for a second he wondered if he was going to puke his guts up. *Why not?* What his pounding head needed was a little bit more indignity just for shits 'n grins.

When he was finally able to stumble from the bathroom, he found his two best friends and de facto brothers waiting for him. The conversation he knew they were about to have would have been better without the hangover, but there was no use crying over spilt milk or an empty bottle as the case might be.

Drae, the cool headed analytical one of their group, went first. "I wouldn't even know where to start so how about you just tell us what brought this on."

"And what we can do to help," Cam added.

Alex folded onto the sofa like a rag doll losing its stuffing. A strange feeling grabbed ahold of him, almost like he wanted to cry. The very thought freaked him out more than the indulgent hangover. Guys did not boo hoo like chicks. *Fucking hell, man.* Talk about indignity. Emotional blubbering wasn't his style.

With his head against the back of the sofa, Alex flung his arm over his face to cover his eyes. He struggled against the tingling in his nose that went along with the battle he was waging to fend off some uncool and very unmanly waterworks. *Fuck.*

Swallowing the lump that formed in his throat he sat up and heaved a deep sigh, letting loose with the first thing that came to his mind.

"The anniversary is next month."

"Shit," Drae growled.

Cam followed up with a pithy, "Goddammit."

A couple of intense, silent minutes passed as each man considered what that meant.

"Alex," Cam grumbled, about to say his piece. Alex didn't let him, it would be a waste without knowing it all.

"Wait. There's more," he told them.

This was the hard part. He wasn't sure what to say, how much to tell them. It wasn't that he was trying to keep anything from the two people he knew would always have his back, no matter what. But this was emotional landmine territory for all of them—especially him—and they didn't even know the half of it.

"I met Meghan in Germany when I was at Landstuhl Medical Center. Actually, that's wrong. We didn't meet until yesterday."

"Uh. *Okay*," Drae said calmly although the confusion in his reply was obvious.

"Shit. This is coming out all wrong."

Cam passed Alex his coffee mug and told him, "That's okay, man. Just say whatever it is. We'll figure out the details as you go along."

He didn't mean for his voice to sound shaky but it did. "I wrote to her. As the C.O. Hated writing those fucking letters." Cam and Drae wore expressions that let Alex know they understood what he was referring to.

"Oh, fuck," Cam muttered as the realization of where this was going dawned on him.

"Yeah, dude. *Oh fuck*, only it's worse than that. Remember The Kid? David. David Anderson was his name, and she was engaged to him. I wrote her one of those bullshit screeds about service, sacrifice, and war. We exchanged a bunch of letters. Kept it up after I came back to the states. It was a bad time for me—the surgeries, rehab, and therapy. I looked forward to her letters, because they took my mind off everything else."

Drae looked like he was having a coronary. "Holy shit Alex."

"Right?" Alex answered with a snort of disbelieving agreement.

"You've been in touch with her all this time?" Cam asked.

"Yes and no. After my discharge it was mostly an annual Christmas card. Nothing more."

"So, this visit is *what*?" Leave it to Drae to ask for clarification.

Alex just looked at him, I mean what else could he do or say? There was no fucking way he could explain the connection those letters had forged.

"She doesn't know," he murmured, ominous and low. "Thinks I'm some sort of shining hero because that's how The Kid talked about me. Shit got out of hand last night after you guys left."

Drae again. The man should have been a prosecutor. "Meaning?"

"We were in the hot tub and…"

"Wait! You were in the fucking Jacuzzi last night with a gorgeous woman? Oh, come on. You *never* use that thing." Cam sounded stunned. A little like how Alex felt.

"She thought it would help my leg and, well I ….." He clammed up after that. No way was he going to admit that wanting to see her in a bathing suit had been the deciding factor in his getting into that tub. Neither of his brothers were stupid and the way they both leered at him let Alex know they did the math on their own and came up with the missing words.

"Fuck you both," he growled.

"So, that's what you mean by shit got out of hand? Like how far out of hand and why the hell would you think that? She's a beautiful woman. You're not half-bad yourself although that shitty attitude could use a little work. So what's the big fucking deal?" Drae asked.

"The big fucking deal, as you so eloquently put it, is she'd be married by now if I hadn't fucked up her life."

They exploded the minute he said he'd fucked up her life. "Bro!" Cam barked. "You did *not* fuck up anyone's life. That goddamn bomber was insane and nothing you did or didn't do would have made any difference."

"Fuck!" hollered Drae for good measure.

They'd been down this road before. His brothers knew he held himself ultimately responsible for what happened that day. Years of trying to convince him otherwise only led to a stalemate. Alex felt he knew the truth—knew in his heart that if he hadn't ordered a raid on a remote village, the dickhead insurgents who waited for bad shit like that to happen so they could fire up the locals wouldn't have managed to talk a widow with a young son into strapping explosives to her body. To make it all that much worse in Alex's head, less than twenty minutes before the explosion one of the bad asses who handled interrogations reported on recent intel that suggested a possible strike against their base.

Common sense told him that twenty minutes was like the blink of an eye in a war zone and even if he'd known five *days* earlier, the intel had been so sketchy that thinking a trusted local, especially a woman with a kid, would be a threat would have been the last thing anyone suspected. The top brass agreed and determined that nothing could have been done to change what happened. They even gave him a fucking medal afterwards because of his injuries.

But for Alex, there was no escaping the haunting what ifs. What if the raid hadn't gone bad? What if he'd had more warning of a possible attack? What if? What if?

In the end, the only thing he knew for sure was the body count. David Anderson's name was on that list. Kissing Meghan had been nothing short of disrespectful to a dead man. There was no way to seek absolution for his actions. Not then. Not now. In a word, he was *fucked*.

"Meghan came here to thank me for helping her through a tough time. I think she wanted closure or something like that. The last thing she needs is some fucked-up asshole with a guilty conscience."

"God-fucking-dammit!" Drae growled. "You have nothing to be guilty about. And you're no more fucked-up than either of us. Maybe you should remember that. I seem to recall you giving both of us shit for thinking similar thoughts and yet look at us now. I've never been happier and fucking Cam actually smiles now for Christ's sake. That has to count for something! C'mon Alex. Maybe this girl is your redemption. I fucking hate that you see things that way but really, what if Meghan is meant to heal that wound?"

Alex snarled and pinned Drae to the spot with a fierce glare. "I don't know what to think. Maybe if I did there wouldn't be an empty bottle of Glenfiddich headed to the recycling bin."

"Look," Drae continued. "You don't have to tell us what *shit getting out of hand* means, but I have one question. Was the lady opposed?"

Alex gritted his teeth. No, she hadn't been opposed. If he hadn't pushed her away there was little doubt that shit really *would* have gotten out of hand.

"Okay then. I'm taking that silence as a 'no'. *Dude.* Take it from someone who's been there. Trust your feelings, man. Shut down that brain of yours and go from the heart. If in the end you're as lucky as Cam and I were, you'll be glad you did."

"Oh, I'm sure he'll find some way to fuck it up. After all, we both did! Thank God our women knew better." Cam slammed his empty mug down and gestured for the door. "C'mon. Let's go see what Ria's whipping up for breakfast. And Alex, chill the fuck out man. We've got you covered. Having the Three Stooges along for breakfast will give you and Meghan a breather, okay? Oh, and dude? Go take a shower and put some clothes on. You smell like old gym socks, and the half-naked with sweats hanging off your dick look isn't all that flattering."

Alex flipped them both off with a wry grin. "You guys suck."

Their laughter could be heard far beyond the walls of the study. Maybe the conversation hadn't solved anything, but Alex felt better now that they knew the whole story. He only hoped that when it came time to face Meghan, he didn't see hurt in her eyes—hurt for the way he'd treated her or hurt for realizing it was him who had cost her the man she loved.

Chapter 8

NOW THAT SHE DIDN'T have a work schedule to stick to, Meghan tried to sleep in and wake up much slower than she had when getting her ass in gear and at school well before her first class of the day had been a top priority. It was another rare luxury in her new life.

But this morning, no amount of slowly rousing was going to take the edge off a shit-tacular night. Why was it that just when you wanted your brain to turn off, it fired up an endless loop of images and emotions that made it damn near impossible to relax? She had a sleep hangover. That gross, knot-in-the-stomach, fuzzy-headed reaction to having tossed, turned, and basically fretted through the night. *Ugh.*

Staring at the wood beams crossing the ceiling above her head, she tried taking a series of deep, meditative breaths hoping to clear her mind and bring a sense of calm, but nothing was helping. Not when all she could think about was Alex and the incredible kiss they'd shared. Especially when that tingling, sexy memory was quickly followed by the humiliating memory of being dismissed from his presence like a naughty child.

Get your ass out of here. Don't look back. I'm not worth it. What the hell had all that been about? There wasn't any doubt that an undercurrent of something powerful had been going on between them and the strength of the hard-on she'd felt when he hauled her onto his lap made a lie of pretending otherwise. She totally got that they were in a weird situation, but his reaction had been extreme.

Scurrying away from the mortifying scene in the hot tub had felt like a walk of shame. She'd been shocked when he pulled away and worried that her lack of expertise had turned him off. All the guys she dated after David had been nice, uncomplicated. Translation—they were boring as hell.

Because she'd been engaged, it was expected that Meghan knew her way around a man's body. But nothing could have been further from the truth. The physical relationship with her fiancé had been respectful and tame, something she'd chalked up to her youth and the fact that David had been her brother Michael's best friend. And that was a big part of the problem.

Except for a handful of hormonal make-out sessions, her engagement had ended with Meghan still hanging on to her virginal status. Almost two years later, when she'd gotten hammered on a booze cruise with a bunch of grad school chums and had finally gotten up the nerve to sleep with a muscle-bound jock, she'd been annoyed that he hadn't even realized he was her first. Men were so dumb at times. Especially the younger ones.

The experience had been less than stellar and once the deed was done she'd walked away wondering what all the fuss was about. The whole thing had been tawdry and cheap, helped along by a river of fancy umbrella drinks. Maybe that was why she hadn't put any real effort into dating. Oh, she accepted the occasional invitation and even pursued a potential relationship with an ambitious architect she met through her coaching services. He was pleasant and laidback and though it hadn't worked out, the experience helped her define what she needed in an intimate relationship, and it wasn't *nice* or *easy*. No. She wanted heart pounding, panty drenching passion. The type that fries your brain. In other words, exactly what she'd experienced for a few brief moments with Alex.

How friggin' cruel was it that just when she'd finally felt a little bit of the arousal she dreamed about, the guy pushed her away. Meghan turned her face into the pillow and groaned. Maybe staying at the Villa wasn't such a good idea. He had told her to get out and not look back.

Thing was, though, she wasn't a quitter. Running just wasn't in her wheelhouse, but it didn't help that she was seriously attracted to a man she'd thought would be nothing more than a blip on her radar screen.

Throwing back the covers, she sat up, swung her legs off the bed, and just sat there, wishing for just a second that her mom was around. They were exceptionally close, but even so, Meghan hadn't ever confided her fears and concerns about David. She couldn't bring herself to share such intimacies, but right now, she could really use another woman's perspective.

As if on cue, her tummy growled, sending her into the bathroom to wash up and get dressed so she could go in search of breakfast. Deciding on a well-worn pair of jeans that clung to her curves like a second skin and a simple t-shirt, she gave her reflection one last glance. Not bad for having gotten no sleep.

If Alex was cool and distant, she'd make the best of it. Maybe hang around a day or so, get that horseback riding lesson Gus promised, then go her merry way. It wasn't running so much as it was conceding defeat. She'd do it if she had to but not happily. There was something about Alex Marquez that invaded her soul and made her want things. Things that got her wild side churning.

DRAE AND CAM HUDDLED together at the far side of the kitchen watching Alex putter aimlessly. Neither of them missed the fact that he kept his eyes on the doorway, probably waiting for his guest to appear.

"Second breakfast is not my thing," Cam grumped as he picked at a plate of bacon and a stack of flapjacks from Ria's over-the-top breakfast buffet. Apparently everyone wanted to impress the sexy gym teacher Alex was losing his shit over.

Drae dropped his plate on the breakfast bar and nodded in agreement. "Just keep eating, man."

"All this food is going to make me fat."

Drae laughed at Cam's dark scowl, watching as he pushed the food around the plate. "Shut the fuck up, man," he chuckled. "My wife is in full nesting mode. She loves all that domestic shit! There's no way she'd let me out of the house without having breakfast first so this is killing me too."

Nodding toward Alex, Drae commented, "At least he cleaned up. Can't remember the last time I saw him that messed up. This situation blows, Cam."

"He's been carrying this guilt for way too long but fuck me if I know what to do about it." Cam considered his former commanding officer with shrewd eyes. "Did you even suspect he was corresponding with The Kid's fiancée? I sure as shit didn't."

"Are you kidding?" Drae spit out. "He's such a closed book, and it's not like I stick my nose into his personal life. It is surprising though, considering the load of bullshit he tells himself about what happened."

Brody suddenly appeared out of thin air and made immediately for the buffet, piling up a plate before joining them.

"Mornin'," he muttered. Always a man of few words, their K9 guru, also former Special Forces, threw them both a quizzical look as he noted Alex's prowling. "What's up with him?"

"You know Alex. Always something on his mind. Probably building a fucking robot from scratch in his head." Cam's answer gave nothing away but he and Drae quickly glanced at each other anyway. It wasn't going to take long for everyone to pick up on the heavy vibe rolling off the man.

Turning to Drae, Brody told him, "Been keeping my eye out for the perfect pup, like you asked. Think the missus would like a big, goofy Labrador? One of the female pups seems to have *fuck with the St. John's* written all over her."

All three shook their heads and laughed at Brody's mocking words.

Looking shell-shocked Drae admitted, "I must have been out of my mind to think about getting a puppy. Don't know that a baby and a puppy at the same time is such a great idea."

Cam made a gesture with his hands that mimicked tiny violins playing and cried, "Wah, wah!" That got an even bigger laugh, which caught Alex's scowling attention.

At the dark look Brody muttered just loud enough for the other two to hear, "Looks like more than a fucking robot if you ask me."

"Hi." The tentative female voice got the whole room of men turning toward the sound.

"You're up," whispered Cam to Drae as he pushed him with his elbow.

Reacting quickly, Drae put on his very best suave and debonair expression and hauled ass in Meghan's direction. "Mornin' pretty lady! Grab a plate and dig in. Ever tasted sourdough flapjacks? They're one of Ria's specialties. I think she's trying to impress you because she never makes 'em for just the bunch of us." He kept it light and friendly, hoping to give the uncomfortable tension in the air some competition.

"Thanks," she muttered, grabbing a plate and sliding one of the enormous flapjacks into the center. "This thing is enough for two people."

"Maybe there's someone you could share it with," Drae answered smoothly. He didn't miss the way her eyes immediately flicked toward Alex, who stood silently brooding on the other side of the enormous room.

Stupid fucker. What the hell was he doing? Drae tried not to roll his eyes. Was this what he and Cam had put Alex through when they were knee deep in angst over the women who eventually became their wives?

The normally tight-lipped K9 guru chose that moment to become a chatty fly in the ointment. "G'mornin' Ma'am," he muttered to Meghan. "Can I help you with that?" He all but pushed Drae aside in order to take the plate Meghan was holding as he started up an inane conversation while piling all kinds of food on her dish.

"Gus is looking forward to getting your ass up….uh, I mean helping you learn to ride."

Drae almost smacked him for being such a dumb fuck. He noted the darkening scowl overtaking Alex's features as he silently watched the interaction between Brody and Meghan. *Damn it.* This wasn't going as he and Cam hoped.

Meghan wished the butterflies performing an Olympic routine in her belly would settle down. Facing an unruly group of kids on a basketball court was easier than navigating this obstacle course of unfamiliar emotions.

Used to being the only girl in a room full of guys, she had instantly noted all the players present. She wondered if Draegyn and Cameron were on hand to provide some kind of buffer between her and Alex. She wouldn't be surprised if that were the case. Everything she knew about the three men suggested an unbreakable fraternity that she, quite frankly, admired. Meghan was comfortable around that sort of bond; it was something she'd been exposed to her entire life. With every male member of her family being a cop, an EMT or a fireman, she understood the solidarity of their relationship.

Brody's presence and obvious interest in her was, however, unexpected. Draegyn's body language when he'd been pushed aside had not gone unnoticed. His innocent suggestion that she share her flapjack with someone had *not* been an invitation for the K9 dude to step in, and he seriously looked like he was going to strangle Brody when he did.

It didn't help alleviate her anxiety that the only person she wanted to be with at that moment was keeping his distance. Damn. She'd been worried about just such behavior. Some part of her wanted Alex to stride across the room, flatten Brody, plant a hot, wet kiss on her, and drag her off to God knows where so they could finish what they'd started last night. Judging by the way he was scowling at her, that wasn't going to happen any time soon.

Turning her attention to Brody she responded to his statement about the riding lesson with her usual brand of sass mixed with a good dose of *BBBB*.

"I'm looking forward to it! I hope Gus knows what he's in for. This fappy backside has never been in a saddle before!"

Brody looked bemused. "Fappy?"

She laughed. "Never heard that before? Must be a Boston thing!"

"What's it mean?"

"Oh, you know….fappy. As in fat and happy!" She giggled at the look of shock on his face.

Across the room Alex slapped his hand with a resounding thud on a counter and glared like she'd just declared all Special Forces Vets pussies. She jumped, startled at his reaction.

"You are in no way *fat!*" he growled.

Brody, Draegyn, and Cameron each wore an expression that translated to *WHAT THE FUCK?* Cam especially looked as if his eyebrows couldn't have gone any higher on his forehead. She was guessing that the Major was not usually prone to such outbursts. Okay then. Maybe this was a good sign. *Hmm.*

Taking the bull by the horns – *ah, she loved a Western metaphor* – Meghan turned her full attention on Alex and flashed him a calm smile.

"Good morning to you too, Major." Now let's see what he did with that.

She had to bite the inside of her mouth to keep from laughing when she saw a look of exasperation flash across his face. *Oooooh,* so he'd been trying to keep his distance but hadn't quite managed. A surge of female satisfaction lit up her insides.

Moving with obvious reluctance into their midst, Meghan couldn't help but admire the way he carried himself. He looked just as handsome and sexy this morning with his messy hair and burly presence as he had last night. She did however detect a tinge of green around the gills and wondered what he'd done after they parted. No stranger to the aftermath of having tied one on, she looked a bit closer and caught the telltale bloodshot eyes. Maybe pushing her away hadn't been what he really wanted after all. Either that or he hated her guts and couldn't wait for her to be gone. Somehow she doubted that was the case. Having felt a very distinctive erection pressed into the seam of her backside last night disproved the hate her guts scenario.

God, she was just so drawn to him in such a primal way. She'd never, ever experienced such skin tightening awareness of another human being. Was it weird that she wanted him so desperately after only knowing him for a day? Okay, so maybe putting it that way wasn't entirely accurate. She might have only known him physically for a single day but the letters they'd exchanged had given her an insight into who he was as a man. There was simply no denying that she liked the person she knew and was drawn to who she saw.

Taking her breakfast plate from Brody's hands, she saw him give the man a look that suggested he back the hell up—and fast. She wanted to jump into to the air and scream *Yee Haw!* There was nothing like a territorial Alpha to make a girl feel all tingly inside. When he turned his bloodshot gaze on her, she melted just a little bit.

"Good morning," he grumped. *Lord, but he was cute.* "C'mon over here and eat your breakfast in peace," he told her, gesturing with his hand toward the table.

Turning his attention on the other three he sniped, "Don't any of you have something better to do?" She almost fell down laughing at how quickly the room cleared. When Dad speaks, the kids listen.

He sat across from her pushing some scrambled eggs around his plate. Probably not a good choice for a hangover, but he put on a good show. Having him so close was making her deliciously aware of him on an almost cellular level. For some ungodly reason a scene from an old movie flashed in her mind causing her to restrain the impulse to kick off her sandals and run her foot up his leg under the table. He'd no doubt choke to death from shock if she tried.

Clearing his throat he asked, "So. You ready to get up on a horse?"

Okay—so discussing what happened last night wasn't on the agenda. She was good with that. Maybe he regretted how things ended. They'd moved too fast and he'd gotten spooked. If she had any god-damn sense she'd be spooked too, but his powerful pull on her senses wiped out what good sense she still had.

She smirked and rolled her eyes telling him, "I have no idea if I'm ready! Guess we'll know in a little bit, huh?"

He nodded. She sighed. A man of few words. *Great.*

"There's not much opportunity to learn to ride where I'm from, but I've always wanted to try. Got a thing for cowboys!" she added with a silly leer that seemed to loosen him up just a tad.

"Ah. I get it now. That's why you want to hang around for the Cowboy Festival. Didn't make much sense at first."

Shoveling forkfuls of flapjack into her mouth, she smiled between bites. "It's the curse of having brothers. It was either Cowboys or GI Joe."

He snickered at that. "I grew up around the Cowboys. Must be why I ended up a real, live GI Joe."

"Do you ride?" she asked.

He shrugged, dropped his fork, and pushed the uneaten plate away. "I used to. Was compulsory as a kid around here. Sometimes I still get in the saddle but ..."

"Mmm," she said. "It's hard on your leg?"

"Yeah. It's not so much the riding as the aftermath. Pisses me the fuck off."

"If I don't fall on my fappy ass, will you ride with me sometime?"

The look he shot at her took her breath away.

"Meghan. *Shit*," he barked. "You are not fat. I don't care if it's just an expression—don't talk about yourself that way."

There was nothing a woman wanted to hear more than that the man she was panting after didn't think she was a chunk. She beamed at him but needled him just a teeny bit more to see what happened.

"Alex, really. Have you *seen* my ass? I mean, c'mon."

"Well, it drove me to finish off a bottle of Scotch last night so I suppose that's your answer."

As she cleared her plate she tried not to grin at him like a lunatic. *Oh my friggin' God*, was all she could think.

Chapter 9

AFTER A MORNING HOLED up in his tech cave doing absolutely nothing under the ever watchful and slightly amused eyes of his assistant, Alex finally threw in the towel.

"Where ya' off to, boss?" Tori asked as he shut down his computer and strode for the door. She had a *butter wouldn't melt in her mouth* innocence to her tone that he knew damn well was a put on. He felt everyone watching him and Meghan like insects under a microscope.

Throwing her a bit of brotherly side shade, he stopped to answer her question with a sigh of resignation.

"Well, Mrs. St. John. If you must know, *and clearly you do*, I am going down to the stables to see if Gus has managed to teach my guest how to handle a horse without getting her kicked in the head. Or worse."

Tori knew him well enough not to openly tease him so she adopted a businesslike expression and asked him to, "Tell Meghan I said hello."

Exasperated, he shook his head and left the room muttering under his breath about women. Detouring his growing fascination for his houseguest with an infusion of alcohol hadn't worked. Try as he might, even with a constant mantra that he couldn't cross that line, all he could think about was how her lips tasted and how mouthwateringly gorgeous her ass was. He was in such deep shit that he couldn't think straight.

Alex knew they'd have to talk about what happened in the hot tub. With every day that passed, the anniversary of the bombing that almost killed him, and did, in fact, take the life of her fiancé, got closer. He hated talking about what happened, even with Drae and Cam, but she had a right to know what went down. Maybe that was why she was here. The universe was making him face, in a very blunt way, the cost of his actions. Or non-actions as the case might be.

Being attracted to a woman who had suffered because of him seemed like the ultimate *fuck you,* and a punishment he hadn't seen coming. Even though he'd already known that there would be no happily ever after for him, it still stung like a bitch that he fell so hard and so fast for the one female on the whole planet he absolutely could not pursue. And fall he most certainly had.

While he absently tapped away on the computer all morning, what he was really doing was thinking about Meghan. Actually, thinking was an understatement. He'd been flat-out fantasizing about her. The gods had a fucked-up sense of humor tempting him with her. She was everything he'd ever dreamed of in a woman and then some.

The curves she kept referring to as making her fat were nothing short of jaw dropping. Add to that the face of an angel, an Irish one at that, and a personality full of wit and intelligence, and you had the ingredients for a made-to-order goddess. He felt completely at ease around her even though she made him all hot and bothered. He wondered if this was how it had been for Cam and Drae. The thought tore at his heart. They deserved their happiness. He still had a lifetime of penance to serve for the failings in his past.

The minute he walked through the house on his way to the stable, Zeus came trotting to his side. He wondered if Meghan liked dogs then quickly squashed the thought. It didn't matter, she was only a guest. One who would eventually leave.

The big Lab must have sensed his troubled thoughts because she nosed his hand and tried to jump in front of his legs to get his attention. This dog had been a balm for his soul when he settled into the Villa and started building the Justice Agency. She was treated like a princess, one of the canine variety, a distinction she'd earned by her devotion to Alex.

When they arrived at the stable, Alex immediately spotted Meghan up on one of the American Quarter Horses - perfect for a beginning rider. The handsome mount named Sasha was trotting slowly around the riding ring with Gus standing in the middle talking horse and rider through their paces.

Meghan looked fantastic in the saddle, her gorgeous auburn curls pulled back in a sloppy ponytail, with the backside he'd been fantasizing about moving up and down, her thighs gripping the sides of the horse, and her feet planted firmly in the stirrups. She was a natural. It didn't do any good to pretend he didn't wonder what her thighs would feel like wrapped around his hips as he pounded into her. Trying to ignore the shit-kicking case of lust he was experiencing was a total waste of time.

Lost in his private musings starring a naked and delectable Irish goddess he didn't at first notice the rest of the scene before him until he heard someone shout out, "You go girl!"

A dark frown and clenched jaw later, he saw a crowd had gathered along the split rail fence to watch Meghan take her first ride. Alex knew he was being an idiot, but all he could think of was that he wanted her all to himself. Seeing other people watch her didn't sit well with him. Especially when one of those people was Brody.

He liked the dog trainer. A lot. Jensen was one of the countless veterans who the Agency brought on board and like so many others, Alex included, he came with a shit load of issues. In Brody's case it was a crippling case of PTSD that almost derailed his entire life until the work he did with the canines gave him a place to focus his energies. He didn't stay at the compound full-time; in fact he was only around from late June until mid-December and then his other life called him away.

He was a good-looking guy. One of those laidback surfer dude types on the outside—he was the complete opposite of Alex's brawny presence. Although suddenly comparing himself to the younger man seemed a bit weird, it didn't take a genius to figure out why. When he'd seen Brody trying to chat Meghan up at breakfast, he'd almost exploded. Morphing into the Incredible Hulk over some polite conversation between the two had been a reaction that surprised Alex. Seeing him here though, watching her as she rode, fired up a fierce sense of possessiveness that wasn't going to help the situation.

Zeus let out an adorable *woof* when she saw the K9 guru. Brody was one of the people who spoiled the dog rotten and while she didn't leave Alex's side, as any female would, she wanted all of her admirers to see she was there. He scratched the Lab behind her ears earning him an adoring gaze from her big brown eyes. "Not you too, girl," he chuckled. Seemed he was doomed to fight Brody for this female too.

Hearing the dog's bark, Jensen looked over and saw them. He quickly ambled over and gave Zeus an enthusiastic greeting, crouching down to rub the dog's chest while lavishing praise for how pretty she was. The damn dog sat there with her tail thumping in the dirt as she stretched her neck up for more scratches. All Alex could do was sigh.

Trying not to be an unreasonable asshole but not able to stop the words that tumbled out of his mouth, Alex gritted his teeth and told him, "You gotta steal all my women, Jensen?" He'd never seen anyone move as fast as Brody did when he shot to his feet and met Alex's glare.

"Shit, Alex. I wasn't trying to be a prick this morning." He looked toward the riding ring as Gus was leading Meghan and Sasha into the stable. "She's a teacher, man. I just thought…well, actually….*fuck*." He seemed genuinely pained that Alex had called him out for an innocent conversation.

Jensen was one of those silent types who didn't talk much about his other life but he, Drae, and Cam were among a select few who knew that when he left Arizona, it was to head back east where he taught a winter semester English course to second language learners at a community college. Remembering that made Alex feel like a jerk.

Slapping Brody on the back he looked him dead in the eye and said, "Sorry man. I'm the prick. Professional courtesy. Teacher talk, right?" It was the best he could do without a full-blown apology. Jensen nodded and patted Zeus on the head one last time.

"I was just yanking your chain," Alex added. Watching as the half-door on the stable swung shut he asked him, "How'd she do?"

Brody seemed relieved that the tense moment had passed reminding Alex that he needed to get his shit together before his attitude upset the teamwork he and his brothers had worked so hard to maintain within the agency.

"I think Sasha scared the crap out of her at first but she's a great horse. Sweet temperament. Gentle."

Alex threw back his head and laughed. "I was asking about Meghan, not the damn horse!"

Patting Zeus on the head he asked Brody to take her back to the house and get her settled. "I've got something to take care of here."

"GUS, THAT WAS FANTASTIC!" Meghan cried as she swung her leg over the horse and eased out of the saddle. "Can I ride her again?"

Gus smiled and laughed. "Of course you can. She likes you, I can tell."

"Really?" Meghan asked. "I think she's wonderful." Rubbing her hand up and down the beautiful sorrel-colored horse's neck, she giggled softly when Sasha's muzzle pushed against her face.

It was the affectionate moment between horse and rider, which Alex commented on when he strode into the barn. "Made a friend have you?" he chuckled as he came upon them.

Meghan's head shot up at the sound of Alex's voice and greeted him with a broad smile that wrapped neatly around his heart.

"Oh Alex! It was awesome. She's such a sweetie. Thank you so much for letting me ride her."

"Don't thank me. It was old Gus over there," he said as the horse master quietly led the Quarter horse away for a good brushing and something to eat. "He knows better than anyone how to match a rider and a horse, but I'm delighted you enjoyed yourself."

As she walked toward him she made the cutest face. "Uh oh."

"What?" he asked.

"My butt's sore. Or maybe it's my thighs. I can't quite tell yet."

She slapped her hands on both spots to brush off some dirt and in doing so did this sexy shimmy of her hips that sucked all the oxygen out of his body. Alex struggled to stay standing while his dick got so hard, so fast, he almost dropped to his knees. It didn't help that he wanted to slowly slide her jeans down over her ass and get her naked from the waist down so he could bend her over and fuck her hard and fast. So hard that she really would be sore afterward.

Apparently, the oxygen deprivation also robbed him of coherent words. "Uh. *Yeah.* Um, uh—want to walk or sit down?" Jesus Christ, he sounded like a twelve-year-old struggling to talk to a pretty girl.

She looked at him as though he had half a screw loose, then shook her head like she was clearing her thoughts. "Believe it or not, I'd like to sit on something soft that doesn't move for a little bit."

He wanted to offer his lap but had the smarts not to be such an ass. That didn't mean however that he didn't have an equally great idea.

"C'mon Calamity Jane," he said smiling as he held out his hand to her. "Let me introduce you to the comfort to be found on a bale of hay."

She grabbed onto his hand without hesitation, causing an explosion like fireworks to fly into his shoulder when they touched. Maybe the hay bale wasn't such a good idea if they were going to create sparks every time they came in contact. He could just imagine the whole place burning to the ground from the heat they created.

"Did you know horses don't burp?"

"What?" he laughed good-naturedly. "Sounds like something Gus made up."

"Oh no!" she assured him. "I looked it up on Google."

"For real?"

She squeezed his hand and leaned closer, telling him in a serious mock whisper, "It's a teacher thing. I Google just about everything."

He led her to the rear of the stable, near the tack room where a stall was piled with hay bales. Grabbing a horse blanket he threw it over a two bale stack at the foot of a much higher stack and invited her to sit down. It was almost like a hay couch made just for them.

"Comfortable?" he asked her as she wiggled that majestic ass of hers until she found the perfect spot. When she was settled, she patted the empty space at her side for him to join her. He practically dove on top of her right then and there.

The minute he sat beside her she raised her legs up straight and giggled. "Look! I've got cowboy boots! Lacey leant them to me."

"Very nice but you'll need a pair of your own if you want to be a real cowgirl. There's a place not far from here where we can go to get you properly kitted out. Boots. Hat. Gloves. You name it."

Her gasp of delight wrapped around his heart a second before she threw herself onto his chest and squeezed the living daylights out of him in a bear hug.

"Thank you sooooo much, Alex. This is much better than sitting in a hotel room and watching things from the sidelines."

He couldn't breathe and not from the intensity of her hug. The moment she plastered herself against him he caught a whiff of her sweet scent mixed with sweat and the smell of horses, all of which blended perfectly into one huge wallop of sensory overload.

"Meghan," he growled.

She loosened her embrace and looked at him with a question forming on her lips. "Wha…?"

He ground out an earthy swear word and grabbed her by the nape of her neck, aggressively pulling her into him as his mouth crashed onto hers.

There was nothing gentle or persuasive about this kiss. It was one hundred percent demand as he devoured her mouth, thrusting his tongue past her lips. She answered a heartbeat later, clutching the front of his shirt and moaning into his mouth.

She tasted like chocolate and coffee and something else he couldn't quite pin down. Sucking on her tongue he invited her to explore his mouth, grunting his approval when she flicked her tongue quickly against his.

Still holding her by the nape of her neck, he shifted his hand to fist her ponytail of curls and yanked her head back as his mouth backed off so she could catch her breath. Not wanting to lose a second of opportunity to greedily consume everything she had to offer, he latched onto her neck as he held her still. She responded with a surprised yelp followed by a deep shudder as she arched her head back giving him total access.

With her hands crushed between them she grabbed at his shirt and held on tight as he licked her delicious skin from ear to collarbone with the flat of his tongue, then sank his teeth into the soft spot where her neck joined her shoulder. Pulling a hand free she put it on his head, spearing her fingers into his hair and encouraged him on.

Moving back to her mouth, Alex nipped and licked at her lips as she panted and quivered against him. When her other arm slid around his back and dug her fingernails into him he lost it.

Still fisting her hair, he pushed his free hand under her ass and pulled her forward enough that he could press his body down into hers. God almighty, she fit his perfectly. He kneaded her bottom through her jeans and thoroughly mapped every inch of her backside.

They were half reclining, as he let his desire for her have free reign, kissing her voraciously, thrusting his tongue in an approximation of what he wanted to do with another part of his anatomy. When she lifted one of her legs and wrapped it possessively around his hips, he was a goner.

She wasn't going anywhere, not with his hard, muscular body pinning her to the hay stack, so he released her hair and did the only thing he could with his free hand – he reached for one of her voluptuous breasts and got lost in the exquisite sensation of massaging the soft mound that was way more than a simple handful. He was groaning, and she was whimpering. It was magic.

Chapter 10

MEGHAN WAS ON FIRE. Like seriously, a ten-alarm blaze. He might be kissing her reluctantly, but that didn't stop him from going deep. His wide tongue sweeping along hers and exploring the recesses of her mouth produced not just a torrent of saliva but a different kind of flood between her legs.

When she'd wrapped a leg around his thighs and pressed against him, her panties drenched with arousal. It was wild, hot, and very, very sexy. If they hadn't been in an awkward position and in a spot where anyone could come upon them at any minute, she would have been shamelessly grinding against the bulge she felt pressed against her core.

His lips feasted on her quivering mouth. She loved the way his beard scraped against her skin but nothing prepared her for how it felt when he fondled her breast. Even through her clothing she could sense the heat coming off his hands and the power of his touch.

She knew they were quickly getting out of control, but she didn't want to stop. The inferno they'd created with their desire was strong and powerful. Meghan shuddered thinking about what it would be like to feel his naked body against her own. He was demanding and aggressive, and she loved every second of it. She might be a Ball Busting Boston Bitch but at this moment, she was putty in his hands. She felt shameless in her greedy need for more. A hand on her ass, another molding her breast to his touch and his tongue moving seductively in her mouth—she was lost.

A sound found its way into her consciousness that wasn't her moaning or his earthy grunts. He must have heard it too because they both started, coming back to reality at the same moment. As the intensity of the response to what they were doing to each other started to back off, Meghan wanted to scream in frustration that this perfect moment was being forced to an end.

His mouth slowly pulled away from hers but his hand remained on her backside, holding her firmly against him, as the other gradually released her breast. Still pinned together he looked into her eyes for a long moment as they each struggled to catch their breath.

He didn't push her away this time. Instead he stayed on top of her even after she dropped her leg from around his thigh. She realized her nails had been digging into his back and she'd again been energetically clutching at his hair so she reluctantly eased both her hands but didn't remove them.

In a voice made rough with arousal he told her, "You tempt me in ways that wreck my resolve to keep away from you."

She answered, surprised how husky and seductive she sounded. "But I don't want you to. Stay away that is."

He looked almost pained by her words. "You should, Meghan. I swear to God that you should."

She didn't understand. "Do you want to hurt me?" she asked. It was the only question that made sense to her.

"No. Of course not." Well, he did. But not in the way she meant.

"Then why should I want you to stay away, Alex? *Why*? Please tell me what's going on."

He laid his forehead against hers for a brief second and then sat up slowly, bringing her shaking body with him. She didn't like the look of bleak desolation that crossed his face. It pained her to see him like that.

"Does this have something to do with David?" she whispered as he tried to right them on the hay bale. "It does. I can feel it." She bit down on her lip and struggled with a truth she'd never spoken before. Maybe it was time.

He looked at her and nodded solemnly when she mentioned David's name, then sighed deeply and glanced away. "I'm not quite the war hero you think, sweetheart."

Meghan melted a little bit at the term of endearment he used. She'd never been anyone's sweetheart before. Did he know how much he gave away with that one word? She doubted it. He was trying too hard to fight what was happening between them. It told her a lot about how affected he was by the way they went up in flames each time they touched.

"Alex," she muttered slowly. "I think there's something I should tell you about me and David."

The sound they heard moments earlier was getting louder. Their private interlude was quickly coming to an end. He stood up, holding out his hand to assist her from the hay bale. Facing her as he was, she had a clear view of the massive bulge straining against the front of his pants. She looked at it and then up at him with wide eyes. When she wet her lips with her tongue he muttered darkly under his breath. "Shit."

Hauling her unceremoniously to her feet, he grabbed her chin with strong fingers and dove onto her mouth for a bruising kiss that left little doubt how turned on he was or how completely unresisting she was. When the kiss ended, he lingered long enough to run his tongue along her pulsing lips, making her groan aloud.

"We need to talk but not here and not now."

She nodded and told him, "I'm having lunch with the ladies and then we're going to work out an exercise program that they can do for the rest of their pregnancies."

"That's nice of you. I'm sure they'll get a kick out of it. Tori and Lacey are sort of outnumbered around here so having another woman around is like a slice of heaven for them."

"Are you kidding? Helping is what I do best. I'm thrilled to share what I know and coming from a testosterone-dominated environment myself, I know all too well how it feels to be odd man out. Or woman out, actually."

He smiled at her. The moment passing between them felt so achingly perfect.

"Will everyone be at the main house again for dinner?"

"Not if I don't want them to be," he answered quickly.

"Maybe we can talk later then."

He leaned in and kissed her on the forehead. "Let's just play this by ear and see what happens."

She might not have a shitload of experience with men, but she did have the benefit of having lived her whole life with a crew of strong-willed brothers and a very opinionated father—she knew a male-evasion when she heard one.

"You're going to have to tell me sooner or later."

"I know," he said. "It's not easy for me to talk about. Need some time to work it out in my head."

She reached up and feathered his messy hair away from his forehead then cupped her hand against the side of his face. "Don't push me away again, alright?"

"You may want to push *me* away, Meghan."

"Oh, I seriously doubt that Major. You underestimate my tenacity. It's an Irish thing. We redheads don't scare all that easily."

AFTER A LIGHT LUNCH with Tori and Lacey, Meghan hauled out her laptop and started running them through a series of videos she had on her hard drive that specifically addressed the benefits of yoga stretches for all types of physical conditions.

She was concerned about the edema Tori had, but her mind was quickly eased when she told her the doctor said it wouldn't be so much of an issue if only she'd learn to stay off her feet. He also told her some regular exercise would help alleviate the swelling. As her belly got bigger she might experience even more swelling so starting a simple yoga routine now would actually be good to help keep the blood flowing properly throughout her body.

Meghan enjoyed their time together. Both ladies were smart, funny, and clearly head over heels in love with their husbands. They were also fiercely protective of all things Justice, particularly Alex.

"May we ask you something, Meghan?" Lacey questioned as she and Tori exchanged a look.

"Uh. Okay," she answered not sure where this was going.

"How is it that you know Alex? He didn't say last night, and we're curious. You two seem to be pretty familiar with one another but…" She shrugged, letting the rest of her comment hang in the ether.

Damn. Meghan hadn't seen that coming. Had Alex explained their history to Cameron and Draegyn? She didn't know for sure. Everything felt very complicated all of a sudden. How much should she say?

"Um. I don't know how to answer that ladies."

"It's a simple question, Meghan."

She couldn't help the exaggerated chuckle that rumbled from her chest. "Simple? *Shit.* Nothing's simple with someone like Alex."

"High five and an amen to that!" Tori giggled. "You should try being holed up with him in his bat cave all day. He's brilliant, in a scary, *are you fucking kidding* me way. You'd be amazed at the well-known people and high powered organizations that come around begging for his expertise."

"But the man's an island unto himself," Lacey added. "It's like he knows something the rest of us mere mortals don't. Everyone that is except our husbands." Both women nodded to each other in agreement. "Also, the fact that you're staying in the main house and not at the Casita is a huge tell on Alex's part."

"Casita?" Meghan asked.

"Yeah. There's a sweet little guest cottage out behind the big house. It's for the brothers' use only. It's where Alex's sisters and mom stay when they're here. Drae's family too. I lived there when I first came to the Villa. Even my husband commented on how out of character it was for Alex to have you stay in the main house."

That was a lot of information to take in. Meghan hesitated and then asked, "Is it me or does the room really get silent when he walks in?"

Tori answered with wide eyes and an exaggerated nod. "No, you're not imagining that. He's like power incarnate or something. People stop, get quiet, and look up because he's so …..*yikes*. I don't even know what word fits."

Lacey rubbed her tummy and smiled. "He's Alex. 'Nuff said. But that's kind of why we're so curious. You appear out of nowhere and suddenly the absentminded professor is the one who's silent and looks up when *you* walk in the room."

"Really?" Meghan squeaked. Holy shit. Was that how people saw them after only a few short hours in their company? She'd shared a meal with these people and that was it, but somehow they'd picked up on the heavy undercurrent. Hell, they didn't even know about the scene in the hot tub or how she'd almost gotten naked with him in the barn. Damn. She could feel a telltale blush firing up across her pale Irish skin.

"Jeez Meghan," Lacey chided. "Your face is almost the color of your hair! Got anything to confess?"

"Oh my Lord," she answered shaking her head with embarrassment. "You ladies are just bad!"

They both roared with laughter. "Bad boys. Bad girls. *Hmm.* Seems like the perfect match, don't you think?" Tori chortled. "C'mon Irish. Out with it. Can't fool us. We know a sister bad girl when we meet her!"

"Oh shit! I surrender," Meghan cried. "You're clearly not going to give up so I'll just say this. I've known Alex since the end of his time in the service, and we'll have to leave it at that. The rest of the story is his to tell."

"I knew it!" Tori chirped excitedly.

"Wait a minute, wait a minute," Lacey protested. "You said you've *known* him. Is that a cerebral knowing or a physical one?"

Tori giggled at her sister-in-law. "Using the big words, are we?"

Lacey shrugged. "She's a teacher. I thought it appropriate to break out some of those five dollar expressions for good measure." She fixed Meghan with a look and added, "Care to answer?"

"Wow. You're good."

Lacey snorted out a laugh. "We've both been through it. Once that lightning bolt hits, the Justice men get serious and territorial fast. Alex's sudden personality change suggests that while you may know each other, this is the first time he's had to deal with you in person."

Meghan considered what she said. Serious and territorial? Didn't feel that way when he was growling at her to *get out of here* or taunting her with cryptic remarks like *maybe you'll push me away*. She sighed. Tori and Lacey were staring at her waiting for a response so the sigh changed to a smirk and she said, "Bull's-eye."

Tori clapped her hands together with glee. "Oooh, this is so cool. We're getting a new sister!"

"Whoa, whoa, whoa!" Meghan roared. "Don't go jumping the gun. What's going on is complicated. Like more complicated than you could ever imagine."

"Darlin'," Lacey purred. "You are preaching to the choir." She and Tori looked at each other and smiled. "We know complicated, believe me. Frankly, I don't think anything less than complicated would do for the Justice men."

"Alright, alright. Enough of this," Meghan insisted. "Let's focus on getting you two mommies set up with a simple exercise program and leave the *complicated* stuff for another time."

Later, as Meghan was gathering her stuff for the short ride back to the main house, she pulled Tori aside and asked what she meant when she mentioned Alex's bat cave.

"Oh, it's just a term the guys use to yank Alex's chain. It means the tech zone where he works. Where we work together. It's an enormous cavernous space, kind of dark and always on the cold side because of the ton of electronics he's got running in there. Think of it like a home office only more like a science lab than a paper repository."

"Do you think it would be alright if I stuck my head in and looked around?"

"Are you kidding? Alex loves talking tech. He's amazing, actually. When I first started working for him, he was involved in a hologram project that got a bunch of dark op super spy shorts in a bunch. He's a natural nerd. It's organic with him. Want me to take you in for a look?"

"Is that allowed? I mean will Alex be okay with that? I don't want to nose around if it's none of my business."

Tori seemed to consider that for a moment but quickly reassured her, "If you ask smart questions, and I'm thinking with your education background that's a given, he'll be beyond thrilled. Alex needs to be challenged. I don't think he'd be satisfied with just tits and ass."

"Oh, I've got the T & A covered, that's for sure," Meghan said.

"But I sure would like to get a look inside the bat cave."

Tori put her arm through Meghan's and smiled. "Well, come on then. Let's leave Lacey to her afternoon siesta and go rattle a few chains in Alex's face. Will be fun!"

Meghan wondered what she'd just got herself into.

ALEX WAS UP TO his eyeballs in data and starting to feel the strain from too much time staring at a monitor. After leaving Meghan so she could have her time with the girls, he'd immersed himself in work to keep from replaying the way she'd melted underneath him when he pressed her back into the hay bales or the way she'd whimpered and moaned while he helped himself to her mouth. Oh yeah, and her ass and boobs too. Try as he might, he just couldn't stop himself. She called to him on some primal level. Got his blood pumping and dick hard with only her presence.

He wondered if she was aware of the looming anniversary of the bombing. Each year as the date rolled around it was hard to ignore. Referring to it as an anniversary never sat well with him but what else could it be called?

That first year after his life had gone to hell, he'd been in rehab when the day came. Drae and Cam had gone to the center outside Phoenix where he'd fought to put his life back together and regain the use of his leg. Spiriting him away from the watchful eyes of the therapists and doctors, they'd headed for an old-time honky tonk bar where they'd gotten shitfaced and nearly caused a scene when a drunken game of darts got out of hand.

Each year since then they spent the day trying to forget what happened, mostly with too much liquor. Instead of hurling dangerous objects through the air, they hunkered down for a video game marathon that usually ended with a round of naked, inebriated howling at the moon.

How would they handle it now that there were wives in the mix and the unexpected presence of a woman who was, in many ways, collateral damage from the bombing? This was why he needed to have a serious talk with Meghan. He couldn't keep up the push me, pull me scenes he was putting her through—not without hurting her even more. He'd done enough to fuck up her life. She had a right to know the whole story, even if it meant she hated him in the end.

He almost jumped out of his damn skin when he heard a softly voiced, "Hi," right next to his ear. What the fuck? Had he conjured her up from his thoughts?

"Oh, I'm sorry. Did I startle you?" she asked. The uncertainty in her voice told him he'd probably jumped half a mile.

"You scared the fucking shit out of me. What are you doing here?"

"Dammit, Alex. I'm sorry I disturbed you. Tori said it would be alright if I came in and looked around, but I'll leave you to it and catch you later." She turned toward the exit and took maybe half a step before Alex pulled her back.

He was perched on a high backed stool and when he yanked her into him, she fit neatly into the V of his spread thighs coming to rest against his chest. Once again, his blood started pumping and his cock twitched just from her close proximity.

There was nothing gentle about the way he gathered her close and pushed her head toward his with the hand he immediately fisted into her hair. Kissing her like a madman he laid waste to her mouth as if the power of her lips would banish his dark thoughts.

There was no hesitancy on her part; she softened against him opening her mouth to his lusty assault, wrapping her arms about his neck as she hung on while he plundered deep.

He heard an amused cough from the shadows that let him know they weren't alone. *Fuck.* Pulling his tongue out of Meghan's mouth and setting her off him was like Chinese water torture. Right at that moment, Alex wished Tori would go the hell away.

While Meghan pulled herself together after their unexpected explosion of passion, he glared at Drae's wife. Tori got the message and hightailed it out of there with a slight wave and an embarrassed expression. He was glad to see the back of her but the moment with Meghan was lost. *Just as well*, he thought. Fucking her on his desk was not an option no matter how much his throbbing cock tried to change that decision.

"You're welcome here anytime. Sorry I barked at you. You took me by surprise is all." They might not be kissing anymore, but he refused to relinquish the tight hold he had on her body. With her between his thighs, those spectacular tits of hers were pressed against his chest. He'd be a damn fool to let her move away.

Making a snap decision he asked, "Want to go for a drive? There's a really cool rock formation not far from here. You can bring your camera and get a few good shots."

She looked flustered, and he hoped it was from the kiss. There was something satisfying and primitive about the way she responded to his possessive domination. He could tell it wasn't something she was used to, and the thought was more than thrilling.

"I'd love that," she murmured huskily. The rapid rise and fall of her chest told him she had gone just as ballistic as he had. "I'll just go grab my camera, and I want to get changed too. These jeans are too much in this heat."

Palming her backside, he looked into her eyes. "Baby, it's your ass that brings the heat. You make a simple pair of jeans look good. Damn good." He punctuated his words with the squeeze of a big handful of her butt.

MEGHAN ZIPPED THROUGH A quick change of clothes and a much needed freshening up after a morning of riding and an hour spent demonstrating yoga stretches. Just the thought of getting in a truck and being alone with Alex got her juices flowing. She was almost embarrassed by how wet she got every time he touched her. It was really disconcerting since nothing like that had ever happened before.

Oh sure. Sexy love scenes in a movie and the occasional racy passage in a book could get her worked up, as could the little bullet vibrator she resorted to when her female flesh begged for release. But never, *ever* had the touch or kisses of a guy ever done to her what Alex did. The man sent her senses aflame with a look.

And that damn beard. *God.* She loved the way it felt when he kissed her. There was something so very male about it. Same for his enormous hands and the broad solid chest she enjoyed being crushed to. All of this was so unexpected. Him. Her primitive response to him. The way they fell on each other every chance they got.

She chose a simple cotton sundress with thin straps and a smocked bodice that clung to the outline of her breasts. On a whim she went braless because the straps on the dress were too thin to hide an under-garment. *Yeah, right.* It was more like going sans bra meant if she got the chance to push his face into her chest, maybe he'd do to her boobs what he'd been doing to her mouth—namely devour them. The thought of his bearded face pressed against her pale flesh made her shiver.

Skipping down the stairs with camera in hand, she all but ran into the driveway when she saw the big dark grey truck idling right outside the front door. He hadn't mentioned doing any walking and since she doubted in this heat that he wanted to go stomping about, she wore simple flip flops but left her hair loose and flowing about her shoulders. To say she was excited wasn't doing justice to the occasion.

He was waiting for her by the side of the truck, clutching an iP-hone in his hand as he tapped the keyboard with an intense look of con-centration on his face. He looked hot. Sexy hot, not temperature hot. In a t-shirt and jeans that accentuated his rugged, outdoorsy appeal, she slowed down to admire how the cotton tee stretched taut against his chest and the way the faded jeans clung to his manhood in all the right places.

Looking up as she shut the wide front door, his face brightened when he saw her then smoldered appreciation as he checked her out from toes to head.

"Your chariot awaits, my lady," he murmured at her approach. Hauling open the passenger door so he could help her step up into the cab, Meghan was stunned to find a big Labrador sitting in the middle of the wide bench seat.

"I hope you like dogs, Meghan," he laughed. "She runs to the truck whenever she hears my keys rattling. Couldn't tell her to stay unless I wanted a female with hurt feelings on my hands."

Meghan laughed and hopped gracefully into the truck as the big dog eyed her cautiously.

"Uh oh. Hope I don't piss your girlfriend off! You better run around, get in quick and introduce us before she takes a bite out of me."

After getting her settled comfortably he did just that, swinging into the driver's seat and patting the dog on the head.

"Zeus," he chuckled, "meet Meghan." The dog looked at her for a minute then leaned over and licked Meghan's face. She'd been accepted, but that didn't mean the Lab was going to relinquish her position at Alex's side. Hell, the damn animal was all but in his lap as he put the truck in drive and pulled away from the house.

The humor in the situation got them both laughing. "Well, this is a first," Meghan joked. "Don't think I've ever had to compete with a canine before."

They drove along down a bumpy dirt road that stretched far behind where Drae and Cameron's houses were located until they were a long way from the main compound. Alex chatted happily about the history of the area telling her the Villa and surrounding acres had been in his family since the early 1800's.

"You don't exactly fit the Spanish mold Alex. Why is that?"

He smiled. "Easy. My grandfather was one hundred percent Spaniard. He married a sweet English rose, my grandmother Annabella. They had two sons—my dad Cristian and my uncle Eduardo. Eduardo was the eldest but he went into the priesthood so that left all the hereditary holdings to my dad. Cristian, in turn, married a true southern California girl, my mother Ashleigh. They had the golden son—that would be me—and my two sisters. We grew up in Sedona while my grandparents still lived here. When they passed away, Dad inherited everything which is how I come to have the Arizona property."

"Where are your parents and sisters now?"

"They're in Spain actually and have been for the last decade. Our family runs a vineyard. It's a good life—everyone's happy and healthy. But all that English and American DNA means my sisters and I are pretty far removed from our Spanish bloodline."

"How did the hereditary Don of a Spanish family end up in Special Forces? Seems like an odd road to take."

"I had just earned a degree in science and technology from NYU when the World Trade Center was attacked. After living in New York City for four years I took the attack personally. Like so many others, I put my personal life on hold to serve my country. My rather unique skill sets back in the early days of the war came to the attention of the Special Forces folks. You can fill in the blanks from there. It's a fairly straightforward story. Patriotism. Duty. Love of Country."

"Nine eleven was a very big deal for my family too. With so many fireman and cops, it hit home really hard. I admire your service, Alex."

He didn't say anything for a really long time. "What are you thinking?" she asked.

It took a minute for him to answer as the truck continued bouncing down the dusty dirt road. "It all started out in such bright, shining terms. By the time it ended there'd been too much harsh reality, too much death, too much sacrifice. And for what? A war that never fucking ends in a country that doesn't give a shit about our so-called help."

Zeus chose that moment to lick her master's face. Meghan wondered if she picked up on the bleak tone in his voice and wanted to comfort him. She reached out and ran her hand up and down the beautiful dog's neck in solidarity for the man they both clearly cared about.

TORI WAS TITTERING ON like a magpie, filling her sister-in-law in on all the juicy deets of what she'd witnessed in the tech cave.

"Oh my God, Lacey! It was so adorable. She walked up behind him, said something and BAM! Two seconds later he was all over her like a rash. Don't mind telling you I got a little hot and bothered watching them. I've never seen him like that but oh lord! That man knows how to kiss a girl."

"Are you serious? Just like that? Poor Alex. He's got it bad, huh?"

Tori plunked down on the sofa and put her feet up on an ottoman while Lacey curled up the best her pregnant tummy would allow on the neighboring loveseat.

"I like her, don't you?" Lacey asked. "She's almost like a female version of him if you think about it. Smart. Well educated. In no way a wimp. And seriously, that body! Holy cow, huh?"

"Well let me tell you something, if you'd seen the way he grabbed onto her it'd be a safe bet to say he likes the curvy girl thing very much!"

The both laughed and sighed, the way girlfriends do when they're talking about romance. After a few minutes Lacey got serious.

"So. What do you think? How soon will it take Big Daddy to screw things up? After all, we've both been there, done that with these Justice brothers."

"Hmmm. You have a good point," Tori replied. "Draegyn was the Crown Prince of Denial and like you've said, Cameron was a runner. I wonder what fuckery Alex has up his sleeve."

"Men! *Right?*" Lacey chuckled.

"Uh oh. What are you two ladies up to? It's never good when I walk in a room and hear my wife chastising the male sex in that tone." Cameron smiled indulgently at his Ponytail and leaned over to plant a quick kiss on her mouth.

"Your old lady and I were discussing Alex," Tori told him.

"And Meghan," Lacey added. "Tori says they got into a seriously hot clinch up in the bat cave. Lots of touchy-feely stuff and loads of tongue."

Tori barked out a laugh bigger than her waif-like body. "Wait a minute! I don't remember saying anything about tongue."

"It was implied," Lacey shot back with a wink.

Cameron sat next to his wife and put an arm around her shoulders as he leaned in and rubbed his face against her belly. "Mommy's meddling!" he growled against the bump.

"Well someone has to. We were just trying to figure out how long it'll take Alex to put his foot in it."

"It's complicated," Cameron replied growing suddenly serious.

"I'd say that's interesting, brother-in-law, because Meghan used the exact same word when we asked how she knew Alex."

Cam shot Tori a surprised look. "Really? *Humph.*"

"Oh my God. You know something, don't you honey?" Lacey asked.

He sighed and said, "I know plenty but I'm not going to discuss it in this ladies sewing circle you've got going on. Besides, Alex is entitled to his privacy, as is Meghan."

Tori eased her feet off the ottoman and stood up. "I think that's my cue to go find my husband and use my powers of persuasion so he'll tell me what's going on." Looking at Lacey she added, "I take it you'll be applying the same pressure to your other half?" At Lacey's jerky nod she smiled. "Then we can compare notes later."

When they were alone, Lacey cuddled close to her hunky husband and nuzzled her face into his neck. "I love the way you smell when you're all hot and sweaty. Did you and Draegyn get the visitors settled in the dorms? I saw Ria and Ben unloading a ton of supplies yesterday getting ready for their arrival. Who is it this time?"

Absently stroking his big hand across his wife's protruding belly he answered lazily, clearly distracted by other things. "It's a rental. Bunch of spooks. They're using the facilities for their own refresher training. Not much for Justice to do but provide a place for them to hole up and plenty of conference space. Let's not talk business, baby. I've got other things on my mind." His hand was slowly creeping under the flowing maternity dress she had on.

"I'm glad you're home," she murmured. "Want your wife to scrub your back in the shower?"

He leered at her as his hand slid down between her thighs and rubbed against her mound. "My wife can feel free to scrub way more than my back."

"Mmm. I like the way that sounds. But first..."

Cameron laughed out loud and grinned at her. "I knew it! Just lulling me in with sexy promises. Biding your time to ask a bunch of nosy female questions. Might as well go for it woman so we can move on to much more pleasurable things."

She smiled at the man she loved with all her heart and soul. "Is it so wrong to want everyone to have the kind of happiness that we do?"

"No. But you're asking me to talk about things that aren't easy to discuss."

"Understood. I'll make this easy then. Just tell me how Alex knows Meghan. That's enough for now."

Cameron sighed and put his head on the back of the loveseat. It was still damn hard to share after a lifetime of brooding silence. But he was getting better at it. Lacey had healed his broken soul in every way that mattered. He knew he could trust her completely. It was a great feeling.

"She was engaged to one of the guys who died in the blast. He wrote to her, as the Commanding Officer, and they became pen pals during his rehab. Lotsa years pass and they kept in touch, but not in a substantive way. She was here in Arizona and came by to thank him for his words when her fiancé ate it. And the rest, as they say, is history."

"Wow," Lacey sighed. "Thanks my love. I think you've earned way more than some back scrubbing."

Cameron stood and easily pulled his wife to her feet. "Come on baby. Let's go make some magic in the shower."

ALEX PARKED THE TRUCK in a secluded spot that gave them a magnificent panoramic view of the red sandstone rocks glowing in the late afternoon sun. It was one of his favorite spots—where he came when he needed to breathe. It was quiet and beautiful. He supposed his trips here were like a personal meditation. He'd never brought anyone but Zeus so the significance of showing his private power spot to Meghan wasn't lost on him.

While she readied her camera he stepped from the truck, opened the back tailgate, and called Zeus from the cab. The dog was used to the routine of this trip and immediately hopped into the rear bed of the truck with ease. Ever the good dad, he flipped open the storage box to retrieve her travel blanket and a bowl in which he emptied a bottle of water.

Leaning against the tailgate, he tossed Zeus a morsel from a bag of dog treats and watched as Meghan started snapping away with her camera. It really was a stunning vista, worthy of being photographed, but not nearly as enticing as what she was wearing. Was she trying to make him crazy or was he doing it to himself?

After seriously appreciating the way she wore a pair of jeans, he was equally as admiring of the summery dress she had on. He very much preferred a woman to look like a woman and not a pant-suited approximation of a guy. Probably the result of too many years in uniform where even the female soldiers wore the same dull serviceable gear—he was finding her feminine style undeniably stimulating.

He thought of his feisty Spanish grandmother who had been quite a beauty in her time. One day he overheard her passing on some grandmotherly wisdom to his sisters that had cracked him up. She'd told them that real men expected their women to be ladies in public and harlots in private. The sentiment proved to be more than true in Alex's case.

Meghan eventually wandered over to him, scrolling through the pictures she'd taken and showed him one that really was spectacular.

"I can't get over all the colors in the landscape. Anyone who thinks the desert is boring is either blind or dumb."

He replied, "I love it here. No matter how many times I come to this spot, I see something different." Right then he was referring to how she looked against the desert backdrop—committing everything about it to memory. "Could you send me that jpeg, Meghan? I'd like to blow it up and hang it in my study."

Looking surprised, she said, "Seriously?"

"Yeah. You have a photographer's eye. It's cool how you captured the saguaro cactus in the foreground against the afternoon sun lighting up the rock formations."

"Thanks," she said, clearly pleased with his comment. "I've got thousands of pictures from my adventures that I pick through and put in digital scrapbooking pages. I'm glad you like this one. It's definitely a keeper."

It startled him when she sat on the tailgate and in one fluid move, tucked her legs under her bottom and stood up. *Shit.* If he leaned a little to the left, he'd probably get a good view of what was under her dress. Moving back a few paces she started clicking away, and then guilelessly began snapping overhead shots that looked down at him where he leaned, feeding doggie treats to Zeus.

"What the hell are you doing woman?" he teased.

She grinned mischievously. "Couldn't help it. You've got the look of a cowboy dressed in your jeans and boots with the desert in the background. Maybe I'll Photoshop in a hat and a horse on a tether later!" she joked.

He snorted with amusement and flashed her a wry grin. "I look like a king-size dork in a Stetson, but I do have one if that's what floats your boat."

The image of him wearing nothing but a cowboy hat, slam fucking her from behind against the side of the truck flared in her mind, making her blush beet red.

She nearly died of embarrassment when he noticed and chuckled. "I know a dirty thought when I see one, Meghan. Care to share?"

"No, I do not!" She laughed primly as though naughty thoughts were something ladies did not speak of. She shot him a pout when he threw back his head and laughed.

Perching precariously on the wheel well in the bed of the truck, she caught a flare in his eyes. He quickly looked away, clearing his throat in the process, making her wonder if she'd given him a panty flash when she sat down.

To her surprise, Zeus moved closer and leaned against her leg protectively. Girl power? The thought was more than just a little amusing. While the female Lab had been accepting of her presence, she suspected if the damn dog wanted to, she could really be a problem. Alex and Zeus clearly adored each other.

Leaning down, she wrapped her arms around the dog's neck and nuzzled into her shiny coat, whispering, "We're going to be good friends, you and I." The dog responded with a quick lick along the side of her face making her giggle as she sat back, muttering, "Yay! Dog kisses!" Meghan was stunned when she looked at Alex and found him, iPhone in hand, taking a picture of his own.

"What are you doing?" she barked with laughter.

"Are you kidding? That's going up on Facebook! Bragging rights. Me and two beautiful females, alone in the desert." He wagged his eyebrows suggestively making her laugh all the harder.

Putting out his hand, he said, "C'mon lady. Jump down and let's hide in the truck for a bit. It's hotter than the lobby of hell right now and your shoulders are starting to turn pink. Gotta get you out of the sun."

God. He was so damn cute. When she took his hand, a tingle of excitement shot up her arm making her nipples peak and rub against the smocking on her dress. The best part though was how he put his hands on her waist and swung her out of the truck bed to land at his feet. Some deliciously female contrivance made her wobble slightly so she could put her hands on his shoulders for balance.

With him gripping her waist and her hands on his body, they were in perfect alignment for a kiss. She was thrilled when he went for it. This time, unlike their previous kisses, he took her lips tenderly, almost reverently, tasting and nibbling on her mouth as if she were a gourmet delicacy. It was heaven.

It didn't last long. He hadn't been kidding about the sun and the heat. Shuffling her along to the door of the truck, he opened it and held her camera while she shimmied in. When he lifted into the driver's seat and slammed the door, she welcomed the air conditioning.

"Better get you some sunscreen," he told her with a heavy, serious tone.

"Oh, I'm good. Slimed head to toe with some good old-fashioned SPF One Million. The curse o' the Emerald Isle," she quipped in a dramatic Irish brogue.

He ran a finger along one of her straps and moved it enough to see a sunburn line forming on her shoulders. The look he gave her suggested that even a million wasn't enough sun protection for her pale skin.

"I need a parasol," she told him. She'd been looking for something suitable but hadn't found anything yet.

"A what?" he asked.

"You know—a parasol. Think umbrella, but not."

"An umbrella but not an umbrella?"

"Exactly!" she laughed.

He chuckled. "And women wonder why men don't understand them."

She grinned at him. "Google it when you get a chance and all will become clear."

He adjusted the flow on the air vents and asked, "Cooled off yet?"

"Uh, sure. Whatever." Maybe her skin had cooled down but the simmering sexual excitement? Not so much.

"Hmmm. Didn't sound all that convincing. Wanna try again?"

Meghan knew her naughty side was pushing to the front of the line to answer but instead of cutting it off before she did something stupid, she just went with it.

"My skin has cooled off nicely, Major." She let the innuendo of more hang in the air.

He picked up on it. "But....?"

"*But*. Being this close to you, with nobody around for miles, makes me hot in other ways."

His eyes literally bugged out of his head. "Meghan..." he growled, low and deep, the red-flag apparent in his voice.

"Mmm," she cut in. "I think we've been down this road before. First you growl a warning and then I moan your name because really, I'm dying for you to kiss me again."

It almost killed her when he didn't say anything. She could see that his respiration had picked up by the rapid rise and fall of his chest, but other than that, he was still and silent.

"I'm being too pushy, aren't I? God. I feel like such a tool," she groaned hiding her face in her hands. "Forget what I said. I can tell I'm making you uncomfortable, but I can't pretend I'm not wildly attracted to you, Major."

"Dammit, Meghan. The feeling is mutual, and you know it, but it's so fucking complicated ..."

"Why is it complicated? When do I get to know what the hell is going on in that mind of yours? Telling me you fucked up my life one minute then kissing me like your salvation depended on it...well, you're putting out mixed signals."

She caught his slight wince when she mentioned salvation and stored the impression away for later consideration. Meghan wasn't sure with her limited experience that she was woman enough for such a complex man. He was fighting the attraction, and she didn't know why or what she should do about it, if anything. Maybe it just wasn't meant to be.

But if that was the case, why had the trajectory of her life brought her to this secluded corner of the Sonoran Desert? To get her heart ripped out the first time she genuinely felt drawn to someone? That didn't seem quite fair. It wasn't like she'd been on a mission to seduce a man she only knew through letters. Far from it. What was happening between them could not have been anticipated. When she arrived on his doorstep it was to settle an old debt based on gratitude. That her feelings turned wickedly intimate in supersonic time was a complete and total surprise.

He looked at her, his eyes piercing and haunted. She could see the conflict reflected there. Her presence was causing him pain and though she still didn't know why, she liked him too much to ignore his suffering.

"Maybe we should call it a day," she whispered as agony flooded her soul.

"No," he grumbled. "Even if you left right now, it wouldn't stop me from wanting you. I don't think anything could change that."

Her mouth dropped open at his blunt honesty.

"I can't help wanting to push you down on this seat, right now, and rip your panties off with my teeth so I can taste every inch of your magnificent body. From the second you walked through my door I've thought of nothing but being inside you, Meghan. I want to fuck you so hard that you won't be able to walk afterward. Be so deep that you'll feel the imprint of my cock forever. Watching you come has become like an obsession, and I don't know what to do about it."

Her female core tightened with each word until the ache became almost unbearable. She was practically panting and deeply aware of the arousal drenching the panties he wanted to tear to shreds. If he felt that way, what was holding him back? It wasn't like she hadn't willingly gone into his arms every chance she got.

Maybe she should tell him how turned on his words made her. Tell him that all those feelings he was experiencing were mutual. "Alex," she murmured, putting her hand on his thigh.

"Oh Christ—don't touch me," he growled. "I can't do this. It's not right. For you."

"Why don't you let me decide what's best for me?"

"Because you don't know the truth. Because you don't see the dark hole inside me. Because every fucked-up thing from my past would suck the light right out of you and I've taken enough already. Because the things I want to do to you would make you run for the hills."

He was killing her with his torment and doubts. She wanted to take whatever it was that ripped apart his soul and make it better. Did he think she would honestly run away from him if the power of his need was unleashed? She wasn't stupid, and she was more than convinced that was part of why she was so drawn to him. Meghan wanted him to take her. To pin her down and control her. Make her scream his name while he was buried in her body. She knew without a doubt he'd be friggin' glorious in his domination; all primitive male and powerful. The thought gave her the chills.

Scooting closer, she put a hand against his cheek so he had to look at her. If it was the last thing she ever did, Meghan was going to take away the look of utter despair in his eyes.

Feeling that he needed her to give herself to him she whispered, "You haven't taken anything. I'm giving it to you. All of it. All of me. *Whatever* you need, I'm yours."

She kissed him gently on the mouth. A lover's kiss full of emotion—trusting, innocent—as she meant it to be. Sensing he was a stranger to tenderness, Meghan responded with an overdose of it as she put her hand on the nape of his neck and pressed wet, open mouth kisses all over his face, telling him with her lips how much she wanted to be with him. Give herself over to his passion.

"Let me love you, baby," she purred in his ear as she felt a great shudder tear through him that fired her up even more. Wrenching the t-shirt from his jeans, she wasted no time putting her hands against his skin.

Sucking gently on the lobe of his ear she whispered, "I want to touch you Alex. Want to feel your body pressed to mine."

He was trembling, trying valiantly to stay in control. She wasn't having it. He might not realize it yet, but this big man with the tortured soul belonged to her in every way a man could. She was sure of it.

When his head fell back and a groan rumbled up from his chest, she put her mouth on his neck and bit down hard as her hands swept under his t-shirt, greedily caressing his hair-covered, hard-muscled chest. It was Meghan's turn to shudder when her fingers found the hard nubs of his nipples. It wasn't enough. She needed to see him too.

Mangling the t-shirt in desperate hands, she managed to push it over his head, forcing him to pull his arms through the sleeves. Damn. He really was magnificent with his huge muscular chest made so very appealing with a covering of dark body hair that matched the beard on his face.

She crawled onto his lap, straddling him with ease as her sundress bunched around her the top of thighs. His hands grabbed her hips and held on tight. The unmistakable proof of the desire he was trying to avoid was pressed against her mound. Only her damp panties and his jeans kept their bodies apart.

With her hands mapping every inch of his torso, she fell on his mouth in a ravenous frenzy, nipping and biting at his full bottom lip, sucking it into her mouth as soft moans of pleasure filled the truck. Kissing Alex was like exploring paradise. He tasted like the sun, his breath hot as the Arizona desert. When their tongues mated he growled, deep and low. And then the kiss became his.

A flare of want that reminded her how undeniably male he was overtook her senses. As he deepened the kiss, Meghan fell into his powerful magnetism. Her fingers pinched his nipples, earning a grunt of approval while he clutched at her hips as he ground his erection against her heated center.

The air in the truck became heavy as they built a raging inferno of lust and desire. There wasn't enough air conditioning in the world to cool the heat coming off their bodies. Meghan was raking her fingers through the hair on his chest, moving across his abdomen on a beeline to the snap of his jeans when he grabbed a fistful of her curls and jerked her head back. She cried out, not from the aggressive way he commanded her but from the loss of his lips against hers. She struggled to get back at his mouth but he wouldn't allow it.

Afraid he meant to stop what was happening, she used her nails on the flesh of his stomach before going straight for the bulge she was sitting on. When her hand moved between their bodies and stroked him through his jeans he roared like an animal in heat, brought his hands to the top of her dress and yanked the bodice down over her heaving breasts, snapping the flimsy straps in the process.

She gasped her approval. He'd stopped kissing her, stopped moving altogether, and it wasn't until she searched his face for a reason that she understood why. He was staring at her naked breasts with a look so hot, it was a miracle she didn't go up in flames.

Seeing his desire, she desperately wanted him to touch her—to taste her aching flesh, and take her pebbled nipples into his mouth.

Feeling sexy and exquisitely female, she cupped her generous mounds in both hands, offering them to him. Her shocking wanton response felt perfect in the moment.

"Jesus, Meghan. Your tits are fantastic." He pushed her hands away, replacing them with his own. Caressing and massaging the bountiful globes he muttered, "Fuck, baby. Gotta taste," as he pointed one of her engorged nipples at his mouth and lowered his head to feast on her flesh.

Placing a wet kiss on the tip of her breast, he flicked his tongue back and forth against the nipple begging for his attention. When his lips wrapped around the sensitive bud and sucked it into his mouth, her wail of pleasure echoed in the cab of the truck.

Meghan was quickly coming undone. Spearing her fingers into his hair she held his head at her breast, encouraging, wanting more. He didn't disappoint. The greedy snuffling noises made by his mouth as he suckled her flesh drove her wild and caused a hot wet flood of sweet desire between her legs.

She cried, "Ah, God," when he increased the suction The move was so sexy she gripped his head in frantic want, moving his mouth to her other breast where he repeated the voracious pattern of kissing, licking, and sucking. Within moments she was shaking and trembling, grinding onto his lap in a feverish dance of desire.

When he finally released her flesh he looked at her with naked lust shining in his eyes. On a deep, throaty growl he said things that made her whimper. "You're so fucking hot. Is your pussy wet and aching?"

He didn't bite her panties off, but he did reach under her dress, tearing the miniscule satin thong from her body. Palming her mound he groaned at the moisture that covered his fingers. She dove onto his mouth again, clutching desperately at his shoulders as she ground her hips against his hand, furiously kissing him with a passion that made her mind go fuzzy.

Sliding a finger inside her, he bit at her tongue until she couldn't take anymore. She fell onto his chest and moaned as he worked a second finger into her passage, dripping with desire for him and hungry for his total possession.

"Baby, baby," she cried over and over. "Oh God, *please*."

His chest was heaving as if he was running a marathon. She'd never known anything to be so primal and exciting. Suddenly he growled a command in a voice raw with need, "Release me."

She couldn't get his pants unzipped fast enough. In a frenzy of movement, some of them awkward as hell, she pulled, yanked, and pushed at his jeans as he shifted, lifting his hips until she shoved them below his knees while his fingers worked their magic inside her.

When he pulled his fingers from her body he growled something about her being wet but she couldn't focus on his words. The desperate desires of her body had taken over and the only thing she knew was a piercing need to take his heated hardness inside until the aching emptiness was filled with his flesh.

He held his cock at the base and guided her hips into position as she trembled and panted. "Fuck me Meghan. Push your beautiful wet pussy onto my cock and take all of it."

She lost her shit completely right then and there. When she felt the lips of her sex stretch open to accommodate the fat head of his cock, she groaned and shook from head to toe. In fact, she was shaking so hard it was a wonder the Cal Tech earthquake sensors didn't go off.

His voice sounded hoarse and breathless. "Yeah, baby. That's it. Come on. All of it, Meghan," he growled. "Don't stop, don't stop," he commanded her as she lowered inch by magnificent inch, easing his enormous swollen cock into her wet depths.

"Ah, shit," he groaned. "You're so fucking tight." Putting his hands on her hips he pushed down hard and swift. Meghan was moaning. It hurt at first, taking his great size a challenge. Finally, when he was fully seated inside she leaned in and bit his shoulder as waves of pleasure radiated out from her core.

Alex wrapped his arms around her and held on tight, telling her, "Don't move, baby. Just feel." His hips rolled slowly against her in rhythmic surges that enflamed the sensitive bundle of nerves in her clit.

It was transcendent. Straddling his hips, his cock pulsing inside her. He wasn't thrusting, it wasn't necessary. Just feeling him so deep within her had Meghan's inner muscles tightening unbearably.

He felt it too and groaned. "Fuck. *Oh Fuck*," he cried. "You're gonna come just from me being inside you."

He was right. Her sex fisted his cock over and over and over, contracting around his pulsing flesh, milking him in a building frenzy that threatened to blow her world apart.

It wasn't enough, she needed the friction of his body against hers so she ground her pussy on him in a circular motion that had him reaching for her ass to control the movements. His cock reacted by swelling, filling her so completely she cried out in wonder.

"Come for me Meghan. Come all over my cock," he groaned.

When her orgasm hit she got swept away as the violent pulsing detonated his climax as well. They were barely moving but that didn't stop the ragged spasms from lengthening instead of subsiding as she rode waves of indescribable pleasure.

He was firmly lodged so deep inside her tight passage that she felt every jerk and pulse as his come spurted into her to be welcomed by a fresh surge of creamy nectar that gushed along his length in heated response.

She was lying on his chest, crying uncontrollably in a maelstrom of pleasure that left her weak and shaken. Nothing would ever be the same in her world after that.

Chapter 13

ALEX WAS IN A state of shock. Meghan lay trembling against him with her magnificent breasts pressed into his chest and his arms locked possessively around her. Still buried in her glorious heat, he was aware of the moisture seeping from her body onto his groin, a stark and very sexy reminder of what had just happened.

She'd called him *baby*. Told him with her words, and in no uncertain terms with her body, how much she wanted him. He hadn't been able to stop his response, letting every sweet unbearable sensation overtake him until there was nothing left but his hard cock buried in the hot velvet depths of her pussy. Nothing had ever felt so right. For the first time in forever he felt complete, whole. The darkness had given way to something pure and joyful, and he lost himself in the beauty of the moment.

As long as he lived he'd never be able to erase the memory of Meghan shuddering on top of him as she came. The way they'd propelled so quickly into an earth-shattering climax by the strength of her powerful inner muscles alone. Not even the daunting task of fucking her on the seat of his truck had made any difference.

Unfortunately, reality blazed with a vengeance in his head as every haunting thought that made him into an emotional recluse came hurtling home. The face of a soldier bubbled up from deep in his memory and tore at his soul as images of Meghan making love to her young fiancé made him sick to his stomach. He'd taken that from her and replaced it with his sex buried in her sweet body. It felt like the ultimate betrayal to a man who lost his life on Alex's watch.

Something ripped open inside him and a feral howl of pain erupted from his throat. "Oh God, no. *No*." A savage despair had him in its merciless grip. He couldn't breathe, couldn't believe what he'd done. He was beyond damned.

The atmosphere inside the truck changed in an instant as he struggled to lift her off his lap in his frantic haste to get some air and dial back the revulsion threatening to take him down. Meghan shot from his lap like a cannonball when his tortured roar split the air.

Suddenly, the door flew open and she scrambled away from him in such haste that she fell from the truck onto the dry desert ground, landing awkwardly on her knees. The sight of the exquisite beauty crawling to get away from him with her ass in the air and her naked breasts swaying with every movement damned him to hell.

Releasing an endless stream of self-castigating words, he slid from the truck, pulling up his jeans as he moved. It should be him on his knees in the dust, not her. What in holy fuck had he done?

Meghan couldn't believe what was happening. One second she'd been lying spent and happy on Alex's broad chest, listening to the pounding of his heart, blissfully wrapped in a cocoon of contentment, and the next her heart was being brutally ripped from her chest. His tortured cry and the "no" that shattered her euphoria brought her crashing back to earth with a violent thud. It was his frantic efforts to throw her body off his that was the topper. She thought she might be sick.

When she fell out of the truck and pitched forward as her knees came in contact with the ground, she tried to right herself with her hands only to have them scrape painfully against the dirt and stones. With her dress bunched around her stomach she felt exposed and vulnerable, a far cry from moments earlier when she thought she'd touched a piece of paradise.

She felt him trying to help her up but the humiliation of her position and the dawning realization that he'd instantly regretted what happened made her desperate to get away from him. Far away. She wouldn't cry in front of him but that didn't stop Meghan from the howling wails of agony sounding in her soul.

Slapping his hands away she flipped onto her bottom, horrified that her naked ass was sitting on the desert floor while her scraped knees and hands shot starbursts of pain along her nerve endings. Distraught, she yanked the smocked bodice of her dress over exposed breasts, wincing from the mangled flesh on her hands. Could this horrible moment get any worse?

Alex crouched down and quickly pulled her into his arms, picking her up from the dirt. She heard a shallow grunt that sounded a lot like discomfort rumble from his chest followed by a definite limp in his gait as he walked her to the side of the truck and placed her gently on the seat. She was no lightweight and despite his hard muscled body she knew the effort of moving her off the ground had caused pain to flare from his old wounds. *Good*, she thought. *I hope carrying me cripples the son-of-a-bitch.* It was what he deserved.

Your knees are scraped," he muttered as his hands slid down her legs to inspect her injuries. Taking her hands in his he turned her palms up and grimaced at the sight of torn flesh that greeted his eyes. She was furious. And hurt. And she didn't mean physically.

Brushing away some dirt and tiny pieces of stone stuck to her flesh, he lifted one of her hands to his mouth as if he was going to kiss the abrasions away, but she snatched it back and snarled at him with shock and disillusionment dripping from her words. "Leave me alone. Get away. You've done enough." She didn't care when his expression registered a pained look at her reaction. *Fuck him*, she thought.

"Meghan," he began, but she didn't want to hear whatever he was going to say. His actions spoke louder than any words ever could.

"Shut up Alex. Just shut the hell up and let me be."

He nodded, looking like a man who had just been handed a jail sentence but told her, "It's not what you think."

She freaked. "You don't know what I think you dick!" Her voice was overly loud in the silence around them but she didn't give a shit about any of that.

Her hysteria rising with each second, she hurled the only accusation she could think of at him. "My mother always told me, *a woman could have any man she wants because a man will fuck any woman who's willing*. Looks like I learned that lesson a day late and a dollar short."

"No," he barked. "That's not what just happened here. Please don't think that."

She pushed him away with a strength that surprised her. "Um, I think you saying, *fuck me Meghan*, describes exactly what just happened. Don't worry, Major. You're off the hook. I started it, and I finished it."

Scooting across the seat until she was plastered against the passenger side door, she did what she could to rearrange her clothing and restore some dignity to her situation.

"I want to go back to the house. Now."

Alex looked at her with dark eyes but didn't argue or say anything else. He grabbed the t-shirt she'd ripped off him and pulled it back over his head before turning toward the rear of the truck where Zeus still lazed. She heard the tailgate slam shut and a second later the big dog climbed into the cab and hesitated.

In one of those unbelievably surreal moments, the dog moved away from Alex and came to rest against Meghan's side, placing a paw upon her thigh and licking her face. It was sweet and protective and made a statement of female solidarity that had an *in your face* quality directed at the man left gaping at the side of the truck. She loved that big dumb dog with a vengeance from that second forward.

The long drive back to the Villa happened in complete silence with Meghan huddled against the side of the truck, as far away from Alex as she could get and Zeus acting as a buffer. She sensed the dog staring at her master with what she hoped was doggie disgust. Girl power indeed.

When the truck pulled into the driveway at last, Meghan scrambled hastily from her seat; vigorously slamming the passenger door after Zeus jumped down at her side. Shooting Alex a damning look before whirling away, she was so lost in fury she barely registered the people standing around watching the strange scene unfold.

With Zeus trotting protectively alongside, she stomped furiously past the startled onlookers and stormed into the house making sure to slam the front door as she did. The fact that her dress was barely staying up, courtesy of the torn straps, or that her underwear was God knows where made her angry retreat all the more dramatic.

Back in the driveway, Tori who had been unloading a stack of cowboy hats from the back of an electric cart for the agency's visiting clients, watched Meghan stomp away and saw the defeated expression on Alex's face.

Well, that hadn't taken long, she thought. Judging by the angry hurt emanating off the woman who just ignored everyone standing around, and by the fact that Zeus had clearly defected, told her a hell of a lot.

These Justice boys had an uncanny ability to fuck up the best thing that ever happened to them. It had only taken forty-eight hours for Alex to put his foot in it. Tori sighed knowing she and Lacey had their work cut out for them if they were going to save the situation.

Catching her husband's gaze as he stood silently slack-jawed watching the scene play out in front of them, she rolled her eyes and shook her head. When Alex turned away and stormed off in the direction of the pool, she noted his pained limp and saw how he clutched his hands into fists at his side.

Carmen, who had been helping her with the dozens of western hats, also watched what happened; only her face registered pained concern tinged with displeasure at the man whose back was quickly moving away from them. He hadn't said a single word to any of them. In fact, he seemed to barely register that they were even on the same planet as he.

With raised eyebrows Tori gestured with her head to Draegyn who nodded in silent response before following after his brother. She knew her boss well enough to know he wasn't going to share whatever had gone on between him and the angry redhead but he'd need the support of her husband.

She hesitated, considering what her best move was, then asked Carmen to finish with the hats before putting a hand on her bump for support as she scurried after Meghan. Somehow she knew that letting the situation cool off wasn't in everyone's best interest. Going by the pained fury on Irish's face, she wouldn't be all that surprised to find her throwing shit into a suitcase. She needed to act fast to keep that from happening.

MEGHAN MADE FOR HER room in haste with Zeus right by her side. The minute the door slammed behind her she flung herself on the bed, letting loose the tears she'd been holding back. She wasn't normally a crier but the waves of conflicting emotion battering her erupted in a torrent of hiccupping sobs that seemed to be endless.

Foolish romantic fantasies aside, no woman wanted to hear ugly regret coming out of the mouth of a man whose body was still deep inside her own. When she told him how her mother had always said a man would fuck anyone who let him, she hadn't been kidding. And that was pretty much how she felt.

He hadn't tried to take more than she was willing to give. No. That had been her. She'd practically forced herself upon him. God, what an idiot she'd been. Once he'd come inside her, he reacted so quickly that she'd been stunned. What had she done?

Zeus hopped up on the bed and curled against her shaking body as she sobbed uncontrollably. There was something comforting about the dog's head lying on her back as she shook and cried her eyes out. At least someone cared.

A quiet knock sounded at her door that she chose to ignore, fearing it was Alex come to make nice. She was so devastated that *nice* was permanently off the agenda.

After a minute, the knock came again only this time she heard Tori's voice. "Sweetie, can I come in?"

She nodded but no sound came from her mouth. Meghan felt empty and scared. Feeling as though she'd behaved like a right royal slut was messing with her mind. Thankfully, Tori didn't wait to be let in and slowly opened the door to peek inside. Finding Meghan sprawled on the bed was enough to get her moving quickly to her side, concern etched on her face.

"Oh, dammit Irish. Are you okay? Why the tears sweetie?"

Meghan sat up and furiously wiped the tears away. "I made such an unbelievable fool of myself Tori," she wailed.

Shooing the dog from the bed, Tori climbed onto the mattress and handed her a box of tissues from the nightstand.

"I highly doubt that, Meghan" she murmured, a thoughtful look shining from her eyes. Reaching out, she pulled on one of the torn straps that were supposed to be holding up her bodice and smirked.

Meghan blew her nose with a stuffy sounding honk and tried to get it together. "I need a shower," she eventually moaned, aware that she looked like hell and still wore the evidence of their sweaty sexually charged encounter on her skin.

Tori snorted out a half laugh and said, "That bad is it?"

"Well, my dress is torn, and I'm sitting here without any under-wear so you do the math."

The last thing Meghan expected was the grin that broke out across the other woman's face.

"Two questions Irish and then you can run to the shower."

Meghan sniffed and shrugged her shoulders. "Why not? Everyone might as well know what a slut I am."

Tori smiled and patted her shoulder reassuringly. "Believe me when I tell you that nobody is going to think that. Not anyone who knows Alex anyway. That distinction is his if I'm correct."

She nodded and looked away, wishing a sinkhole would open up and swallow her whole.

"Okay. First. Was there a condom anywhere in this situation?"

Meghan gaped at her with wide, horrified eyes at how irresponsi-ble she'd been but managed to croak out, "It's okay. I'm on the pill."

Tori visibly loosened up. "Second. Does Alex know this?"

The horror only deepened as she offered a negative nod. "Uh, it didn't exactly come up in conversation."

"*Sooooo* what… he had his head up his ass? That's not like him at all."

"Oh my fucking God Tori!" she wailed as a new wave off misery washed over her and the tears started up again. "It was all me. I started it and believe me—even if I wasn't on the pill, it would have happened anyway. What's wrong with me?"

Tori rubbed her back as she cried it out, then pulled a couple of tissues from the box and handed them to her.

"I can tell you what's wrong, Irish. You fell hard and incredibly fast for a Justice Brother. Welcome to the club sweetie."

"It was my fault," she whispered. "He's made it abundantly clear that he didn't really want me. In fact he's been trying awfully hard to make me back off."

The other woman snorted in amusement again. "Let me guess—he tried to make you back off in a push me pull me sort of way, right?"

"Yeah. How did you know?"

She smiled and stuck out her hand as if they were meeting for the first time. "Hi. I'm Victoria St. John. *That's* how I know. Do you think it was any different for me? Or Lacey? You will never meet three more extraordinary men than Draegyn, Cameron, and Alex but oh my Lord are they one fucked-up unit. But you need to talk to him about this. If I know my boss, he's probably wallowing in remorse and wondering how the hell to bring it up."

"This is unfamiliar territory for me. I don't have any experience in these matters. Plus, I'm embarrassed by how out of control I got."

"Well, I'm kinda glad to hear that. The experience thing, I mean. Look," Tori said, "my husband told me a little bit about how you came to know our fearless Big Daddy. I'm really sorry Irish. Losing someone that way must have been terrible. The Justice brothers are unusual men. Alex is like the conscience of the group while Draegyn is the intellect and Cameron the soulful brooding heart. Ever see the *Wizard of Oz*?"

Meghan nodded while trying to wrap her mind around the unusual reference.

"My hunky husband is the Scarecrow without a brain. Cam is the Tin Man searching for his heart and Alex, well Alex is the Lion. His challenge is finding the courage to overcome what he sees as a shit ton of failings. The kind that haunt you. Is this starting to make sense?"

Oh God, it was. Why hadn't she seen it before? He felt responsible for David's death and had tried to say so a bunch of times. Making love to her was something his soldier's conscience couldn't handle. That was what the pained *no* had been about. He'd disrespected the memory of one of his men by being with her. Plus, he wouldn't know that their lack of precaution wouldn't turn in to a shit show.

"Tori. You said Draegyn told you how Alex and I met. I want you to know that no matter what Alex thinks now, I was never going to marry David. I can't tell you why, but I swear. It wasn't going to happen. I cared for him, yes. Maybe even loved him. I knew him most of my life and despite what appearances may suggest, our so-called engagement was a moment in time spurred on by a war and something else."

"Does Alex know this?"

"I've tried to tell him but he won't listen. It's like he has this picture carved in stone inside his head where David's dead, somehow he's responsible, and being attracted to me is like pissing on a dead man's grave."

Tori thought about that for a moment and told her, "Maybe you should try and find out what that *somehow* means and go from there. I'm thinking that's what is driving him to keep you at arm's length." Taking in how she looked, the other woman smiled. "Doesn't look like he was all that successful at it either and before you say another word," she insisted as she put up her hand to stop whatever Meghan had been about to say, "there's no possible way you made a fool of yourself. If you think you seduced an unwilling man, think again. I knew that first night we met from watching him track your every movement that he was a goner."

Meghan sniffed again and gave her a watery smile. "Really?"

"Yes, sweetie. Really *truly* really. Now go get your shower and put on something pretty. Ria and Ben have a cookout planned and you don't want to show up looking like someone ran over your dog. And speaking of dogs, what's up with Zeus?"

Meghan looked at the big dog that sat by the bed watching them and giggled. "I think she's mad at him."

Tori scuttled off the bed and scratched the dog behind the ears. "I always did like her. She knows what's up."

They both laughed at that, and Meghan felt a measure of calm return to her senses. She was done crying, and she wasn't going to run. Tori was right. She had to find out why her hesitant lover was so damn conflicted. Maybe if she told him her truth, he'd share his.

"DON'T SAY A FUCKING word Drae," Alex muttered darkly when he came up for air to find the man standing at the end of the pool where Alex had flung himself after retreating from the scene with Meghan in the driveway.

Drae snickered and crossed his arms over his chest fixing Alex with a mocking look. "Dude. Your clothes are in a pile; I find you naked and swimming like you're trying to escape the devil. Not saying anything isn't an option."

Heaving a sigh, Alex hauled himself out of the water and wrapped a towel around his hips before collapsing on a nearby lounger. His leg was fucking killing him whether from the strain of picking Meghan up off the ground or from sheer guilt for having been such a complete dick. Both were viable options.

"I fucked up bad, bro," he muttered to his friend.

"*Uh.* No shit Sherlock," Drae sneered. "You put Cam and I to shame with how fast you managed to fuck yourself up your own ass. I think you set a new land speed record with this girl. You might want to consider an asbestos suit because that's one seriously pissed off lady. Unless I'm woefully mistaken, and I doubt that I am, I'd say you're in for some well-deserved fire breathing."

Ah shit. Drae was so right. He was fucked. She was furious and hurt too. If she turned on him it would be nothing less than he deserved.

"Want to talk about it?"

Alex snorted in frustrated amusement and glared at his brother. "Did *you* wanna talk about it when it was you being a complete ass-hat?"

"*Mmm*, probably not," Drae answered solemnly. "But then again, my situation wasn't quite as fucked-up or as tied to the past as yours is."

Alex threw his arm over his face to block out the sun and to shield his expression from the knowing eyes of someone who knew him too well.

Standing over him so his body cast a shadow, Drae went for the gusto, making Alex wince at the frank way he spoke.

"*Alex.* Fucking get over it, man. You are *not* responsible for what happened to her fiancé. There was not a single thing you could have done to stop what happened."

"The botched raid…" Alex started, but Drae was having none of it.

"That's tired bullshit, and you know it. If it hadn't been that raid, it would have been something else—something equally unexplainable. Those dickheads would use any excuse—fuck, they had no problem making shit up—to force what happened. Come hell or high water, they were going to eventually get explosives inside the perimeter. Yeah, people died. It's part of embracing the suck, man. We all watched those body bags fly out, but at some point you gotta let it go."

"She thinks I'm some sort of war hero."

Drae burst out laughing. "No she doesn't you asshole. That's your fucking ego talking. Meghan knows the score. Didn't she tell us that her entire family was a bunch of first responders? Do you honestly think that you're the only guy to ever think he's responsible for bad shit when it happens? Give her some credit, man. The girl has a great head on her shoulders, and I'm sure if you just explain why this is so hard for you, she'll understand."

There was a lot of truth to what Drae was saying. That was why he was the intellect in the family. He might be a cold-hearted bastard at times with the sort of nerves of steel that gets idolized in comic books, but he was also deeply intuitive.

"Time to pull it together, Dad," he mocked. "The kids want a mommy."

"Jesus. Don't even joke about that."

"I wasn't joking. Now pull it together and stop with the wah-wah shit. You've got a lady to talk down off the ledge. Ben's had the smoker going all afternoon and we're supposed to meet up in an hour for a family cookout."

"OH MY GOD! SHE'S so adorable," Lacey squealed with delight when she saw the puppy Brody was introducing to Tori and Drae. "What are you going to name her?"

The couple laughed and answered in unison, "Raven."

"You do realize she's a *blond* Lab, right?" Cam quipped. "Raven seems an odd choice."

Drae roared with laughter. "Excuse me, but Zeus for a female canine? Seems like we're just keeping with tradition."

"Well played, bro," Cam answered with a snicker. "Well played."

While Tori and Lacey cuddled and cooed over the new addition to Family Justice, Drae and Cam went to the big wood table set up for their cookout dinner and sat across from each other, cold beer in hand.

"So I missed all the fun earlier, huh?" Cam smirked.

"It wasn't pretty," Drae told him. "When they got back, Meghan had that freshly mauled look, and she slammed every door in her path. Tonight oughta be fascinating."

"Think he's in love with this girl?"

Drae almost choked on the beer he was swallowing. "What the fuck, man? How unreal is it that we both have pregnant wives and we're sitting around talking about love? Go figure."

"Guys," Brody called out. "And ladies too, sorry but I gotta roll. My crew is having a tough time with one of the Shepherds. Enjoy the puppy Tori!" On his way out he slapped Drae on the shoulder and whispered, "Good luck. Puppies are a handful, y'know."

Drae smirked and said, "That's what you're for Jensen."

Alex passed Brody as he left and the two men nodded at each other but didn't speak. After having ripped his head off over absolutely nothing, Alex was wise enough to steer clear of the dog trainer. Something about the good-looking loner being around Meghan didn't sit well with him. He knew he was being unreasonable, but especially after what had gone down earlier, he didn't give a shit.

After greeting the ladies present and saying all the appropriate things about the new puppy, he went to join the men who sat shooting the shit while Ben and Gus fussed with the grill. Betty had gone into town but Carmen, Ria, and Meghan were nowhere to be found. He wondered what the hell that was all about.

Didn't take long to find out when his housekeeper appeared wearing an expression directed solely at him, which suggested he go fuck himself. Ria, on the other hand, ignored him completely. To make matters worse, Zeus who had been ambling along by their sides also dissed him, choosing to investigate the new puppy instead of sitting adoringly at his feet. And Meghan was a no-show. Fucking fantastic.

When Ben shot him a murderous look as his wife stood close whispering fuck knows what, he almost groaned out loud. Whatever this was, it wasn't good. For him.

"Let's eat everybody," Gus called out as the family took their places at the big outdoor table.

Alex gritted his teeth but took his place at the head of the table as a bead of sweat rolled down his back. Scraping his hands through his hair, he hunched over with a dark scowl on his face aware that Meghan's absence was not lost on anyone. He couldn't remember ever having to endure such a painfully silent meal.

There wasn't any use in ignoring the fucking elephant in the room, especially not with the meaningful glares being sent his way.

Everyone around the table was surprised by his outburst, even Alex, when he'd finally had enough.

"Alright, goddammit. You can all stop with the dirty looks."

Carmen's *fuck you* look never wavered, something she'd never done before. He tasted the distinctive flavor of shoe leather as the image of his foot protruding from his mouth lit up his mind. *Shit.* Ria, Lacey, Tori, and even Zeus were also looking at him in a way that made him squirm. Apparently they were all on Team Meghan. Besides the one black look Ben had shot him, the men were wisely staying silent. That was what happened when women got added to the mix. Even Gus—the old fucker said nothing and seemed to be taking his cues from the testy housekeeper. Great.

Alex stood up and tossed his napkin onto the table. Looking to Carmen who seemed to be the lead bitch in this scenario he barked, "Where the fuck is she?" No one misunderstood the question or the meaning behind it.

Seemingly satisfied that she'd managed to rattle his cage, Carmen smiled sweetly then smirked right to his damn face. "She has a headache," was all she said although she made the term headache sound like, *she's putting bullets in a gun to blow your damn head off you fucking idiot.*

A headache? Women actually used that stupid excuse for real? Alex knew that *headache* was code for *bite me.*

Turning, he stormed from the group, hearing the distinct titter of laughter as he marched away.

He was at her door in record time, just barely managing to stop from flinging it open without knocking first. Trying to reign in the aggression coursing through his body was a lost cause although he didn't know why he was pissed off and that was part of the problem. It was his damn need for control he was sure of it. He wanted her with him and by not joining them for dinner she had provoked him beyond words. Headache, yeah right. More like a female manipulation; something he was having none of.

The moment he rapped on the door with his knuckles, he remembered that it was his rejection of the beautiful woman after she'd given herself to him that brought this situation about. That didn't stop him from wanting an explanation. This type of behavior wasn't what he'd come to expect from Meghan. The woman had brass balls so why was she playing the headache game?

When she didn't answer the door he simply pushed it open and strode in like he owned the place. Which he did but that wasn't the point. The primal man inside him had staked a claim on the red-haired woman when he buried his dick inside her hot wet heat and that was all he could focus on.

It took a few seconds once he entered the room to realize he'd made a huge mistake. The curtains were drawn making the atmosphere shadowy and silent. He saw her right away, curled on her side in the bed, with her knees drawn up and a hand covering her eyes.

Moving to her side he reached out and ran his hand across her hip making her moan out loud.

"Jesus, Meghan," he hissed, alarmed and chastised at the same time. "Are you alright?"

She flopped onto her back and looked at him through narrowed eyes, discomfort etched on her face. The words *ass* and *clown* flared in his mind. She really did have a headache.

Her voice sounded small and thready. "I feel like shit. Too much sun. Too much…well, I don't know. Everything's just too much. Don't be mad."

Mad? He wasn't mad. Okay. Maybe he had been a minute ago but seeing her in such a state instantly wiped all that from his head.

She was wearing one of those flimsy nightie things guys fantasized about, which got his dick throbbing in record time. Nothing but a bit of silk and lace, it barely covered her tits, tying underneath the glorious mounds and stopping at the top of her thighs. He saw matching silk panties peeking out which all but destroyed what little self-control he was clinging to.

After the blinding surge of lust cleared, he immediately saw bright red strips of skin alongside the straps of her nightie that extended down her arms. Her nose was hot pink, and she looked like someone who'd spent way too much time under the blazing Arizona sun. Add to that what happened between them and it was understandable why she was in a funk.

"I was worried about you."

She struggled to sit up making him swiftly move to assist her, bringing him close enough to pick up on that delicious scent of hers that had been fucking with his head from moment one.

Getting her situated against a stack of pillows, he saw a bottle of water on the nightstand and handed it over.

"Drink this, baby. You're dehydrated. Have you taken anything for the headache?"

"Yeah. Carmen gave me a couple of tablets; they just haven't kicked in yet. I took a shower and was starting to dress for dinner when it all hit me."

They were talking but she was avoiding his eyes. He didn't like it. Not one bit.

"Look at me Meghan," he growled at her.

When she finally did he saw so many emotions flash across her expression he didn't know which one to deal with first.

Before he could say anything, she beat him to the punch.

"I'm sorry about earlier."

The comment, innocent as it was, fired up a replay in his head of their provocative coupling and the ugly aftermath.

"You have nothing to be sorry for."

"I shouldn't have forced myself on you like that. It's so unlike me."

He knew that without her saying it.

"There's something you need to know but first, I want to tell you, uh…what I mean is you don't have anything to worry about."

He looked at her searching for meaning. She was blushing so hard her neck looked like it was on fire. She cleared her throat and put on what he suspected was her teacher face.

"The thing is, I'm on the pill. Have god awful periods." The blush deepened. "Anyway. I thought you should know after the way I behaved in the truck."

The way she behaved in the truck? Jesus. Who the hell was she kidding? He let the encounter get completely out of control knowing full well that he should have stopped things before he slid into her body. At least he was sorta sure he could have stopped her. Thing was—she affected him on such a primal level maybe he was kidding himself about that.

"We were both in that truck Meghan, and I don't want to hear any more about it."

She nodded and gave him a worried smile. "Now here's the other thing, Alex…"

He wasn't so sure he wanted to hear what she was going to say. Something about her tone freaked him out.

She must have picked up on what he was feeling because she quickly added, "I know this may be something you don't want to hear but it's important that I say it out loud, okay?"

He nodded but didn't have a clue where this was going.

"It's about David. David and me."

His gut clenched. She was right. He didn't want to hear it especially if what she had to say included regret for having let him inside her body. He might have been a pig for taking her like that but he didn't want to hear about her fiancé or deal with the possibility that she felt as he did, that they'd disrespected the young man's memory by what they'd done.

"Are you sure that talking is a good idea? I'm not a complete prick Meghan. Maybe we should wait till you feel better."

She shifted her position, sitting cross-legged with her forearms resting on her knees while she clutched the water bottle in her hands. He didn't even try not to notice that he had a clear shot of her panties, and she didn't seem to care. With the riot of auburn curls hanging on her shoulders she looked every inch a naughty temptress and it was all he could do not to reach out and touch her. He would have given his eye teeth right then to slide his hand into those silken panties and see if she was as wet as he remembered.

The minute she started talking, he pulled his thoughts out of her underwear and focused.

"I've never spoken of this to a single soul, Alex. But I think you need to hear this as much as I need to say it."

He'd faced almost certain death in combat but nothing scared the shit out of him more than whatever put that sad, confessional tone in her voice.

"David was my teenage crush. He and my brother Mike were BFFs. They were a couple years older than me, and I tagged along after them like a puppy dog, eager to join in their antics. We were always together, hanging out, getting in trouble. And they were my protectors too. You can imagine," she said while pointing at her chest, "that once the girls came on the scene, every horny teenage boy in a twenty mile radius was intent on feeling me up. I think that's why I never dated or looked for a boyfriend. I had Mike and David. Eventually David took on a protective role. To a teenage girl, that protectiveness felt like love. He took me to prom, and my parents loved him; knew his parents too. It was all so predictable. During my first year in college he suddenly announced one day, *like literally one day*, that he was shipping out to the Middle East. He'd been ROTC in college but whatever was going on was way more than reserve officer stuff."

Alex nodded understanding what she was getting at. David hadn't been regular Army. Or even a Marine. He was CIA and a relative newbie to their base in the months after he'd been promoted to commander.

"Your eyes tell a lot Alex, even though you're not saying anything."

All he could do was look at her. It wasn't in his purview to talk about things that went so far above his pay grade.

"Everyone just sort of assumed we were boyfriend and girlfriend so it seemed natural to fall into a relationship even though it wasn't entirely true. He was off in a war zone doing God only knows what and it felt like my duty to be his emotional anchor back in the real world. I wrote long letters full of stupid stuff." She glanced at him and winced. "You'd know all about that."

Alex shifted uncomfortably but said nothing.

"As time went on, our friendship really did grow into something else. As a dreamy-eyed college student I imagined it was love, and he certainly cultivated those feelings. It was like he needed the reassurance or something. It was weird but I didn't realize that until much, much later. Over the next two years he came home a few times, and like the dutiful girlfriend, I was always on hand. Mostly we spent time with his folks—seeing us together gave them some peace, as if he wasn't in constant danger. There wasn't much of anything physical between us to talk about, and I'd always figured it was because I was Mike's little sister. God, I was so painfully naïve."

She looked away from him, but he saw the blush she tried to hide.

"Anyway—to make a long story short, he came home for two months, just in time for my university graduation. We hung out and played like kids. It was so nice. I could tell something was up with him but figured it was whatever he was doing. I was just trying to be the perfect, supportive girlfriend. Coming from a family of first responders it felt like my patriotic duty—keeping the home fires burning and all. Right before the time came for him to leave, he suddenly asked me to marry him, totally out of the blue. I said yes, and everyone was happy. His parents cried, mine were ecstatic. Only Mike seemed less than thrilled."

She stared off into space, lost in her memories.

"Not too long after that I overheard David and Mike in the midst of a fierce argument. Mike screamed at him that it wasn't right that David should use his sister but for what I couldn't figure out. He was furious about something, and I imagined it was because he hadn't sealed the deal with an engagement ring. Later I would see the omission was a warning sign that passed right over my head at the time. After that I headed off to grad school and the letter writing continued only something changed. Shifted. Maybe it was because I was a bit older, wiser, I don't know. But I started to see that when he talked about the future it was in past terms. Like a re-telling of how we grew up. Christmas dinners with his folks, summer camping trips, rooting for the Red Sox. He never ever spoke of kids or having a family. Never shared his dreams for what he thought our future would look like, it was all weirdly anchored in the past. That was also when he started talking about the Justice Team. There were other squads and people he talked about too but it was mainly you guys."

She looked uncomfortable but kept on. "He had a particular fascination with Cameron. Talked about him like he was the second coming of Christ. It creeped me out, and I got jealous. That was when I started *really* reading between the lines and connecting the dots. It wasn't normal that my fiancé would write long, passionate letters about some random dude. I remember one where he referred to him as a hottie. Right then and there, I knew. David was gay. I have no idea whether he'd even admitted it to himself. It was *Don't Ask Don't Tell*. I think Mike suspected, and that was what their argument had been about. He hadn't proposed with a ring like a man in love with his longtime girlfriend should because, well…because I think the proposal was some last ditch hope on his part for a normal life. Maybe if he just went through the motions, *you know*, everything would magically be alright."

Alex was speechless. The story she was sharing wasn't anything like the one he'd created in his imagination. Plus, the part about Cameron was an eye-opener.

"I didn't get the chance though to set things right because he never came home. His parents were devastated. They tried to give me his grandmother's engagement ring because they felt he would have wanted me to have it. I didn't take it of course. Their devastation meant that no matter what, I was never, *ever* going to let my suspicions see the light of day. It was one thing to lose an only child and the promise of his future and all the things to come, and another altogether to find out posthumously that it had all been a lie. Once, and only once, Mike and I talked about it. We got shit-faced drunk sitting in the dugout at the neighborhood Little League field one night. David was his best friend. I was his little sister. He cried. I cried. We said things that needed to be said. I think he was relieved that I suspected. It meant he didn't have to keep that horrible secret alone."

He heard the pain in her voice and died a little inside. The loyalty she showed to David's memory humbled him.

"So you see, David and I were *never* going to be married. We'd never been intimate beyond a few lackluster make-out sessions. You're not shitting on some dead guy's grave by making love to his fiancée. I was still a virgin when he died, crying tears for a man who loved me but just not in that way. Two years later I went out and relieved myself of my virginal status with a drunken, sordid romp while on a cruise with some girlfriends who totally egged me on. They thought they were helping me get over a broken heart. I just wanted to move past the whole thing and screwing some macho asshole was the means to an end and a moment in my life that I'm the least proud of."

WHEN SHE FINISHED, THE silence in the room was deafening. Alex was struggling to wrap his mind around everything she
said. Meghan watched him with an intensity that let him know she'd
had a hard time telling him all that. Now that he understood, a huge
weight felt like it had been lifted from his shoulders.

There were probably things he should say, but his mind was blank.
Sometimes actions speak louder than words so he put his hand on the
nape of her neck and pulled her forward until his lips met hers. His
intention had been to tenderly kiss her but the gentleness was quickly
replaced with a rapacious need that exploded between them with a vengeance. Her admission had loosened him from the restraint he'd been
clinging to.

He plundered her mouth with no remorse. Swirling his tongue
with hers, Alex coaxed a fiery response from her, encouraging her with
his lips to join him in the flames.

Grabbing hold of her he hauled Meghan across his lap kissing her
with a searing passion. Only her slight wince at his touch stopped him

from pinning her to the bed. Remembering her headache and the sun-burn, he eased off until she calmed in his arms. Her need was great, and while he wanted nothing more than to sink inside her delicious heat, Alex knew this wasn't the moment.

True, her confession had given him a measure of peace but there was still a fuck ton of crap he needed to consider. Things he had to make sense of before this went any further. She didn't know the type of passions that drove him, and he wasn't just thinking about the remnants of guilt he felt for his part in David's death. It was time for him to stop running from himself too.

Meghan was shaking like a leaf in a windstorm. Sharing her truth with Alex had been powerful. More so than she expected. His vora-cious kiss had shocked her until she fell into it with helpless abandon. This was what she wanted. His passion. The power of all that mascu-linity focused on her. It made her feel feminine and wicked. Right then she would have gladly done anything he asked of her. The thought was shocking and a little scary. She hadn't known this side of her even ex-isted until he'd unleashed it.

When he ended the kiss she groaned aloud in disappointment and frustration. "Why did you stop?" she cried out.

The look he gave her blazed with desire but he didn't come back to her mouth. Instead he sat perfectly still but kept a hand on one of her legs.

"Thank God you told me that, sweetheart. It was killing me to want you so bad while some other guy's memory hung between us."

He slid his hand between her thighs and ran two fingers along her silk panties.

"I want you Meghan but you should know there's nothing gentle or tender about that want. Right now, this very second, all I can think of is ripping your nightie to shreds and devouring every inch of your body. My tongue wants to feel you come while I lap up your sweet flu-ids. My cock wants to bury inside your wet pussy and fuck you till you scream. I want to take you hard and fast, over and over. There won't be any hearts and flowers when I do, baby. That's not who I am. I like it rough, wild, and dirty as fuck. Wanna make you do things that good girls shouldn't even know about."

Oh my dear sweet God. Rough, wild, and dirty as fuck? She hoped to survive the experience and nothing, *nothing* was going to stop her from giving him everything he wanted. But her head was thumping with the mother of all headaches and wherever the sun had kissed her skin, it felt like fire.

"If my head weren't about to explode I'd want to hear about these things good girls shouldn't know about. Is it anything I can Google?"

He smirked but made no effort to stop touching her. "I will be your search engine, Meghan."

She sighed and shut her eyes resting her head on his shoulder, enjoying the feel of his big hand stroking her thigh and occasionally pressing his fingers against her mound in a way that made her squirm.

"By the way," he said quietly. "Thanks for corrupting my dog and turning her against me. And my housekeeper too."

Meghan smiled against his skin but didn't open her eyes. "That's what you get for being an ass. There wasn't anyone in that driveway when we got back who saw the both of us and didn't immediately know what happened." She liked the way his chest rumbled when he chuckled.

"This conversation most definitely is not over, but I can see you've had enough for tonight."

"*Mmm.* I think maybe the ibuprofen is starting to take the edge off." She wiggled on his lap and snuggled into his chest. She might be a so-called *good girl* but she knew how to get his attention.

He shifted and slid from underneath her, pushing her down onto the bed, searing her with a look that was so hot and lust-filled she whimpered softly.

"Close your eyes and relax, baby. Let me help you feel better."

And then the kisses started. Light sweeps of his mouth, sweet and slow, all over her face made Meghan purr with delight. The contrast of his soft lips and rough beard was delicious and sexy.

With eyes shut, her other senses were heightened. Each touch and heated breath on her skin intensified Meghan's awareness. When his tongue swept the shell of her ear a volcano of need erupted inside her.

He was seducing her senses and doing a damn fine job of it, too. Pushing his hands into her hair he feathered her curls onto the pillow. In her mind's eye she saw him laying her out just so as if preparing her for his pleasure. The thought was erotic and provocative.

A long, deep sigh moved through her body as she surrendered to his care. He was so big and powerful that this softened approach was mesmerizing in its simplicity. He still hadn't kissed her on the lips.

She felt the scrape of his beard on her cheek as he leaned close to her ear, whispering huskily, "You're fucking beautiful Meghan."

The touch of his lips, when they caressed her neck, made her tremble and shake as goosebumps prickled along her skin. God, it was heavenly. Pressing warm, moist kisses across her collarbone and up her neck to her chin he slowly stoked the flames of her arousal until she wriggled and moaned in earnest.

When he finally turned his attention to her mouth, she responded instantly, desperate for more. Meghan kept her eyes closed as he'd commanded but turned toward his huge body, lifting her leg and wrapping it across his backside. Even through his jeans she could feel the heat coming off him.

He feasted slowly on her lips in a wet, deep kiss that turned her to mush. His thick tongue inside her mouth, sliding sinuously against hers, set off sparks along her nerve endings. He was playing her, and she knew it, gauging her response, driving her insane with just his mouth until she was almost out-of-control.

She didn't expect him to draw back and ease her leg from his waist, but he did. Meghan moaned her disappointment and almost opened her eyes when frustration gripped her senses until she heard his low, growl.

"Lie still. Don't move or speak." He was asking a lot but she complied, gasping when he took both her wrists in his hand and raised her arms above her head, anchoring them to the bed with the power of his touch. "Keep these here," he murmured. All of his movements were slow but demanding. His control over her body was a definite turn on.

She startled when she felt his fingers press against her mouth until two slid between her lips and went deep. The move shocked and titillated at the same time. Feeling his hot breath close to her face, Meghan knew he was watching his fingers move in and out of her mouth making her quiver as she sucked on them and swirled her tongue the way she would if it was his cock.

"Good girl," he murmured.

Oh my God.

His fingers moved to her chin and then her neck, as his caress swept down the middle of her heaving chest until they met the fabric of her delicate nightie. She expected he would stroke her breasts, her nipples puckering almost painfully with anticipation, but he merely continued moving lower, his light touch rocking her senses.

Holding still became its own torture when Alex's hand swept across her stomach, going lower still until his hand was intimately cupping the mound of her femininity. Meghan jumped when his mouth suddenly began suckling on her neck, as his firm touch remained wedged between her legs. She turned her head to give him more access, relishing the sensation of his lips and beard on her flesh. It became almost impossible to keep her arms above her head until her fingers found a space between the headboard and mattress where she could hold on and still obey his command.

"Your panties are damp, baby," she heard him growl. All the while, he pressed harder against her mound, then released in slow pulses that were driving her wild. Meghan gritted her teeth, trying to stay still but his caress was too much. She quite literally couldn't help the roll of her hips as her sensitive flesh sought a more intimate contact with his hand.

The moment she moved though, he snatched his hand away, making her groan from the loss of his glorious touch.

"You must stay still Meghan…or I'll have to stop."

She grabbed onto the headboard and tried to quell the shaking in her limbs. There was no way she'd survive if he stopped.

Long moments passed, the only movement and sound in the room coming from her chest as it rose and fell on deep, shuddering gasps. Meghan was ready to beg for more, if only she could speak.

Having ignored her beaded nipples until now, he tweaked one with a sharp pinch, rolling it between his fingertips, murmuring, "Obedience will always be rewarded."

Was it possible to come just from the sound of his deep, sexy voice and a few deliberate touches?

With neat efficiency, she felt her panties being removed and bit down hard on her lip to stop from reacting. When she felt the cool evening air on her bared skin, her body slipped into a sensory overload that only increased with each passing moment.

Alex was pretty sure Meghan's headache had ceased to be an issue about the time he put his fingers in her mouth. With all of her senses focused on what he was making her feel, it was an easy way to disconnect her from the thumping in her head and the discomfort of the sunburn.

That didn't mean however that he wasn't also intent on his own pleasure too. He'd told her in blunt terms how he wanted her. Dirty as fuck actually didn't even come close to what was driving him, but it was a good start. Had he expected her to cringe at his lewd words? Maybe. When she didn't even flinch at his wicked description of taking her hard, fast, and rough, he practically beat his chest in primal satisfaction.

Looking at her, as she lay totally compliant to his desires, he was mesmerized by her exquisite beauty. With her riot of curls spread out about her shoulders and her arms stretched seductively above her head, she looked every inch the maidenly sacrifice to the carnality of his heavy desires. Leaving her short, silky sheer nightie on and not exposing her amazing tits had been a stroke of genius. It threw her off and added a bit of unfulfilled desire. For both of them.

When he slid the matching panties down her legs and tossed them aside, he almost lost his intention to focus solely on her pleasure when his dick reacted with strong pulsing throbs that stole his breath. This morning in the truck he hadn't seen anything but her naked breasts but now, seeing her glorious femininity exposed to his voracious gaze, well, it was nothing short of mind-blowing.

She had curves in all the right places and a surprisingly tiny waist that accentuated the womanly flare of her hips. Alex's heart thumped in his chest when he saw the fluffy curls guarding her pussy from his gaze. He wasn't a fan of the nude trend, relishing her natural look and the way the pale flesh of her thighs made her mound look like a decadent auburn-hued treat. He was *so* going to enjoy what came next.

Should he press her legs open or demand she spread them wide? *Decisions, decisions.* So far she had responded well to his verbal commands, pleasing him with her willingness to let him take total control of everything. Even her response. He hoped she liked this part of the erotic game they were playing because he seriously got off on dominating her in every way possible.

"Meghan," he grunted. She jumped at the demand in his voice. "Open your legs for me."

He watched her slowly and very shyly parted her thighs. Alex couldn't help the lascivious smile that broke across his face. This was new territory for her. He'd sensed her surprising lack of experience this morning and been floored by it. How a woman who was so undeniably sexy and drop dead gorgeous could remain sexually naïve was a fucking crime. It was also something that turned him on beyond measure. She was a carnal blank canvas; one he intended to enjoy.

Time to test her shyness. "Wider, babe. A lot wider. Show me that beautiful pussy."

God. Watching as she bit her lip and seeing those fantastic deep rosy nipples pressing against the flimsy nightie as she demurely met his demands was beyond anything his imagination could have worked up. Especially once he caught sight of her pink center. With her legs widening, the lips of her sex parted and he saw the entirety of her sweet pussy for the first time. It was incredible. He wanted time to stand still so he could just stare at it, at her, stretched out before him, panting with unfulfilled desire and so very ripe and ready for his touch.

Alex reclined on his side, his body close to hers but not touching, and enjoyed the view. There was a fine tremor moving along her flesh that excited him. The longer he made her wait for what came next, the more the tremors increased. Arms above her head, her torso barely covered in sheer silk and her legs spread deliciously wide, she was a true goddess. He was half-tempted to keep her like that until the sweet musky scent of her arousal found its way to his senses.

He liked playing with her. *A lot.* Liked the teasing touches and her trembling reaction. Putting his hand under her nightie, he drew small circles on her stomach, extending each caress until his fingers barely touched her soft curls. Her muscles clenched with excitement and expectation. He smiled.

"Are you wet, baby?" She bit back a moan, and he chuckled. She was learning fast. He'd told her not to speak. "*Hmmm.* What a shame I can't hear you beg."

The shaking increased. She was so fucking responsive but he'd tempted her long enough.

There was a light teasing sound to his voice when he leaned close to her ear and murmured, "Do you want me to touch you? See for myself if you're wet?"

Her head nodded so fast he had to chuckle again. His laughter however got caught in his throat when he reached into her sultry heat and ran a single finger along the seam of her sex, finding her flooded with arousal.

"Shit," he ground out as his finger briefly delved deep and found nothing but incredible heat and more moisture. Goddammit she was hot. Sexy hot. Using his middle and forefinger, Alex spread her creamy wetness, lightly grazing the bundle of nerves at her clit, which was swelled with desire. For him.

Alex took his time kissing and licking her with the flat of his tongue, tasting her skin from her neck down the exposed part of her chest to her stomach until his face was at pussy level. He wanted to watch while his fingers played with her sensitive flesh. His cock throbbed its approval.

With one hand he spread apart the slick lips of her sex and groaned at the beauty of her exposed pussy. He liked that her thighs were trembling. He knew he could probably do anything to her, and she would have welcomed it.

At first he thought of teasing her unmercifully. Rimming her passageway and denying her need but there wasn't any hope of that the moment he had her open to his gaze and he saw a droplet of creamy fluid escaping her body. It was far too late for anything drawn out. She was well beyond that point.

Without warning or preamble, Alex shoved a finger inside her, deep and hard. She grunted and a flood of sweet cream erupted in her core, drenching him. *Jesus fucking Christ.*

Still holding her lips open with one hand, he added a second finger, feeling the inner walls of her juicy cunt expand and contract around them as he started a deep, slow stroking while his thumb circled her exposed clit. She was shaking uncontrollably within seconds.

He changed the angle and explored the hot, wet velvet clutching his fingers until he found the bump of her swollen g-spot. Her legs fell open wider and though she didn't exactly move, her hips canted in such a way that his fingers had free access. It was nothing short of glorious.

She smelled fucking amazing, and he wanted to taste her, but Alex decided to save that pleasure for another time. For now it was enough to watch his fingers fuck her while her clit visibly pulsed. It wasn't going to take much to push her into an orgasm.

He bit the inside of her thigh really hard, and she cried out briefly before her response turned into a muffled grunt. Even deep in the throes of arousal, she continued to submit herself to his demands. *Stay still. Don't talk.*

What had he told her? Obedience would be rewarded? He fully intended to make sure that was what happened.

Pushing his fingers against her g-spot, he groaned when she creamed again. "You like that, baby don't you? You've been such a good girl. I'm going to make you come now in a way I guaran-fucking-tee you've never experienced before."

He started rapidly manipulating the sensitive spot inside her as his thumb tapped relentlessly against her swollen clit. She was groaning deep in her chest and her legs were wildly shaking.

"Let it go, Meghan. Just relax and let go. I want to give you an orgasm you'll never forget."

What he was doing to her was so visually erotic that he couldn't stop himself from licking her beautiful clit and sucking it into his mouth, feeling it pulse against his tongue. She was so fucking ready to come, and he was so fucking ready to enjoy her pleasure.

Increasing the pressure on her g-spot while sucking madly on her swollen clit, he sent her up so high she gasped for breath as her body arched off the bed and she quite literally exploded. A flood of liquid that tasted like the rain from a thunderstorm on a hot desert day shot from her cunt. He'd made other women come like that before but nothing compared to Meghan's sweet cries while her inner muscles clenched furiously against his fingers as her astonishing climax went on and on. He could feel the spasms on his tongue making him grunt with satisfaction. No matter what happened after this, right here and right now, she was totally *his*.

Pulling his fingers from her body he noted the creamy proof of her orgasm and quickly moved up her body so he could put his wet fingers into her mouth. He wanted her to taste her own arousal. His body reacted with intense self-satisfaction when she opened her lips, licking and sucking his fingers clean. When she had done as he demanded, he rewarded her yet again with a deep, wet kiss as he enjoyed the taste of come on her own lips.

She was spent. Her arms were limp, and he doubted whether she had the strength to shift her legs. Taking one last minute to ravish her with his eyes, Alex reached for the panties he discarded earlier and slid them back on. When she was covered once again and her legs relaxed, he ground his hand against her core knowing the silk was now drenched with her fluids, then placed a sweet kiss on the curve of her panty covered mound, inhaling deeply to savor the scent of her pleasure.

He rose from the bed and marveled at how beautifully disheveled she looked. Alex felt like a fucking God, having experienced the primal satisfaction of bringing the sexy, Irish goddess to two shuddering orgasms in one day. Reaching for her hands, he brought them to her sides and pulled a soft throw blanket over her body. Her eyes remained closed as he'd commanded.

He bet her headache was a thing of the past. Leaning in he placed two gentle kisses, one against each eye followed by a quick, deep ravishing of her mouth and said, "Next time, Meghan. My dick. Your mouth." She whimpered against his lips. "*Shhh*," he murmured, softly running his fingertips across her temple.

He turned and left her laying there, his hand briefly grinding against his erection knowing that he'd have to take care of it himself once he was alone in his room. It was worth it though. She'd been beautifully submissive—complying with his every desire and command. As he let himself out of her room, he looked at her one last time and smiled.

ALEX AVOIDED GOING BACK to the family gathering, preferring to seek the sanctuary of his bedroom. There was a lot to think about. Besides, some things were meant to be private, something that wasn't always easy when so many people were paying attention.

He didn't doubt for a second that the spectacle he and Meghan made when they returned from their escapade in his truck had provided an almost unending supply of things to whisper about. The only thing more obvious than her hurt and fury were the torn straps of her dress and scrapes marking her knees and palms. The last thing he wanted was for anyone to create the scenario where he'd taken her on her hands and knees in the dirt, but that was exactly what the evidence suggested. No wonder Carmen looked at him like he was the shit on the bottom of her shoes. Women were like that. Cross one and expect to be ganged up on by her entire team.

Funny thing was, in typical guy style—he didn't know Meghan even had a team until today. But he knew it now. Glancing at the empty dog bed tucked in the corner of his room was proof of that. Even Zeus was pissed at him for how he was handling things and that was exactly why he needed to find some clarity, and fast.

It only took two days for the beautiful redhead to turn his life upside down and inside out. Admitting he wanted her was the easy part. It was the way he wanted her that was making him pause. And giving him a never ending hard-on.

Making for his enormous bathroom, Alex stripped off his clothes along the way, arriving butt fucking naked before the half-wall of mirrors that ran the length of the sink area. As always, his eyes immediately fell to the patchwork of scars marking almost his entire left side from just under his ribs to well below the knee. He was damn lucky to be alive and have the full use of his leg too.

It really had been touch and go in those first harrowing months after he was injured. Oddly, Meghan had been a part of his recovery. Taking that into consideration, he probably shouldn't even be a little surprised that the universe had seen fit to throw them at each other, even after all these years.

For the first time in his life Alex tried to see himself through someone else's eyes. Being born with a self-confidence that made others look like errand boys, he'd always carried himself with smug assurance knowing he was good-looking enough to attract the ladies with ease.

Years of training and discipline had honed his physique into a seriously hard-bodied machine. Flexing his muscles in the mirror he smirked at his reflection. Bulging biceps and the broad chest of a warrior tapered to a pretty impressive six-pack. Except for the scars, his trim waist and solid hips were not bad either. He had a muscular ass, the result of the never ending physical workouts and therapy he relied upon to keep his leg in good shape, and a set of thighs that would rival any athlete. All in all, he was pretty fucking hot for a thirty-six-year-old guy who didn't give a shit what he looked like.

Reaching into the shower he adjusted the controls and let the hot water fill the glass enclosed cubicle with steam—just the way he liked it. Meghan had been right about the warm water of the Jacuzzi being good for his aches and pains but why he never used it was odd. Until he really thought about it. There was nothing that said *lonely guy* louder than sitting alone in a hot tub. She was changing the way he looked at so many things.

Stepping under the pounding steam, Alex started to relax the minute the water rolled down his body. Relax yes. Lose the hard-on, no.

Grabbing a squeeze bottle of his preferred bodywash and dumping a huge glob into his hand, he vigorously rubbed it into the hair on his chest creating a covering of suds that dripped lower until it was coating his dick too. He thought of the moment in the truck when she'd straddled his hips and slowly lowered herself until he'd used his strength to push her rather forcefully into taking the whole of him.

He didn't need an anatomy lesson to know he was big and that taking him like that had been a challenge for her. She'd been almost unbearably tight and those two factors—his size and her practically untouched body—had led to a coupling the likes of which he'd never known. There hadn't been any thrusting or grinding, just the incredible sensation of being squeezed by her luscious cunt. It had been enough to send them both hurtling into an orgasm that had been uniquely satisfying.

Remembering how she had climbed on him, biting his neck and raking her fingers on his abdomen made Alex reach for his hungry cock as it stretched upward and bobbed against his skin in the pounding water.

Pouring some more soap into his hand he palmed his rigid staff and fantasized about teaching her the endless ways she could pleasure that part of his body. With her hands. With her lips and mouth, especially with her tongue. He bet she'd be damn good at it too if the way she'd bent so easily to his will in her bedroom earlier was any indication.

Stroking his hand slowly against his firm flesh, Alex let his imagination run wild. He didn't want a spinner; some skinny model type who munched on lettuce leaves, eager to perform all sorts of acrobatic moves learned from having been with a long line of guys. No, he preferred Meghan's sex goddess curves and tantalizing innocence. He could mold her into the perfect partner, someone who would welcome his sometimes heavy-handed preferences. The wicked thought made his dick throb in his hand.

And there it was. The reason why he needed to get a grip on what he was feeling. Meghan wasn't built for a no-strings attached sexual fling. She was operating on pure emotion and the fact that she was so fucking eager to please him sent his libido into overdrive. She wasn't just chasing orgasms for her own gratification, something he'd come to accept in the women he'd been involved with. No. She was a different creature altogether.

With his heart pounding heavily in his chest, Alex picked up the tempo, stroking his long shaft, swirling his hand over the head of his cock in a seamless movement. It wasn't what he wanted but was going to have to do. Sagging against the tile wall, he closed his eyes and remembered the way her body had quivered and arched as the orgasm he gave her exploded on his fingers and tongue. With a hoarse grunt he felt his balls tighten. Seconds later a climax started low and built until he released his desire in a series of pulsing throbs that left him satisfied but emotionally empty.

So much for having any goddamn control. The thought made him uneasy. He needed control and lots of it. If the military had taught him just one thing it was that authority was not the same as control; a fact that was brutally brought home during his long months of hospitalization and therapy. He had hated being helpless—hated the feeling that he couldn't control any of what was happening to him. Until he started the Justice Agency, he'd had little control over much of anything. Now, it was a driving motivator in everything he did. Even being a certified mess was an off-shoot of that need. He chose to be that way.

Maybe that was why he'd been so fucked up about Meghan's past. Believing he was responsible for her fiancé's death had gutted him. Failing to actually *have* control had caused so much grief. Now that he knew the truth about their relationship, he was freed from the guilt over something he couldn't change.

And all those thoughts just brought him full circle to the question of what the fuck he was doing where she was concerned. He wanted her, no question about it. But long years of avoiding relationships and feeling like he'd never completely be free of the regret he carried for every fucked-up thing that happened during the war had made him an emotional coward. Something he hated to admit but the truth was what it was.

What if after he let himself feel something for her, she learned to hate him later for all the miserable decisions and sick shit his military service brought? What would be worse? Losing her now or having her turn away from him later? And what if she couldn't accept his emotional needs? *Fuck.* He was a mess.

In a few weeks he'd be staring at the calendar and remembering what had happened. Would she? How would she react to the maudlin anniversary? Did she have similar thoughts or was he torturing himself out of habit? All good questions that he had no answers to.

Toweling off, Alex made a few quick decisions, hoping he wasn't heading for a huge mistake. She was his, plain and simple, and he didn't share. He ached for her. Why else would he have just jerked off in the shower like a horny college student? It had to be all or nothing on both their parts.

Her honesty was refreshing and guileless. That candor damned him because he still hadn't been man enough to open up about his hang-ups despite the fact that she was directly affected by them. She exposed her most secret thoughts—because she thought knowing would ease his mind. Who did that? Someone worth caring about.

That didn't mean he wasn't scared shitless. Was this what Drae and Cam had wrestled with when the L word burst into their lives? Probably. Would explain why both men fucked up in epic terms before growing a set and finally stepping up to the plate. If those two shitheads could do it, then dammit, so could he.

A sound outside his door sent Alex to investigate. *Well, look who it is.* Apparently Zeus hadn't deserted him completely. Letting the dog into his room, she came and sat at his feet and eyeballed him in that way which only a big, dumb Lab could.

"Thanks for not giving up on me, girl," he chuckled while giving her a good scratch behind the ears. Was that what she wanted to hear? Maybe, because after that she went and curled up on her bed and promptly ignored him. *Females, go figure.*

Remembering something Meghan said earlier, Alex pulled on a pair of sweats and grabbed his laptop. Bringing up Google he typed in 'parasol' and clicked search. The lady needed a fucking parasol? Well, he'd find the perfect one if it took the whole damn night.

MEGHAN COULDN'T LIFT A finger. Completely and utterly spent she lay in the shadowed silence of her room running over in her mind the events of the day. It was a lot to take on board.

Alex's territorial behavior at breakfast; her time in the saddle; their make-out session in the barn; the excursion into the desert which ultimately led to her jumping his bones on the front seat of a truck. Then there was everything that came after—his instant regret; her angry and hurt reaction; the scene she'd inadvertently caused in the driveway; Tori's concern; the way Carmen reacted when she'd come to check on her before dinner.

The housekeeper had knocked on her door just as she'd come out of the shower. When Meghan had flounced from the driveway in high dudgeon mode, she hadn't noticed who had witnessed the hissy fit she'd been directing at Alex. The moment she saw the housekeeper's face though, she knew the kindly Latina was more than a little dismayed about what had passed between her boss and his house guest.

Keeping things light and casual wasn't going to happen especially after Carmen caught sight of her scraped knees and the ugly abrasions on her palms.

"Dios, M*eee*s Meghan! What happened to you?"

It had taken enormous effort not to start crying all over again. There didn't seem to be a way to explain so she shrugged and murmured, "I stumbled and fell," knowing from the dark scowl on Carmen's face that she was creating her own picture of what that meant. Soon thereafter the women pulled a first aid kit out of thin air and solemnly set about caring for Meghan's wounds.

Between the emotional overload of having been rejected by the brawny Major and the crying jag that followed, it was Carmen's concern that got the better of her. Her brutal headache wasn't just the result of too much sun. It was everything rolled into one huge stress ball that got her head thumping.

"My head's killing me," she told her, accepting the pain tablets and quickly taking them. "I don't think there's any way I could sit through a meal, Carmen. Would you pass along my regrets to, *uh*.....I mean tell everyone I'm under the weather?"

"Not to worry M*eee*s Meghan," she told her. "I'll take care of it. You lay down and close your eyes."

Grateful for her care and understanding, Meghan tried to relax as the housekeeper pulled the curtains and quietly slid from the room taking Alex's dog with her. It hadn't taken long for her to end up curled in the fetal position as the code ten thumper took her down.

She hadn't expected Alex to appear inquiring if she was alright. He'd been distant, almost angry at first, but eventually softened. The decision made in that moment to unload on him about her backstory with David was nothing short of life changing. Sharing her truth hadn't been easy, but it needed to be done. Once the story was out, she'd felt relief.

Being honest also helped get Alex down off the emotional ledge where her former fiancé was concerned. It had been the right thing to do but still hurt like hell.

What happened after had stunned her. His admission that he wanted her and what that meant—*dirty as fuck* he'd said. She'd never forget hearing those words and how they made her feel. There was more she wanted to say, especially the part about the lack of protection during their spontaneous interlude, but she'd lost the chance to say anything else the moment he told her to close her eyes and let him make her feel better.

And man oh man, had he done just that. Meghan felt confused about the level of trust it required on her to part to so willingly allow him to dominate her as he had. She barely hesitated at every command, something that got her shaking her head. She'd always been so sure of herself. So *large and in charge* as her brothers liked to tease. With Alex though, she surrendered so fast that it seemed completely out-of-character. He affected her that way. And she affected him too. What he'd just done to her body and senses was not much different from how Meghan had pushed his control earlier in the day.

Now that the truth about David wasn't clouding every interaction, maybe they'd be able to make some sense of what they were feeling. She was drawn to him in a big way. And it wasn't a simple hormonal blitz. That she could have handled with no problem. He charmed and fascinated her; challenged how she saw herself; got her thinking about happily ever after.

Whoever said that women were the complicated sex was delusional. It wasn't her who kept pulling away. She still didn't have a handle on whatever fucked-up shit he had going on in his deepest, darkest thoughts, and maybe she never would. But Meghan was not going to give up on him so easily. It occurred to her that all the growling and mixed signals might actually be his mechanism of defense—defense against giving away his trust, to keep from opening up his heart to the possibility of love.

Chapter 17

HE HEARD IT THE minute he walked from his room the next morning. The sound of the piano being put to very good use if what he was hearing was any indication. He knew it was her playing. No one else but him ever sat at the old-fashioned instrument, and she'd been fascinated by it the moment she saw it tucked away in the alcove under the staircase.

Alex slowed his steps and listened. She was doing some runs, learning the way the baby grand responded to her fingers. He'd only had to listen for a few moments to appreciate that she was incredibly talented. And then she began playing a song—something he'd never heard before. It was soulful and haunting, just like her.

He knew she couldn't see him and wouldn't be aware of his presence so he quietly came to the bottom of the stairs where he sat down, with his elbows resting on his knees, closed his eyes, and let the melody sink into his senses. She played beautifully with a confidence that made listening a pleasure.

Sensing the piece was coming to an end, Alex moved behind her, as she played, oblivious to her audience. Watching as she swayed to the music, her beautiful hands moving by rote against the keys, he was transfixed by the passion with which she played.

When the song came to an end, she lifted her hands slowly from the keyboard and sat quietly as the last vibrations faded from the air.

"Meghan, my God. That was beautiful."

He wondered if she'd known he had been listening because she didn't startle at his voice or immediately turn around. When she did, he sucked in a quick breath at the wave of emotion he found in her gaze.

"Thank you. It's one of my favorites."

He went and stood next to the piano and searched her face. "I've never heard that before. Is it something you wrote?"

"Oh Lord, no! I can play almost anything but a composer I am most definitely not. That piece is from an artist I enjoy. It's called "Broken" by David Nevue."

"It was lovely. Just like the woman playing it."

She didn't actually acknowledge the compliment, just waved her hands over the keys and sat back to look at him. "Y'know, I'm never sure with that song whether it makes me happy or sad. Must be why I like it so much. It can be anything you make of it in the moment."

"It's been a long time since someone sat on that bench and played anything so beautiful."

She smiled that time and actually blushed. "I thought you said you played," she teased.

"Well I do, but not like that," he laughed.

"Show me," she said, scooting over to make room for him on the bench.

"Are you challenging me, woman?" The warmth and humor in his voice made her eyes twinkle.

"*Mmm hmm*. Show me what ya' got big guy." She patted the bench and raised her eyebrows. "Unless of course, you're full of shit."

He enjoyed her lighthearted manner. "Blow me," he taunted as he sat down by her side.

He had to laugh when she pointed to her face and chuckled. "This would be a shit eating grin. Now either put up or shut up. We'll discuss getting blown, *later*."

Alex met her wicked grin with one of his own. "Deal. And I'm going to hold you to it, *later*."

"Tell me something I didn't already know," she teased with a dramatic roll of her eyes.

Alex thought for a moment. He wasn't much for Rachmaninoff, but he did have a serious selection of pop music pieces he could whip out with no problem. Wanting to impress her, he decided on an old Elton John composition that reminded him of his college days in New York City.

Meghan watched while Alex readied to play something for her. She'd been touched by his praise and found sharing a love of music with him deeply personal and not just a little seductive. It was a rare man who would admit to being so moved by a simple piano piece.

He surprised her with his choice of songs and his obvious musical talent. Not only could the man play, he could sing too. Something she hadn't expected. Sitting alongside him as his hands played the familiar piece; he treated her to a moving rendition of "Mona Lisas and Mad Hatters", a song she knew well.

Alex Marquez continuously surprised her. His dexterity on the beautiful instrument showed an artistry that delighted her. He was a musician through and through. *My God*, she thought. *There was so much more to him than met the eye.*

When he finished, she beamed at him and elbowed him gently in the ribs. "You dog. What other hidden gifts do you have?"

He seemed pleased with her reaction, took hold of her chin and said, "Well, this one you already know about." And then he kissed her.

"That was nice," she whispered when their lips separated.

He had some kind of light bulb moment after that, telling her, "Look. I've got to head into Sedona on business this morning. Tori is coming along because she wants to do some baby shopping. Would you mind going with us? Drae is tied up with clients, and he's concerned that she'll overdo it and spend too much time on her feet."

"Oh, no problem. I'd be happy to tag along. I can never say no to a shopping excursion."

Alex reached out and took her hand, bringing it slowly to his lips. Placing a kiss on her knuckles that charmed the pants right off her, she practically swooned with glee.

"Thanks, baby. Drae will be relieved, and I'd enjoy your company.

Did you grab breakfast yet?" At her affirmative nod he eased from the bench and gestured toward the kitchen. "Well, I'm gonna stuff my face and then make myself presentable. How about we meet back here in say, forty-five minutes? I'll text Tori and let her know the plan."

"Sounds good. I'll get changed too. Put on my bargain hunting outfit and do some power stretches!"

He barked with laughter and shook his head. "Heaven save me from women clutching a credit card when there's a sale nearby."

WAITING FOR ALEX TO reappear was probably the longest forty-five minutes of her life. Tori had bustled into the hacienda ten minutes ago and was chatting happily about the things she hoped to pick up, telling Meghan her plans for the nursery she was decorating and gushing about her love for a hand-carved cradle her hunky husband had made for their baby. Seeing her joy and hearing how she spoke of Draegyn warmed Meghan's heart.

When Alex finally did stroll down the big stairway from the second floor, she almost vapor locked at his appearance. Used to the bearded and burly presence that he made look so damn good, she was unprepared for a completely different side.

The beard was gone and instead of his usual casual clothes he was wearing a dark blue business suit that was obviously tailor-made to fit him perfectly. She almost giggled like a schoolgirl at how unbelievably sexy he made the serious suit look. If Tori hadn't been right there she would have leapt on him like a crazed fan girl and given him a lip lock he wasn't likely to forget. Damn—he was one handsome dude.

"Ready ladies?" he asked when he hit the bottom step.

Picking her jaw up off the floor, Meghan smirked at him and feigned a swoon while teasing, "Oh God! Be still my beating heart!"

Tori busted out laughing and fanned herself in jest, joining in the fun. "Don't tell my husband I said this Meghan, but he *is* seriously hot, huh?"

Alex's broad smile at their exaggerated reaction to his makeover was cute as hell. Sliding a pair of Ray-Ban aviators on, he flashed his pearly whites and offered each of them an arm.

"C'mon wenches. Time to get this show on the road."

As if his transformation wasn't enough to get Meghan's insides all tingly and warm, when they went to the driveway she saw that today he was driving the top-of-the-line car she'd seen on her arrival. The beautiful S-Class was the ultimate in Mercedes Benz luxury. Meghan was familiar with the amazing car, having purchased one for her parents with her lottery windfall.

She knew all about the hot stone massage seats, the way the rear seating would enable Tori to comfortably recline, the kick-ass audio package, and the unbelievable safety systems that made the car unique. It was first class from top to bottom.

Once they were on the road, she couldn't help but smile. He handled the vehicle a lot like he handled her body—with skill, pushing the limits and then backing off. An instinctive ability that made her sit up and take notice. He looked over at her from time to time and met her smile with one of his own. Yeah, he really was full of surprises.

When they were close to their destination, the three of them mapped out a plan. Alex would drive straight to the office of the legal firm where his meeting was being held and let the ladies take the car for their shopping excursion. They'd meet up in a couple of hours, grab a late lunch, and head back to the Villa.

When the time came for Meghan to slide behind the wheel, he kissed her briefly by the side of the car and helped her get situated then totally blew her mind by insisting they use one of his credit cards that was so exclusive they could literally purchase anything they wanted. Money was hardly an issue for her, but he wouldn't take no for an answer, admonishing Tori to buy whatever her heart desired for the baby with his compliments.

And they did. Over the next few hours they visited a number of high-end boutiques and specialty stores that took shopping for baby to a whole new level. Meghan enjoyed watching Tori bring her nursery vision to life.

With a trunk full of bags and boxes and a bounty of other things ordered for delivery, they returned to the office building where they were to meet Alex. The minute they walked through the door a cheerful receptionist who was clearly anticipating their arrival offered a friendly greeting and directed them to an empty conference room where they could wait while Alex's meeting wrapped up.

When he finally appeared, there was another man with him in an equally gorgeous business suit who looked to be about Alex's age and someone he clearly knew quite well.

"Well, if it isn't Mrs. St. John," the man said with a welcoming smile directed to Tori, who quickly rose and responded with a big hug.

""It's good to see you again, Parker. Draegyn and I had a great time last month at the picnic. Are you guys playing again anytime soon?"

"Actually, I was just trying to get old Thunder Foot here to drag his sorry ass out tonight for a reunion gig at Crazy Pete's."

"Oh my God!" Tori giggled with glee. "For real?"

"Okay. That's enough," Alex replied drolly. "Don't try and use the pregnant woman against me. Not fair, dude. Not fair. And take your paws off Mrs. St. John before I have to knock you the fuck out."

The three laughed in unison as Meghan stood by and watched.

"Come on over here, sweetheart," Alex told Meghan, "and meet one of my oldest friends." She smiled when he called her sweetheart and went to his side, aware that he was looking at her like she was the most beautiful woman on the planet.

Meghan was glad she'd decided to wear the teal-colored bandage style dress that showed off her curves and made her boobs look like a million bucks when she saw appreciation light up Alex's eyes.

Casually putting his arm around her waist, he introduced her to the other man. "Meghan, this is Parker Sullivan. We grew up together, and as it happens, we even went to the same college. Luckily for me and the agency, he's taken over his family's law practice since he knows where quite a few skeletons are buried from our younger, wilder days." His affection for the lawyer was evident.

"Parker, this is the lady I was telling you about. Meghan O'Brien."

He'd been talking about her? *Squee!*

Parker took her hand and gave it a good squeeze. "It's a pleasure to meet you Meghan. You're everything I'd expect when it comes to a woman being even remotely interested in putting up with this guy's bullshit."

Meghan laughed but swiftly removed her hand from his when she felt Alex's reaction tighten at their brief contact. She liked that he was outwardly possessive toward her.

"It's good to meet you too, Parker. Mind if I ask what *thunder foot* refers to?"

Tori chuckled as Parker answered. "He hasn't told you then? Sheesh, Alex. You'd think you were embarrassed by your former notoriety! To answer your question Meghan…back in the day, Alex and I played together in a cover band. Started in high school and kept up through college until other things became more important. I gig with a couple of the other guys for shits 'n grins a couple of times a year but getting this one to join in is like pulling teeth. Maybe you can convince him that an evening spent in a dark bar playing old school rock 'n roll for our devoted and mostly inebriated fans is more fun than it sounds!"

"Seriously?" she asked, looking at Alex for explanation.

"You play dirty," he sneered at his old friend. "First the hormonal pregnant lady and now my girl? Come on dude. I'm still trying to impress her, not scare her the fuck away with an aging rock star fantasy."

Tori chimed in, waving her cell phone at them. "It's settled. I texted my husband, and he's all in for a trip to Crazy Pete's. Sorry boss, but you've been outnumbered on this one." Her snarky smile said it all.

"You will pay for this, Sullivan," Alex ground out.

Meghan couldn't tell if he was truly annoyed at having been maneuvered so neatly or just playing a part.

Slapping him on the back, Parker laughed at his reaction. "We go on at nine o'clock. Hope that's not too late for your old ass. Bring your sticks man and be ready to rock out with your cock out."

Meghan snorted out a disbelieving laugh at the man's pithy remark while Tori chortled gleefully with a delighted and smug look on her face.

"Irish, you are in for a treat!" she said.

Alex's dark scowl suggested he wasn't happy but had no choice but to go along.

"Alright you asshole. You win this round. But I'm gonna seriously consider taking my legal business elsewhere."

"Fuck you, Marquez!" Parker barked with laughter. "Meghan, I'll see you tonight. " And with that the strange encounter ended as Alex made his farewells and hurried them along to the car for the drive back to the Villa.

CRAZY PETE'S ROADHOUSE TURNED out to be exactly what one would expect of an old, slightly rundown bar halfway between Sedona and the sleepy little town close to the Villa. The parking lot was crammed with pick-up trucks, motorcycles, and SUVs with the occasional beater car thrown in.

Inside, the place was a classic hole-in-the-wall with a small stage where the bands played, a dance floor that looked like it had seen its share of boot scooting boogie fun and a long bar that ran along the back wall and down one side.

Hearing that Alex had been coerced into playing a set with his old bandmates, everyone and their brother came along to join in the fun. Cam and Lacey were there with Drae and Tori, of course. There was also Ben and Ria, who commandeered a wobbly table where they set up camp, along with Carmen and Gus who looked suspiciously as though they were on a date. Even Betty had come out, as had Brody and most of his K9 crew. There were also a couple of people Meghan didn't know who worked for the agency.

Alex had bitched non-stop the entire drive home from Sedona but by the time they'd all gathered at the bar he seemed somewhat bemused and adorably happy to have so many people there to support him

The band was actually really, really good—playing a varied set of country rock, old school rock 'n roll and even some newer stuff like one really impressive Soundgarden cover. The alcohol was flowing pretty freely and by the time the last set of the night was gearing up, everyone except the designated drivers and pregnant ladies were pretty toasted.

Meghan had put a lot of thought into her outfit, deciding at the last minute to wear her borrowed cowboy boots along with a short denim skirt that had a flared hem and a simple scoopneck cotton top. With her hair down, hanging in a riot of curls around her shoulders, she almost looked like a Southwestern local.

As the final set of the night started, the Justice crew was dominating the space on the dance floor eagerly awaiting Alex's performance. Parker strode to the microphone and thanked everyone for coming out.

"For you old heads in the audience we have a real treat for you tonight. While it took an act of blackmail to get him here, we are thrilled to bring out our original drummer and king of badassery himself … none other than the legendary Thunder Foot in the flesh."

A loud cheer burst from the gathered crowd that quickly escalated into wild screams, whistles, and applause. "Get your ass out here Marquez and show these good people how it's done!"

Taking the stage, Alex sauntered up to the massive drum kit just vacated by a long-haired guy who bowed low, waving him to the seat, and sat down with an amused expression on his face. She, Tori, and Lacey screamed like the Beatles had just come on the scene when he twirled his sticks and barked out a count as the band ripped in to a rousing rendition of "You Give Love a Bad Name".

The dance floor erupted as everyone went batshit crazy and the good times flowed. Meghan worked up a sweat, dancing her ass off to the loud rock and roll, one song after another. The very pregnant Lacey did a lot of swaying and boob shaking but for the most part it was a wild, drunken, gyrating good time. Even the guys joined in. Turned out Drae had some serious moves as did Brody who stuck close to Meghan.

A couple of songs in, it was Alex's turn at the mic. The hollers and crowd sing-a-long when he pounded out "My Hero" by the Foo Fighters while doing the lead vocal offered Meghan yet another surprising insight to his personality. The way Cameron and Draegyn looked at each other and then at Alex when they sang along got her thinking about everything they'd all been through. It occurred to her that they understood all too well how damn lucky they were to have survived the war together, and also the depth of feeling the two men carried for her Major.

She was seriously impressed by Alex's rock 'n roll presence and totally got how he earned the Thunder Foot nickname. It also occurred to her that hammering the shit out the drums for so long had to be killing his leg.

As the song ended and the place erupted in raucous applause, she saw him reach for a towel and swipe away the sweat sliding down his face and neck. He acknowledged the response of the crowd with a grin but she noticed the tautness around his mouth and tension in his neck. Parker leaned over the drums to say something to which he nodded and twirled his sticks as if nothing was wrong but she knew better. When he looked out at the crowd and found her watching him, some of the strain evaporated when she winked and shot him a smile.

Unfortunately, Brody chose that moment to sling an arm around her shoulders as the Justice crowd crushed in on the dance floor. Alex's expression quickly changed to something dark and menacing. *Poor Brody,* Meghan thought. Alex was going to make him regret being so familiar with her.

The remainder of the long set went by with one awesome performance after another. For a cover band these guys rocked hard. Meghan danced off her alcohol buzz, shaking her ta-tas and waving her hands gleefully in the air with the rest of the ladies until she was ready to collapse.

For their last number of the night, Alex and his homeboys kicked out a blistering rendition of Led Zeppelin's "Rock and Roll", starting with a mighty drumroll that served up a reminder to anyone who doubted his endurance that old Thunder Foot was a serious force to be reckoned with.

It was loud, proud, unabashed old school rock at its very best and got the entire crowd up on their feet, hollering with delight. Meghan couldn't remember the last time she'd gotten so enthused on the dance floor. Even Carmen and Gus were head banging and dancing. Since the song ends with thunderous drums, it gave Alex one last opportunity in the spotlight and then it was over but the laughter, applause, and screaming lingered on.

The band wandered from the stage one by one to wade into the audience, accepting beers and compliments, but Alex didn't move from behind the drums. She saw him sitting there, wiping down with a pained expression on his face. Meghan reacted instantly, making her way to the rear of the stage, hopping up to go stand by his side.

She wanted to help but she also knew it was a pride thing for him that he act like he wasn't about to fall over.

"That was amazing, Alex!" She put a hand on his shoulder and squeezed. "You're one endless surprise after another."

"Thanks," he smirked. "I hope those surprises cast me in a good light."

"Are you kidding?" Meghan laughed. It was good to get him talking. Give him an opportunity to catch his breath and take his mind off the pain. "Let's see. Soldier. Tech nerd," she giggled at that. "Dog lover. Sex god. Piano player, singer, and now drum master. I'd say those are all good things."

"Sex god, is it? I like that," he snickered with a goofy grin.

Meghan tossed her head back and laughed. "Well, *of course* that would be the one thing you'd focus on!"

He laughed with her until she leaned down and landed a big, juicy kiss on his mouth. Pulling back she whispered in his ear, "As you stand up, put your arm around me, and I'll help you off the stage, okay?"

When he nodded and calmly accepted her assistance, she fell for him all over again. He might be big and strong but he was also man enough to know when he needed help. Accepting it from her, in this unusual circumstance with everyone he knew milling around, seemed huge.

"Ready?" she asked, dipping slightly to wrap her arm around his waist. He lurched up off the drum stool with an agonized grunt that tore through her.

Grabbing at her shoulders he muttered a terse, "Fuck," letting her know it was pretty bad. "My foot is numb, and my whole left side is on fire."

She knew what to do. He needed a second for the blood flow to catch up so she pressed against him, offering her body as an anchor, and kissed him slow and deep. Anyone watching would see them in a clinch and not notice he was trembling slightly and hanging on to her for dear life.

"I think I can walk now," he told her after a few minutes, keeping his big arm around her shoulder while she gripped his waist.

"Lean on me if you need to," she said, guiding him off the stage as he carefully stepped down.

Behind the stage there was a dark hallway obscured by a backdrop, where he headed with her help. They'd taken maybe ten steps down the hall when he pushed her into a small cramped room stacked with cases of beer and bar supplies. Shutting the door firmly behind them and poking in the lock he hustled her against the nearest wall, pinned her body under his, and fell on her mouth for a ravaging kiss that set her on fire.

Meghan clutched at his shoulders then speared her fingers into his hair, holding his mouth on hers as he deepened the kiss while he ground his pelvis against her. Kissing him without the beard was a new experience that she liked equally as much as she did the facial hair.

He was all sweaty, his muscles pumped up and hard from the physical exertion of the drumming. The way he covered her body with his was exciting as hell.

The fever he created inside her with the hungry kiss sent Meghan into a frenzy of need. She'd been helping him one minute, focused entirely on giving him some comfort, then out of control with lust the next. How the hell did he do that to her so fast?

She tried telling herself that she was simply taking his mind off the pain by firing up his endorphins to short-circuit the torment, but the truth was she wanted a taste of the rough, wild, and dirty he promised.

They were going at each other in a frenzied way when she felt his hand slide up her thigh. She froze when he reached into her panties and vigorously thrust one of his big fingers inside her. Meghan groaned her pleasure and almost came the second she felt him invade her flesh.

"Jesus, God. You're so wet. Is this for me?" he moaned into her ear when he found her ready for him.

"You know it is," she whimpered as he thrust the finger deep, withdrew, and then thrust again.

"Tell me Meghan. I need to hear you say it."

"That's all you, baby," she groaned. "All you."

The wild kissing started up again as he fingered her while she writhed and moaned in his arms. Just as he'd done the night before, when he withdrew his fingers from her wet heat, he brought them to her mouth so she could taste her arousal. She decided she liked when he did that. Very much. It was primal, erotic, and so very, very basic.

Reaching for his belt, she got it unfastened and the zipper down on his jeans in record time. He startled when she pulled away and dropped to her knees in front of him as she pushed his jeans and briefs down his legs.

He was huge and hard, practically begging for her attention. She didn't really have any friggin' idea what she was doing, but he didn't seem to notice or care. He'd told her, *next time, my dick, your mouth*— so she was going to give him what he wanted.

As she held his hard cock in both hands, while licking and sucking on the head, he gathered her hair and pulled it away from her face— she presumed so he could watch. Wrapping her lips around him, she sucked on his flesh, moving it in and out of her mouth. She'd need some practice before she could take him deep but that didn't stop her from enthusiastically slurping away as saliva flooded her mouth and covered his manhood. She was pleasantly surprised how delicious he tasted.

Within minutes he groaned, "That's enough," and forced her off her knees by pulling on her hair.

As she stood he told her with a lusty growl, "Either take off your panties Meghan or I tear them off you."

She was panting with need as she pushed the silky fabric down her legs, managing to get one foot out before the scrap of material snagged on her other boot. He picked her up and all but threw her onto a stack of beer crates, pushing her knees wide as he stepped between them. Grabbing onto her hair again with one hand, he brought her hips forward with the other, and then guided his cock to her wet opening.

"Wrap your legs around me," he ground out, which she did with haste, desperate to feel him inside her.

Having already told her he didn't do nice, she didn't expect a gentle possession. With an aggressive lunge, he powered into her and went deep in one mighty thrust. She screamed at the invasion, but he quickly covered her mouth to muffle the sound giving Meghan the opportunity to bite down hard on his hand.

When he was all the way in he held still and took his hand away as she whimpered and shook all over.

"Let me know when you're ready, baby."

Meghan grasped his waist and pulled him closer to her body. Even though his penetration hurt like hell, she quickly adjusted to his size, relishing the sensation of warmth that accompanied a gush of arousal from deep inside her.

She closed her eyes and shivered as the sensations rocked her body but he demanded she look at him. "I want you to see who's fucking you."

Every muscle inside her clenched at his words, sending him a signal that she was more than ready for whatever he wanted to give her.

When he began stroking in and out she lost her grip on reality as each of his forceful thrusts ended with a low grunt from deep in his chest. Pulling all the way out, she gasped each time, then moaned on the return.

It got rough, and as the rhythm picked up, wild too. She was aware of her panties dangling from one of her boots as her legs wrapped tight around his thrusting hips. There was nothing she could do but hold on tight as he pounded into her over and over.

Meghan tried to stay quiet as he drove her into a seething climax that threatened to destroy whatever control she had. "Oh God, Alex," she groaned as her insides tightened. She was so wet that she could feel moisture leaking from her body and sliding down her ass.

"Look at me when you come, beautiful," he groaned as the relentless pounding went on.

And then it happened. Her muscles clenched and released in a frenzy of powerful spasms as her body fisted his cock. The primal heat from his lust-filled gaze rocked her over the edge as the powerful orgasm detonated deep inside her, radiating in wave after wave of indescribable pleasure.

"Yes!" he grunted, triumphant. "Your cunt is mine."

After a devastating series of energetic thrusts, she felt his cock swell inside her as his back arched and every vein in his neck stood out in harsh relief against his skin. She watched him through passion-drenched eyes as he found his release, coming deep inside her as his body jerked and pulsed just as the rippling flutters of her climax began to calm.

He'd given her everything he promised. It had been rough, wild, and dirty. When it was over, he slid out of her body and eased her legs down as she shook all over and tried to come back to reality.

Ever the gentleman, he helped put her panties back on, then stood and pushed his come covered cock into his briefs, yanking his jeans up as he leered at her wearing an expression of intense satisfaction. She noted he didn't seemed as pained as he had before they lost their damn minds in a dark and dingy supply room at the back of a seedy bar.

She didn't quite know what to say, so she stayed silent. As did he. It was as if the ferocity of what they'd shared had spoken louder than any words could.

Alex watched Meghan closely. He couldn't believe what they'd done. He hadn't been kidding when he told her she'd scream when he fucked her although she didn't seem upset or in any way put off by the fierce coupling he'd subjected her too. He wasn't proud of the fact that he took her on a stack of beer crates in a public place where anyone could have jimmied open that door with nothing more forceful than a good shove. But he wasn't sorry.

If anything, he was eager to do it all again. Even the part where she'd tried taking him into her mouth. Her inexperience had been evident but that didn't mean her enthusiasm hadn't gone to his head. Both of them.

When she seemed ready, he put his hand low on her back and led her from the back room, along the darkened hallway and out into the back parking lot. He thought that better than suddenly appearing in the bar where everyone and his fucking brother would be able to figure out what they'd been up to.

He marveled at her composure and snickered in his head at how demure and proper she looked as she calmly sashayed over to his truck as if they'd just come from a Bible study class. Only he knew that she'd just gotten her inner slut on and come forcefully while his cock was buried balls deep inside her.

They stood in the darkness leaning against the truck in silence for a few minutes until people started drifting from the bar in their direction. They looked so innocent and calm, giving off the impression that nothing more than a conversation had been taking place.

She smiled at him and reached a hand into his hair, pushing it back from his face. "Last night, my headache. Tonight, your pain. I'm thinking we're on to something here," she chuckled. "And by the way. I'm giving you a new nickname. A better one."

"And what would that be?" he asked.

"Thunder Cock," she said with a wicked leer.

He roared with laughter.

"And maybe next time we can try naked and a bed? That would sure be different, Mister Thunder, sir."

He liked her naughty mind, and the way she had no trouble telling him what she was thinking.

"Oh, I don't know," he teased. "I was thinking something more along the lines of you bent over, legs spread wide, your naked ass for me to enjoy while I fuck you from behind as those magnificent tits of yours sway with each thrust."

"Fuck you, Major," she laughed.

"No. *Fuck you*, Miss O'Brien," he answered with a wicked grin.

As if on cue, Brody walked over to them and asked if they needed a designated driver or if they were cool. Meghan laughed at the question and told him they were good, probably better than a few of the others who were stumbling as everyone navigated the drunk versus sober portion of the evening.

Seeing her answer with a lovely smile got Alex's gut churning with a surge of jealousy that made him stop and think. When it came to his sexy Irish goddess, he wasn't interested in sharing. Not even along the lines of a few friendly words. *Back off Jensen*, his mind barked. *That's my come in her panties, dude.*

"We've got his," he sneered. Brody sensed the warning in his tone and wisely drifted away.

"That wasn't very nice," she chuckled.

"Yeah, well, I don't fucking care. Especially not since I can smell my scent coming off your sweet body, Meghan. I don't share. *Ever*."

She beamed at him like he'd just gotten down on one knee and proposed. For the thousandth time in a few short days he thought,

Women! Go figure.

IT WAS HANGOVER CENTRAL the next morning at the Villa. Even Carmen seemed a bit rough around the edges.

Meghan's hangover was from a combination of alcohol and carnal excess. She was accustomed to drinking the boilermakers. But the sexual indulgence and orgasms? Not so much.

Once they'd returned to the Villa last night and made sure everyone else got where they needed to go in one piece, Alex had walked her to the door of her room but no further. Navigating the unfamiliar territory in which they found themselves was making them both hesitate.

She was confused. Maybe he was too. Was it just sex? Hot, dirty sex at that. Or were they taking baby steps into a real relationship? It was hard to know.

Instead of kissing her goodnight, he'd done that gentlemanly thing he was so damn good at and taken her hand in his, pressed it to his chest for a moment, then left a sweet kiss on her knuckles before turning it over and licking her palm thereby guaranteeing that he'd left her scattered and breathing heavily.

"Goodnight sweet lady," he'd murmured.

"Don't you want to come in?" she'd asked breathlessly.

He smiled that wicked smile that turned her insides to jelly but made no effort to take her up on the obvious offer.

"Yes," he'd said boldly. "*In* is exactly where I'd like to be." The innuendo wasn't lost on her. "But unless you want me to drop you to the floor right here and fuck you till standing or walking is no longer an option, I think we'd better just say goodnight. Oh, and by the way." He pulled something from his back pocket, which she quickly identified as the panties he'd torn off her the day before. "I found these on the floor of my truck. Considered hanging them from the rearview mirror but they're pretty much ripped to shreds."

"Oh goody," she'd giggled. "A souvenir."

And now here it was the following morning, and she didn't quite know what to do with herself. Another riding lesson was out since everyone seemed to be hanging by a thread so maybe doing nothing was looking like her best bet.

Craving the sunshine, she took advantage of the pool, swimming a handful of laps to loosen up then plunked down on a comfortable lounger for a spell. The heat from the sun warmed her skin. It was delicious. Just what her Boston-bred soul needed. She didn't really miss her hometown. Her family, yes. The weather there, *meh*. Meghan really did feel like her visit to the Southwest opened up possibilities that a year ago she would never had entertained.

She was surprised when after a bit she felt a cold, wet nose nudge her leg. Opening her eyes she found Zeus standing by the lounger, tongue hanging out and a goofy dog expression on her face. Looking about, she expected to see Alex somewhere in the vicinity, but he never materialized.

"Where's Daddy?" she asked, scratching the dog's head and kissing her on the snout.

Zeus's response was a wet lick and a raised paw as she basked under the attentive strokes. Apparently she was on her own this morning, much to Meghan's disappointment. *Hmm. He was probably working in the bat cave*, she concluded, and went back to her early morning sun worshipping. Soon it would be too hot for her pale skin so she had to take advantage of the early rays while she could.

Not too long after that Tori appeared near the cabana and called out, "Hey! Irish. Time to get your ass out of the sun unless you want to look like a tomato later. Grab your stuff and come on inside. A package was just delivered for you."

A package? What in the world was that all about? Well, she better go and see, so Meghan gathered her big sun hat and flip flops, slid on a cute cover-up, and headed back to the house—patting her leg in command so Zeus would follow.

When she stepped into the kitchen, there was the usual bustle of activity. Alex had been so right about the space being the heart of his home. Carmen was there along with Gus who looked awfully smitten with the feisty housekeeper. Betty was there too – grabbing a jug of cold drinks from the fridge and the whole crew along with Tori were talking over each other as several conversations seemed to be going on at once.

The minute she appeared, Tori jumped off the stool she'd been sitting on and grabbed something from the counter.

"FedEx delivered this for you," she told her handing over a long box that looked big enough to hold a fishing rod.

"I didn't order anything," Meghan mumbled, confused. Intrigued, she checked the delivery label and sure enough—it was addressed to her. *Hmmmm.*

Ripping open the packaging as everyone gathered around, she found a shipping document that indicated whatever was in the box was a gift but no other details were available except for a short notation in the message box.

It read: *Parasol / 'par e sôl / noun / A light umbrella to give shade from the sun.* She almost choked with delight.

Reaching into the box she pulled out a fantastic antique lace parasol with a wooden handle that was exactly what she would have ordered had she seen it herself. It was charming, feminine, and really, really pretty.

"What is that?" Carmen asked. "An umbrella? What do you need an umbrella for in the middle of the desert?"

Meghan grinned so wide her face almost hurt. "It's called a parasol, actually. An umbrella, but not. Think of it more like protection from the sun rather than from falling raindrops."

She caught Tori's eye, who was nodding with a smug expression on her face and looking at her like she'd just pulled the Hope Diamond from the box.

Alex. The Major. Mister Thunder. Meghan was bursting with delight.

"Where is he?" she asked Tori.

"Ah, yes. About that. He's off the radar today."

"Why? What's going on?"

Tori looked like she was considering what to say next. At the question, everyone else in the vicinity melted away. What the hell?

"He's having a bad day, Irish."

Meghan stiffened trying to read between the lines and failed miserably. "C'mon Mrs. St. John. I'm a teacher for Christ's sake. Don't play the dog ate my homework word games with me."

Tori laughed. "I like you, lady!" she trilled. "No pussyfooting around. You're good for him."

"Uh huh. Whatever. Now answer the damn question."

"Around here, *bad day* is a euphemism for he's probably doubled over in pain and hiding away in a darkened room until it passes. He hates bringing attention to himself that way so we've all learned to talk in code."

The other woman was watching her intently, gauging how she would react to this news. Her protective manner warmed Meghan's heart. Not only did good people who genuinely cared about him surround Alex, Tori's instincts drove home what a fantastic mother she would be.

"On a scale of one to ten, how unmanageable is he when this happens?" she inquired as her brain started working overtime on how she could help.

"This one is off the scale, I'm afraid. Personally, I think he should eat some pain pills and sleep if off but he refuses. Between you and me—it's a combination of powering through and the belief that his physical issues are some sort of penance. Catch my meaning?"

"Understood," Meghan answered as she turned to leave. Grabbing her cell phone at the last second she added, "Give me your digits so I can text you if help is needed."

ALEX WAS IN AGONY. Dark, searing agony. Pain like he hadn't experienced in a long time was wracking his body and battering his soul. Up half the night, he wondered a few times if he was gonna make it—it was that bad.

It did not take a room full of doctors and therapists to tell him what was wrong. It had been ages since he'd put his leg through the hell of a drum session that went on far longer than he could realistically handle. Last night it had been a question of getting through it. In the harsh light of day, he had a whole different outlook.

His back, hip, and leg were in full on spasm. As a result his head was thumping out of control and his unaffected side was tight as could be from overcompensating for the injured half. In short—he could barely move. *Balls.*

It had been worth it even though at the time he'd been a complete douche about playing with his old band. Watching Meghan party her glorious ass off on the dance floor had been pure heaven. That woman knew how to shimmy and shake like a pro. He supposed it was the gym teacher in her soul. She loved being active; that much was clear.

And then there was what happened after. All through the long, painful night, there had been the memories of her sucking on his dick and the incredible sensation of her hot, wet cunt squeezing the fucking come out of him that helped him manage his torment.

But it was late morning now and instead of backing off, his suffering only seemed to be getting worse. Last night his foot had gone numb. Today it felt like someone was sticking needles in it while hot pokers jabbed him all along his left side.

Wearing nothing but the smallest briefs he had, Alex was slumped in a big easy chair as sweat covered him like a second skin. It hurt to have anything on his body, touching his inflamed scars, and in another minute or so he was going to chuck the briefs too. Anything to find even a second of relief.

His phone buzzed alerting him to an incoming message. Thankful for the distraction he opened the text box and stopped dead.

Warning, Will Robinson. I'm coming in.

What the fuck? Five seconds later he looked up and found Meghan standing by the doorway with a cool, assessing expression on her face.

"You shouldn't be here," he grumbled.

"Says you and what army? Shut up Major and let me have a good look at you."

"Seriously Meghan, get the fuck out of here. You don't know. You just don't know."

She snorted at his comment and moved deeper into his room. "Let me take this moment to remind your sorry ass that this is what I'm trained for."

He felt like she was giving him an eyeball MRI. Talk about an odd feeling. She looked him over, head to toe, and if he wasn't mistaken she zeroed in, time and again, on all the trouble spots.

"You look like shit, baby," she husked.

God. He loved it when she called him baby. For a big, burly dude, he had a marshmallow core when it came to this woman.

Sighing, he scraped his hands along his skull, tugging at his hair. "Yeah. And I feel like shit too."

Why was it that just when he felt like nothing could surprise him she went and did just that, surprised him. She knelt down at his feet facing him on his good side and put her palm upon his thigh. It was an innocent move but seeing Meghan on her knees and the way she was looking at him, ramped up every dominant impulse in his pain wracked body. Did she know how provocative her choice of positions was?

"I can help but you have to trust me, Alex."

"Unless you have a magic wand, I'm not sure what anyone could possibly do. It's just a matter of riding it out until the pain passes." His voice didn't sound all that convincing, even to him.

"Well, it's your lucky day, *really*." Pulling out her cell phone she tapped on the screen and rose to her feet. "I'm a licensed massage therapist and as it happens, I have a brand new portable therapy table in my car that I picked up in L.A. It would be my pleasure to break it in by working on you."

He couldn't help the grimace that crossed his face. The idea of being touched in the state he was in didn't sound all that appealing.

She was watching him closely. "Baby, you have to trust me, okay?"

"Who are you texting," he asked, dodging the question.

"I'm having Tori send one of the guys to my car to get the table and bring it up here."

Growling like an animal in pain he bit out, "I don't want anyone to see me like this."

She was on her knees again in a hurry so she could look him directly in the eye without him having to arch his neck to see her. "You didn't even have to say that. Don't worry. They'll leave it in the hallway for me. I'm gonna go put on some clothes and grab some things I need. If you think you're up to it, make sure your bladder is empty and lose the briefs. Wrap a towel around your waist and don't do anything dumb while I'm gone."

He really must be out of his mind with pain because he realized she was in a bathing suit and cover-up only when she said something about getting changed.

"Alex," she said. "Look at me."

He did and almost lost his way in her amazing green eyes.

"I do this for a living. If I didn't think a massage would help, I wouldn't suggest it."

She didn't wait for his reaction, just leaned in, kissed him on the forehead, then rose and hurried from his room, saying over her shoulder, "I'll just be a few minutes."

They turned out to be the longest minutes of his life. Stumbling to the bathroom he'd done as she said and returned to the bedroom with only a towel slung low on his hips. Even that hurt like fucking hell where it came into contact with his spasming muscles and tingling scars.

She returned ten minutes later dressed in a plain t-shirt and a simple skirt made of stretchy material that molded to her curves like a second skin.

It only took a few minutes for her to set up the massage table and lay out her supplies.

With hands resting on her hips she assessed him. "Think you can get onto the table, stomach down, or do you need my help? Oh, and by the way, undo the towel. I want it loose so all it does is drape."

It took every ounce of strength Alex had to move onto the table while she busied herself with other things. He heard the light strains of music from the iPhone she'd plugged into his stereo dock as he tried to relax. She showed him how to lay his arms on a padded rest underneath the table and from the unusual position with his head in a padded oval and his shoulders relaxed, he felt some of the strain leave his upper body.

He didn't know how long he lay there but once her hands started gliding across his skin, he went somewhere in his mind—someplace peaceful and calm. Starting on his neck she kneaded, stroked, and prodded in all the right places as sweet relief started coursing through his body. She was using some kind of oil that felt like liquid velvet, adding to the sensory experience.

The warmth of her hands was like heaven and everywhere her skilled touch focused, his body relaxed and gave up the pain, little by little. She was working on his lower back along his hip, having discreetly moved the towel to expose one butt cheek when he felt her fingers press and rotate on a spot that exploded in pain, followed a heartbeat later by a flood of relief that made him groan.

It was like she'd flipped a switch. One minute he was in agony body and soul, and the next…it was gone. The sudden alleviation of suffering made Alex overly emotional. His body quivered slightly, and he had to shut his eyes to bring himself back under control.

Her magic touch continued down his leg and then began all over again on the other side—his damaged side—starting at his neck and moving slowly downward. No longer tense and filled with burning pain, he relaxed under her hands and gave himself up to her entirely.

She flipped that same switch on the other side and suddenly Alex felt like jumping off the table and going for a run. Something he hadn't been able to do for a very long time. When she told him to turn over, he moved without an awareness of pain for the first time in forever.

The next twenty minutes passed in a blur of contentment. Her touch. The music playing. The oil gliding on his skin wherever she put her hands.

When she was finished, she covered him with a big body towel and told him to lay there while she cleaned up.

He heard her in the bathroom, washing up, and felt his awareness level increase until he swore time slowed down. Returning to his side, she pushed an errant lock of hair off his face as his eyes snapped open and held her in place. Grabbing her hand he told her, "If you ever use your hands on anyone else quite like that, I'll have to kill them."

She looked shell shocked by the comment. He meant every word, but it probably came out all wrong.

MEGHAN WAS TOTALLY UNDONE by the territorial vibe in Alex's voice. "If you ever use your hands on anyone else quite like that, I'll have to kill them." *Whoa.* That sounded more than a little serious.

How could she tell him she'd never experienced anything like what had just passed between them? Desperate to ease his suffering she'd focused the healing power of her hands to draw the pain from his body and infuse him with her love and affection as an exchange of energy took place. *Shit.* She'd fallen for him so completely that she didn't know which revelation rocked her world more; knowing how she felt or hearing the power of possession in his words.

"Can you get up?" she asked. "Swing your legs off the table slowly, and I'll help you stand."

Tossing the towel off, Alex sat up swiftly, flexing his shoulders and arching his back.

"My God, Meghan. What you did. I can't thank you enough sweetheart."

She beamed at him, thrilled to learn he was feeling better. "I'm glad I could help," she murmured, unsure of herself now that she understood her feelings.

Meghan admired his impressive physique as he climbed off the table and headed for the easy chair. He was completely naked and seemingly unconcerned about his state of undress. From behind he looked like one of those drool-worthy models in a magazine. Broad shoulders tapering to a lean waist and an ass that would make a saint blush. It was the front view however that melted her brain into her panties.

There wasn't any use in pretending she saw anything at all except his impressive cock as it rose from a thatch of dark hair swaying proudly with each movement. What she wanted to do to him just then gave new meaning to the expression *happy ending*.

He saw where she was looking and leered at her with a knowing smirk that set her senses on fire.

"That's all you, y'know," he told her pointing at his erection. It was the same expression she'd used last night when he found her wet and ready for him.

She blushed and shrugged, quickly saying, "It's just a physiological reaction to the massage."

"It so is fucking *not*, baby. Come here," he told her with a hand stretched in her direction.

Meghan hesitated. The professional knew she should back off but the woman wanted nothing more than to sink to her knees and explore him with her hands and mouth.

The woman won out. Going to him she slid gracefully to her knees between his spread thighs and watched his face, biting her damn lip the whole time. She felt stupid and inexperienced, not knowing what to do next. Or first. Or second.

She'd put her hair up in a clip for the massage so it didn't get in her way but he quickly made short work of taking it out as her long curls tumbled across her shoulders.

"I love your hair," he murmured. A distinct huskiness to his voice.

There was no way he didn't sense her frustration at being so completely without game when it came to pleasing him this way. She was way too old to be such a novice yet somehow the knowledge that she'd never indulged her carnal desires this way with anyone else made it so very special.

He smiled that devilishly wicked smile that turned her to jelly. "Want to claim your reward, baby?"

Meghan nodded her head enthusiastically and eyed his hardness.

He laughed and said, "Class is in session Miss O'Brien."

Gripping the base of his cock he held it close to her mouth, "Just relax, and do whatever feels good to you."

She looked at him like he was crazy. Wasn't she supposed to be making him feel good?

He read her thoughts and said, "Honey, there's nothing sexier for a man than watching his woman enjoy his body. Whatever way she wants. There's no pre-set agenda."

"But I don't know what I'm doing."

His nostrils flared at her admission and heat from his eyes seared her skin. "Your innocence excites me. I can smell your desire. Would it help if I told you what I'd like? Full on? No holding back?"

Nodding, she searched his face for assurance and felt a surge of confidence invade her senses when he looked back at her with such desire she sucked in a quick breath.

"First. This isn't a challenge. You only do what feels good to you, okay?"

He was stroking his hard shaft, hypnotizing her with each movement of his hand.

"Three simple basics. Kiss. Lick. Suck. In any order. I'm not gonna lie Meghan. The idea of fucking your mouth is a serious turn on. I wanna push my dick into your throat while you suck the come out of me. But that's sorta the advanced shit we need to work up to. I don't want to scare you off but I've been thinking about those sexy lips stretching around my cock. Watching you take all of me."

"Oh shit, Alex," she moaned. "I want that too."

He looked unconvinced so she wrapped her hand around him and learned his flesh while never looking away from his eyes.

"Why are you so surprised? I think about this too. Making love to you with my mouth and lips. Sucking on you. Feeling your hardness slide along my tongue." She shuddered at her own words.

"Take your top off, honey," he muttered. "I want to see your breasts while you take me in your mouth."

Having spent so much of her younger days beating guys off with a stick who wanted nothing more than to get off grabbing at her boobs, Meghan found Alex's clear appreciation of her curves exciting as hell. Being a sucker for pretty lingerie and glad she was wearing a sexy bra that made her tits look fucking fantastic, Meghan reefed the top over her head with speed and tossed it aside. *Yeah.* The girls looked pretty damn awesome if she said so herself.

His look of undisguised arousal as his eyes caressed her breasts with hot longing empowered Meghan. She wasn't just some random piece, willing to be used for his indulgent amusement. This was different, and not just because of the massage that had turned sensual and forbidden. He didn't just want her. He wanted her to enjoy his body and find pleasure in doing so.

Running his hand over her hair in a gesture she found possessive and exciting, Alex pushed the long locks over her shoulders then traced a thumb across her lips. Shutting down the noise in her mind, Meghan relaxed and let instinct rule her passions, opening slightly to suck his thumb into her mouth. She registered a hiss of approval as her tongue swirled against his skin followed by him grasping her chin firmly in his hand as he swiftly leaned down kissing her deeply with lips and tongue.

With his face close to hers he searched her eyes and murmured huskily, "Remember, this is your reward. Not mine. Only what pleases you, Meghan. Understand?"

All but drowning in her newly recognized feelings of love for the man at whose feet she knelt, she nodded and smiled into his handsome face, telling him, "I need to feel your pleasure Alex. Need to hear it. Is that okay?"

Her heart melted when he snorted a deep chuckle and shook his head at her in wonder. "Don't know what I fucking did to deserve you sweetheart. Never regret for a moment about telling me what you need. What you want. It's all *more* than okay and believe me, you'll be hearing plenty."

Turning passion filled eyes to his straining flesh, she marveled at the perfection before her, remembering how it felt to take this powerful part of him inside her. There was nothing different about what she was about to do except this time she'd be welcoming him into her mouth instead of her pussy.

Starting with a soft kiss, Meghan held his shaft in both hands pressing her lips on skin stretched taut by arousal. His desire felt like a badge of honor that brought a gush of heated response into her core.

Meghan brought the fat head of his beautiful cock to her lips, licking at the droplets of arousal that formed, opening her lips to suck just that part of him into her mouth. She marveled at the two opposites invading her senses. The incredible and surprising softness of his skin and the exquisite hardness and strength underneath.

She inhaled the groan of approval rumbling from deep inside him as it reverberated on her tongue. Knowing she had already stirred his passions with one simple move emboldened her. Giving in to her desire, Meghan indulged in a thorough exploration of the plump knob against her lips—licking, sucking, and kissing as he'd instructed.

Soon though, it wasn't enough. Not nearly enough. There was so much more of him to enjoy. When she let go of the shaft and it lay against his stomach, all sorts of wicked thoughts and desires flooded her thoughts. Placing both hands on the insides of his thighs, she pressed them open wider to give her complete access then flicked her tongue briefly on his balls before laving the flat of her tongue along the underside of his cock from root to tip. When his staff twitched from the simple caress she whimpered with delight, returning again and again to the base, repeating the smooth stroking of his flesh.

He didn't disappoint, groaning his pleasure, letting her know what she was doing excited and pleased him. It still wasn't enough. She needed to feel the strength of his manhood between her lips, sliding against her tongue.

Bringing her hands to his flesh, she was surprised to see the trembling in her fingers as equal parts arousal and satisfaction drove her on. She wanted and needed him, yes, but feeling his desire, knowing she was giving him pleasure, took her to a place she'd never been before.

Not knowing how much of his impressive length she could take, Meghan experimented at first with shallow strokes as she suckled on him with growing abandon. God. He tasted so good. Saliva flooded her mouth increasing every glorious sensation a hundredfold.

When she felt his hand on her head again, gathering her hair into his fist, she went a little wild, got overeager in her strokes, taking him too deep too fast making her pull back suddenly as her gag reflex took over.

"Easy, lover," he purred as she struggled with the unwanted response. *Dammit.* She wanted more. It wasn't enough to only take a portion of his magnificent cock when in her mind's eye she saw something much more primitive. Meghan wanted all of him—every hard, glorious inch—throbbing in her throat. She moaned at the thought.

Giving her senses a chance to calm before trying again, she relaxed and swirled her tongue around the shaft in her mouth. When she was ready, Meghan started the slow up and down motion again, moving her head in an erotic figure eight on each stroke as she took him deeper. His grunts let her know he liked the move as much as she enjoyed feeling him dominate her mouth.

"Ah, God," he groaned. "Baby, that looks and feels fucking fantastic." She thrilled knowing he was watching her lips stretch around his hardness, enjoying the way her mouth turned greedy, demanding more and more.

Reaching for the hand he had fisted in her hair she pressed it firmly against her head wanting to feel his power and knowing full well that should he want to, he could force her into taking all of him.

Cupping his balls in one hand, while guiding his staff with the other, Meghan swallowed another rumbling groan that erupted inside him and went for the gusto. Her body was on fire with desire, her insides tightening with each delicious stroke of her mouth. She wondered if it was possible to come from what she was feeling and knew in that moment that there was no doubt that she could. He'd been right. It wasn't just about him. They were equal partners in this exquisitely primal act. She was beyond turned on, desperate to possess every part of him with her mouth while her pussy twitched and throbbed.

The fever inside her increased as she picked up tempo, swallowing as much as she could then withdrawing slowly, suckling him with joyful abandon. On each downward plunge she managed a bit more until she felt the head of his beautiful cock nudge the back of her throat. *Oh God.* He was almost there. Where she wanted him.

Saliva was dripping from her mouth covering the fingers massaging his balls as she bobbed up and down with increasing fervor. Meghan was almost blind with lust, unaware of anything else except his heat and hardness. It was nothing short of magnificent perfection.

In her dazed state it took a moment to realize he was pulling her head away from his swollen flesh. She moaned, resisting his efforts to disengage, unsure what was causing him to back off. She heard him chanting her name as her head cleared.

"Meghan. Baby," he groaned. "Oh God. Your mouth. It's too much. I'm gonna come if you don't stop."

She almost jack-knifed with pure, unadulterated joy when she heard what he was telling her, but he was fucking crazy if he thought for one minute that she was going to back off now. *Nuh-uh. No way.* This was her *true* reward. She wanted to know what it felt like to bring him to his knees, until the desire stole his control and he pumped into her throat, releasing his come deep as an orgasm she'd given to him ripped through his body.

Doubling down on the sucking and thrusting, she knew the moment he understood she wasn't giving in when both his hands went to her head and his hips started to buck into her mouth. Even though she couldn't see, her mind created a devastatingly erotic image of his hands guiding her head as her mouth took him deep while his thighs trembled.

In a moment she'd never forget, Meghan felt her nose brush against the soft hair gathered at the base of his enormous cock as her throat relaxed and welcomed him in. Holding her there briefly with his touch, he let her retreat and catch her breath only to have him push her back down again and again. There wasn't anything rough or scary about his hold on her, in fact she welcomed it.

She was moaning on his cock as it buried in her throat over and over. Meghan was seriously impressed by how deep she was taking him. Her body told her that her enjoyment in sucking him off was what made the difference.

She moaned and felt the reverberations of the sound all along the hard flesh, swelling inside her mouth alerting Meghan to his approaching climax. It was so personal and sensual, feeling him thick with desire. *For her.* A soft whimper escaped her lips a second before she felt him tense then start wildly bucking his hips as his cock battered the back of her throat. She was ecstatic when the first spurts of hot fluid hit her tongue.

Alex was coming and nothing in her previous experience prepared her for the sense of triumph and sweet drugging pleasure that raced through her body. The grunts and groans erupting along with his release wrapped around her senses and held on tight. His hand fell from her head and hung limp at his side.

As he subsided, she could still feel the tremors moving through him. Meghan was overcome with a cascade of emotion. She wanted to do it all over again. Sliding her mouth from him, she licked her lips, enjoying the tangy taste of thunder cock's essence. She smiled at the nickname she'd given him. It fit so perfectly.

Being something of a visual person, she sat back and enjoyed the sight of his cock covered with her saliva and the remnants of his orgasm. While sucking him to completion hadn't been all that rough, it had been wild and dirty so she figured two out of three wasn't so bad.

21

ALEX WAS HAVING CONSIDERABLE difficulty coming back to earth. He'd indulged in his fair share of oral sex over the years but what Meghan had just done to him required a category all its own. Blowjob was such a coarse term that didn't in any way do justice to the sensually charged act the Irish beauty gifted him.

Cracking open an eye he saw her sitting back on her feet, gazing at his dick like she was looking at the most fascinating and wonderful thing she'd ever seen. He hadn't expected that. *Fuck*. He hadn't expected any of what happened. How exactly had she managed to mouth fuck him without it turning into an ugly gagging nightmare? He knew she'd try – it was in her nature to want to give him everything she could. He underestimated her passions, something he wouldn't be foolish enough to do again.

She ran her hands up and down his thighs and purred, "That was amazing!"

Wait. Wasn't that supposed to be his line? Forcing both eyes to open and focus on her, Alex had to bite back a chuckle at the look of total rapture mixed with childish delight blazing on her face.

"Can we do that again?" she asked breathlessly, reaching for his sex as if she hadn't just undone him completely with her ravenous mouth.

"Only if you want to give me a fucking heart attack."

"What?" she asked, clearly startled by the seriousness of his tone. "Did I do something wrong? Hurt you in some way?"

This time, he did laugh. "First, unless your teeth get overzealous, I doubt there's any way to hurt me and second, you did nothing wrong and absolutely everything right. I was just kidding about the heart attack." *But not really,* he thought. The way she got his heart hammering in his chest had been a thousand times heavier than any endorphin rush he experienced on the battlefield.

She looked, well…she looked like a woman who just had a cock stuffed in her mouth. Her lips were slightly swollen and her eyes overly bright. His hands in her hair had made it a tangled mess and those magnificent tits, already a sight to behold, were heaving from her rapid breathing. It all went to his head.

While there was nothing quite like a wild orgasm to make a man feel like he could conquer the world, being pain-free from the extraordinary massage that started all this moved him in ways he couldn't express. He remembered her telling him that the next time they were intimate, she hoped they'd be naked and in a bed. Seemed like an easy wish to make happen. And she deserved it. That and whatever else she fucking wanted.

The unmistakable fact that she got off on his response made being with her the single most erotically satisfying experience of his life. She was totally unique. Was it her uncontrived innocence that made her that way or was it something else? Something entirely to do with her feelings for him?

Even though it was the afternoon of a sunny day, having kept his room shaded as he'd struggled earlier with his pain meant that they were shrouded in near darkness lending an edge to their love play. He wondered how far he could push her. His cock down her throat had been pretty fucking far on that score but still, he wondered.

"Stand up beautiful and strip for me. My cock loves your hot, sexy body."

Alex's mind started working overtime when she rose to her feet and gave him a wicked smile before turning her back to him. Pushing her hands into the waistband of the stretchy skirt she wore, he watched with lascivious delight as she wiggled when she pushed the skirt down over her hips giving him a mouth-watering view of her amazing fucking ass. Her blue lace thong was absolutely perfect. He could sit there and stare at her backside for hours.

Giving him something to think about she ran her fingers along the top of the stretch lace, smoothing it over her skin then slowly pirouetted to face him again, naughty delight shining in her eyes.

Pouting prettily, her lips still puffy from having stretched wide to accommodate his shaft, she covered her breasts with her hands, pushing in from the sides giving the already fabulous mounds an even sexier look. He watched through heavy lids as she reached behind to unhook the sheer white bra, holding it to her as she lifted first one arm, and then the other, from the straps. Finally, she bent over slightly; peeling the cups from her swaying mounds while giving him a look so hot it could have melted through steel.

She clasped her hands behind her back in an innocently childish way as he stared. His sexy goddess knew how to present her tits to their best advantage. The thought of her posing like that for anyone's eyes but his got the beast inside him roaring to life.

What she did next was the stuff of fantasies. Gliding to him she cocked a hip and growled, "Take my panties off with your teeth, Mister Thunder, sir."

Jesus H. Christ. Maybe she actually was going to give him a heart attack. Grabbing her butt cheeks in both hands he hauled her close spreading wet kisses across her belly as he fell to his knees before latching his teeth onto the lace at one hip and tugging it down. Half her mound was exposed so he moved to the other side and repeated the action until the sides hung low while her panties held in place only by the placement of her legs.

Sinking his teeth into the fabric he paused to inhale deeply with his nose pressed into her soft curls, then pulled the scrap of lace down her legs. He looked up at her and saw arousal darkening her green eyes. Keeping their gazes locked, Alex's hands slid the fabric down to her ankles being sure to caress and stroke her skin the whole way. After helping her step out of the panties he scooped them up, crushing them in his hand before bringing them to his face where he buried his nose and breathed deep all while never looking away. Her eyes flared causing him to smirk at her response.

"Go to the bed," he demanded. "Turn around and put your hands on the mattress. Keep your feet shoulder width apart and bend over."

She did what he asked, carefully moving into the position he commanded as he sat and watched. She was so beautifully willing. From his vantage point, even in the shadowed light he saw moisture at the juncture of her thighs when she bent forward. It thrilled him to know she was already wet and ready for him.

Alex knew that anticipation was its own aphrodisiac so he sat and enjoyed the view without making any move to go to her. It was exciting to see her skin prickle and her breathing increase, especially since the shallow pants were making her breasts sway so beautifully. He had half a mind to leave her like that until her arousal got the better of her and her legs buckled. But his reawakened cock was having none of that bullshit.

Going to her, he caressed her ass, smacking it briefly with a few stinging slaps that made her gasp and shake, then with no lead in, he reached between her legs and pushed a thick finger deep into her dripping pussy. Her legs almost gave out but quickly recovered as he stroked the hot wet velvet of her passage.

She collapsed onto her forearms as her head hung down and soft whimpers filled the air. Before too long she was wriggling her ass seeking more contact with his invading finger. Adding a second digit, Alex penetrated her with rapid thrusts marveling at the moisture leaking profusely from her body.

Placing an arm around her waist, he worked at her pussy until he felt the tightening deep inside that signaled she was close to climaxing.

"Squeeze that cunt for me baby. Coat my fingers with your cream."

She let out a low, agonized moan that turned into a throaty growl as her body exploded. He felt the rippling waves of her orgasm on his fingers as he pumped them in and out, glorying in the sound of her dripping response.

Before the last flutters of her release had calmed, he pulled his fingers from her clutching heat and smacked her hard again on the butt.

"Move that ass up on the bed, love. On your back."

Alex smiled watching her struggle with the command. Her orgasms were strong, making her shake as she climbed onto his enormous bed, moving into the center where she lay down on her back, gazing at him with hungry eyes.

He stood there, stroking his dick watching her. "Is this what you wanted, baby? Naked and on the bed where I can fuck you properly?"

She groaned his name. "Alex."

"What?" he chuckled. "One orgasm wasn't enough?"

He joined her on the bed, running his hand from ankle to waist, teasing her with his touch and his words.

She undulated under the caress, and he laughed again. "Greedy baby? Want more?"

He loved hearing her whimper. It was fucking hot, turning him on with a fever of desire.

"I want you to watch while I suck on those pretty pink nipples," he told her while he slowly zeroed in on her heaving breasts.

The moment his tongue flicked on a pebbled nub she moaned and reached for his head. He'd anticipated she'd do that and quickly drew back as she gasped her disappointment.

"Now, now, now. You know better than that. No hands and don't move unless I say you can. Come if you must Meghan but it'll be better if you wait. I want to feel your cunt clutch at my cock when your orgasm hits."

"Dammit Alex," she muttered but did what she was told, releasing him and stretching her arms up over her head.

"That's my good girl," he chuckled. "So obedient. So fucking sexy." He had her just where he wanted.

"Now let's see. Where was I?"

Alex was an educated man. In his youth, he'd traveled the world with his family; been exposed to other cultures, seen most of the world's seven wonders and then some. He and his sisters had been in every major museum around the globe from the Hermitage in St. Petersburg to the Prado in Madrid. The Louvre in Paris and the fabulous Metropolitan in New York. He knew how to appreciate a masterpiece and without a fucking doubt, Meghan's breasts were at the top of that list.

Leaning on an arm, he drank in the visually stunning sight she made, spread out before him with her hands clasped together above her head. Instead of returning to her pretty nipples, he just barely ran his fingertips through the valley between her glorious mounds as she watched. He drew on her skin in wide circular arcs—first one breast and then the other, drifting lower down the center of her stomach to make smaller, lazy circles around her belly button. Seeing her skin quiver at his touch tightened his balls. Had there ever been a woman more responsive than she?

It was a tantalizing tease, making her wait. No hardship there. Not for him. He enjoyed the vision of his big hand against the smooth, rosy beauty of her skin. Her hands earlier on his flesh had been a tortured pleasure. He wanted her to know what that blending of sensations felt like. The sheer enjoyment of being caressed and stroked in contrast to the pulsing want for something more.

When she growled at him and writhed under his touch he had to smile. Making her wait definitely had its advantages. By the time he was done exploring every inch of her amazing body, she'd be so ready he wouldn't have any trouble fitting his large sex with her tight sheath. The shudder that raced along his nerve endings was as delicious as the naked flesh before him.

Making sure she was watching, Alex shot her a hot leer that told her without words how much he desired her. Still leaning on an arm, he cupped one bountiful breast, weighing it with his free hand, molding it to his touch, his thumb moving across her hard nipple as a sharp hiss tore from her throat.

He got serious after that, bending over her, using his teeth to nip sharply at the distended bud, flicking it with his tongue, drawing just the sensitive tip between his lips. The hard suction he used made her squirm and moan, nearly driving him over the edge of the control he was fighting to maintain.

Parting her thighs, Alex crawled between them and pushed her knees up as he sat back on his haunches and surveyed the beauty before him. From that position he had complete dominance over her body, reaching out to caress her tits with mounting fervor, he leaned in to tease each sexy bud with his mouth, teeth, and lips.

His senses were overloading at an alarming rate of speed. The taste of her flesh, her soft moans, and sexy whimpers, it was almost too much. Easing his big body onto hers, he gritted his teeth when his brain registered the wet heat between her spread thighs where it rubbed against his groin. *Shit.* It certainly didn't help things when she ground against him. She was more than ready for him, but he still held back. There was so much more he wanted to feel and do before finally claiming her.

With his hands on either side of her head, Alex held her in place for a devastating kiss that set the stage for what was about to happen. Her mouth opened without pause, inviting him in as he stroked the deepest recesses with his tongue. His hungry lips destroyed hers, nipping and sucking greedily as the passion between them exploded.

The feel of those fucking magnificent breasts crushed against his chest and her hips wiggling as she dug her heels into the mattress briefly wiped his mind of reason. It wouldn't be any hardship on his part at all to plunge into her heat and, quite simply, fuck her into total submission. But they'd already been down that road. What had he told her? Rough, wild, and dirty. Yeah. She'd shown a willingness to do just that. But he was going for something much more sensual this time. Slow. Deep. Endless.

Releasing her mouth he kept kissing her wherever his lips landed. Sliding down her neck and across her collarbone, over every quivering inch of her tits, down across her belly and into the soft curls that guarded her pussy. She cried out when his tongue parted her folds and licked her slit over and over. The woman was delicious, her pussy dripping with desire. When his lips and tongue zeroed in on her hardened clit, Alex relished her delicate flesh with all the enjoyment of a gourmet treat. Pushing his hands under her sensational ass, he lifted her into his mouth and feasted with abandon until she was crying and begging for relief.

Enough was enough. His cock was at DEFCON status—hard and aching with need for the woman writhing underneath him.

"What is it you need, lover? Is that beautiful cunt ready to be fucked?" She reacted to his lewd words with a naughty roll of her hips letting him know she was more than ready for whatever he intended to give her.

She was gasping his name. "Alex. *Please.* Oh God, please."

"Tell me Meghan. What do you need? Say the words, baby. I want to hear your desire," he growled low and deep.

The plaintive wail she let out startled him with its carnality. "Please let me touch you, *please*." Her begging shredded his control.

Moving into position he met her hungry gaze and nodded. She immediately wrapped her arms and legs around him, digging her nails into the skin on his back as her thighs gripped him with amazing strength. Watching her go a little crazy as she clawed at his back, grinding her hips on him with a wild, hungry look on her face made his cock twitch.

With one arm holding on tight she wrapped the other around his neck, spearing her sharp female talons into his hair and bit down hard on his neck. It felt like a claiming, and he reared up growling like a beast in heat.

Fuck. He was on fire. She was killing him. He wanted to go slow and maybe he would but right now he just wanted to take her hard. Make her cry out. Let her know who she belonged to.

"Say it, baby," he demanded. "Tell me what I want to hear."

With her legs wrapped around his hips, she was squirming like mad, trying to catch his throbbing cock with her demanding pussy. The lady knew what she wanted, and if he wasn't going to give it to her, she was going to take it. She was fucking magnificent when she was out of control.

She moved her lips from his neck close to his ear and groaned. "I want you. Now. Inside me. *Inside* me, Alex. Please."

Aww. She begged so prettily. Alex spread his thighs wide for maximum leverage and moved the throbbing head of his cock to her wet entrance. She whimpered sweetly knowing what was coming next.

He wanted her to talk dirty, not just say she wanted him so he held there, keeping her on a knife's edge of anticipation.

"C'mon lover. Say it. *Scream it.* Cry it."

She tried to impale herself on his cock, but he held her at bay. He made a low, guttural sound and demanded she tell him in no uncertain terms what she needed.

"Say the words Meghan. Now!"

He won. He knew he would. She wanted him so badly there was no way she wouldn't give him what he needed.

"Fuck me, baby," she finally groaned. "Fuck me, *please*."

His grunt of satisfaction split the air as he reared back and thrust forward in a plunge so forceful he moved both their bodies further up the bed. She let out a primal scream that did more than hint at his complete domination of her body. He was deep inside her but it still wasn't enough. Grabbing her hips he pulled her underneath him at an angle that forced her legs open wider as he sank in deeper still until the head of his cock nudged her womb. A flood of super-heated wetness greeted him, coating his sex with the unmistakable proof of her desire. He roared his approval, flexed his hips, and surged again.

Something snapped inside Alex. He was delirious, the heat from their desire was consuming him. She was his. Totally fucking his. In that moment he vowed that his cock, and only his cock, would ever be buried inside her hungry cunt.

"Mine," he groaned over and over as he started a slow stroking, his hips moving with a fluid motion made possible by her healing touch. Alex didn't bother to restrain his satisfied moans as he drew out of her body and then slid back in, grunting with each nudge of her cervix.

"Shit, baby. Your cunt is fucking beautiful," he groaned. "God-dammit Meghan. You fuck like a goddess." He pretty much hit the trifecta of lewdness with what he said. That she responded to his crude words enflamed his senses.

Having already come once, it wasn't all that difficult to bring her to the crest again. Keeping up a slow, steady pace, she met every one of his deep thrusts, shimmying against him while he was planted deep inside. And judging from her shaky whimper each time, that little move-ment was getting her closer and closer to completion.

Alex sucked on her neck, thoroughly enjoying her response to the sensuous fucking, encouraging her with his body to take whatever she needed from him. When he felt her cunt tighten like a fist around his dick he marked her with his teeth as she whimpered and shook under him.

"Baby needs to come," he growled in her ear, approval in his voice. "C'mon lover. Move that ass and fuck me hard."

Yep. That pretty much sent her flying high. He tried to take it all in. The spasms that started at the head of his cock and moved along his length. The creamy flood that started with her orgasm. Her luscious cunt squeezing his sex. Her grunts and cries as she undulated on his staff. She held nothing back.

It was her hands gripping his ass though that tattooed his brain. She had him in a death grip that was sure to leave bruises, forcing him deeper. Her loss of control was fucking awesome.

Alex didn't think anything he'd ever seen or experienced in all his thirty-six years was quite as indescribably glorious as Meghan climaxing underneath him. When the strong flutters inside her began to lessen he grunted with satisfaction.

He wasn't finished though. Not by a long shot. That first one had been for her. He knew she'd craved a slow, torturous possession that he was happy to give. But she was in for a shock if she thought for one second that was going to be it.

Before she had a chance to recover, he grabbed her legs and put her calves upon his shoulders; opening her up to the pounding he was about to subject her to. When she realized the vulnerable position she was in, Meghan groaned and scored her fingernails down his chest, clutching at his cock with her incredible inner muscles in randy encouragement.

Wild and rough did not do justice to what happened after that. With his back free from pain and his hips able to flex and thrust without discomfort, Alex went for broke. Slamming into her with a ferocity that had him howling with unleashed primal lust, he hammered away until sweat was literally pouring off him from the effort. Her pussy dripped with renewed need, adding to the obscene sounds coming from their intense fucking.

"Again," he growled at her. "Come for me again, baby."

He reached between them, found her swollen nub and rolled it between his fingers. Her arms flew wide, clutching frantically at the sheets while her back arched and a deep flush spread across her chest up her neck to her face.

He fucked her even harder, grunting like an animal, rubbing her clit as her creamy response drenched his fingers.

And then reality slipped away. She started screaming. He heard her crying his name over and over. His balls tightened and cock swelled until he was sure it was going to explode. She spasmed so forcefully he almost blacked out from the strength of her cunt milking him.

Alex's orgasm started in the balls of his feet, gathering intensity as the sensation raced up his legs, shooting into his groin while all the blood and every sensation in his body rushed into his cock. He could actually feel his sex jerking wildly inside her, spurting his essence deep as he groaned in wonder.

It didn't stop there. How could it? For long moments afterward they continued grinding against each other, desperate to suck every feeling possible from the wanton experience. She matched his carnal need with her own.

In the aftermath, he eased her legs from his shoulders and gathered her trembling body close as she softly cried in his arms. Neither one of them would ever be the same after what they'd just shared.

Chapter 22

IT WAS WELL AFTER sunset when Meghan awoke in the warm cocoon of Alex's bed. The air was heavy with the remnants of their passion and pretty much every muscle in her body ached from his commanding possession.

She was more than just a bit stunned by everything that was happening to her. Something about his mastery of her body made her feel small and breakable. Not easy for a big girl with an even bigger and ballsier attitude. The vulgar language and crude demands hadn't turned her off—in fact, if anything, they had her responding with a lustful appreciation that surprised her. Although nothing shocked her more than the realization that she was hopelessly in love with Alex Marquez.

A sly smile lit up her face remembering how eager she'd been to make love to him with her mouth and how she'd unashamedly begged to do it again. Same for her pleading cries imploring him to fuck her. Who was that wicked woman who so enthusiastically demanded her lover's possession? Meghan never dreamed she could act that way; be so open and vocal about her desires.

But through it all, he never spoke of his feelings. Oh sure, he made no effort to conceal his attraction to her. Being told she fucked like a goddess hadn't exactly been a bummer. That didn't mean she wasn't self-conscious about her newly realized love for the man in whose arms she snuggled. Especially since she didn't know just where she stood with him.

What was she supposed to do now that they were lovers? Was this one of those vacation romances that would end once it was time for her to leave? Did screwing each other's brains out at every opportunity even qualify as a romance?

What was the accepted protocol in these situations? Sighing, Meghan conceded that she just didn't know. *So much for being a grown-up*, she thought. Feeling completely out of her depth she started to worry about how broken she'd be if all this ended up just being a sexual dalliance on his part.

They were good together and definitely good in bed. Was that enough? Somehow she doubted it. Any thought of him being that way with another woman made her deeply uncomfortable. Actually, that was an understatement. It made her want to throw up followed quickly by thoughts of violence. He was hers dammit. What a pair the two of them made with him threatening to kill anyone she touched and her entertaining aggression toward some nameless, faceless females. *Good God.*

The warm male body beside her stirred. Before he came fully awake she indulged her senses with his scent and the way his huge body felt pressed to hers. There would never be anyone to equal this man. Not for her.

"*Mmm.* What's this?" he asked groggily as the arm around her waist grabbed a handful of her ass and squeezed.

Meghan snuggled closer and inhaled deeply while wiggling into his touch. "I believe the answer is, *yours.*"

He swatted her butt and chuckled. "Damn right that's the answer."

It was a nice moment. Simple. Unhurried. Sweet.

He turned toward her and smiled. "Just so you know, I love it when you call me *baby.*"

Meghan blinked. Had she heard him right or was that her mind engaging in some wishful thinking?

"I'm serious Meghan," he said when he saw the look of uncertainty she felt flash on her face. "You said it in the truck and … well, it turned me on. No one's ever said that before."

Her previous thoughts about doing bodily harm to anyone seeking to replace her in Alex's arms bloomed again in her mind. "Good. Glad to hear it, *baby*. And for the record," she smirked knowing she was about to throw his own words back at him, "I'll kill anyone who so much as thinks about calling you that." It was as close to an expression of possession that she could make without adding, *I love you. You're mine.*

He swatted her butt and laughed. "I don't think you have much to worry about where that's concerned."

Stretching, he kept his arms folded around her and sighed. "What time is it?"

She peeked at the clock on his nightstand and murmured, "*Ugh.* It's after eight. I'm surprised no one sent out a search party for us."

Alex snorted and said, "Believe me babe, nobody was dumb enough to even consider knocking on that door."

She hid her face in his neck and groaned. "Shit. Do you think everyone knows what we've been doing?"

He laughed and hugged her closer. "You *do* know that at one point, maybe even twice, you were all but screaming the house down, right?"

She didn't answer. I mean, what did you say after a statement like that? She had been screaming. "You weren't exactly quiet yourself," she said after a moment.

He kissed her. Slowly. Lots of tongue. Just the way she liked it.

"You bring out the beast in me lady. So if I was loud, it was *your* fault."

"What?" she squealed in faux outrage. "Oh my God. You poor thing."

"I know a good way you can make it up to me," he leered.

"This oughta be rich," she joked. Meghan liked these quiet, uncomplicated moments. Yet another way they were good together. "You were saying, Mister Thunder Cock, sir?"

She was pretty sure his expression qualified for shit eating grin status.

He rather pointedly glanced over his shoulder at the bedposts and nodded as if formulating a plan. Being pretty quick on the uptake, after all she was a teacher, used to staying one step ahead of the fuckery laid at her feet by a passel of young teenagers—she was pretty damn sure she knew what his dirty mind was thinking. And she loved it.

"You. Spread eagle and tied to the bed. Preferably on your stomach so that naughty mouth of yours can't distract me. Ass up and naked of course."

Alrighty then. She certainly got close to what she imagined he was thinking but the *ass up* part was a revelation.

Her face went back into his neck to hide her smile but she could tell by the low rumble of laughter coming from his chest that while he hadn't seen her grin, he certainly felt it against his skin.

"C'mon my sexy Irish fuck goddess."

Oh jeez, she almost jumped on him again with that statement. Fuck goddess. *Wow.* She'd wear that wicked badge with pride.

"Let's get your glorious ass in the shower. I think we both need a good scrub down."

HE SURPRISED HER BY behaving in the shower. Maybe it was the husky wince she let out when he reached between her legs with a handful of suds that held off whatever hope she had of an amorous replay of earlier. Meghan hadn't realized how sore she was until that moment.

Every man wanted to think of himself as well-endowed but Alex sort of took that to another level. She knew that not just from having him penetrate her vaginally but also from her oral ravishment of his impressive cock. The guy was huge, and she wasn't even kidding. Of course, he was big all over, so no surprise there. Big hands. Big body. Big appetite. Was she woman enough to satisfy his powerful sexual needs? Well one thing was certain; she'd willingly exhaust herself trying. Good news was that she too apparently liked it rough, wild, and dirty as fuck.

He let her wash his body and didn't shy away from the soapy exploration of his aforementioned cock but he did stop her from taking it any further, telling her, "I'm going to play the gentleman and refrain from dragging your ass back to my bed. *This time*. Your body needs time to adjust." Pretending to check his watch, he smirked at her and added, "What do you think? Couple of hours do?"

Meghan stood there under the pounding water, her hair hanging in wet ringlets down her back, their suds covered bodies pressed intimately together, and smiled. "Are we going to start sneaking into each other's rooms, then?"

"Sneaking? *Fuck no*. There'll be no hiding from what's going on sweetheart. If I want to throw you on the dining room table and fuck your ass into oblivion, then that's what I'm going to do. And frankly, I don't give a good goddamn who knows about it."

Meghan's insides clenched at his provocative words. "Well, if that's the case you're lucky my brothers aren't around. Hearing you use the words fuck, ass, and oblivion in a single sentence when referring to their saintly sister is sure to earn you a can of Boston Whoop Ass."

"Alright woman. Enough with the scare tactics. I'm a fucking Special Forces motherfucker with an ass kicking posse of my own."

She laughed as they slid from the shower and wrapped up in big fluffy towels. "I'm curious Alex."

"About what?" he asked.

"How many times can you use the word *fuck* or a derivative thereof in a single sentence? You're pretty good at it, y'know."

"Oh shit," he groaned. "My mother and sisters would unhappily agree with you on that." He shrugged. "It's a guy thing made a thousand times worse by years in the service. Once I get going it's like the word has a life all its own. After a couple of drinks I pretty much start using it like a comma in every sentence."

Back in his bedroom Meghan surveyed her clothes, which were spread here and there around the room and frowned. "Do you have something I can put on?"

"No. I prefer your ass naked and your tits bouncing in my face."

Dropping the towel to the floor she sighed melodramatically and said, "Well, I suppose if it doesn't bother you then, I can walk back to my room stark naked and hope there's no one watching."

"Only if you're begging for a spanking," he told her with a glimmer in his eyes.

Jesus. He was killing her. Tied to the bed, ass up, and now threats of a spanking? She launched herself into his arms and kissed him like a fucking nymphomaniac before eventually releasing his mouth and stepping back.

Grabbing her by the nape of her neck, he marched her into his wardrobe and yanked a button-down shirt off a hanger, covering her quickly while muttering all the while about her being the death of him. She liked it when he got all caveman like.

"My turn," she said winking at him. Looking around at his clothes she settled on a pair of jeans and a dark V-neck t-shirt then asked with her eyes where his underwear was. Pointing to one of the built-in drawers, she pulled it open and took her damn good time rifling through his briefs until she found a pair she liked.

Knowing his scars sometimes made clothes uncomfortable, he preferred form fitting and extremely skimpy cotton briefs that showcased his powerful masculinity the way a skin-tight Speedo would, which was fine by her.

Kneeling at his feet with a totally innocent expression, she helped him step into the underwear, then as slowly as humanly possible shimmied them up his legs, palming his impressive bulge once it was covered. Planting a swift kiss on his cotton-covered manhood, she reached for his jeans while he watched her every move with a hooded expression.

Getting his jeans on was almost as much fun as the briefs. Pulling the zipper up proved a bit of a challenge though. All women had to worry about was damp panties when they got aroused. It was a completely different story for guys. Figuring slow and steady was the best way to proceed, she finally pulled the tab over the last of the zipper's teeth and yanked on the waistband so she could slip the button through its hole.

Standing before him, Meghan bit the inside of her mouth to keep from smiling at the hot leer plastered on his face. When she reached for the t-shirt she accidentally nudged the prominent bulge under his zipper, muttering a completely shameless, "Ooopsie," followed by a very intentional sweep of her hand across his tight ass.

"Oh, you are *so* getting spanked woman," he groaned.

This time she didn't even try to hide the smile. She bunched up the t-shirt just like she would when dressing one of her young nieces or nephews and held it up for him to slide his arms into. From there it was a swift tug over his head and then he was covered. *Dammit.*

His hair was a mess from the shower, not that it ever really looked all the groomed and she ran her fingers rather possessively through the unruly mop, forcing it into some semblance of order.

"Tell me something Meghan."

She looked at him with an amused expression and said, "What?"

"If I were to put my hand between your legs right now, would you be wet?"

"Seriously?" she barked. "*Seriously*? You want to know if I'm *wet*? Are you standing anywhere near me, baby? Cause that's where the answer lies. All you have to do is walk in the room and yes. Wet would be a good description."

She enjoyed the lascivious grin and the way he leaned into her and breathed deep. It made her shudder with awareness. She knew, even after the shower, he could pick up his scent clinging to her skin. It was part of her now. Much to her chagrin, she felt a trickle of arousal roll down her thigh. He asked if she was wet. Who the hell was he kidding? Being so close to his powerful masculinity gave new meaning to the expression *wet and willing*.

She blushed the same color as her hair, making him laugh. "That bad, huh? Pretending again to consult his invisible watch, he teased her. "Hold that thought beautiful."

Swatting her playfully on the butt he said, "C'mon. Let's get you some real clothes before I forget to be nice."

Meghan threw back her head and laughed. Nice? This was nice? Damn. She was in serious trouble if he ever decided to screw being nice.

THE HOUSE WAS QUIET and deserted when they finally made their way downstairs, something Alex was extremely grateful for. Ordinarily he enjoyed being surrounded by Family Justice but right now he was completely in the moment with his beautiful lover and wasn't in the mood to share or make nice.

He also noticed that Zeus was nowhere to be found, supposing that she was down in the kennel with Brody or had made herself at home with Drae or Cam. All surefire signals that everyone knew what had been going on in the master suite.

Carmen, true to form, had left an elaborate note detailing every single burp and fart that occurred once Meghan had gone to his room along with instructions for heating up the meal Ria left for them.

None of that really mattered though. Walking down the stairs together, hand-in-hand, Alex was filled with a calm he'd never sought and frankly, didn't know was possible. She did that for him. What was that saying about music soothing the savage beast? Yeah, well whatever it was, Meghan was his music.

"Oh Alex, I forgot!" she cried, grabbing something off the counter. "The parasol—*I love it*," she gushed. "See how pretty it is?" she asked as she pushed it open and twirled the pretty lace umbrella.

He smiled at her enthusiasm. Watching her dance around with the gift he'd spent hours searching for on the internet was a delight. It made him feel like a prince that he'd picked the right one. All he'd done was look for the prettiest and most feminine one he could find—something that matched the woman it was intended for.

It suddenly occurred to him that the girly parasol represented a first for him. He'd never bothered with gifts for anyone he'd been involved with before. *Fuck.* Not even his college girlfriend had gotten more than a half-assed Hallmark card out of him. Yet here it was, day three of knowing this particular woman, and he was falling all over himself with gestures. Wait till she got a load of the cowboy hat and boots he'd ordered for her.

"Hey. I have an idea. How about tomorrow we take the agency plane and go check out the Grand Canyon?" Alex wasn't sure where that impetuous thought came from and didn't care. She wanted to see the big ol' hole in the ground so he intended to make sure she did. "Wasn't that on your bucket list of things to do?"

She giggled and threw her arms around his neck, pressing her voluptuous body against his.

"You have a plane? Why am I not surprised?"

It felt fantastic to stand there with his arms wrapped around her as she beamed at him with those bewitching green eyes.

"We can even make it a family affair if you'd like. I'm sure Tori and Lacey would get a kick out it too. Actually, fuck just flying over it in the plane. I have a buddy who can hook us up with a first class tour. Whatever you want, sweetheart. Loads of photo ops. The whole enchilada."

She said something that sounded like, "I'd love that," but the actual words got eaten up in a blazing kiss that went on and on and oh yeah, on some more. He didn't make any attempt to stop until the sound of her stomach growling made its way into his brain.

"Oh God!" she laughed. "That wasn't very sexy, was it? Maybe you'd better feed me if you want me to keep my strength up."

He didn't miss the innuendo in her words.

"Aren't you all demanding?" he teased. "Wait. Let me rephrase that." He cleared his throat like he was about to recite Shakespeare. "Aren't you all fucking demanding? There," he teased. "Got one well-placed fuck in that sentence for good measure."

"Well, one good fuck deserves another, don't you think?"

She was priceless. "Grab some plates while I heat up our dinner. You can sit on my lap while I feed your naughty mouth, and we can discuss your terms of surrender for later."

"Surrender? What exactly does that mean?" she asked.

He grinned and wagged his eyebrows. "I'm saving the best for last."

THEIR TOUR OF THE rugged beauty of the Arizona desert and the western rim of the Grand Canyon had been everything Meghan hoped it would be. In the end it had been just her and Alex since Lacey didn't want to fly and Tori had stayed behind in pregnant solidarity.

They'd flown to the canyon then boarded a private helicopter for a personal tour from a friend of Alex's who was an incredible tour guide. He told them when to get the camera ready and narrated an endless stream of consciousness about the canyon that delighted her field trip mentality. She had no idea how many movies had been filmed there, from *Thelma & Louise* to the Griswald's on vacation. It was just the most fantastic day.

And the best part? Alex had possession of her hand whenever she wasn't snapping pictures. He just held on and wouldn't let go. It was so ridiculously sweet that her insides melted each time their palms made contact.

Things only went from awesome to off the charts amazing after that. Dismissing each of her arguments and refusing to take no for answer, Alex had moved her lock, stock, and barrel into the master suite from that night forward. No one questioned the new sleeping arrangement any more than they did their emerging relationship. If anything, Meghan felt a quiet delight coming at them in waves each time they appeared together.

To her complete shock he practically walked away from any agency responsibilities in order to focus entirely on her. She'd even overheard him several times saying *let Tori handle it* when some work related issue or crisis came up. In every way that mattered, she had his undivided attention.

And so it went for the next few weeks. They laughed like children, got into all sorts of mischief, rode together, took day trips, explored the natural wonders in that part of the world, even played board games at night when the house was quiet and they were all alone. It was, in a word, heaven.

Every couple of days she would indulge him with one of her special body massages, which inevitably gave way to other, more erotic diversions. Spending each night in his big bed had been quite a revelation too. She found the sleeping arrangements incredibly intimate, even without the mind-blowing sex.

They made love non-stop; upon awakening every morning, throughout the day—sometimes in the strangest spots—and late into the night. Alex was inexhaustible on that score. Losing their clothes with alarming speed whenever the fancy struck had been an eye-opening experience for her. He'd taken her on the wide stairway, up against almost every wall in the house, on the dining room table, and several times in the pool cabana. It made her blush just thinking about it.

And it wasn't always him. They were equal partners in expressing their passions. She had instigated more than a few randy encounters, especially enjoying one particularly memorable naked romp on a blanket in the desert at sunset. She'd gotten on all fours and begged him to take her out in the open with the glory of nature as a witness, and he'd eagerly complied. She'd never forget Alex pulling on her head with an immense fistful of her hair as he fucked her hard while she cried out her pleasure.

He'd treated her like a rare and delicate flower when her monthly cycle came, seeing to her every comfort and need. Were all men so solicitous of their lovers during those out-of-body times? She didn't know but secretly hoped his caring was the exception rather than the rule. He'd given her his own version of a massage, even rubbing her feet when her discomfort had been palpable. What man did that?

When the annual cowboy festival took place he'd surprised her with a gorgeous pair of hand tooled boots and a western hat that made her jump into his arms with unabashed delight. Everyone got in on the fun as the entire Family Justice enjoyed the parades, rodeos, cook-offs, and general cowboy fun that Meghan had so looked forward to.

That was another of those occasions when their love play had tripped into legendary territory. Showing his romantic side, Alex booked them for several nights in a stunning private cottage at the L'Auberge in Sedona. They'd indulged every sense with gourmet meals served creek side, cuddling next to a wood burning fireplace, and enjoyed an outdoor couple's massage with only the sound of their contented sighs and the quiet waters of the creek. It had been like a honeymoon in a way—just the two of them. Out of place and time, wrapped in each other, exploring what was happening between them. When it was over and time to step back into daily life, they returned to the Villa and the warm embrace of the people and familiar routines found there.

Meghan's reverie of the past month was interrupted by the shrill intrusion of her phone buzzing. Wearing a rueful expression at having her happy thoughts so rudely cut off, she glanced at the screen and saw it was Lacey texting about some pictures Meghan had taken.

Ah yes. The pictures. She smiled thinking of the day she'd spent with the pregnant sisters-in-law. They'd cajoled and prodded her into agreeing to shoot some intimate photos depicting their gloriously ripe bodies in various states of undress. The photos were sweet and romantic showing the women at their best. Others were semi or completely nude, not too unlike some well publicized celebrity pregnancy photos.

Meghan had been cropping and photo shopping the hundreds of images, which was why Lacey had contacted her. She'd promised to bring her laptop down to the cabin after lunch so they could view the photos together while the men were off doing whatever it was they did when clients were in the compound.

Tori fell in love with a stunning shot showing her reclining on an antique chaise that had been draped with a beautiful deep red throw highlighting her coloring and gorgeous glow. Her beautiful naked belly was on display with one arm behind her head and the other covering her bare breasts. With a leg crooked just so to protect her modesty, she looked like a sexy vamp, only one with a baby growing inside her.

Lacey had chosen an equally provocative pose in black & white, showing her wrapped or rather partially unwrapped in a swirl of see-through silk that pooled about her feet. With her long blond hair tumbling over her shoulders and covering a breast made heavy by pregnancy, she looked naughty but angelic.

It was there that Alex found her many hours later—hanging out with her new friends, laughing as girlfriends do, and full of female mischief.

"I HAVE SOMETHING FOR you," he whispered.

Alex was playing with Meghan in a room full of people, hard with wanting, but really, when wasn't he? It had been quite the revelation over the past couple of weeks to realize that with each passing day, his voracious appetite for devouring this woman at every opportunity was only getting stronger. And more intense. Sometimes it seemed as though he had a constant hard-on. Not even fucking the shit out of her was enough to get his greedy cock to back down even for a little while. It would be amusing if it weren't so bloody frustrating.

This was something they did well—the sexy love play that started almost as soon as their most recent climax had ended. It was as provocative and naughty as it was sensual and alluring. The looks. Touches. Even a well-placed sigh became part of what they did to each other. He particularly enjoyed saying suggestive things that only she could hear when others were around. She had this way of looking totally innocent no matter what lewd comment he threw her way. This playtime was one of the things that excited him about their time together.

She smiled, running her tongue over her lips with a naughty wink.

They were gathered at Cam's house for a movie night, cuddled up on a wide loveseat that left no space between them. He watched her glance at his lap and smirked at her when she looked back at him with a wry grin.

"Not that," he growled low and deep next to her ear.

When she returned his smirk with a raised brow he chuckled. "Okay. That too. But first, something in a pretty box for you to unwrap."

He enjoyed watching her green eyes sparkle as she made an exaggerated pout. "I suppose this means I have to wait till later." Sighing heavily she burrowed into his body as he slung an arm about her shoulders in the darkened theater room. "You're an awful tease," she purred.

The movie had just started when he took her hand and pushed it onto the hard bulge in his jeans and held it there. "Hold that thought," he told her with a wicked leer. She rolled her eyes but grabbed on with a forceful grip.

Alex was a demanding and creative lover. His need to master her, to be in absolute control, reduced her to a quivering mess. And damn if he didn't do it extremely well too. *He totally owns that master and control thing*, she thought. It was easy to understand why people looked to him as a leader. The guy in charge. It was in his fucking DNA.

Meghan sighed, contentment and excitement dancing inside her. She looked forward to their private play. Snuggling together in the dark with others close by was shockingly exciting and terribly challenging because continuing to watch the movie lost its appeal when all she could concentrate on was the blinding need to straddle her burly lover and grind them into a tumultuous orgasm. But he'd taught her that dragging out the arousal, waiting, denying the gratification only heightened the senses.

One of the ways he drew out the anticipation was by showering her with gifts, big and small—some specifically for those times when they indulged in sensual games that never failed to leave her breathless. Just the other day he'd given her a magnificent rope of pearls that he demanded she wear—with nothing else—as she rode him while he controlled her with the long strand wrapped several times around her neck like a collar. Wearing them, the pearls had made her feel elegant and sexy but when he used them as a reminder of his mastery over her she'd been turned on by the symbolism and would never look at pearls the same ever again.

She knew before they even arrived at Cam's for movie night that he had something planned. He'd texted her earlier when she'd been in the barn brushing down the pony she'd ridden, and there was something titillating about casually glancing at her phone and seeing the words *Prepare yourself to be fucked hard tonight. Till you cry and beg for more.* Her pussy clenched every time he did that—sent her a message or whispered something seductive while others were present.

Nothing about what they did or said surprised her. Not really. Yeah, it was terribly erotic and flat-out dirty most of the time, but he'd been honest about his need for rough and wild, and Meghan had happily submitted to his powerful sexuality. For him, she played the lady with a wanton side to perfection. It was liberating, actually. She even loved when he called her his fuck goddess.

It was mid-August and Meghan had been living a sensual fantasy starring her sexy Major for the last six weeks. If anything really bothered her it was that in all that time they never spoke of what came next—never touched on the fact that she was a visitor and not a permanent resident in the Villa *or* his bed. Enjoying their powerfully seductive dream meant she didn't exactly want to ruin things with anything that resembled reality. Somehow she'd become a modern day version of Scarlett O'Hara, another feisty Irishwoman who was famous for saying she'd think about this or that tomorrow.

He was the devil though. Getting through a two-hour movie with his hard cock pressing against her palm and the promise of making her cry till she begged for more hanging in the air, she would be wet and aching for him by the time she got to unwrap her gift. The man knew how to play her so well.

Meghan got him back for teasing her about halfway through the screening when she'd quietly undone the button on his jeans and slid the zipper down far enough for her to slide her fingers against his naked skin. In the darkened room no one was the wiser, plus she didn't doubt for a second that the other two couples were probably engaging in their own private teasing games. All three of the Justice men were seriously oversexed, much to the delight of the women at their sides.

Even Lacey, who was heavily pregnant and counting down the

final weeks before the birth of her child, displayed an insatiable desire for her gorgeous husband. Meghan suspected all those things she heard about pregnant women and their crazy hormones were true, since at times Cam looked like he'd been thoroughly ravished by a she-beast. Everyone laughed about it, making ribald comments when he turned up with love bites all over his neck or some pretty interesting scratches on his back.

As if to make the point, when the movie was finally over and the lights came back up, the distinctive sound of zippers being pulled up was heard with all three men sporting hilariously sheepish grins on their faces.

By the time she and Alex had said their good-byes and hurried back to the main house, Meghan's panties were soaked. He didn't even have to touch her to get her wet—just the anticipation of what was to come was enough.

They lingered downstairs long enough to haggle over whether it would be Jameson's or Glenfiddich with Alex getting his way of course. Grabbing two large tumblers of whiskey they headed to the privacy of Alex's enormous bedroom where Meghan immediately spied two beautifully wrapped boxes on her pillow. She grinned at him and moistened her lips. He leered at her, but she made no move to pick up either box. Waiting was part of their playtime. Until he gave permission, she'd have to be satisfied with looking but not touching. He played his part of dominant lover with exquisite precision, never failing to reward her compliance of his wishes.

Somewhere deep in her heart Meghan knew this game they indulged in had wrecked her for any other man. She was his—totally and without reservation. The thought should probably scare the shit out of her, but it didn't. He definitely understood and respected that it was she who allowed him to exercise such complete control over her. Nothing was forced or taken for granted. She gave willingly every time.

Clinking their glasses together, Alex drank heavily of the fragrant alcohol, watching as she did the same. There was a twinkle of mischief in his eyes that made her heart pound.

Pushing her into the en suite with the attached dressing room he playfully swatted her ass and told her, "Put on something naughty, lover. And don't forget the heels and stockings."

Ah, yes. As if their playtimes weren't off the chart hot enough, he'd gifted her an endless supply of sexy lingerie that never failed to take things to an eleven.

Meghan set her glass down on a table and molded her body to his with her hands upon his chest. He liked when she acquiesced with a little show of sensual docility. Moving against him with a flirtatious wiggle, she asked breathlessly, "Tell me your pleasure, baby. Naughty comes in many forms."

He shot her a lecherous look that made her skin tingle.

"White and virginal?" When he didn't react she pouted and said, "No?"

"Hmmm." Meghan stared at his mouth with the sensual lips curled in playful delight and sighed as she pretended to think.

"Sheer black lace?" Still nothing. She liked this game.

Even though her portion of his big closet was overflowing with sexy finery he'd personally selected, she'd also acquired a thing or two intended to knock his socks off which he knew nothing about.

Palming the bulge in his pants she whispered in his ear, "I have just the thing," before swiftly turning away from him. The moment she went to leave his side though he pulled her back and swatted her butt playfully then grabbed a handful of ass and squeezed.

"Let me check something first," he growled, quickly slipping his hand under her wrap around dress and reaching into her dampened panties before she could react. She knew what he would find. Her body always gave her away, no matter how calm or relaxed she appeared.

"Fuck, you're so wet," he groaned. Thrusting a finger inside her, she gasped at the intrusion and forced herself to stay still so she wouldn't grind her aching pussy against his hand.

When he removed his hand, he slowly and deliberately inserted the finger covered in her fluid into his mouth while his eyes never left hers. "Hurry," he ground out as she stared with longing at his lips.

Meghan almost ran into the dressing room as Alex started moving around the bedroom readying their private sanctuary for the love play to come. The last thing she saw when she peeked, he was lighting several candles in deep glass hurricane holders that illuminated the bedroom with low gleaming light.

WAITING FOR HER TO come back tested Alex's patience. He'd been thinking about tonight all day, wondering what her reaction would be to the gifts he'd left on her pillow. He thoroughly enjoyed surprising her with everything and anything he could think of and not just a treasure trove of sexy lingerie.

Knowing she had the ability to buy anything she wanted, he thought long and hard about every present. He wanted the emotion to mean more to her than the value. From some silly Southwestern refrigerator magnets to a gold necklace meant to hang down her back with a sparkling emerald at the end—everything was intended to get a response. Hell, he'd even managed to track down a first edition signed by the author of a Harry Potter book that earned him quite a sexy thank you.

Tonight's gifts though were far different and meant to convey something very private between just the two of them. He doubted she'd be sharing what was so beautifully gift-wrapped.

When Meghan finally appeared, Alex almost forgot everything

he'd planned. She was wearing something he'd never seen before—an emerald green corset with deep, plunging cups, trimmed in black lace that was cinched tight enough to highlight her glorious curves and tiny waist. A pair of indecently flimsy sheer green panties made his mouth water, as did the very sexy lace topped thigh high stockings and black peep-toe pumps with a dainty bow on the heel. The look was feminine, seductive, and hotter than hell.

She'd left her hair down in a riot of curls that tumbled about her shoulders and when he looked closely, he noted she was also wearing the delicate back necklace and a pair of small emerald and diamond tear drop earrings he'd given her during their stay in Sedona.

The woman was so fucking gorgeous he couldn't move. Her eyes sparkled with desire as he slowly took in every inch of her appearance. He liked seeing her like this, his sexy Irish beauty dressed up for his pleasure. Later, after he'd ravished her in every way he could, she'd be a disheveled mess and become the fuck goddess at whose feet he worshipped.

While she'd been gone, Alex had changed into a pair of black silk bottoms that did absolutely nothing to disguise the throbbing erection she inspired. While he'd been enjoying the view she provided, Meghan had been checking him out as well. He liked the way her gaze fired up when her eyes roamed over his broad, hair-covered chest. After she told him how much she liked it when he didn't shave for days at a time, he'd been sporting scruffy facial hair that she deemed sexy as fuck.

Stalking slowly closer to him, he was transfixed by her stunning elegance. Just out of arm's reach she stopped and stood, with legs apart, hands on hips, and a wicked pout. Her scent reached out and grabbed his senses by the balls, making him groan with lusty desire.

"Turn around," he husked. "Let me see everything my beauty."

Meghan smiled and wet her lips, then flipped her hair from one shoulder with a flirty gesture that made his dick even harder. Pirouetting slowly on the sexy, 'fuck-me heels', she turned around and gave him a memorable view of her backside that was barely covered by the sheer panties. The laces of the corset were pulled tight leaving two long strands of ribbon hanging in the crevice of her ass. The back necklace rested on bare skin above the corset with the dainty emerald twinkling in the candle light. She was nothing short of magnificent. When she returned to face him, his eyes burned with arousal.

"Are you ready to see what's in the boxes on your pillow?"

Swinging her hips with a sexy sway that nearly brought him to his knees, she walked to the bed and picked up both boxes.

"Shall I open both now?" she asked. He caught the sound of breathless want in her voice. Remembering that she'd been dripping with desire, he smiled knowingly and motioned her forward.

"Sit on my lap sweetheart, and we'll open them together."

She immediately went to him as he sat in a wide overstuffed chair, drifting gracefully onto his lap and crossing her legs, adopting a seductive posture so the plunging cups of the corset made her tits plump in his face.

Taking a flat box from her hands that he laid aside, he motioned to the other and murmured, "Start with that one." As she deftly worked at the wrapping, he grazed his fingers on the bare skin of her back, enjoying the way her flesh prickled at his touch.

Once all the wrapping was removed she met his eyes. The intimacy of the gift-giving had her chest rising and falling rapidly with suspense but she didn't rush, preferring to play out the excitement with longing looks and shy smiles.

When she lifted the lid off the box he watched her face. At first, she seemed confused, and he enjoyed watching how her mind tried to make a connection. Finally she lifted out what looked like a swatch of material and fingered the satin until it suddenly dawned on her what she was holding. Her sharp gasp told him she knew exactly what he'd given her. When her eyes darted back to his, he saw a flash of green fire that pleased him very, very much.

Taking the satin from her, he smiled into her surprised face. "They're called boudoir cuffs."

Alex was quite proud of this particular gift. Beautiful and elegant, the black satin cuffs were sewn with small crystals that twinkled in the glow of the candles. Trimmed in black lace with ribbon ties for proper fit, the fabric cuffs had a beaded removable chain that would bind her hands together when attached. Without the chain they looked like a chic fashion accessory with a naughty twist.

He fitted each one to her wrists and tied the ribbons as she sat there on his lap watching with a veiled expression.

"We'll leave the chain off for now," he told her as he inspected the way they looked before pressing a wet kiss into each of her palms.

The way she was breathing gave her away. As he'd tied the cuffs on, Alex noticed an increase in her respirations made deliciously obvious by her spectacular breasts as they rose and fell with each choppy breath. She was surprised, and maybe a bit nervous, by the obvious intention behind the cuffs, but she was also quite turned on. He felt the heat radiating off her body where she sat on his lap as she exuded waves of arousal, specifically from between her thighs.

"They look good on you," he murmured. "Very sexy."

She surprised him with a quick kiss by lips that quivered on his.

When she drew back she held up her hands and inspected the elegant cuffs, touching the sparkling crystals with trembling fingers. He enjoyed watching the play of emotions flit across her face. She gave so much away with her expression.

Reaching for the flat box, he pressed it into her hands. "Next," he teased as he sat back and let the ensuing moment unfold as it was meant to.

This time she was less precise about removing the wrapping, making quick work of tearing the paper off and tossing it and the small ribbon aside. Lifting the lid and parting the delicate tissue paper she really did gasp this time when she found a matching satin and lace blindfold.

He didn't give her any time to think. "I'm going to enjoy fucking you hard and rough with your hands restrained and your eyes covered so you'll not know what's coming next."

She shivered on his lap and turned lust-filled eyes on him.

"Have any questions?" he purred as his fingers drew across the skin of her breasts where they plumped out of the corset.

When she shook her head and glanced at the bed, he knew she was ready to play.

"Walk to the bed Meghan, but don't turn around. I want to enjoy your sexy ass."

She glanced at him, and he leered knowingly at the flash of apprehension in her eyes. He could set her mind at ease and tell her he wasn't especially interested in fucking her anally. Unless it was something she really wanted to explore, he'd just as soon pass. Drooling over her ass and teasing her with his fingers and mouth was one thing, but making her cry as his cock pounded into her that way didn't have much appeal for him. But he didn't say anything, preferring to absorb her exquisite tension because it excited the fuck out of him.

He let her stand there in silence for several minutes as he simply savored her magnificent backside and the way she looked in her decadent lingerie. He liked pushing her boundaries, testing her limits. The cuffs and blindfold were meant to drive home the command he had over her body. She could choose not to wear either, but he knew she wouldn't. Meghan liked giving in to his pleasures. He might never get enough of her sweet surrender.

Alex had to clear his throat when he told her to take her panties off. She wasn't the only one turned on and aching. Watching her slide the flimsy silk down her thighs was incredibly sensual. She moved with a delicate gracefulness that belied her athletic build. The picture she made with the glittering jewelry on her back, ribbons from her corset tickling the seam of her ass, her legs slightly parted with the sexy hose, and decadent heels had him reaching for his cock.

Taking his time about it, he eventually went and stood behind her. Close enough that she would feel his warm breath on her skin. Spreading his fingers wide, he grabbed a handful of her lush backside, caressing the pale skin with an unhurried thoroughness that made her moan.

Fisting a section of her auburn curls, Alex yanked her head back as she let out a startled yelp. With her neck forcefully arched and his hand teasing the flesh of her derrière, he groaned next to her ear. "I love your ass." He smiled when she shivered from head to toe.

Alex ran his tongue along the sensitive skin of her exposed neck. When she started breathing erratically he claimed his prize—latching his teeth into her flesh, marking what was his.

Untying the ribbon lacing on her naughty corset was pure delight. He liked unwrapping this particular present. As he worked the ties he murmured to her about what lay ahead, gauging her response to his words, curious what would get a reaction.

"I wasn't sure at first, but seeing you in your jewelry and the sexy heels, I think on your knees, legs spread wide, and back arched will do nicely."

He chuckled as she wantonly shimmied her ass against his hardness.

"Ah. So my baby likes that, hmmm? You're such a hot piece of ass Meghan. My dick twitches with desire when you express your passion."

Her head swung forward as a soft whimper escaped her lips. He'd taught her to be quiet unless he gave permission to speak. It was a simple power play that she seemed to enjoy. It forced all her awareness on him.

When the corset was loosened, he barely touched her skin as he flipped the lace straps off her shoulders and peeled the green fabric from her body. God almighty. What a sight she made wearing nothing but his jewelry, the wicked satin cuffs, and those damn sexy stockings and high heels that made him hard as steel. The dainty bows on the back of her 'fuck-me shoes' was a nice, feminine touch. A subtle reminder that his lady was also very wicked.

Leaving her side for a brief moment, Alex retrieved the blindfold and short chain that he'd attach to the cuffs to restrain her hands. He gave her the blindfold to hold. Another subtle power play. Letting her handle the satin fabric before covering her eyes would fill her head with images and increase the allure.

"Put your hands behind your back, baby," he commanded in a voice that said he wasn't messing around.

While she wasn't being given permission to talk, he had told her in blunt terms that she should communicate with him in other ways. Every moan and quiver told him so much. As did the tension in her shoulders or the way she paused when some unexpected command or new sensation washed over her.

She hesitated for the briefest moment, enough time for Alex's mouth to quirk with amusement. As always, her display of nerves turned him on. Giving in with obvious reluctance, she crossed her hands behind her back but she turned her head and sought his eyes. This was what made her perfection. She needed to see his desire. Without that connection, she struggled to obey his commands.

He kissed her sweetly letting his tongue slip briefly between her lips. Reading her response, Alex knew that this time at least, restraining her hands behind her back was a step too far for his Irish temptress, but he rewarded her willingness by taking advantage of how the position forced her breasts into a particularly seductive pose. With one hand holding hers low on her back he teased the pebbled nipples on each glorious mound with his other hand and whispered into her ear.

"I feel your desire baby. And your hesitation too. This time we'll use the cuffs the easy way." She shuddered under his touch. It was such a small concession but one that he knew would make her want to please him even more.

Swatting her ass with a resounding slap that echoed in the candle lit room he growled low and menacing. "I *will* have your consent to this Meghan. When you're ready. I desire you helpless, hands bound behind your back, unable to see, focused on nothing but your arousal. Maybe I'll tie your legs too."

He thought it was cute as fucking hell when she whimpered and bit her lip. There was something about a hard slap on the ass that never failed to get a reaction from her. He'd yet to give her a full on spanking, preferring to stoke the flames of her curiosity with teases and taunts. By the time he got her over his lap with that mesmerizing ass of hers up in the air, she'd be begging for it.

Thinking about her ass on his lap got his sex throbbing like a motherfucker. He needed to feel her hands on his flesh. *Now.* He suddenly pulled away from her and dropped her hands. "Undress me," he demanded in a voice made rough with passion.

His sexy Irish goddess knew what to do. Since he was only wearing bottoms, she quickly pulled the tie that held them on his hips and pushed the silken fabric to the floor. When his cock sprang free she caressed him with her eyes and wet her lips in a way that drove all thought from his brain.

Her eyes sought his, seeking permission. Kicking the bottoms aside, Alex moved into a firm stance while he pushed two fingers into her mouth. When she closed her eyes and groaned, sucking greedily, he feathered his free hand across her stomach and into the mass of curls between her legs.

"I know what you want. Your body hides nothing from me." Finding her clit was easy, she was so wet and swollen with arousal that the sexy nub practically leaped into his touch. He rolled it between his fingers. In seconds she was shaking all over.

Yanking his hands free he pushed her down to the floor. "On your knees woman," he growled. Grabbing his cock he stroked it several times just inches from her face. The way she looked at him with eyes full of lust and need was so hot—he could feel it on his skin.

With a trembling hand he swept the head of his staff along the seam of her mouth as she pursed her lips and groaned. Alex never had to ask for her outrageously sexy mouth on his cock. She all but pleaded for it morning, noon, and night. It made him hot as hell knowing his woman not only enjoyed sucking on him but that she got seriously turned on too. Watching her take him deep in her mouth was fucking glorious.

"Should I make you beg?" he chuckled. She shot him a naughty look and let her lips relax, pulling the sensitive head of his cock into the suction of her mouth. That shut him up damn quick.

When she reached for his hard flesh, the crystals on her satin cuffs flashed in the candlelight. "Open that mouth wide, baby," he demanded, "and put your hands on your tits. I want to watch you fondle yourself while my cock gets a tongue bath." The leer he gave her did not miss its mark. His twitching flesh absorbed the sly smile on her lips.

There was something hot and decadent about their positions. Him standing with his cock jutting from his hard-muscled body, her on her knees before him, hands molded to her bountiful breasts. When she licked him with her tongue his cock reacted. The woman had a wicked mouth.

Alex stood there, watching the scene at his feet, his eyes glazed with desire. Without the aid of her hands, she had to catch the head of his hard staff with her lips, which she did with a deep groan of satisfaction. Watching her open wide and suck him into her warm, wet mouth was almost torture. He wanted to grab her head and fuck her mouth with heart-pounding abandon but he didn't. This was just a warm-up for what was to come.

While she worked on his flesh and played with her tits, he spoke to her softly. Telling her how sexy she was. How much he loved what she was doing. Praising her passion and encouraging her to enjoy herself.

"I love when you go deep and moan on my cock."

When she did just that he hissed and shook from the glorious sensations she was causing. His eyes almost popped out of his head when she let his staff slide from her mouth so she could suck along the length with wet kisses that drove him insane with need.

This was something he'd discovered that she liked very much, teasing him with her tongue. Lapping at his hardness until his cock quivered and jumped with each caress. As she licked him Alex groaned his delight, his butt clenching with the force of his arousal.

They were both breathing heavy when she suddenly made an O with her lips and sucked him in slow and deep. Watching his cock slide along her tongue until he felt it nudge the back of her throat was hypnotic. He staggered briefly as the devastating impact of her greedy mouth shot along his nerve endings.

"*Fuck* Meghan," he growled. She answered with a desperate moan and just like that he was beyond his limit.

Pulling out of her mouth, he grabbed a handful of hair and forced her to stand. A bright pink flush washed her cheeks and her eyes held a smoky haze of arousal that darkened them to a midnight green. Crushing her to him with his hand against her head, he devoured her mouth, thrusting his tongue where his cock had just been.

This wasn't going to be a gentle fuck. He'd certainly warned her; plus the cuffs and blindfold made his intentions crystal clear. Reaching for the beaded chain that would bind her hands together, he quickly restrained her then leaned down and suckled fiercely on each of her pebbled pink nipples until she cried out and writhed against him.

He was almost at the point of no return and reluctantly decided the blindfold would have to wait for another time. The unmistakable scent of her arousal had him by the balls and nothing short of a brutal pounding was going to satisfy his desire.

"On the fucking bed Meghan. *Now*," he growled.

He had to give her credit; even with her hands restrained she managed to get into position without any assistance from him. Watching her swing that magnificent ass as she spread her legs wide and rested on arms tied at the wrist, was exactly the image he'd been fantasizing about. With her chest on the mattress and her hands above her head he had a clear view of her beautiful pussy. Primal male triumph made him growl like an animal when he saw proof of her arousal trickle down a thigh.

Joining her on the bed, Alex watched a sensual shudder move through her body as he ran his tongue along the path of her fluid

"Baby, you are so wet. My cock is going to enjoy this."

She whimpered at his words and turned her head so she could look back at him as he moved into position.

"I like seeing your pretty eyes watching." And he did. Desire flared as he drowned in her exquisite lust-filled expression making Alex feel like a fucking god.

She whimpered some more. *Enough was enough,* he thought as he lined up his throbbing cock with her entrance and plunged deep in one forceful thrust. A hoarse grunt rumbled from his chest.

Grabbing onto her voluptuous hips, he didn't give her time to adjust to the penetration. That wasn't what he promised—rough and hard was what he told her to expect, and that was exactly what she would get.

Holding firmly enough to leave bruises, Alex thundered into her, over and over. The pounding went on and on. He felt powerful, intense—demanding her cunt to surrender to his claim on her body. Letting the beast inside off its carefully leashed tether was mind-blowing. Heat pulsed in his groin as he absorbed the primal energy driving him on.

Running a hand possessively up her back, Alex pushed her chest down and forced her knees further apart making her arch onto his cock as he thrust without mercy into her wet depths. The longer it went on the more primitive he became. Grabbing a fistful of her hair and yanking her head back, she cried out and fucked him with an energetic enthusiasm that tested his control.

She was fucking magnificent. Meghan's cunt clutched and pulsed as he moaned with satisfaction. "My baby likes it rough and hard." Her response was to come with such intensity that her muscles seized his sex and held on like a vise. Alex gloried in the rush of heated cream that bathed his cock.

"Fuck," he roared, still pounding relentlessly, churning her fluid response into a sexy sound that made him shiver. The primal pleasure intensified as sweat poured off him. Grunting forcefully with each thrust, she whimpered softly in answer. He loved the sounds she made.

Keeping his grip on her hair, he never lost his rhythm, sinking deep over and over as he reached around to vigorously tweak her swollen clit. Her pussy knew its master as she shook with renewed arousal. Needing to hear her pleasure, he demanded in a rough voice that she tell him what she wanted. Teaching her to talk dirty had been one of his first triumphs with the woman whose body fit so perfectly to his.

She grunted and moaned. "*Alex.*" She made his name sound like prayer. "Make me come again, baby. Please. *Please*...." she cried. Watching her gorgeous ass undulate as he thundered into her was nothing short of phenomenal.

Come again? With pleasure, he thought. Rolling her clit one final time, he swung his hand back and smacked her ass with a resounding thud. She writhed and gasped. He did it again.

"Move that ass Meghan. Take me deep, baby." He smacked her again and again until she cried out. Her legs were trembling as she feverishly impaled herself on his insatiable cock.

A bead of sweat made its way down his neck and along his spine as her sheath tightened and then tightened some more. Before long she was gasping his name. With one last lusty smack on her ass he plunged deep and held still as his swollen cock nudged her cervix. She screamed and shook all over as another orgasm exploded inside her.

"Yes," he cried triumphantly. "Come for me my beautiful fuck goddess. Come all over my cock." She did. And it was a beautiful sight to behold.

Leaving control behind, Alex thundered home in a blistering assault of relentless thrusts until his orgasm finally detonated. He pumped into her willing body, as his balls emptied and his cock jerked.

His beautiful Meghan in her black stocking and heels with her hands bound and her ass in the air, cried softly when his completion hit, thanking him over and over.

"Oh God Alex. I love it when you come inside me." And that was exactly what he wanted to hear.

"Only for you, baby. Only for you," he groaned.

THERE WERE SOUNDS THAT triggered things inside Alex. Sounds and sensations, which unleashed a torrent of dark memories, threatening to steal his sanity. Simple sounds like Velcro ripping open could get his nerves on edge. And then there were the other sounds, like the hollow thud of a gun butt hitting flesh or the popping noise from a bullet tearing into a body. Sometimes he didn't know how he lived with that shit in his head.

When the opera of war took center stage in his dreams, it was his own personal hell that had no end. A memory and a nightmare intersected in those night terrors—percussion waves and the heated air from an explosion choked off the oxygen until it suffocated as the force of the blast turned your body into a missile, throwing you like a ragdoll against an immoveable object, where you crumbled to the ground and debris covered everyone and everything. Consciousness faded and black oblivion took over.

And then the pain and the fear took hold when the darkness began to recede. In the end you didn't know which was worse—the physical and mental reaction to the explosion, or the never ending aftermath. In his nightmare, a jumble of voices and ominous sounds rang in his head. Snippets from just before the flashing boom, then the eerie muted silence, followed long agonizing moments later by shouts, screams, and curses. And then the precise staccato of military speak. Directives, responses, orders flying, more shouting, then doctors, nurses, medics. Short, detached, exact.

It was those auditory cues; the frayed threads of a life torn to shreds, that were bouncing around in his brain when Alex's eyes shot open. Going from nightmare to wakefulness in a nanosecond, he was barely aware of the present as the past clung to him like a cold, wet blanket.

Every molecule and atom in his body was either on fire or pulsing in pain. Even though he knew he was at home in Arizona, his senses were clogged with the taste and smells from a time long ago that turned his stomach and made his breathing labored and harsh. *Fuck.*

He didn't remember sitting up or getting out of bed. Couldn't re-call how he dressed himself or anything else he did before finding him-self in the tech room. Lights were flickering around him, technology humming, but he heard and felt nothing. Nothing at all until he flipped on his computer and hit the log in keys. And just like that a different sort of bomb went off in his head.

The first thing that flashed on the screen was the date in bold letters and a list of names, some with jpeg thumbnails. They were all there in black and white. A maudlin butcher's list of the dead sent from the past to haunt him in the present.

Something tore open inside him the minute that fucking list of names appeared to remind him what today was. Anger, hurt, and loss detonated in Alex's core, mimicking the explosion. After weeks of calm, and maybe even happiness, the harsh brutal reminder ripped a hole so big in his psyche, he fell completely into it.

Bellowing like a wounded animal, he roared until the veins popped on his neck, grabbing a hold of the laptop and sending it crashing to the floor. Hurling his desk chair next, it slammed into the wall followed in short order by any object in his vicinity that wasn't nailed down.

A fury enveloped him. It was one thing to mark this day year after year—that he was used to—but this time the loss was deeper, more profound, because it included something different. Someone new. Life had been the cruelest bitch of all by letting him have a taste of happiness and then mocking him with the cold, hard reminder of who he was, what he'd done, where he'd been.

Storming from the room in a blind rage, Alex made like a man possessed for the front door, flinging it wide and stepping into the early morning light with a dark savagery etched on every inch of his body. He wanted to fucking kill someone. Wanted to strike out at the entire world for everything he'd lost and all the damage he'd done.

Jumping into his truck, he started the engine and peeled out of the driveway in a cloud of dust, roaring down the drive as if the hounds of hell were chasing him.

MEGHAN STRETCHED SLOWLY, STILL cocooned in the warmth of Alex's big bed. His scent wrapped around her like a blanket. Memories of the night flashed in her mind. A small smile curled her lips as she remembered how he'd taken her with a ferocity that had been a total turn on. She'd responded to him in such a primal way. Thinking about it made her shudder with pleasure. He was a magnificent beast. *Her* magnificent beast.

Reaching for him, she was surprised to find herself alone in the bed. Thinking he was in the bathroom or maybe getting dressed, Meghan lay there and luxuriated in the aftermath of their lovemaking. Could anything be sweeter than replaying such a bawdy encounter? She didn't think so. He'd been masterful and demanding. Playing her emotions the entire day until she'd been ripe and ready for whatever he threw at her.

Smiling, she remembered the sexy boudoir cuffs and the way she'd crawled with hands restrained onto the bed and raised her naked backside in the air for him to use as he pleased. He had turned her into a wanton and try as she might to feel weird about that fact, she couldn't.

She'd been with him every step of the way, even crying out for more when he fucked her aggressively.

Sitting up, she pushed the messy tangle of her hair away from her face and looked around. As far as could be told, Alex was nowhere in the vicinity. She wondered where he'd wandered off to. It was still early. Early enough that she doubted anyone from the agency had need for him.

Hmmm. What was going on, she wondered.

Twenty minutes later, freshly showered and dressed, Meghan tip-toed into the kitchen thinking to surprise him at coffee but the house was silent and empty. Maybe the tech cave?

Making her way down a series of corridors, she pushed open the large doors to the cave and went in search of him. With no lights on except the ones that flickered from the tons of electrical equipment spread around the space, she was baffled by his absence.

And then she saw it. His corner of tech-heaven had been reduced to rubble. The only thing that hadn't been slammed into the wall or sent crashing to the floor was the desk itself. Everything else was in pieces. What the hell had happened?

Sprinting back to the bedroom like a fire was chasing her down, Meghan quickly found her phone and called Alex's cell. When it went straight to voicemail without ringing, she knew he wasn't communicating. On reflex, she connected next with Tori's cell phone. Something was definitely not right. With panic spreading through her body, she hoped Alex's assistant would have some answers.

"Meghan. Good Lord Irish. Do you know what time it is?" grumbled the groggy, half-asleep voice that answered.

"Tori. Is Alex with you?" she blurted out.

She could almost feel Tori shaking her head to clear the cobwebs of sleep from her mind. "Um. No. Draegyn's in the shower though, but I haven't seen or heard from Alex. Why? What's wrong?"

Meghan didn't quite know how to answer that question.

"Can you come up here? To the house, I mean. Something's wrong."

"With Alex? What do you mean Irish?"

"Look," Meghan said jerkily. "Just get here as soon as you can. Okay?"

"Okay, okay. We'll be there in a few."

Meghan heard Tori calling out to her husband as she hit the end button to terminate the call.

Dammit. She was beside herself. Something was terribly wrong, she could feel it. When the St. John's arrived a half hour later, Meghan was pacing back and forth by the front door, wringing her hands and trying not to entertain every horrible scenario that popped into her head.

The expression on Draegyn's face told her he wasn't exactly surprised that something was going on. In fact, he had a somber, almost dour look that felt like a foreboding. Meghan swallowed the huge lump forming in her throat as he came toward her.

"What's up?" he asked tightly with Tori following close on his heels.

Unable to form words, she just pointed toward the tech room and waved them on. Scurrying quickly, the minute Drae saw the carnage he loosed a terse, "Fuck," and turned quickly toward his wife.

"C'mon computer wizard," he murmured. "That laptop looks like toast but I know you can access whatever he was looking at. Get me a screenshot of his computer, babe."

Meghan saw Tori hesitate and bite her lip as she shot her husband an anxious frown. Drae quickly told her, "And no, I don't give a fuck and neither should you that he'll be pissed you hacked into his personal shit. Screw that. The goddamn NSA is probably watching everything he does anyway."

It took Tori less than two minutes to do as her husband asked. The minute the date flashed on the screen with the damning document list—nothing but names and a couple of jpegs—he was swearing like it was his job. Without hesitating he pulled his phone from a pocket and tapped on the screen. She heard the sound of ringing and realized he had it on speakerphone. *Oh thank God*, Meghan hoped silently. Maybe he knew how to get in touch with Alex.

A pissed off growling voice answered, but not Alex's.

"Suck my dick St. John. Why the fuck are you calling at this hour?"

Drae winced but answered quickly. "Alex is off the reservation Cam. Check the date and then get your ass up here. Fast. This doesn't look good."

She heard Cam mutter, "Fuck," followed by silence. A minute

went by during which he must have checked the date and time, then he said, "Got it. *RTB*. I'll be right there." And the phone went dead.

Meghan's anxiety got the better of her. "What's going on Drae? RTB? What does that mean? Why did you say Alex was off the reservation?" The questions came fast and furious. Tears clogged her throat when Tori put an arm around her waist. "Please tell me what's happening."

Drae looked at her for a hard minute, his ice blue eyes cold and assessing. He was frightening her but good. A cold shiver swirled in her senses making Meghan start to tremble uncontrollably.

Tori finally spoke up. "Draegyn," was all she said but she did it in that tone wives use when they want their husbands to pay attention. He sucked in a huge breath of air and seemed to pull himself together.

"RTB means return to base. It's an expression from our military days. Cam will be here in record time." He looked around again at the mess in the office and frowned. "Alex off the reservation just means he's not here. Something definitely happened when he came down here and saw what day it is."

Turning to his wife he asked, "Did he search for that list or was it...?"

Before he got any further with the question Tori chimed in. "He had it scheduled for the welcome screen when he logged in today."

"Motherfucker," he mumbled. "Why does he do this to himself?" he asked out loud, pacing restlessly, his eyes intense and hard.

Meghan had enough. She didn't know what anyone was talking about. Her nerves snapped and she cried out, "What the fuck is going on?"

Draegyn and Tori looked at her stunned. Drae groaned and shook his head.

"Sorry Meghan. I can see this is freaking you out so I should warn you that it's probably going to get a lot worse before it gets any better."

"Is Alex alright?" she asked in a thready voice overcome with anxiety. "What can I do?"

Drae waved his hand at the broken equipment and grimaced. "It's the anniversary of the bombing. The list on his computer was the names of everyone who died."

Her "Oh," formed on her face, but she wasn't sure if the word actually came out of her mouth. The anniversary. *Shit.* David died on this day all those years ago. Cold fear started making its way into her nervous system. This was the thing that lived in the shadows of Alex's conscience where dark thoughts and terrible memories constantly threatened to steal his soul.

"Is he okay Drae? Please tell me."

Draegyn moved to her side and wrapped her in a hug. Tori came in from behind and wrapped her arms around Meghan's waist enveloping her in an affectionate emotional sandwich.

Drae assured her, "He's going to be fine honey. Don't you worry. Cam and I know what to do."

Turning to his wife he said, "You ladies should hang out together. Lacey can't really be running around, and it'd be best if you just let us handle things from here. Okay?"

What was Meghan supposed to do? She was scared and confused but not a stranger to the dynamic behind what was happening right before her eyes. Her father was a cop, two of her brothers were firemen, and the other an EMT. She knew all too well about guilt and survivor's remorse and the shitstorm those emotions could cause. It killed her to think of Alex going through that.

Last night was fading into memory, and being replaced with things that were scaring the shit out of her. There was nothing to do but wait and see what happened next.

MEGHAN WAS NUMB AND panicked when she let Tori bundle her into an electric cart for the drive to Lacey's cabin. They passed Cam along the way as he sped by without a wave. It was all Meghan could do not to turn around and return to the house. She didn't know what help she'd be but she wanted to be in on whatever Cam and Drae were going to do.

Tori reached out a squeezed her hand reassuringly. "Let the men handle this one, Irish. I told you how complicated these Justice brothers are. I don't have enough knowledge to offer an opinion, and I doubt Lacey does either about whatever this is, but I bet they've been down the road before."

Meghan nodded but turned and watched as Cam's truck disappeared around a bend in the lane. She felt helpless. And even worse, she hadn't ever spoken of her feelings to Alex—telling him how she felt might have helped. Them not talking about what they were doing or looking at the future had been a critical mistake. She loved him. Like crazy, bat-shit, all encompassing, tie me to the bed and have your way with me, love. And he needed to know that.

Lacey was on the front porch when they arrived at the cabin. She looked like they all felt. Worried. Confused. It was going to be one hell of a day.

HOURS LATER DRAE AND Cam were still working the angles and coming up empty.

"Still no answer?" Cam asked

Drae shook his head in the negative and disconnected the phone call. They just looked at each other but said nothing for a long time.

"He's an asshole for disconnecting the GPS on the truck. We'll never track him without it," Cam bit out tersely. Picking up one of Zeus's toys that laid nearby, Cam started tossing the small rubber ball against the floor, angling so it then ricocheted off a wood door. The rhythmic sounds drowned out the silence of their thoughts.

"What the fuck, man," muttered Drae. "I actually thought we were beyond this, didn't you?" he asked with a look of sad disbelief all over his face. "He's been so wrapped up in Meghan these last few week. Guess it was wishful thinking but I really thought...*shit*."

"I know *exactly* what you thought, and I was right there with you. She's been good for him. First time *ever* that he hasn't been all up in everyone else's grill about every little thing." Cam punctuating his words with a fierce toss of the ball, the angry sound echoing his frustration.

"Wanna go track the back forty? See if he's skulking out in the desert?" Drae knew they were grasping at straws.

Cam thought about it for the hundredth time and came up with the same answer. "No. He doesn't want to be found. Alex knows damn well that's the first place we'd look which is why we're still here, pounding sand. I can track anyone but him. The man taught me most everything I know. He isn't Tori, dude. He's not gonna suddenly leave a trail a mile wide that we can follow."

Drae laughed at the memory of them banding together to track his wayward wife when she did a flit after he'd fucked up one too many times. At least that drama had a happy ending. This situation with Alex didn't feel like it was going to be that easy. "What do you think set him off, bro? Every other year he's been a dick, yeah. But this, I don't know, man. This is different."

"He's got something to lose now that he didn't before," Cam murmured quietly.

"Meghan," Drae added, nodding. "Did he ever tell you what the deal was with her fiancé? Something must have gone down because one minute he was fighting the attraction and the next she moved into his room."

"Hmmm, good point. Somehow I think our wives may hold some clues on that score, and if they don't, maybe we should just ask the lady. Whatever caused his explosion of rage this morning has everything to do with her, I'm sure of it. And from what you said, she's unglued and seems stunned by his behavior so I'm betting they didn't have a fight or anything like that."

Drae headed for the door and waved at him to follow. "Alright, Cam. Let's go shine an interrogation lamp on the women and see what we can flush out. Hanging around here waiting for him to show himself is getting us nowhere."

SHE MIGHT BE SITTING upright in a chair but internally, Meghan was in the fetal position, overcome with anxiety as the awful day unfolded. Tori and Lacey were being sweet and supportive, making jokes about men and how thick they could sometimes be—sharing their personal stories with her. Bawdy tales of the tempestuous road their relationships with their husbands took before each found their happily ever after.

Meghan didn't need a guidebook to know her happily ever after just got wiped the hell out. She wasn't stupid. She knew that the years Alex spent in the Special Forces had not been wasted on knitting sweaters for the underprivileged. Bad guys died, and so did his comrades. Civilians got tagged and bagged too, collateral damage.

Stuff like that never really gets forgotten, and if she knew anything at all about her Major, it was that he carried enormous emotional and moral burdens about those times. She thought about the architect she'd dated briefly who seemed so uncomplicated and downright dull. He'd never had to make peace with double-tapping some enemy insurgent or calling a raid on a village where women and children were used as shields.

With her brain working overtime Meghan was plagued with memories of David. She recalled him sharing horrific stories about desperate firefights and the mental anguish knowing the bullets he was firing would be taking lives. After a while though she noticed the anguish was replaced by acceptance and finally by an air of nonchalance. Death in a war zone was every day.

In Alex's case it wasn't just about his own actions. It was complicated by what he ordered others to do. And suffer through. And deal with. All sobering thoughts.

And then there was what today represented. She'd totally forgotten. How could that be? What did that say about her? Her conscience was feeling itchy. Coming to Arizona had been about honoring David's memory and finding closure for that chapter in her life. Over the last few weeks she'd been so wrapped up in the excitement and passion of her affair with Alex that memories of her former fiancé had faded to nothing.

But Alex hadn't forgotten. Or maybe he had and that was what this morning's rampage had been about. Had he been so caught up in their newfound connection that he failed to recognize the day's significance? It pained her that the one thing proving to be Alex's hard limit was something she was so much a part of. She didn't know what to think. Didn't know what to do.

Around lunchtime Draegyn and Cameron arrived looking somber. Meghan's heart sank. Drae approached her asking, "Meghan, can we talk?"

She was numb and panicked at the same time but managed a weak nod. Everyone gathered around her, the husbands exchanging meaningful looks with their wives and no one looking comfortable.

Clearing his throat, Draegyn spoke in a gentle tone, while Tori stood at his side with her hand upon his shoulder. "We don't want to nose around your personal life Meghan but you should know that Alex told Cam and me a little bit about his feelings concerning your fiancé. We liked David. He was a great kid."

"Thanks," she murmured. "He spoke of Team Justice quite a bit." She couldn't help but glance at Cameron when she said that. His movie star good looks were a reminder of David's man crush and what that had meant to Meghan. She was sure Alex hadn't divulged to either of his brothers what she'd admitted about her fiancé's sexuality, and she wasn't going to let them in on it now.

"Well," Drae said sounding uncomfortable as he questioned her, "the reason I'm bringing it up is because Alex was pretty fucking conflicted when you arrived. But somewhere along the way that changed. Can you tell us why?"

Meghan considered the question and rolled a shoulder. "As I told Tori, whatever you may think, despite the engagement, David and I were *never* going to be married."

Looking at Cam again she blushed and dropped her eyes. She knew what they were really asking. It was a guy's question, the one that dealt with honor and doing the right thing. She didn't have much choice but to blurt out what they needed to know so they'd understand that she and Alex had gotten beyond his moral dilemma about sleeping with her based on who David had been to all of them.

"Look," she bit out. "David and I. We were never intimate if that's what you want to know. This is something Alex is aware of, and really—I don't want to say any more on the subject."

She watched Cameron and Draegyn look at each other with what appeared to be relief. *Cross that assumption off the list*, she thought.

"Okay," Drae murmured softly. It was clear he felt like a dick for asking. "We've all noticed that you and our fearless leader have gotten unusually close."

"This isn't my fault!" Meghan threw at them anxiously.

"No, no, no," Cam cut in. "Meghan please. We aren't implying he took off because of you. I think what my shithead brother was trying to say was, we've all been enjoying watching you two get together. I don't think any of us have ever seen him so happy." They all looked at one another and nodded in agreement. "We're just trying to piece together what may have caused this morning's events. Everything seemed fine last night."

Meghan groaned and put her head in her hands. "I don't know what happened. I don't know what changed. Last night was…well, whatever, and then I woke up and he was gone."

She leapt off her seat and started pacing like a caged animal. Restless, nervous energy was invading her system. "Maybe I should have seen this coming. I don't know! To be honest, I forgot all about what today meant, and I feel horrible about that. Maybe Alex feels the same way. Maybe what we were doing, or rather, what's been happening between us these last weeks was a distraction. Or a mistake. *Jesus*. I just don't know."

Cam and Drae looked at each other. "I think we got what we came for. Thanks Meghan. We'll take it from here."

"Guys," Meghan choked out as anxiety clogged her voice. "What should I do?"

Cam told her, "Don't do anything for now. You've actually clarified a few things that will give us a place to start."

Going to his wife, he kissed Lacey on the forehead and smiled. "You ladies just hang in there. We'll be in touch when we know something, and I'm sure I don't need to remind you that if you hear anything from Alex to let us know immediately."

After they left the house and were climbing into his truck, Cam turned to Drae and said, "Bull's-eye. He's beating himself up because for once in his fucking life he was happy and actually living. Forgetting was an act of betrayal."

Drae nodded. "I have an idea. Remember the house where his grandparents lived? I think we should check there. It's likely that he'd go someplace familiar if he was hurting."

ALEX FELT LIKE SHIT. His life was crumbling, and he didn't know what to do about it. He needed the world to slow the fuck down so he could get a grip on what was happening.

Pacing or rather prowling around the sprawling home that had been the scene of countless happy family times, he was assailed with thoughts of his grandparents who counted honor and integrity among a man's most essential attributes. Right now, he had neither.

Dammit. With so many conflicting thoughts and emotions swirling inside him Alex thought he might explode. *He'd certainly already had one epic blow up today,* he thought cringing at the recall of trashing his office in a blind fucking rage. He still couldn't believe that he'd forgotten what today represented. What the hell was wrong with him?

And that was what was really ripping him up. He'd done a lot of shit and seen so much evil and depravity during his years at war that the only way for him to deal with it all and not lose his fucking soul was to condense every sick, bloody, deadly event into one. A little like CliffsNotes—everything rolled into a single day where he would remember and yeah, beat himself up. It was his burden to bear after all.

But he hadn't remembered. In fact, he hadn't slowed his roll at all the last couple of weeks. It was as if the peace and happiness he'd gotten a taste of with Meghan had wiped his pain and guilt clean. Alex knew it was fucked-up to feel this way but he couldn't accept what that meant in the bigger picture. He needed to remember. Needed the pain. Needed to do the penance. Without it, what had it all been for in the end? To render so much horror inconsequential didn't sit well on his conscience.

When he'd floored it away from the Villa, it seemed like the devil himself was behind the wheel. It had taken endless miles of driving before he came back to the present and by then he couldn't turn around and go back. Alex didn't want to face Meghan, or anyone, for that matter. Not until he got everything straight in his head. That was how he'd ended up at his grandparents' house outside Sedona. It had been ages since he'd been there, but it seemed like the perfect place to go and lick his wounds.

He knew that Drae and Cam would find him. *Eventually.* It was their way, after all. Though he had a blood family he adored and cherished, his battlefield brothers were the glue that held his adult life together. No matter what fucked-up shit any of them did, they'd always been there for each other.

Some part of Alex was surprised that neither of them had spoken up about today as it got closer. In the past, their way of dealing with it was to set aside the maudlin anniversary for remembrance and male bonding. Why hadn't they said anything this time?

Snorting with unease, Alex knew the answer before the question was fully formed. They'd seen what was going on between him and Meghan and probably hoped he'd forget altogether. Drae especially had been urging him for some time to let the past go once and for all. What some saw as unemotional and cold when it came to Draegyn's attitude was actually his analytical side. He had a logical mind that gave him a leg up on those who ran on emotion and instinct. As far as he was concerned, the past couldn't be altered or changed. Acceptance with a big dollop of *get the fuck over it* was his answer.

Well, there was nothing for him to do now except wallow in his self-imposed hell and find a way to move forward. He'd have to have some answers before they showed up to confront him. Though he didn't have a clue how he was going to deal with the shitstorm he'd unleashed, Alex knew one thing for sure. Meghan was the deal breaker. Whatever he decided, she was going to be affected by the outcome.

MID-AFTERNOON, DRAE AND CAM slowly made their way into the residential neighborhood where Alex's grandparents had lived. After they got on the road and headed toward the city, Drae contacted Betty and had gotten her to give up the address. By the time he'd made the call and heard the agency's office manager's concerned voice on the phone, he knew that word of Alex's outburst had spread through the core of Family Justice.

It wasn't any kind of a surprise when they'd turned down the street indicated on their GPS and found Alex's truck parked in the driveway at his grandparents' home.

"Okay. What's our plan," Cam asked Drae as they parked and eyed the property. Concern dripped from every word.

Drae exhaled on a deep sigh and said, "Balls to the wall, man. This is a big one. Dad's got a case of itchy conscience. We probably should have been prepared for this. It was bound to happen eventually."

"Fuck my life," Cam muttered as he struggled to pull a backpack from behind them in the truck cab. "You take the lead. I'm going to hold back and slap a tracking sensor on his damn truck so if he decides to tear off again, we'll be able to follow his sorry ass."

"Smart move. What else you have in that bag of tricks? Don't suppose there's a tranquilizer dart gun?" Drae's mocking question got them both laughing.

"Fuck the tranquilizers," Cam chuckled. "If he's a surly confrontational bastard, I'll just knock him out. Would serve him right."

"Well, if it comes to that, hit him twice. I still owe the son-of-a-bitch for cold cocking me the morning my charming wife disappeared."

"Alright," Cam said briskly. "Let's get this show on the road."

Levering out of the massive truck, they made their way to the front door with Cam inconspicuously pausing near Alex's vehicle as he pressed a sensor into the wheel well. They must have looked like undercover cops the way they surveyed the front of the house with Cam keeping watch on the street as Drae pounded on the front door.

"Open up, Alex. You have till the count of ten then we break the door down."

Both men were slightly shocked when the door immediately opened. "Settle down boys," Alex complained. "The neighbors will think this is a home invasion if you keep barking like that."

Once inside the house Cam dropped the backpack he carried on a table as Alex calmly closed the door and turned toward them. Drae was already assessing the situation with shrewd eyes and his arms crossed decisively across his chest.

Alex frowned at them and sniped in a warning tone. "I'm not drunk or in any need of intervention so ease off and back down." *Shit*, he thought as he stomped away from the disapproving glare of his brothers to throw himself onto a sofa in the living room. He fucking hated the very idea of the conversation they were about to have.

"It took you long enough," he muttered as Cam and Drae followed and sat opposite him in two easy chairs. "Figured you'd be here hours ago."

"Yeah," Cam answered drily. "Well, we had some damage control to do at home before we could traipse after your miserable ass."

Alex tensed at the obvious taunt meant to remind him that the scene he'd caused had ramifications for them all.

Drae got in the next swipe. "How much bullshit do we have to wade through before you spit out what the hell is going on? I've got a pregnant wife texting me every half hour demanding answers. Don't know what's worse. That or you and this sorry charade."

Ah, the cold analytical dickhead. Why not? Alex shifted uncomfortably in his seat and looked away from the censure in the man's eyes.

"And that," Cam chuckled, "would be the elephant in the room. You're up Dad. Better make this good or you'll have *two* unhappy pregnant women to fend off."

Scraping his hand against his scalp, Alex sat forward and stared at the two men. "I fucked up."

"How do you figure?" Drae asked. "And make the answer actually part of the problem. Don't distract me with nonsense, Alex."

He shrugged and shook his head. It was too late for nonsense, and they all knew it. "Forgetting wasn't something I'd ever imagined would be possible, but I had. Forgotten, that is." Sighing, he fell back on the sofa and covered his eyes with a hand before rubbing it against his beard. When it fell away, he kept his eyes closed but let the rest of it come rushing out of his mouth.

"Had that fucking dream. You know the one. Damn nightmare is on some sort of programmed loop in my head. Anyway, it shook me up. Habit got me into the office and when my computer fired up the first thing I saw was the date and a list of the dead. It was like throwing gasoline on a fire." He paused, remembering the violent outburst that followed. "It was pretty bad, huh?" he asked next.

Cam answered calmly, "Yep. Looked like a smash and grab, dude."

"You're a fucking masochist Alex. *Seriously*. Why the hell would you set up that grisly reminder to appear on your computer?" Drae sounded like he was reeling in his temper, but Alex got the message loud and clear. He'd done this to himself.

"You know, I was right there with you for the longest time, man. Letting the past fuck with my head, thinking I had to embrace the suck and live a half life because of all the shit in my past," Cam said offering a surprising glimpse into his former mindset.

"Yeah, man," Drae added. "We've all been there done that shit, Alex. Dragging that crap along only shackles us to the past."

Alex knew what they were getting at, but there was one huge difference. "It's different for me. You were both dealing with family shit. Stuff you didn't ask for."

"Oh Jesus Christ," Drae muttered. "This again."

Shooting his brother a glare that spoke volumes, Alex hit out at him verbally. "I made choices and people died. It's not about anything being done *to* me. It's about what I did. What I didn't do."

His mind worked overtime on one word—control. Unlike Drae and Cam who had been victims more or less of some ugly family shit, Alex had been in control of his circumstance. While none of it was anything he would have chosen, taking orders and giving them was the deciding factor and that was the thing he could never forget.

"For fuck's sake Alex. This is getting old. I know you think you had some sort of control over what went on then, but you didn't. None of us did. Shit happened. People died. Was it all wrong? *Fuck yeah* it was. But we didn't ask for anything that happened in that goddamn war. We were playing by immoral rules dictated by bad guys and circumstance. That you feel so strongly about something totally out of *anyone's* control is testament to the honorable man you are. Can't that be enough for you?" Drae was almost yelling, his voice choked with bitter emotion.

Alex jumped up from the sofa and stalked to the front window. "I forgot!" he barked. "Don't you get it? *Fuck*," he roared, pain and regret booming in the silence. "If I can forget, what's that say? That all those people died for nothing? That nobody remembers the horror?"

"Dude," Cam interjected. "That's what this is really all about, isn't it? For the first time, *like ever*, you were happy. It was no half life you were living. You're human and that red-haired spitfire brought you back to life. About time, I should add."

It took a mental count of ten for Alex to compose himself before responding. "What's it say about me that someone who's *passing through* pushed me so far from center?"

"She's doing a whole lot more than passing through, Alex. Are you blind?" Drae shook his head and scowled at him. "Please tell me you weren't dumb enough to move her lock, stock, and barrel into your bed on a whim."

"Shut up, Drae," Alex snapped. "You don't know what you're talking about."

"Oh, that's fucking rich coming from you. You spend your days in a cave with my wife who it should be noted, I married on a drunken tear in Vegas. Want to try telling me again that I don't know what I'm talking about? I'm the fucking master of denial, and if I recall correctly, that particular ass hat was bestowed on me by Cam who had the distinction of wearing it first."

"Meghan's not the issue, Lieutenant," Alex barked at Drae. The energy in the room was so intense it was ringing in his ears.

"Fuck you, Major because she *so* is."

Alex felt like a caged animal. This was about him, not some woman he was sleeping with. Without realizing it, his wincing expression at the way he'd just categorized her place in his life did not go unnoticed by his brothers.

"Alright you two. That's enough," Cam cut in. "Let's get to some sort of wrap-up here. Alex is beating himself up. He says it's not about having fallen for a woman. And we disagree. Does that pretty much sum it up?"

Alex almost took issue with the words *fallen for a woman*, but wisely shut up. He didn't want to compound his moral failings with a bitter lie.

"Okay then," Cam continued when nobody said anything. "Where do we go from here?"

"Go home, Alex," Drae muttered through a clenched jaw. "Go home and fix this mess before you lose your chance to actually be a man and not some whiney pussy with an overly active conscience."

He wasn't ready to do any of that. The thought of facing Meghan made ice settle in the pit of his stomach. Alex was so thrown by how quickly her presence in his life had turned everything upside down that he knew thinking clearly wasn't an option. But this was different from when Tori and Lacey had appeared in their lives. Each of them came to the Villa on long-term status. Meghan was, by her own words, passing through. When she left and went on with her life, he'd have nothing. Not even the enormous shit pile of guilt and mindful penance he wallowed in. Today was an example of what that actually meant.

Making a swift decision, Alex informed Cam and Drae, "I'll be back tomorrow. There's still some shit I have to get straight in my head."

Cam went and put his hand on Alex's shoulder and gave a small squeeze. "Look, we'll stay with you man. We're in this together, and it wasn't all that long ago when you said something similar to me."

Alex shook his head but managed a weak smile. "No, I've got this Cam, but thanks for the offer. You two have wives and shit to deal with. Best to get moving so you can be home before dark. Don't worry about me."

Although he should have seen it coming, Alex wasn't prepared when Drae with all his cut to the chase charm went for his throat. "What should we tell Meghan? She's pretty upset and confused."

Alex inwardly cringed at the censure in his brother's eyes. "Tell her..." He didn't have any clue what to say next.

"Yeah?"

"On second thought, don't tell her anything. No use in spoiling her vacation with a lot of garbage that she didn't sign on for."

Drae's face told him if he could have smacked him upside the head right then, he would have. Alex knew he was coming to a series of conclusions that the other two men wouldn't like or support but so be it. Meghan's whole life was ahead of her while his had pretty much been shot to hell years ago. She was on a magnificent adventure, and he was just a way station on that journey. Best to cut the cord quickly and neatly. No messages. No pretensions of false hope.

FOLLOWING AN AFTERNOON FILLED with tense emotion, Meghan left Tori and Lacey at the cabin to return to the main house. She was a big girl and didn't need any babysitters to watch over her. Each time she'd tried Alex's cell phone it went straight to voice-mail, a solid indicator that he had nothing to say. It was time for her to come back to reality.

Letting herself into Alex's bedroom all she could do was groan when she saw that the bed had been made and the room straightened. In all the time she'd spent there, Meghan had been careful not to leave evidence of their erotic playtime scattered about for Carmen to deal with. It was bad enough that everyone knew what was going on without also providing a comic book view complete with sexy lingerie and blindfolds to raise eyebrows.

After discovering Alex wasn't by her side in the big bed this morning, she'd gone looking for him, sure that they'd be back to straighten things up long before Carmen did her daily rounds. Catching sight of the freshly made bed had Meghan's eyes frantically searching the room for her corset when she spied it neatly folded along with her thigh high stockings and shoes on an ottoman in the dressing room. The boudoir cuffs and blindfold sat nearby along with Alex's black silk pajama bottoms. *Oh shit*, it really couldn't get any worse than that.

In the dressing room, she looked at all the sexy silk and lace in the drawers and felt her heart clutch. Every bit of it was meant for Alex's eyes only, a thought that brought an onslaught of hot tears.

She couldn't stay in his bed, in his room, without him being there. It didn't feel right. Nor did keeping any of the gifts he'd been lavishing on her for weeks. He was gone, by his own choosing, and knowing that changed everything. Maybe it was a good thing that she hadn't divulged how she felt. Admitting she was falling in love with him only for Alex to leave and not look back would have been more terrible than words could convey.

Swiftly gathering the few items of clothing she'd brought and her stash of toiletries from the bathroom, Meghan cleared her presence from his room then stopped and gave the space one last look. She surmised from pieces of her earlier conversation with Cameron and Draegyn that Alex going off the rails today of all days had most likely been the result of him being distracted by their affair. She hated calling what they'd been doing by that trashy term, but if it had been more, he wouldn't have reacted so badly.

In the end though, she understood. All of it and that was why she saw no good in trying to fight it. *Hell.* Surrounded as she'd been her entire life by good, honest, caring men who put their welfare second to the needs of others, she had a special understanding of the heavy burden that a man like Alex would carry. Honor, duty, sacrifice; even remorse for those times when circumstances went horribly wrong—these were things she knew well. He'd just never be able to accept a lesser version of himself. Now, while their relationship was new and exciting, it was one thing but later on, he'd come to resent her for taking him so far from his sense of center.

"I'm so sorry, baby," she sighed into the empty room. The solid wall of silence answering the lament pretty much summed up her predicament. Closing the door firmly behind her, Meghan walked with leaden feet back to the guest room and made mental preparations for the departure she knew wasn't that far off.

BY THE TIME ALEX drove down the long drive to his home the next day, he was fighting a lump of dread that had settled in his gut. *Time to face the piper*, he thought while parking his truck near the front door and dragging his unwilling body into the house.

The first thing he noticed was the eerie quiet. He'd gotten so used to Meghan's boisterous presence and the way people flocked to her that finding his surroundings hung with the unpleasant silence of a mausoleum gave him pause. *Shit.* This was going to be harder than he imagined.

Dropping his keys on the front table and grabbing a stack of mail Carmen had left for him, he made his way slowly up the wide staircase with feet weighed down by regret and something that was starting to feel like heartache.

Pausing outside the door to his room, Alex prayed to a God he wasn't sure was listening that Meghan wouldn't be waiting for him on the other side. He doubted his resolve to make a clean break if he found himself alone with her. Knowing that was the only course open to him, for her sake he had to do the honorable thing and act like a man.

A coward's relief coursed through him when he noted that the bed hadn't been slept in and found he was alone in the big room. Alex tried to pretend that pulling away from her was the best thing for everyone involved only to stumble on his own foolish thoughts when he spied the sexy lingerie she'd worn that last night they'd been together folded neatly in the dressing room.

Warning bells started clanging in his head, knowing how Meghan was about keeping their bedroom activities private. She would never leave those cuffs or the blindfold laying out for Carmen to see. A tic started twitching near his eye as he hurried into the bathroom, instantly noting that all evidence of Meghan having been there was gone. Returning to the dressing room, Alex began yanking open drawers only to find them overflowing with the endless wardrobe of lingerie and sleepwear he'd given her. A quick glance in the near empty closet told him she'd taken only what she came with. His chest tightened and a bitter taste rushed into his mouth at what it meant.

He'd seen her SUV in the driveway so he knew she was still at the Villa. After his appalling behavior she must have sensed what was coming and taken the initiative to start putting up a wall between them. *Was for the best*, he thought although why his chest hurt he wasn't sure. Maybe it was because he could still smell her. It was as if her scent clung to everything.

Glancing at the bed pictures flashed of him and Meghan in every corner of the room. His mind was filled with visions of her face, the way her voice softened when she called him baby. How she looked spread out on his bed, writhing and screaming in ecstasy. *Fuck.* His hands were shaking and a sense of loneliness hammered in his gut.

Alex dropped into a chair and closed his eyes. How could he stand being in the room without her? Spending night after night in the very place where so many intimate memories drenched the air was expecting too much.

"THANKS FOR LISTENING TO my complaining," Brody told Meghan with a wry half-grin. Rolling a shoulder, he studied the floor for a second in that way guys did when they accidentally wandered into the unfamiliar waters of emotional sharing. "I just figured that another teacher would understand my dilemma."

Wincing, she offered a self-conscious eye roll. "Yeah, well… teachers united, right? With so many people taking shots at the profession these days, it gets harder and harder to keep sight of what drew us to the field in the first place."

Brody chuckled. "Students more interested in challenging authority than learning."

"Amen to that," she agreed with a snort and a headshake.

"Do you miss it? The kids, I mean. Not all that school district tug-of-war bullshit."

"God, Brody. I don't know how to answer that," she admitted. "There was so much about being a teacher that I loved and wouldn't trade the experiences I had or the challenges faced for anything." Meghan threw the brooding veteran a hard glance. "But the politics and the atmosphere of confrontation and aggression from the kids, parents, colleagues, and especially the MFers who controlled the money….. well, it leeches the joy right away. You know?" Her reply was a statement more than an actual question.

Brody huffed, his exhale all sneer and nothing else. "Yeah. I hear that. Me?" he spat. "I had enough of that tired shit in the Marines. No way could I teach full-time like you did. This suits me better."

Meghan enjoyed talking to the surprisingly bookish loner with the familiar East Coast twang. The entire Justice Family was interesting. Everything about their dynamic fascinated her. But Brody was the odd piece. The entire puzzle didn't come together quite right without him, but somehow he was always a smidge askew. Getting to know him wasn't easy. He was about as closed off as a person could get. Learning he had a whole other life far from here as a teacher had surprised her.

"That's why the community college gig is so perfect. It's a job share with another instructor who can't commit to full-time. Teaching one semester lets me keep my hand in but still gives me the freedom to, well…" he said with a mocking smile and a half-shrug.

She smiled and nudged him jokingly with her shoulder. "Oh you boys! I see what goes on around here and know perfectly well what the attraction is!" Chuckling with glee she poked him good-naturedly in the ribs. "This place reeks of testosterone, admit it! It's like summer camp for mercenaries, spies, and geeks."

They laughed together, big whoops of lighthearted high spirits. When her giggles died down, Meghan released a mournful sigh. *I'll miss this*, she thought. All of the people she'd met during her stay in Arizona had touched her in one way or another. Feeling her time here coming to an end, unhappiness must have flashed in her expression.

In one of those horrifying moments where timing was everything, Brody frowned at her glum face and reached out to comfort her with a friendly hug. Did it go on a few seconds too long? Maybe. All she knew was a sound brought them quickly to attention and in that moment Meghan knew her fate was sealed. Standing in the doorway was her tortured lover, in all his stern, forbidding Major glory. The hard expression on his face, and the bitter look in his eye, as he took in the sight of Brody and her in mid-hug, sucked all the air from the room.

Happy to see he was back and in one piece, it was reflex and habit that propelled her instantly in his direction but he stopped her with a terse greeting that felt more like a slap than a kiss hello.

"Good afternoon, Meghan. I'm delighted to see you found a way to amuse yourself while I was away." Ignoring her the next second, he turned what actually looked like a friendly eye on Brody, his tone lightened when he addressed the other man. "Jensen. Glad I ran into you. Thought I'd stop by the barn later and look in on the kennel. Time to evaluate those shepherds so we can start pairing them with potential owners."

Brody, for his part, looked shell-shocked. Meghan wasn't ignorant of the territorial vibe Alex had put out where she was concerned. To see him now, acting as if she was a tourist passing through, around a man he had specifically snarled away, was uncomfortable and confusing. Looking anxiously between Meghan and Alex, poor Brody had the air of someone who desperately wanted to be anywhere but here.

"That's great, Alex," he answered flatly. The teacher in her envisioned him in a Swiss t-shirt as he valiantly tried to stay neutral. "I gave Betty some files that she promised to get over to you about a couple of the pups. We should definitely talk."

Oh, this was ridiculous, Meghan fumed inwardly. Men are so stupid. So the big, bad Major wanted to play the ignore card. He probably figured she'd cry and cling and get all dramatic on his sorry ass. And Brody. *Good Lord.* He was acting like he got caught with his hand in the cookie jar. It was a damn hug for Pete's sake. *Whatever.* She knew the score and none of this was a surprise. She was a complication so Alex was simply going to emotionally withdraw. *Fuck.* He wasn't even original. She sighed, disappointed and hurt.

Reverting to type, Meghan startled everyone by clapping her hands once, then rubbed them together like she would to get the attention of classroom full of boisterous students. "Well, I'm outta here," she chirped with a mocking smile and two raised brows into their shocked faces. "You boys have fun." The sarcasm dripping from her voice could in no way be misunderstood or taken the wrong way. Score one for the teacher.

And with that she pirouetted gracefully, did a complete one eighty, and swept from the room.

ALEX WAS PRETTY SURE Meghan's parting shot, the implied *fuck you*, would be her final word for the day. But he discovered that wouldn't be the case, not that he'd be that lucky, when she appeared at the dinner table with that traitor Zeus at her side once again.

Matter of fact, the entire cast of Family Justice, except for Brody who he'd already fucked with, had starring roles. Cam and Lacey were on hand as were Drae and Tori along with their rambunctious pup Raven who was making Zeus crazy. Betty appeared with Gus who was actively sharking around Carmen, and eventually Ben showed up with Ria in tow. *Oh joy*, he thought. The gang was all here.

For the first time in his life, Alex Marquez felt like the odd man out. The point was driven home with cruel precision when he appeared in the arched doorway and everyone turned and looked at him. The entire crew, *his* entire crew, was gathered around Meghan. She was like the sun, and they were planets, swirling in her gravitational pull. Alex was churning internally. He needed everything to be the way it had always been. It was the only way he could cling to his illusion of power and remain in control. From the moment she appeared on his doorstep, he had been slowly losing the carefully maintained checks and balances he relied on.

The meal had been a miserable farce. He presided over a table divided, and it was killing him. Alex felt damned. In a rare moment, he let his guard down and said the first dumb-ass thought that came to his mind, regardless of how callous and mean-spirited his words sounded. He didn't doubt for a second that he was going to hell for his rude behavior. *Fuck.* If his mother or sisters had been there, he'd really have been in deep shit.

Settling back in his chair, he propped his feet out straight beneath the table and appeared to all the world, relaxed. Looking round the table he met everyone's gaze then turned to Meghan last and said, "So, Meghan. What's left on the bucket list? Is there anything else you'd like to check off before you go on your way?"

Until then, he'd never really considered what that expression, *hearing crickets*, meant. He knew now. The room became silent and the air so heavy that he swore everything downshifted into slow motion. Drae and Cam looked at him with faces frozen in absolute astonishment at the unforgivable lack of decorum he'd just subjected them to. In his mind's eye, he envisioned the ceremonial passing of the ass hat award to him from both men.

For her part, Meghan sat completely still with no outward show of emotion or reaction of any sort whatsoever to the obvious dismissal he'd so boldly thrown at her in public. There wasn't a person present who wasn't gaping at him with expressions that ranged from fury to shock to disappointment.

Just when the deafening silence threatened to get ugly, she spoke. "At least I *have* a bucket list," she began, a warning tenor in her voice. "Pity the fool who has no dreams and only focuses on the past." The look she gave him was dripping with false sympathy. The same look you'd give someone who was too fucking stupid for words.

"As for your intentionally insensitive question, don't you worry about little old me, Major. I know when my welcome's up. You didn't need to embarrass your friends like this."

Shame washed through Alex. She'd totally put him in his place by challenging his unseemly behavior. He'd been a coward. Afraid to face her privately for fear of losing his strictly imposed self-restraint, he'd clung to his master of control delusions and acted like a dick. He was shaken when she stood up and threw her napkin on to the table near his plate. The expression on her face let him know she was going to have her say in front of everyone, and he'd have to sit there and take it 'cause this hellish situation was of his own making. It didn't help that in his mind, as she geared up to lay into him, she looked like some fiery Celtic goddess with blazing emerald eyes and the type of breathtaking beauty that robs men of their sense.

"You know, Major, what you're doing here is so predictable. I expected better from you. At least something original. Not the oldest *dude* fallback in the book." Her contemptuous expression hit him square between the eyes.

Glancing at the women gathered who collectively looked like they were plotting his imminent demise she went for the gold. "C'mon ladies, you know what I'm talking about, right? The one where Mr. Macho gets spooked when actual feelings for a woman bite him on the ass so he acts like a dick as though sleeping with her had been an optional activity at summer camp." Alex felt every single person at the table squirm at her blunt honesty.

"I get that my being here upset your perfectly managed little apple cart but why is that such a bad thing? Is it because shit was so great for you, before? *Pfft.* Honestly, you're pathetic. By shutting me out you're throwing away something that won't ever come around again. Good job. Now you and your superior intellect can live happily ever after—*alone.* Hope that works out for you, asshole." Her green eyes were shooting sparks of scorn that Alex swore singed his skin.

He watched her walk away from him, felt a constriction in his chest, and chalked it up as the inevitable. She would have left eventually, he tried to convince himself. Better now than later. Later when it would have killed him outright, instead of now when it was just gutting him.

The solid, impenetrable wall of stillness that descended around him was the only thing that kept Alex from shattering into a million pieces as every single person left behind after her bull's-eye performance glared at him in disbelief.

Later, isolated and alone in his room, he'd had to endure the sound of one person after another stomping past his door all evening on their way to the guest room, no doubt to say their good-byes to the woman he'd rather dramatically pushed away.

In full martyr mode he'd gathered whatever she'd left behind from their time together, all the lingerie, jewelry, and gifts, and had them taken to her room by a scowling Carmen. He imagined that by removing all reminders of their time together he'd have his space back without her presence oozing from every nook and cranny.

She left the next morning. Early. Carmen went out of her way to twist the knife by tersely informing him his guest had left behind anything and everything that he had given her. Even the parasol. Ignoring the statement she was making he focused instead on being petulant about her dismissal of what had been gifts.

Now that she was gone he was going to press the reset button, reboot his life, and slide back into familiar routines. He'd get used to being alone again. It might take some doing, but he'd find a way to wipe her from his memory. He'd have to if he had any hope of surviving.

THERE WAS NO JOY left in her extended road trip so Meghan
didn't even try to pretend otherwise. After driving away from the Villa
de Valleja-Marquez, she let an hour or so eat up the road under her tires
and then pulled over. She'd been in such a hurry to get away from the
hacienda that all she did was load her crap into the back of her SUV
and head out. No route in mind. No destination set.

Finding a gas station with a convenience store attached and a little greasy spoon luncheonette where she stopped to get her bearings,
Meghan was numb from the aftermath of Alex's dismissive performance. He didn't have the balls to speak with her privately—something that pissed her off big time. But still, she understood. He was
scared. Life change wasn't what either of them had expected when
things between them first exploded.

But it was more than sexual attraction, she was sure of it. At least
for her that was true. But Alex got spooked and bolted. Now look at
the mess they were in. Some part of her wanted to hold out hope that
he'd come to his senses but the man who treated her like shit yesterday

in front of everyone had been so intent on pushing her away that she'd had no choice but to throw in the towel.

Wandering aimlessly through the aisles of the tiny store, she tossed all sorts of items into her basket—candy, pastries, gum, a couple of juices for the cooler, some ice, even a few magazines. Random supplies she'd need now that she was on the road again. After gassing up and cleaning the windshield she pulled up a mapping app and started entering data into the navigation system. Even with the most direct route possible, it was still going to take a week to get home. While Meghan didn't relish being alone with her thoughts in a car for that long, she conceded it was probably for the best. She'd have time to think and come up with a plausible story to tell her family and decide what on earth she could possibly do next.

"YOU'RE KILLING ME PONYTAIL," Cam whispered in his wife's ear as he held her against him in the warm lap pool. Coming quickly to the end of her pregnancy, Lacey's back constantly ached so they took every advantage of the relief she found by relaxing weightless in the water.

"I can't help it," she mumbled quietly. "Couldn't you have stopped him? He's made it that much more difficult to get her back by being such a...*sheesh*. Such a guy."

"Believe me, if we'd known what he was going to do, one of us would have knocked him the fuck out before those words left his mouth."

Because the pool area was private, his gorgeously pregnant wife had donned a simple halter-bathing top, which barely contained her ripe breasts and a pair of bikini bottoms that rode under her huge bump leaving the sexy tummy swollen with child bared to his eyes and hands. Cam stroked his big hands on the protruding bulge where his son or daughter lay. He loved Lacey's rounded belly. To him it was pretty much the sexiest thing he'd ever seen.

"Are you so sure that getting her back is even a possibility," he questioned anxiously. "I know you've been talking to her. What's she saying?"

When his normally chatty wife didn't say anything, just floated silently between his legs with her back resting on his chest, he had his answer. *Women*, he thought wryly. They certainly did stick together when it came to one of their own.

Turning her, he settled his quiet wife on his lap, lifted her chin with his finger and stared deep.

"Out with it, wife," he gently drawled. Still nothing. "I can't help if you don't tell me what's going on," he persisted.

Lacey sighed and nodded but a worried frown lingered on her face. "She's being all stoic, which only makes Tori and me crazy. Thinks Alex is better off without her. Some rubbish about tortured alphas and survivor guilt."

Wow, Cam thought. Meghan understood their Big Daddy even better than he imagined. She was just as bad as him though. Had he been this bloody stupid when it had been him and Lacey hanging by a thread? Luckily, his Ponytail had refused to give up on him. In Alex's case though, he'd pushed the poor woman caught in the crossfire pretty far away and her background with a family of cops and firemen meant she actually bought into his conflicted soul bullshit. What a fucking mess.

"She looks horrible too. Like the light's gone out of her eyes."

"Now, come on honey. It's only because you're internet chatting. I'm sure her eyes are just fine."

"Cameron," his wife replied tartly. "You know perfectly well what I'm getting at. Plus Tori says Alex is being impossible at work. And by impossible you know I mean a bunch of swear words I'd rather our child didn't hear me say."

Cam groaned at the reminder of Alex's shitty attitude. Drae had been bitching up a storm all morning about the very same thing. He even threatened to march into the bat cave and knock Alex's fucking teeth out if he kept on pissing Victoria off. Drae was incredibly protective and territorial when it came to his pregnant wife, an impulse he and his brother shared. Their fearless leader was going to get his ass kicked if he didn't watch it.

"I want her here when the baby comes."

Cam gritted his teeth when he saw Lacey's lower lip tremble. *Aw fuck,* he thought wryly. Leave it to the pregnant water nymph nestled in his arms to land the most direct shot possible.

"I swear to Christ honey, if you start crying, somebody is gonna die, and it won't be pretty."

Lacey snuggled into his chest and laid her head on his shoulder. Cam kept a protective hand on her tummy as his mind worked overtime on the problem at hand. With their due date just around the corner, there wasn't a lot of time to maneuver.

"Talk to him again. You and Draegyn." She put her hand on the side of his face so he would look at her. "He made sure we had our happy ending. Tori and Drae too. It's his turn, okay?"

"Understood Ponytail," he murmured, kissing her softly on the forehead.

Looks like he and Drae were up to bat at the bottom of the ninth inning. No time to swing wildly or run around without some sort of strategy for bringing this ridiculous situation home.

"TORI," ALEX MUTTERED HARSHLY. "I'm flying to Washington next week."

His assistant looked up from the stack of papers she was working on with bewilderment in her eyes. "Whatever for?" she questioned. "I thought you hated all that D.C. wonky stuff."

"Yeah, I do," he replied with a dismissive shrug. "Command performance. One I can't ignore."

"Oh," she said with a grave look. "Um, I mean, what do you need from me?"

Alex was exhausted trying to act like everything was fine. It had been weeks since he'd had his unseemly hissy fit and thrown away the only thing that had brought him even a moment's peace in a very long time. In short, he was in a living hell going through the daily motions, pretending that he gave half a shit.

He didn't need to go to Washington, and it wasn't for a command performance. Like the emotional pussy he was, Alex was filling the empty spaces in his life with random bullshit he hoped would distract him from the truth. The awful truth that he missed his Irish fuck goddess and didn't know how long he could go on like this before he went insane.

When the opportunity came up to do a bit of geek networking at a security symposium, he gladly signed on even though the thought made him roll his eyes and shake his head. He wasn't in the fucking mood to play nice with others right now but he couldn't stay at the Villa much longer without driving everyone around him nuts. He knew Tori was at the end of her rope with his surly attitude, and it was just a matter of time before Drae, Cam, or both of them tried to rip his head off for being such an obstinate dick. Retreat seemed like a viable option and maybe the change of scenery would help.

Yeah, right. Who the fuck was he kidding? He could pretend all he wanted about symposiums and changes of scenery but it was all a deflection for what was really going on. By taking the agency jet to Washington, he'd be on the other side of the country and that much closer to where Meghan was.

Things had in no way reset after she left. There had been no re-boot. No return to normal. He'd been a tremendous douche but was still so fucking conflicted and tormented he didn't know which way was up. At this point he needed fucking satellite imaging to find his own ass.

"There won't be much of anything for you to do while I'm gone. You'll have a bit of downtime. Give you a chance to work on the nursery." *There. That sounded reasonable, right?* He was being Mister Magnanimous so why did he still feel like shit?

Leaning back in his swivel chair, Alex stared at the ceiling and didn't notice his assistant's quiet approach until she was almost on top of him.

Wearing a concerned expression, Tori murmured gently, "How much longer are you going to be the tortured victim, Boss?"

Alex fixed her with a blank stare as if doing so would magically make her back off.

"Oh. Nice try," she snorted. "You honestly think that's going to work on a St. John? I have to put up with that crap from my husband but not from you."

"I'm not a victim," he grumbled.

"Oh fuck yeah, you are," she snapped. Sometimes he forgot how quickly those pregnancy hormones could take over a conversation. *Shit.*

"I know you think you're the master of your own fate, but honestly Alex—could your head be any further up your own ass?"

He sighed and rolled his head on his neck to ease the tension. "Lady, something tells me I'm going to be forced to hear you out so just go for it. Get the lecture over with so I can get back to what I was doing."

"That's just it, Boss! You aren't actually *doing* anything." She was waving her arms in frustrated arcs that ended with a both hands planted firmly at her waist while she tut-tutted and shook her head at him. "Did you really think you could fool me? You haven't done one damn thing in the weeks since Meghan left." He flinched hearing her name, but Tori just kept on ranting.

"You've been engaging in classic nerd denial behavior. Yesterday, you spent the whole damn day updating the calendar and contact list on your phone. The *entire* day, Alex. It was your stupid phone for heaven's sake. And what was all that bullshit about searching for productivity apps? You downloaded four games that I highly doubt have anything to do with work."

She was right but that didn't mean he wanted to hear it. "What the fuck do you want me to do, Mrs. St. John?" he growled harshly.

Tori threw up her hands in disgust and glared at him like he was the dumbest fuck on the planet. "Really?" she sneered. "If that's how you're going to play it I'll get right to the point. Grow a set of balls Major and fucking get over yourself. Get up off your butt and go bring Meghan back here and do it before she figures out that she's better off without your tortured alpha shit."

"Tortured alpha shit?" he barked. "What in the hell is that supposed to mean?"

Speaking to him like a four-year-old, she spelled it out in terms even he could understand. Because she was a little thing to begin with, being handed one's ass by an indignant elf with a baby bump was actually kinda cute, but it didn't diminish the impact of her response.

In a tone that felt like ice slithering along his spine she gave it to him good. "*Alpha*, as in male; denoting the dominant role. *Tortured* as in conflicted and tormented by things over which one has no control. *Shit* as in unpleasant personal garbage. Questions?"

"Yeah, I have a question," he snarled. "How'd you come up with that less than flattering takedown of my character?"

"I didn't," she replied mockingly.

Gritting his teeth he sniped, "This better not be more of Drae's bullshit."

"It's not. Come on Alex. You're a smart guy. Do I really have to spell this out for you?"

Oh fuck. He walked right into that one. Really? That was how Meghan saw him—as some pitiful tortured alpha?

The one thing he'd gotten really good at the last few weeks was being silent, and that was what he stuck with now. Say nothing. He was fucked up in the head and with every minute, more and more regret and confusion was added to what was going on inside him.

"Boss. Ask me about her," Tori begged. "Come on. Just ask. You *know* we've been talking. Please. *Just ask.* It's a first step."

Alex couldn't look at Tori after that. He just hung his head and wallowed in his private hell until she eventually gave up. Patting him on the shoulder before she left him in peace, she offered a parting shot. "Why is it so hard for you to see the obvious?"

Why, indeed?

LATER THAT AFTERNOON, CARMEN signed for a large package that came by ground delivery. The huge box was tall and wide but not very deep, and had obviously piqued his housekeeper's curiosity. She was guarding it like a national treasure when he made his way right before dinner from his tech room into the main part of the house.

"Meeester Alex, something has arrived for you," she announced just as Drae and Cam happened to walk through the front door.

"Whatcha got there, bro?" Cam asked, eyeing the impressive box. "Flat screen TV?"

"I have no idea," Alex grumbled. "Don't remember ordering anything."

Whatever the box contained, it was wrapped up like Fort Knox. "What the fuck," Alex mumbled, trying not to rip the packaging to shreds. "Need a damn chainsaw to break in to this thing." When at last he was able to slide a wood stretcher from the box he was annoyed and even grumpier. "This better be good," he bit out to no one in particular.

Drae laughed and gestured at the mysterious object with a nod of his head. "Maybe that's your presidential award for being King of the Douches."

Alex scowled at his audience when Carmen found Drae's snarky comment funny. His brothers managed to needle him every chance they got. *Fuckers.*

Took but moments to remove the final layer of protective wrapping and what met his eye when the task was completed, stopped Alex dead in his tracks.

There, in a beautiful wood frame was a huge Southwestern photograph that he recognized immediately. It was the shot Meghan had taken that first time he'd driven her into the desert. He remembered complimenting her on the perspective with a cactus in the foreground and the magnificent vista of red rocks and blue sky in the background. The colors were so vibrant a casual viewer might question whether it had been enhanced but Alex was there when the shot was taken and remembered with clarity the dazzling colors and majestic panorama.

"Good Lord," Cam gasped. "That's amazing."

"I know where that was taken," Carmen mumbled quietly as she stared at the huge framed photo with awe on her face. When she looked back at him, Alex swore he saw censure flash across her expression. She knew. *How could she not,* he admitted silently. Carmen knew everything that went on at the Villa.

"Hey," Drae added, "You're onto something Carmen. Isn't that out by the flats at red rock?"

Alex stood numbly, nodding his head. *Meghan.* He'd asked her that day to send him the jpeg. Looked like she went a couple steps further than that. The enormous frame would dominate whatever wall on which it hung. Her photograph was meant to impress, and it most certainly did.

It was then that he saw a small white envelope attached to the back that he abruptly grabbed and ripped open with all the finesse of a kid on Christmas morning. Inside was a card with Meghan's distinctive handwriting on which she'd written, *'What lies behind us, and what lies before us, are tiny matters compared to what lies within us – Ralph Waldo Emerson'.*

He swallowed the tension constricting his throat as a deep frown etched his brow. With one quote, just eighteen simple words, she'd driven home her belief that the strength of a person's character counted more than any demons from the past or future worries. Her unyielding faith in him was staggering. And what had he done? Pushed her away like a damn fool.

"I have work to do," Carmen mumbled. Alex looked up when she spoke in time to see her give Drae and Cam a stern, forbidding look.

It was a meaningful exchange, but Alex couldn't react to it. He could only stand, numb and in awe of the *in your face* statement his Meghan had made. That day in the desert had changed his life. Hers too. Their coming together opened floodgates of potential more meaningful than any shadows from the past. *Oh God.* A raw, uncomfortable anxiety was growing in the pit of his stomach.

Alex had no idea how long he stood, immobile, glued to the same spot, arms weightless and no strength to his body whatsoever, a deep misery claiming his senses. After a bit, awareness started filtering into his brain. He felt Cam on one side of him and Drae, the other. Standing close as brothers would, ready to catch him when he fell. He straightened abruptly, his spine charged with heat as his emotions started coming back online.

"What have I done?" he questioned anxiously, swinging back and forth between Cam and Drae. "*Fuck,*" he groaned.

Drae put a hand on his shoulder. "Take it from one who knows.

Getting there was half the battle," he told him solemnly.

"You ready to get honest, Major?" Cam asked.

Alex clutched his chest as a huge, overwhelming surge of emotion shot into his center. Why hadn't he seen it before? This was exactly what Drae and Cam had been through. For each of them there came that moment when all the internal bullshit had to fade away, when they faced the undeniable fact that the chance to claim their soul partner was almost gone, due in no small part to their own foolish actions.

"I'm in love with her," he proclaimed. When the two men by his side didn't respond to his declaration he said it again, with gravitas. "Did you fuckers hear me? I said, *I'm in love with her!*"

"Duh," Cam snorted.

"Ah, so Captain Obvious has made an appearance," Drae quipped.

Alex flipped them both off. Suddenly, he knew what he needed to do. Okay, so maybe that wasn't entirely true, but he knew he had to do something. *Anything.*

"Oh fuck, man," Drae muttered good-naturedly. "I know that look."

Cam laughed and smacked Alex hard on the back. "Hey man, I dig that expression. Always means shit's about to get real. Team Justice to the rescue?" he joked.

With a rueful grimace, Drae pulled his phone out and swiped at the screen. "If I'm not mistaken, Team Justice will require the assistance of the Ladies League," he chuckled. "Get ready for the pregnancy brigade gentlemen. Things are about to get interesting."

WHEN TORI AND LACEY arrived on the scene, they took in the enormous framed photograph and the small hand-written card with its damning message and stood quietly. The silence in the room was so thick you could hack at it with an axe.

"You're an ass Alex Marquez," Tori eventually bit out deridingly.

Lacey made that clucking noise, which spoke of something just this side of pity, and shook her head. "Feel stupid now, do we? *Hmmm*?"

The irony of the situation did not escape Alex. For what seemed like forever he, Draegyn, and Cameron have been a force to be reckoned with. When the three brothers banded together, there was nothing that couldn't be done. Along the way a female counterpoint to their trio had been forming. Tori and Lacey, who forever after he would refer to in his head as the Justice Sisters, were just as formidable a force, ready to fight for their missing partner.

Clearing his throat, Alex felt like he'd hit a wall going about a thousand miles an hour. Tori had taunted him, almost pleaded with him to just ask about Meghan. He wasn't stupid. Okay, maybe he was, where the fairer sex was concerned. But he knew enough to realize that opening a dialogue and asking was one of those tests that meant something to women. All he had to do was stick a toe in the door and maybe it wouldn't slam shut forever. Was it really that simple?

There were a million things he could say or ask but only one question really mattered. In the end, it wasn't about him and his tired, old crybaby shit at all. What he really cared about was Meghan and nothing else.

"What's she up to?" *No, wait. That wasn't enough.* "I mean, is she okay?" *Jesus.* He sounded like a mumbling twit.

Something about what he said must have been right because Tori beamed at him and put her hand on his forearm. "She misses you, and that's all that matters."

Alex grabbed at his chest like he'd been shot. "Don't fuck with me Mrs. St. John," he begged. "I need the truth."

Lacey quickly spoke up with clear, calm eloquence. "That *is* the truth, Alex. Even after what you did—pushing her away and acting like a pig—she misses you."

And there it was. He'd been an insufferable dick. Clinging to things well past their expiration date. It all made sense now. For years, he'd punished himself for stuff he never really had control over no matter what bullshit he tried to believe. Alex had always known that authority wasn't the same thing as control but hadn't fully internalized what that meant. By going away when he practically demanded she leave, Meghan had left him with his pathetic need intact to be the one with the power; but without her in his life, the brutal truth was it was all so very empty, hollow, and meaningless.

He also knew that missing him wasn't the same as forgiving. Or needing. He'd have to bring something tangible and real to the table if he hoped to fix the mess he'd made. Being someone with zero experience in these matters, he turned to his sisters-in-law for guidance. "What should I do?"

Tori and Lacey smiled. Drae and Cam exhaled a huge sigh of relief.

"Um," Alex mumbled before they could answer, anxiously, scraping his fingers through his hair. He didn't care who the fuck knew he was a total head case about this woman. It was the truth. "When you talk to Meghan, will you....I mean, are you going to let her know I asked?"

Suddenly he was the center of an affectionate pregnant sandwich as two bellies pressed in on him from either side with both women hugging him tight. Feeling their approval and unconditional love kept his feet on the ledge. Maybe he didn't have to jump headfirst into oblivion after all.

"Alright, alright," Cam chuckled. "Jesus ladies. Let the man breathe," he teased, peeling his wife off Alex's body.

Tori stayed close though, still hugging as hard as her little rounded body would let her. "Don't do anything, Boss. I mean it," she chided. "You'll put your foot in it for sure. Let me talk to her and see which way the wind is blowing. It's getting late on the East Coast but I'm going to try calling her in a bit."

Alex hugged her back. "Thanks babe. I'll owe you one."

"No, Dad. Not necessary." Her sweet smile warmed his heart. When Drae came and slung an arm about his wife's shoulders, the husband and wife exchanged a meaningful look.

"We just want you to be happy, Alex. If anything, we're paying *you* back for helping us when we lost our way." Drae nodded at his wife's well-spoken sentiment.

Squeezing his hand for reassurance she promised to let him know after she'd reached Meghan but reminded him not to expect too much at first. He knew he'd hurt her but hearing the warning in Tori's words made his blood run cold. *Please God,* he silently prayed. Don't let it be too late.

"MOM," MEGHAN GROANED AS she pressed her head into her hands. "Please stop with the questions. I don't want to talk about it, so drop the whole thing, okay?"

Snorting furiously, Maggie O'Brien bit back, "I most certainly will not, young lady. And you'd do well to remember who you're talking to, missy. I can get your father up here in two minutes." The tone in her voice and fire in her mother's eyes were intended to make a point. Yep. *Bull's-eye*, she thought. *Dammit.*

Defeated by the old threat, Meghan gave in. Nothing was worse than seeing disappointment in her father's eyes so she braced herself for the onslaught of questions coming her way. She wasn't mad or even annoyed. It was just that she didn't have any answers. None that made sense, anyway.

"Meghan Elizabeth O'Brien. I'm surprised you would even try and keep anything from me. When I left you in California, your plan was to wander around the Southwest for a while before moving on to New Orleans."

Meghan was uncomfortable being reminded of her original plans. So much had changed since the spa retreat with her mom.

"And the next thing I know, you're staying at some private hacienda in the desert. No explanation. Nothing. Now here you are, back in Boston with your tail between your legs, and *no comment* plastered on your face." Her mother wiped her hands on the apron she wore and sighed, exasperated at Meghan.

"*Mo stoirín*," Maggie O'Brien whispered the old Irish saying that meant 'my little darling.' As the only girl in the family, the expression was a special endearment just for her. "It's been weeks, darling. You're not eating or sleeping, and you walk around here like a thousand pound weight is strapped to your back. This isn't like you Meggie."

She winced at her mother's apt description.

In a gentle voice her mother prompted, "Tell me about this Major you're trying so hard not to speak about."

Leave it to Ma to zero in on the substance right away. Meghan looked away and searched for the best answer to the simple question. Everything about the room they were in screamed comfortable. It was familiar and solid, just like her childhood. But the matter of Alex Marquez was none of those things. Not comfortable. Certainly not solid and completely *un*-familiar.

Collapsing in a soft overstuffed chair like a puppet whose strings were suddenly cut, Meghan swung her legs over the arm and sat sideways, a brooding frown on her face. Picking at imaginary lint on her clothes, she smoothed her top and heaved a deep sigh. "His name is Alex. Alexander Valleja-Marquez."

Her mother's eyebrows shot up. "Well that sounds rather old worldly."

Meghan snorted in amusement. Old worldly. Yeah, on the outside maybe. Inside however beat the heart of a primal warrior. She couldn't see herself explaining that to her mom.

Shrugging, she tried acting like it was no big deal. "Yeah. He's some sort of ancestral Spanish Don. The hacienda dates back in his family to the early eighteen hundreds and is more like an entire village on hundreds of acres than a simple home."

"How is it you came to be staying with a Spanish Don in the middle of the desert? You're leaving an awful lot out, daughter."

She looked into her mother's face and dropped the bomb in the story. "He was David's commanding officer in Afghanistan." Letting the facts sink in, Meghan gave it a minute then kept talking.

"He wrote to me about David's military service a couple of months after his funeral. We exchanged some letters and still send a card during the holidays. I knew he lived outside Sedona and decided to pay a visit. That's the simplest way of explaining how we know each other."

"Why on God's green earth would you decide to pay a visit?" her mother asked incredulously.

There was no way she was going to be able to keep anything secret from her mom now that she was, more or less, letting the cat out of the bag.

"Mom, don't freak out but…David was gay."

Her mother's shocked gasp filled the air.

Meghan hurried to fill in the blanks while she watched her mother grapple with that bit of news. "I didn't even realize it till after he went back overseas that last time. And for the record, Mike knows. We talked about it. It's way complicated and to be honest, I'm not even sure David had admitted it to himself. But all the signs were there." She hurried out the rest of the story before she lost her nerve. "We never did anything more than hold hands and a little kissing. He was never going to marry me, and it's important you know that. I've kept this a secret all these years, because I didn't want to harm his memory."

"Oh, daughter," her mother cried in a pained whisper. "You poor thing having to keep such a secret. I'm sorry you had to go through that. David was a nice boy. I understand why you stayed quiet."

"Yeah, well…here's the thing Ma. I only told you that so you don't judge Alex harshly."

"Why would I do that? I don't even know the man."

Meghan felt her nose start to itch and her lip tremble as she fought back the torrent of tears threatening her composure.

"*Ohhhhh*," her mothered murmured, coming swiftly to her side as she laid her hand reassuringly upon her head. "You've got a case of the hots for this Major character." Seeing her old school Irish mother smirk at her in understanding was priceless.

"Ma! Come on!" Meghan cried out. "The hots? Jeez Louise. You and that naughty book club you belong to," she chuckled shaking her head.

"Don't you be dissing my book club, young lady," Maggie giggled. "I've learned all sorts of things. I can be hip too, y'know. Don't tell Da, but I've got a ton of wicked erotica on my Kindle." In a conspiratorial whisper she added, "I've read all the Fifty Shades books."

Meghan looked at her mother like she was crazy. "Ma, c'mon," she groaned while shaking her head.

"What? You think I don't know about these things? Ask me anything!" she laughed. "I even know about the Kegel Balls," she announced proudly.

Meghan was sure she was going to die of embarrassment. "Ma, seriously, *enough*."

"Well, if you'd rather I changed the subject, maybe you can tell me if this Major is the reason you came back here looking so miserable?"

It was useless to avoid the truth. Her mother would see right through any attempt to pretend otherwise. "*Mmmm hmmm*. But it's complicated."

Maggie O'Brien sat in a chair alongside her daughter and stared off into space for a bit. "Did I ever tell you what a royal pain your da was before we got together?"

Surprised, Meghan sat forward and faced her mom. "No. I thought you said it was love at first sight."

"Oh, it was," her mom replied with a giggle snort. "But that doesn't mean it was easy *or* uncomplicated." She rolled her eyes and made a mocking face. "He's a man, after all, Meghan Elizabeth, and the whole lot of them can be so exasperating! And just so we're clear—they are *all* complicated."

"I hear that," she agreed with a grunt.

"Let's just say your da needed some help to find his way. He's lucky my father didn't knock his head off."

"Mom, I don't know what to do. He's got all these issue because of the war that have him wrapped so tight emotionally, he can't see the damn forest for the trees."

"What kind of issues? Are you talking serious PTSD?"

"No. Nothing like you mean. It's survivor's guilt mostly. Like Uncle Damian had. He doesn't think he should be happy because somehow if he is, it means he's letting all those people down. Like they'd all be forgotten."

"Is that why you left?"

"Yeah, but to be honest, I would have eventually murdered him if I'd stayed. The man gives new meaning to being a brick wall," Meghan murmured. "He needs time to figure it out on his own. Maybe he'll get there and maybe he won't. I still don't know."

"Have you been talking to him since you left? Is that who I see you chatting with on the phone or your laptop at all hours?"

Meghan shook her head and groaned. "No. I made friends with some women at the Villa. That's who I've been on the phone with but I haven't talked to him. We had a sort of—*confrontation* before I left. We didn't even say good-bye." Her voice trailed off to nothing, remembering that last day.

Her mom mumbled a drawn out, "Mmm…" She'd given her a lot of information to take on board.

After a minute of powerful silence, green eyes met green eyes, making Meghan swallow a thickening in her throat. She was Maggie O'Brien's only daughter. Once she was trapped in the tractor beam of her mother's knowing gaze, she couldn't look away as she heard her ma ask, "Are you in love with his man?"

Direct and to the point. Meghan admired the shrewd way she'd been backed into a corner. Her mom was good. She'd have to remember this maneuver for when she had her own kids to deal with.

"Yes." There really wasn't anything else to say, so she didn't.

Maggie suddenly laughed and gave Meghan a little tap on her knees. "I hope your Major has back-up my dear, because when your da and brothers hear this, there's a Spanish Don about to get his butt kicked. Nobody around here is stupid." She chuckled. "This confrontation you speak of—that's code for *fight*, yes? And if I'm not mad crazy, I'm guessing your Boston Bad Bitch attitude and mouth didn't take any prisoners. Even so, make no mistake. None of the O'Brien's will sit back and let some stranger holed up in the desert give you grief."

"Mom!" Meghan yelled, panicked. "You can't tell them any of this. Are you crazy?"

"Oh sweetie, *really*? When I said everyone was worried about you, I was serious. Deval is being especially worrisome. You know he can't stand it when you're upset."

Maggie leaned in and gave her daughter a brief hug. "Better man up, my daughter. I'll handle Da, but your brothers have a right to know what's going on with their only sister and even with all your bitching, you wouldn't have it any other way. Your family is part of who you are. The man who gets your heart is going to have to understand that."

And there they were—little nuggets of mom wisdom that cut right through everything.

"He's got back-up, Mom," she assured her. "In fact, he's got his own amazing family who are just as great and awesome as the O'Brien clan."

"Well good! He's going to need them. Be prepared to explain this to the whole fam damily at Sunday dinner."

Meghan bit back a smile and shook her head. She loved how her mom tried to be cute with her non-swears. Yeah, the whole damn family indeed. Something to look forward to.

IT WAS ALMOST MIDNIGHT when she heard the faint hum of a cellphone buzzing. Sitting cross-legged on the floor at the foot of the loveseat in her bedroom alcove with her laptop and camera nearby, Meghan struggled to reach for the phone before it woke everyone else up. She'd been mindlessly organizing her photo files and had flung it aside earlier.

Rolling to her side with fingers stretched as far as they could reach, she finally made contact with the corner of the humming object and scooped it closer till she could snatch it up. Trying awkwardly to right her position, she quickly pressed the call button, then bobbled the phone next to her ear.

"Aargh," she groaned when she nearly lost her balance, the phone, and her sense of humor as she pitched forward awkwardly. "Shit," her pithy swear made it into the mouthpiece a second before she answered properly. "Hello?"

"Irish!" Meghan's heart clutched when she heard Tori's excited voice. "Damn glad that I caught you up. You *are* still up I hope," she chuckled.

"Sleep is not my friend these days," Meghan grumped.

"Well, I have some news. An update, really. Maybe it will help you sleep a little better."

Meghan cut her off. It was late and while sleep was an elusive thing, that didn't mean she wasn't pretty wiped out. She was tired and miserable enough that she knew even the best news in the world wasn't going to change that. And besides, if this was going to be about Alex, she was feeling so raw and out-of-sorts that she wasn't sure she wanted to hear it.

"Not tonight, Tori. Okay?"

The voice coming over the phone sounded worried and also a bit surprised. "Um, sure Meghan. Did I catch you at a bad time?"

Lord but she wished it were that simple. Blowing a deep sigh, Meghan drew her knees up and used them as an armrest. "Bad time, bad day. Take your pick. I hate men, by the way."

"Yikes," Tori chirped. "That doesn't sound good. What brought this on?"

"My fucking brothers," she mumbled into the phone. "Would you believe that my mother lost her damn mind and told them about...well, you know."

"Uh—she told them about what? Your visit here?"

"Oh for heaven's sake Tori. She told them that some lothario out in the Arizona desert seduced their sister, sullied her innocence, and then dumped her when the kinky fun times were over. You know. The sort of dramatic big bad wolf story intended to get them all fired up."

"Are you serious?" Tori wheezed. "Holy shitballz Irish. I hope you're exaggerating, even if it is just a little."

Meghan moaned into the phone. "They're my *brothers*. No matter what she says, that's what they'll hear. And God only knows what she's telling my father. Tomorrow is Sunday and everyone will be over for family dinner. I have no doubt that I'm going to be getting an earful of Irish outrage and indignation."

There was a long stretch of silence that broke when Tori mumbled a heartfelt, "I'm so sorry."

Meghan sighed and squeezed her eyes shut to stop the tears threatening to break free. "He broke my heart." It was all she could say.

"I know."

"I still love him."

"I know that, too."

Shit. Her nose stung while she fought back the tears. Sniffing loud enough for Tori to hear she added, "God, Tori. I feel like crap, and I'm falling apart physically. It's more than I can take." The last words came out in a shallow whisper that gave away much.

"Sweetie," Tori asked gently. "Have you given any more thought to calling Alex? Maybe try to talk to him?"

This time she sniffed really loud as her lip trembled. "*Fuck* him. He didn't say good-bye."

Tori groaned. "I could say something here about his head being up his ass but it'd be a waste of time. He's a man, Irish. And a Justice Brother. Remember the Cowardly Lion searching for courage? For redemption from the past? I just know he'll get there eventually. Just hang onto that, okay? And don't give up. Not now."

Meghan pushed up off the floor and sprawled across the loveseat as she remembered Tori saying she'd called with an update.

"H*mmmm*. You're up to something Mrs. St. John. I can hear it in your voice."

Tori burst out laughing on the other end. "Christ, girlfriend. I *wish* I were up to something. You two are driving me and Lacey batshit. As it is, I can only offer up a bit of inside information. What you choose to do with it is up to you."

"Go on…"

"Well, it turns out that Big Daddy is taking the agency plane to the East Coast."

"What?" Meghan's heart started thudding in her chest.

"*Mmmm hmmm.* You heard me. Alex is headed to your coast. He's doing some classified security 'whateveryouwannacallit' in Washington. I Googled the distance between Boston and D.C. It's less than five hundred miles. A short plane trip or even a train ride."

She didn't respond right away; just sorta let the information sink in.

"Irish? You still there?"

"Yeah."

"What're you thinking?"

What was she thinking? Now there was the million dollar question. She'd had an overabundance of time to think when she made the drive from Arizona to Boston. He had freaked out—she understood that. At first she clung to the belief that if she'd just told him about her feelings it would have made a difference. But as the weeks went by and he didn't even try to reach out to her, she'd begun to replace that narrative with one that was anchored in the notion that she'd been spared more pain by not revealing what a romantic fool she'd been. It was the proverbial rock and a hard place. The two warring points of view were eating her alive.

"He's not coming east to see me, Tori," she whined petulantly. "Not really. No matter what your imagination tells you. And I'm sure it's not even a little bit unusual for him or anyone from the agency to be in high demand by Washington."

She heard Tori sigh and hesitate. "You're forcing my hand, Meghan. My husband will spank me for what I'm about to tell you, but I think you have a right to know even though Draegyn doesn't think I should meddle. Alex, well…he, um—he asked about you. And before you say any more about his trip, we both know it'd practically take an act of Congress to persuade him to willingly step in the middle of all that military and national security shit. He's going because it's where you are."

"What did he ask, Tori?"

"Well, first of all, the framed photograph arrived. Well played, Irish, well played. He looked like a man in need of oxygen once he saw the card with it. After everyone had a chance to rub it in a little he sucked it up and asked if you were alright. He knew when he asked, what a big deal it was." After a quick pause she added, "Sweetie, Alex knows he fucked up. *Big time.* His only thought was concern about you. That means something, doesn't it?"

Shit. This crying business was getting old. "What did you tell him?"

"Are you kidding? I told him the damn truth. That you miss him. And since I might as well spill all the friggin' beans, he knows we've been talking and flat-out asked if I'd tell you. About his asking how you are."

"I'm not going to D.C., Tori," Meghan interjected passionately. "No way. Fuck that noise."

Tori snorted with obvious delight. "Good! Don't you dare make this easy for him. Just hang tough a little longer, okay? He'll reach out to you Irish. I know he will." Meghan cringed hearing the slight ring of hopeful wishing in her friend's voice.

"Can I ask a question, Mrs. St. John?"

"Uh oh," came the lighthearted reply. "What did I do?"

Meghan grinned. She'd come to really love the feisty, brilliantly intelligent little woman with the vocabulary of a shit-kicking Marine. It felt like having a sister. Tori was loyal to a fault where the Justice family was concerned. Knowing that she'd take care of Alex once she'd left had helped ease some of her anguish about leaving Arizona behind.

A squeaking embarrassed cough shot from her throat. "Were you, um... serious before? About the spanking?" It might have been an off-hand comment but Meghan's curiosity was piqued. When she heard Tori hysterically giggling she couldn't help but laugh right back. "Don't read anything into the question," she shrieked with a hiccup of giggles.

"Oh my God, Irish. Is Big Daddy a bad boy in the bedroom?" She could imagine Tori practically falling over with glee. "I fucking love this! And the answer to your question is most definitely, yes. My demanding, Alpha husband finds spanking to be a way of handling my smart mouth."

Meghan howled with laughter. Tori's smart-ass mouth was practically a legend at the Villa. "Oh, that's clearly working out so well,
huh?"

"*Pff.* These Justice men. Oversexed, naughty boys in my opinion.
It's the same for Lacey. I say enjoy yourself and remember one thing
sweetie…when it comes to who's really in control, it's you wielding
the real power when you allow him to be lord and master."

Wow. She was good. Meghan had to choke back a sigh. Lord and
master, indeed. "I love you Mrs. St. John."

"I love you too Irish. Now stop your sulking and tighten your laces
sweetie because your shit's about to get real. And remember, when you
finally see Alex, it's tits out, okay?"

What wasn't to love about such a hilariously ribald and yet oh so
true statement? Especially when it came out of the naughty mouth of
an adorably pregnant elf.

"Message received, Mrs. St. John. Tits out. The girls send their
regards and promise to make a statement as requested."

They both giggled, then grew silent. It was time to hang up.

"Give the bump a pat for me." Meghan sighed, and then pressed
the end button on the phone.

AFTER THE KIDS WERE excused from the table along with their mom following Sunday dinner to go hang with Pop in his basement handy room where all manner of cool things were always in store for visiting grandchildren, the remaining adult contingent of Meghan's immediate family closed in on her.

"So, let me get this straight. Some dickwad Lawrence of Arabia out in the desert is begging for a Boston beat-down?" It was Deval scowling furiously and sounding like a bully. *Fabulous.* Meghan felt the start of a stress headache bumping around inside her head.

Mike chimed in next. "This Special Forces asshole needs to get his butt kicked. And Dev," he continued, nodding in his brother's direction, "I think it was Desert *Rat* not Lawrence of Arabia."

The obvious slam at Alex's honor made Meghan flinch. It pretty much went downhill from there as she endured an endless barrage of smack talk from her siblings.

Finn waited until his older brothers were finished thumping their chests, then flashed her a harsh look, dramatically cracking his knuckles for emphasis. "How do I find this guy, sis?"

Meghan groaned and sat back in her chair taking in, one by one, the furious looks on all the faces turned in her direction. Her mother's pained expression didn't help things.

"Nobody's getting a Boston beat down, and you can stop with the shitty character slurs. Just let me handle my own life and back the hell up."

Feeling her fury rising Meghan regarded this whole farce of a family meeting as nothing more than an opportunity for her swaggering siblings to try and run her life.

"Meggie's right," her mother declared, bringing the entire discussion to a screeching halt. "She's a big girl and knows what's best for her. You boys will have to learn to play nice with others." The look she gave each of her three boys meant business.

Knowing her mother was just as meddlesome as her brothers were controlling, Meghan rolled her eyes behind her mother's back. Crossing her arms defensively across her chest she visibly sulked like a bratty teenager. At one point she got in a good shot at Dev. Finding him staring at her, she wrinkled her nose and furiously stuck out her tongue just like she did when they were kids. *Pfftt.* He infuriated her the most—always had and always will. Though he was the brother she adored the most, his heavy-handed interference in her life had always made her crazy. Maybe because he was the oldest, Deval thought it was his job to keep his siblings safe and out of trouble. With her though, as the only girl, he'd taken it a bit too far sometimes.

As if the matter of her meddling brothers wasn't enough to stress her out, there was the matter of Alex. The Major. She missed him so much it hurt. With Tori's information about an impending trip to the East Coast hanging in her mind, she was struggling to keep calm.

After Tori's call last night, when she finally went to bed, sleep eluded her once again as her entire being churned with anxiety. Would he contact her? *Oh God.* What if he didn't? What had happened to him in the weeks they'd been apart? All night long that was how it went. An endless cascade of questions and fears chasing her.

By breakfast time, she was exhausted and emotionally ragged, felt like shit and about as miserable as a person could be. In the end it all came down to one thing. She loved him. The truth wouldn't be denied, and she couldn't hide from it if she hoped to survive with her sanity intact.

It was all on the line. Her heart and soul, their future. She had to hope her Major had found his way. It'd probably kill her if ..... *if what*? If he didn't love her? If he went away without seeing her? If he couldn't find closure for the past? There were so many 'ifs'.

She continued to sulk for the remainder of the evening until, family dinner over, the boys made moves to depart, calling the kids to clean up and say their good-byes. She couldn't let them leave without having the final word. It was her right dammit, as their only sister and if ever there was a time to make that point, it was now.

"Ma, guys….c'mon back here a minute, will ya?" Four pairs of curious eyes met her determined expression. Time to remind everyone who she was. Meghan O'Brien. Goddamn gym teacher for heaven's sake who could hold her own in a drinking game, kick some serious ass if she had to, and of course the fact that hands down, she was a true Boston bitch of the ball busting variety. Feeling mad irritated, she glared at them with an uncompromising expression.

"Listen carefully, all of you. Ma, this includes you too." Meghan's eyebrow arched high in clear warning. Only a fool wouldn't see she was wicked serious.

"If anyone here so much as breathes on Alex Marquez, I will make you wish you hadn't."

"Ah. Stuff a sock in it, Meggie," Mike chortled.

"No!" she demanded with a stern finger pointing in their direction. Everyone looked shocked at her outburst. "He's *mine*. Do I make myself clear? You know the rules—do *not* fuck with what's mine." Glancing at her mother, she murmured, "Sorry Ma, but the f-word was necessary."

"Oh, no, no," her mother answered with a surprisingly smug expression on her face as she waved her hands indicating she wanted no part of an unnecessary apology. "I think everyone got the message. I certainly did. You did too, right boys?" she asked innocently as she vigorously nodded her head.

Leveling Meghan with a meaningful mom stare she continued, "Thanks for clarifying things, my dear. I'll make sure to tell Da later that the Arizona Zorro is yours. Special emphasis on the *yours*. He'll be glad to hear it." The mocking tone in her mother's voice couldn't be overlooked. "Seriously daughter, it was him you needed to worry about, not these three," she taunted while waving at her brawny sons. "If this mysterious desert soldier knows what's good for him, he needs to man up with your father or you can kiss family peace on the ass."

She couldn't hide her grimace. Her parents used a tag team approach with their kids. Generally, Ma did the talking, the negotiating, the interrogating. She'd then parse whatever information Da needed and go from there. They rarely descended at the same time on her or any of her siblings. The two-pronged approach was so much more effective. Hearing her mother remind her that her other parent had yet to weigh in on the matter got her stress levels percolating.

The anxiety headache pulled up a stool and sat down, determined to stick around for a good long while. It occurred to her that she'd probably need a mouth guard soon, as well, to protect her teeth from the constant grinding and clenching.

ALEX FELT LIKE AN old man and not because his injuries were acting up. Blaming his current state of malaise on that old saw wasn't going to cut it this time. There was no way he could avoid what was going on. Every fiber and sinew in his entire body seemed to have shut down until he was left with the sensation that his skin was too heavy to hold up. Plus, he was twitchy and downright grumpy. Might as well plant his miserable ass in a chair on the front lawn from where he could rail at the kids on the street like a cantankerous old fuck. In short—he was a mess.

Glancing around the room with an admittedly cynical eye he grew even wearier at the reminder of what he'd gotten himself into. Day three of a week-long event for him and about forty others, an intense group of bad ass motherfuckers, almost exclusively ex-military, who made up the cream-of-the-crop so to speak, in each of their areas of expertise. Bunch of Terminator-type private security people not too un-like Team Justice, some Men in Black spooks, black ops guys, merce-naries, someone he knew to be one of the best hackers on the continent, and two black widow lipstick lesbians who were pretty fucking scary. It was like a Who's Who in in the civilian worlds of counter-intel and security. A shudder of revulsion raced through him. He nodded slightly, confirming that he really did hate all this shit, and let the honesty of how he felt get some oxygen. He was done having his head up his ass.

While he hated being a part of anything that had the power to yank his Special Forces chain, he'd also accepted that he brought all this on himself. Desperate for any crazy plan or ploy to reconnect with Meghan, he'd grasped at straws and really bitten the bullet when he accepted the request that he participate in the Washington D.C. event.

Pfft. Not much of control junkie now, are we? Pondering the irony of his situation he knew it wouldn't take much for him to willingly don women's clothes and walk a runway if it meant he could see his beautiful Irish goddess just one more time. Even though he'd need a figurative Silkwood Shower to wash away his jaded bitterness at hav-ing to get involved in this crap, it was a small price to pay for what he thought would be step one of Operation Meghan. As usual with pretty much anything involving the fiery woman who consumed his every waking moment and dominated his dreams, he could make all the plans he wanted but where she was involved, the outcome was never quite what he'd envisioned.

After flying into D.C. and getting settled, he'd calmed down con-siderably following weeks of escalating tension at home that threat-ened to explode in epic fashion if he didn't get his shit together. Just knowing he was on the same coast as Meghan gave him a few moments to breathe calmly again. When the symposium got underway he kind of paid attention during the meet and greet and orientation, because despite his disdain for the proceedings, some of the folks present were of value to the agency and vice versa. Though he gave a *back the fuck off* vibe, most of the others present had beat a hasty path in his direction early on. Clearly, his reputation preceded him.

By day two however, he fell so deep into his thoughts that he'd barely connected more than a handful of times the entire day with what-ever was going on. All he could focus on was Meghan and figuring out what step two should be in his attempt to re-establish some sort of connection. Running a loop of never ending options in his head he picked apart everything. No hair-brained idea was too crazy to consider.

The notion of flying to Boston and flat-out catching her off guard with his appearance was carefully vetted. He considered every conceivable scenario about how it would play out and in the final analysis decided the surprise frontal assault was a very bad idea. After the way he'd behaved the last time he saw her, she'd rip his balls off for what he put her through.

Texting seemed like a viable alternative. Sort of like a foot in the door. A simple, 'Yoo hoo, I'm over here'. Maybe combining a text with something like a big floral delivery was worth considering. Somehow, though, he doubted it.

This was what I'd been reduced to. Conscious of his unsettled state, Alex sighed heavily. What the hell was he doing; pretending to be professionally interested in something he had no taste for then quite literally checking out mentally so he could engage in this endless internal emotional hand wringing? *Some bad ass*, he snickered silently. All it took was a fistful of red curls, a set of mouth-watering tits, and the type of fleshy curves that make you want to grab on tight. He was toast.

By the day's end he'd decided to just man the fuck up and call her. He was being a total pussy. His whole world tilted slightly the day she walked through his door. Whatever the hell he thought about his future had been blown to smithereens when a bewitching pair of wicked green eyes locked on his. It took those same eyes glaring at him with a mixture of hurt and disappointment when he pushed her away to wake him the hell up and eventually force him to tackle the landmines in his past. He still wasn't quite there, but did that ever really happen? He somehow doubted with all the fucked-up shit that went on in the world that every good guy like him got to tie up brutal realities with a nice neat bow.

The minute he was free, Alex had hurried to his hotel with the simpleminded focus of getting Meghan on the damn phone. *Enough.* She belonged to him dammit, and he wanted what was his. Groveling would take place if he had to. Hell, even thinking about her sultry voice got him so emotional he'd gladly cry if it would make a difference. Whatever it took—he was going to get her back.

Fifteen minutes later, he'd crashed and burned in spectacular fashion. Running on adrenaline and the upside of a wild emotional swing, it took three taps on his phone to connect with Meghan. It wasn't until he heard the call ringing through that he realized he didn't have a clue what to say. With panic starting to zing through his nerves it took a good long moment to comprehend that she wasn't picking up.

What the fuck? He hadn't considered that as a possibility. Uncertainty, swift and uncompromising, stole his breath. Had she seen his name on her caller ID and chosen not to answer? Assailed with doubt, he was in no way prepared when the call went to voicemail. Remembering that Tori had told him not to expect too much at first, an icy chill of fear ran the length of his spine.

He hated voicemail, and being caught off guard this way made it even worse. He wanted to talk to Meghan, goddammit, not leave some lame fucking message. He needed to hear her voice so he would know how she was. When the beep signaled to start the message, it sounded like a gunshot aimed directly at his head.

"Uh, hi." *Shit.* "It's uh, me. Um, Alex."

Why did every silent, tongue-tied second feel like an eternity? Pinching the bridge of his nose as if the sharp twinge would magically make him smoothly eloquent, he searched for something to say. This was not how he thought a simple call would unfold.

Clearing his throat he choked out some more inane words. "Yeah, so I'm here. I mean….well, actually by *here* I mean D.C."

Oh my God. This was going in the shitter pretty damn fast. Could he sound any more like a mindless lunatic?

"Uh, anyway. Since we're in the same time zone I thought…um." Alex was mentally loading bullets into a gun to blow his stupid head off when this ridiculous call ended. When exactly did *um, yeah,* and *uh* become such a big part of his vocabulary? Rolling his eyes he thought, *'and I've been a commanding officer?'* Jesus. Wonders never ceased.

Since clearly there weren't two available coherent thoughts to string together in his message he threw in the towel. "Meghan. It's Alex." And then he pressed the disconnect button to terminate the call.

"Well, that went well," he'd sneered as he poured himself several fingers of whiskey. Two hours later, when he didn't immediately hear back from her, he'd been well on his way to a righteous hangover. No wonder he felt like shit today. His entire evening had become one monumental pity party. She hated him or at the very least didn't feel like speaking to him.

Having Meghan turn away from him was like being gutted. Feeling like a fraud and a wimp, he thought about his pathetic lifelong insistence on being the one in control. What a joke. Who the hell was he kidding? At this moment, he was powerless, impotent, barely able to crawl—so undone by how things were turning out. It was his naughty Irish fuck goddess who was the one with all the power. Didn't help that he'd been a day late and a dollar short in figuring that out. By giving herself over to his powerful desires and letting him have his control fantasy, she'd turned his emotional life on its head. And now that she was gone, he had nothing. *I am so fucked*, he thought.

The idea of calling Tori and crying like a little girl crossed his mind. So too did contacting Drae directly and asking for his help. He could use 007's cool, analytical presence right about now.

No wonder he felt a hundred years old. Too much stress. Definitely more alcohol and less real food than was wise. A raging guilty conscience. The sudden and unfamiliar loss of confidence. The absence of his normal support team. Oh yeah, and a tightening in his groin that refused to settle down. *Fucked* didn't actually cover how he felt.

Rubbing his hand absently across his chest, as he narrowed his gaze on the cast of characters sharing his space, Alex wondered whether he should even bother continuing with this farce. He wasn't the man these folks imagined he was. Not in his current state, anyway.

Toughing it out for another two days was less than appealing. So was waiting around like a lovesick fool for some glimmer of hope from Boston. But when all was said and done, he didn't have much choice but to let things play out as they were meant to.

That didn't mean that he had to endure alone. It would be wrong to isolate from the people closest to him when ultimately, they too would be affected by whatever happened with him and Meghan. They'd be pissed to find out he needed them but hadn't let them know. Remembering how each of his Justice brothers had needed help at critical points in their relationships with their women, Alex gave in and admitted that this time around he was the one needing back-up. An odd predicament for a bad-tempered, know-it-all who built a life carefully structured to keep any and all emotions at bay.

His need for Meghan had broken down those walls. He was overcome with the deluge of feelings her presence in his life invited. It was heart-pounding, kiss-me-till-I'm-dying passion wrapped in a perfect cloud of love. He couldn't breathe without her in his life. It sounded so simple when he put it like that.

MEGHAN KNEW THE TOLL being sucked from her body from the anxiety, lack of sleep, and almost total absence of food had gone off the charts when by Monday morning she felt like she'd been dragged through a knothole backwards. Her throat was sore, it was hard to swallow, and she was on fire but freezing cold. In addition to the thumping in her head, every inch of her body ached.

Shaking from the fever, she huddled under a mound of blankets and tried to sleep off her symptoms as if they'd magically disappear. It was now Wednesday night, and she was slowly making her way back to the land of the living.

For days a fever cocoon had wrapped tight around her that seemed to be fueled by the memories of her time in Arizona. They were like montages. Sometimes gritty. Sometimes focused and clear. All with a pulsing thrum of want, like a heartbeat. She recalled the sound of Alex's voice when he was in absentminded professor mode and how quickly she could get it to change into something deeper, darker, tinged with reminders of the man's potent masculinity, by doing nothing more than being close to him.

As illness wracked her body, her mind replayed each intimate moment down to the smallest detail. How it felt to be pulled onto his lap. The wonder she always experienced each time it happened because being a big girl, she'd always thought lap-sitting was for the tiny and petite. Discovering that her brawny lover got off on having her lush ass sitting on his groin had freed her so much that wiggling about and squirming against his Herculean body had become her go-to move.

It was all there in her fevered thoughts, playing out like an erotic movie on the backs of her closed eyelids. His scent. How she loved using his spicy shower gel because it made her feel like a part of him was clinging to her skin. In the confines of a steamy shower, even without him present, that scent had a way of grabbing onto her senses and not letting go. She couldn't remember how many times she leaned against the smooth tile wall as a heavy mist of steam and condensation gathered in the enclosure infused with the essence of his scent—turning her inside out with need. There was something mystical and otherworldly about feeling as though Alex's essence was always with her. In desperate want she would snake her hand through the showering water down across her stomach through the dripping red ringlets guarding the puffy folds of her sex.

One time she'd even acted it out while he watched with eyes so hot they scorched her skin. She'd felt sexy and wanton standing naked with water sluicing off the curves of her voluptuous body, one hand holding a mounded breast and the other between her legs, head back, eyes glazed with arousal as deep shudders rocked her from head to toe. She could hear him breathing heavily in the confined space, reveling in each excited hiss as she fondled herself for his pleasure and absorbed his earthy grunt of male satisfaction that filled her senses at the moment of her climax. He did that to her. Knowing his desires and wants, she found it beyond exciting to have him watching as she writhed against a wall while bringing herself to orgasm.

There were hundreds of fever-driven flashes just like that playing out in her dreams, most ending in a morphed image—a specific moment from their first time in his truck, something that was seared on her soul. He'd seemed stunned by her desperate need when she'd rode him like a bull, legs pressed against his sides absorbing the movement of his heaving chest as she lowered her greedy body onto his, inch by agonizing inch. The look of absolute wonder on his face once she had taken all of him and the momentary flash of vulnerability she found in his eyes kept replaying over and over in her thoughts. It was the moment that changed everything.

What was left after the fever finished burning through her system was a body tortured with an achy tension and a mind struggling to contain the aftermath of uncovering all those memories. It had all felt so real. Waking to realize it was just her dreams, Meghan curled into a tight ball and felt her heart break all over again. He pushed her away. He didn't want her, at least not enough to fight for her. It was agony in her soul.

God, she yearned for him so damn much. No wonder she'd gotten sick. The missing and the blunt, visceral depth of her need were killing her. So was the horror of the rejection she felt because he hadn't come after her. Deep in her heart of hearts, Meghan had to admit that was what she'd been hoping for. That he'd see that while life could certainly suck sometimes and be difficult and messy, without her it was going to be even suckier and a thousand times more difficult and messy. She needed him to believe that they were better together than apart; that two halves really do make a whole; that the end result was worth the fight to get there. When he didn't—her heart quietly shattered into a million pieces, all sharp and deadly, pressing into her soul.

Making it worse was remembering that the moments when they awoke together in the sanctuary of his enormous bed. Meghan loved the intimacy of it. Them sleeping together. Waking up next to his solid presence, the heat rolling off his body. Sometimes she would lay still and quiet, marking him with her eyes, taking in every exposed inch of flesh. In the quiet stillness of the early morning those visual tributes felt sacred and beautiful. He was magnificent, and he was hers.

The best part of all though was that moment when his eyes fluttered open, and he'd turn his head to search for her. In that brief first glance when their eyes met she would catch glimpses into the vulnerability he tried so carefully to control. Reliving those flashes, her soul cried out. How could he let her go? And not just let her go—send her away with brutal backhanded snark.

Throwing off the covers she growled and struggled to sit up. *Fuck.* Feeling weak as a baby, hollow and empty, her head started to swim. She wanted to cry. Just then her eyes fell on her cell phone. Didn't surprise her in the least to see she'd been sleeping with the damn thing clutched close. At this point it represented the only lifeline she had left that could connect her to Alex.

Tapping on the screen with weak, trembling fingers she checked for emails, noted the day and time then tossed it away. Wednesday. No email. If the information Tori had texted was right, he'd been in D.C. since late Sunday.

Ugh, she groaned, flinging back onto the pillow top mattress to stare wretchedly at the ceiling. She was overwhelmed with awareness that he was nearby even if a couple hundred miles away. It was like she could feel him. She had to hope it was her imagination because if it wasn't and she really and truly could connect to him like that she was beyond fucked. There was just no way she'd survive.

"I'M NOT SURPRISED TO hear you couldn't get through to her," Tori said over the phone when Alex broke down and called her Wednesday night. It was getting late on the East Coast, the perfect time to catch his sister-in-law so he'd dialed her up and immediately begun fretting to her about Meghan not taking his call.

Not surprised? Fuck. That wasn't what he wanted to hear. Barking like an angry dog he asked, "Why aren't you surprised? Did she tell you she wouldn't speak to me?" Alex was suddenly filled with insecurity and fear.

"Oh, no Alex. No!" came her instant response. "You misunderstand. I just meant that it was no surprise you didn't get through because I also ended up hearing her lovely outgoing voicemail message when I checked in earlier. It's not just you she didn't answer for. I'm absolutely sure she'd take your call, Boss. Please calm down."

That was just it. He couldn't calm the fuck down to save his life. His inner turmoil was like a ping pong ball—flying all over the place— back and forth, being relentlessly pounded with unsettling thoughts.

Motherfucker. He wanted Meghan. All this bullshit was driving him over the edge. He needed her to stop the freefall he was in. Needed her sweet, giving heart and soft, lush curves to break his fall. He'd had enough. He was going to go get what was his.

"I'm going to Boston, Tori. This is insane. Sitting here in Washington, hating every minute of what I'm doing even if it is good for the agency and killing myself with doubt about Meghan isn't helping the situation. She either wants me or she doesn't."

The groan that came through the phone let him know he'd said that last part like an arrogant prick.

"Alex," she bit out in a tone clearly intended as a voice of adult authority that would serve her well once she became a mother. "Let me take this moment to remind you that ultimatums won't work. She either wants you or she doesn't? Are you high?" she all but screeched. "You didn't give a hot damn that she wanted you when you sent her away like a nuisance fan girl you'd grown tired of. So fuck you Major. I suggest you stand down and catch your breath before you make this worse."

Alex started to crumble. Tori was right. He couldn't just puff up his chest, snap his fingers and demand Meghan submit to his he-man authority. Without thinking he reached for his manhood, subliminally protecting his balls from her wrath should he try such a bone-headed approach.

"Holy fuck, Mrs. St. John. Help me out here, lady. I just can't…" He couldn't even finish the sentence. After a long silent hesitation he added, "Do this. I can't do this. It's killing me." He said that last part in a pained whisper.

Several long moments ticked by with Alex clutching the phone to his ear, eyes closed, a sad, tormented expression glued to his face.

In a voice that sounded like it had been lifted from the grave he murmured, "I need her, Tori. Nothing matters without her. Until she came along, I thought my whole world would forever be defined by the past; believed I'd spend an entire lifetime doing penance for things I had no control over. She gave me back the dream of a future. Drae said he thought she was my salvation, that through Meghan I'd stumbled on the most unexpected and unearned redemption ever imagined. I think he was right." Groaning as he grabbed at his chest to stop his heart from falling to pieces he said, "I won't make it without her. *Please.* Please tell me what to do." He'd never felt as exposed or helpless as he did in that moment.

He heard Tori sniff then clear her throat. Was she crying? "Tori?" he croaked. There it was, that sniff again. *Fuck.*

"You made it, Major," she choked out after another heavier throat clearing. "You made it to the other side of a huge leap of faith that took more courage and balls than anything you did in that damn war. Admitting proves you're the man we all know you are. If that's the way you feel and you are certain to the depth of your soul that this woman belongs to you, then yes Alex. You go and get her. My only suggestion is you get used to using the one word I still haven't heard you say."

"Love," he croaked. "You want me to admit I love her."

"No Big Daddy," she chuckled. "It's not me who needs you to admit it. I'm just saying—bitches like romance."

He smiled at the irreverent teasing in her tone. "Okay. Understood. Bitches like romance. Got it."

They laughed together for a few moments then Tori giggled and said, "My lord and master is home so this call is over. You've got this now, Boss?" she asked.

He chortled with a grin. "Probably not. I seem to keep fucking things up without even trying but I feel better having talked with you. Thanks sis."

"Get off the damn phone," he heard Drae growl a second before a sharp sound and Tori's startled gasp shot through the phone.

"Uh, bye Al..." and then the phone went dead. He laughed and shook his head as a visual of Drae smacking his wife's butt before grabbing the phone from her and disconnecting the call filled his head.

For the millionth time he thanked the universe for his Justice family. Tori and Drae plus Cam and Lacey and the children each couple was bringing into the world would enrich that family immeasurably. He desperately hoped before too long he'd be bringing his Irish goddess into the fold.

He didn't know it but back home in Arizona, after Drae had terminated their phone call then subdued his feisty wife with an incendiary kiss, she had winked at him saucily and said, "Pack your bag, Double-Oh-Sexy. Dad needs his boys so you and Cam will have to go wheels up in short order. Time's a-wasting and Alex on his own is a recipe for guy-fuckery that only a team approach can manage."

"YOU LOOK BETTER TODAY, *mo stoirín,*" Meghan heard her mother say as she gingerly folded onto the wood bench behind the rustic old table that gave their family breakfast nook a charming Irish pub vibe.

Pfft. She might look better but she still felt like shit.

"Where is everybody?" Meghan asked.

Pushing a plate of shortbread scones across the table and nodding at her to eat something, Ma scurried to the Keurig and went about making an aromatic mug of Meghan's favorite coffee blend.

"Da is down at the station but he'll be back soon. He's been worried about you, daughter. Learning about his baby girl and her Latin gigolo was one thing. Watching while you slowly fade to nothing, only to end up sick and miserable, well—it's expecting too much of him I'm afraid. He'll be wanting a word with you when he gets home today."

Dun dun, dun. In her head she heard the mocking trill of the tone crime shows used at dramatic moments. Anxious to push past the bout of nerves her mother's pronouncement fired up, Meghan wrinkled her nose and forgot her manners all in the same second.

"For the sake of St. Patrick himself, will you all please stop with the snappy slurs. Lawrence of Arabia, Desert Rat, Zorro, and now gigolo. C'mon. Give it a rest," she grumped, taking a vicious bite of a scone that sent crumbs cascading down her front.

What she got in return for her moment of churlishness was Maggie O'Brien's raised eyebrow and an exaggerated tut that made her feel like a naughty child. Manners were everything in an Irish household. Speaking irreverently to her parent in such a tone would have earned her a lengthy time out as a youngster and possibly even a good spanking.

When her thoughts did a frantic one-eighty and an erotic spanking tableau starring her ass in a sexy purple thong and Alex's big hand fired up in her head, Meghan blushed furiously and tried to look anywhere but at her mother. It took a mountain of effort not to roll her eyes at how easily her mind went into the naughty fuckery zone.

"Darling, I've been thinking," her mother said as she sat across the table and snagged a scone. "Maybe what we need is some retail therapy for what ails you."

"I don't think shopping is going to make me feel any better, Ma."

Her mother smiled and wrinkled her nose playfully. "It's always been my opinion that some well thought out lingerie and the proper dress can make or break certain situations."

Meghan almost choked to death on the scone. Had her mother always been such a vamp or was she just now sharing this side of herself now that she knew her daughter was in love?

Ignoring her daughter's cough or the way she guzzled the coffee to manage the choking fit, her ma kept on talking as if nothing were amiss.

"This calls for something white, I think. Despite being sick you still have a nice golden glow from your time in the Southwest sun. You always did look angelic in white Meggie. And it'll make your beautiful hair really stand out. And of course there's nothing like white or blush silk undies." Her mother's beaming smile was disconcerting.

Meghan thought of her Major's preference for sexy lingerie and swallowed hard. It was Thursday dammit, and she still hadn't heard from him. Her nerves were rocky enough from having been sick but worrying that he wouldn't contact her was making things worse. Maybe doing as her mother suggested and indulging in a new outfit that she could employ to knock his socks off was a good diversion and a bit of positive thinking.

"I think you may be on to something, Ma," Meghan murmured. "Wanna go to one of those flashy new Southie boutiques and set my credit card on fire?"

"What's this I hear about fires and credit cards?" boomed a deep voice with a distinct Irish brogue.

"Patrick," her mother purred in that special way she did whenever she addressed her husband. While it had always been there for her to see, Meghan was just this second opening her eyes to the deeper relationship between her unflappable and ladylike mother and handsome, spirited father.

Rising from the table, Maggie O'Brien hurried to her husband's side and welcomed him with a kiss. And not some quick peck on the cheek either. This was something Meghan and her siblings were used to. Her parents were a deeply affectionate couple. But seeing them now, arms wrapped around each other for a sweet embrace and a lingering kiss, Meghan couldn't have loved them anymore if she tried. They'd been the best example a little girl could have ever hoped for when it came to imagining what true love looked like.

Meghan saw from the corner of her eye how her dad helped himself to a good handful of her mother's backside just before he turned to fix her with a shrewd and assessing gaze.

"You look better Meggie," he said. Lowering onto the bench next to her, he leaned in for a father daughter smooch then grabbed onto her hand. "How're you feeling baby girl?"

Meghan smiled into her father's kind eyes. Patrick O'Brien was her hero. She couldn't imagine a better father. Only she had the ability to wheedle her way around his sometimes gruff exterior with ease, but she supposed that would be true of most fathers where their little girls were concerned. Her only Daddy issues were that she knew what it was like to be loved unconditionally.

Suddenly she recalled how as a young girl playing make believe with her dolls and with romance and weddings filling her foolish head she'd dreamed of finding a boy who would be the equal to her handsome, charming father. Only such a person would deserve her love.

It didn't take but a split second to slot her hunky Major into that role. They were both good men. Loyal, hard-working, intense. Her parents made a fetching couple. Maggie's green eyes, Marilyn Monroe curves, and wicked laugh blended well with her dad's dashing good looks complete with a set of dimples that softened his otherwise serious expression plus he had the brawny build of a seasoned police officer. None of that description was all that dissimilar to how she and Alex must appear. The thought rattled her cage a tiny bit.

"Cat got your tongue?" he teased when Meghan didn't answer straight away.

She blushed and shook her head. "Sorry Dad. I was just thinking about how much I love you guys. And to answer your question, yes, I do feel better. Nothing like one of Ma's wicked scones and a trough of coffee to bring a person back from the dead."

"I'm glad you're back to your old self," he chuckled. "I hear you threatened the unholy trinity with dire consequences if they fucked with your mysterious boyfriend. Where'd you get such a naughty mouth I wonder, *hmm*?"

"Oh gee, Da. Let me think a moment." Meghan giggled because it was well known that her dad had a black belt in swearing.

"Well, be that as it may, your mother tells me that you've gone and fallen for this man but that he pretty much needs a serious talking to where you're concerned. Is that true?"

Was it true? Her mother had been right when she said that her overprotective family came along in the deal and that whoever earned her heart was going to have to accept that. She tried to imagine a conversation between Paddy O'Brien and Alex Marquez. They'd probably argue over their tastes in whiskey but beside that they were fairly well-matched.

Scooting closer to lay her head on her father's comforting shoulder, Meghan sighed. "Oh, Da. I don't know if a talking to will help much."

A long moment of silence passed that she was sure had her parents sharing meaningful looks back and forth.

Drawing her into a mighty hug, her father's love and strength felt like the best balm of all.

"I think what you need Meggie girl is a neighborhood stroll with your dad. We'll walk and talk like we did when you were a little girl. How's that sound?"

Walk and talk with her dad. Just the two of them. God, could he be any more perfect?

"Let me get dressed, okay?"

And so off they went, father and daughter, making the rounds through the south Boston neighborhood where Meghan grew up. They walked and talked for a long time with her dad asking the occasional question while she rambled on endlessly about her trip to Arizona and the man who was turning her life upside down.

She told her dad everything she could about the compound and the numbers of veterans the agency helped. With an overabundance of enthusiasm she went on and on about the interesting cast of characters who comprised Family Justice and giggled like a schoolgirl about her horseback riding lessons and how she'd even tried her hand a time or two at target shooting. It felt good to let all of it out.

At her dad's insistence they stopped at an old-time ice cream parlor near their home, taking a seat at an outdoor table where they could people watch and continue their conversation. It was just about the best way she could imagine to spend an afternoon.

"Still a vanilla girl, I see," her dad chuckled as he watched her inhale a huge dish of plain ice cream. "You never were one for all the extras although I remember a time when Finn tried his damnedest to convince you that mint chocolate chip dripping with syrup would make you smarter."

"Once an idiot, always an idiot," Meghan snarked between mouthfuls of the cold, creamy treat. "Remember the time he played 'close your eyes and open your mouth' and I was dumb enough to do what he said?"

Her dad barked a laugh, his eyes twinkling with merriment. "You screamed and cried like the world was ending when he stuck a fluffy dandelion cluster on your tongue."

"Shithead," she mumbled. Arching an eyebrow and trying to look like she meant business, Meghan's sardonic side appeared. "Fool me once, you know?"

Patrick O'Brien took a long time licking a spoonful of ice cream before he reacted to her words.

"I certainly hope you learned to be more discriminating about what you put on that sharp tongue of yours and to not be so eager to do as told."

The comment, rich with innuendo, made her all but choke on the ice cream.

"Aw, come on. Really? What is it with you and Ma these days? She's talking to me about sex toys and you're …well, jeez Da. I don't even know how to decipher what you just said."

He laughed at her reaction and waggled his brows. "Your ma was going on and on about those damn Kegel Balls, I'm guessing. You have

Aunt Heather to thank for that."

Meghan groaned and pretended to smack her head on the table. "You guys are killing me."

And with that, the kidding around came to an end, and her father got serious as a heart attack.

"Meggie, darling, you've always been in charge of yourself, a trait that has served you well as you've grown into an amazing woman. Your mother and I couldn't be more proud. The way you've handled everything—David dying, going after a career, even how you dealt with all that lottery money. You're a credit to the O'Brien name."

Putting her spoon down, she offered her dad a watery smile edged with the tears his praise summoned. "Thanks, Dad. It means a lot to hear that from you."

"I hope you know what you're doing," he added a moment later when he sat back and stared at her. "The way you talk about your time in the Southwest is pretty telling baby girl. Why don't we stop dancing around what's not being said and get down to business?"

Here it comes, she thought. The parental lecture. There was no way her dad, with his protective instincts, was going to sit idly by while a man he didn't know and had never even met turned his daughter's world inside out.

Prepared for some heavy words of wisdom she was completely shocked when he started talking but didn't come close to saying what she expected.

"It's clear from everything you've told me that this Major of yours is quite a guy. So why in the hell are you sleeping in your childhood bedroom and making yourself all kinds of sick while this paragon of virtue sits alone a couple of thousand miles away? If he's what you want Meggie, it's up to you to do something about the distance."

She hoped her face wouldn't freeze forever with the look of absolute wonder and dumbfounded surprise she felt. Was her dad basically telling her to buck the hell up and go claim the man who had sent her away? *How exactly does one do that*, she wondered.

"Let me tell you something about love, daughter. It's rarely easy, always a challenge, and sometimes messy as hell. I hear what you've said about why you left. Survivor's guilt is a heavy burden. The fact that your Major feels it so deeply makes me like him even more. It means he has a moral center. What more could a parent hope for when it comes to the man who steals a daughter's heart?"

"Oh, Da," Meghan murmured.

"Straight up baby girl. Don't listen to any of the romantic crap your ma is dishing out these days—especially if her advice was to stand your ground and make him come to you. From a male viewpoint, that's asking for trouble. Men rarely if ever see the forest for the trees where a woman is concerned."

"What are you saying, Dad?"

Her father gave her a look of such love and caring that Meghan almost burst out crying.

"I'm not saying you should jump on a plane and fly halfway across the damn continent but maybe a simple phone call would be a good idea. No communication is the devil's handiwork, Meggie. You'll never know if you don't at least try."

Biting her lip, she looked away and tried to wrap her mind around what he was saying. Her gaze returned to his when he reached across the small table and took her hands in his.

"Tell me what you're thinking, child. Maybe I can help."

"He's not in Arizona, Dad," she blurted out, eager to tell her father everything.

"Where is he then?" he asked gently. She wondered if he could sense her conflict.

"Well….uh. Actually he's here. On the East Coast. Down in D.C. to be exact."

She watched, fascinated, as her big, handsome father tried to stifle what looked like an impending laugh. "He's followed you here, then?"

Shrugging, Meghan held on tighter to her father's hand. "I don't know, did he?"

"What's your heart tell you Meggie girl?"

Ever since Tori's phone call when she let her know that Alex was travelling east, Meghan had been clinging to the hope that this was his way of inching closer.

Her father must have read her thoughts because he squeezed her hands before letting go and sitting back.

"I get to say this because as a male of the species I know with certainty that when it comes to the women we love, men in general are mad clueless, my daughter. If I'm not mistaken, he's trying to bridge the gulf between you two and probably doesn't know what to do next. I'd say being in Washington was his way of getting the ball rolling. Maybe the next step is up to you."

"FUCKING HATE THAT THERE'S never anything on TV," Alex grumbled to an empty hotel room.

Furiously clicking through the channels at a rapid clip, he searched for something, anything, to take his mind off the ugly mess he'd made of his life.

He'd been in D.C. for almost a full week, on a fool's errand to repair his relationship with Meghan. But after a failed phone call and a nonsensical voicemail message he was no further along to meeting that goal than he was while at home in the desert. She hadn't picked up his call or responded to his message, not that he'd had the fucking sense to ask for a callback. In short, after a week of bullshit he was no closer to finding a solution.

By some miracle he'd managed to get through the security symposium without either wrecking his or the agency's reputation and hadn't done anything so stupid that it couldn't be fixed later. Thank God there was just one more session the next morning and then he was free. But free to do what exactly he still didn't know.

Settling on the mindless diversion of a shopping channel, he sprawled across the stiff, uncomfortable sofa in his room and brooded. Just as his thoughts started veering into self-pity mode, three rapid knocks sounded at his door.

Had he called for room service? Shit. He didn't know. This whole situation was fucking with his head so bad that he couldn't remember what he was doing between one moment and the next.

Bitchy and miserable, he went to answer just barely remembering to make sure he had clothes on before yanking the hotel room door open. Not that he cared one way or the other but it wouldn't do for the Justice CEO to cause a scene in front of hotel staff with some naked fuckery that would only embarrass the agency.

Just as his hand connected with the door knob he heard a low, ominous voice bark, "Alex Marquez. FBI. Open the door."

What the fuck? Jesus Christ. Just what he didn't need.

Jaw clenched, he opened the door with a curious expression plastered on his face, expecting to see vested agents with guns drawn on the other side only to find Draegyn and Cameron standing in the empty hallway literally hanging on to each other in a fit of silent laughing. *Motherfuckers.*

"Oh man!" Cam hooted. "Wish you could see your face."

Drae was howling with delight and slapping Cam on the back as if they'd just pulled off the best prank ever.

"Fuck," Drae muttered. "You're right Cam. I shoulda been ready with my phone to snap a picture. Put it up on the agency web site as a 'caption this'."

"What the hell is wrong with you two?" Alex bellowed as he stepped aside to let them in. He might not appreciate the joke but he sure was glad to see them.

Immediately taking over his space like unwanted college roommates, Drae pointed to the TV and snickered.

"What up Dad? You thinking about buying a set of hand-painted stemware?" he mocked. "I like the ones with the birds." Motioning to Cam he said, "Get over here bro and take a look. What do you think? The birds or the flowers?"

"Whatever pussy boy wants is fine by me," Cam tossed out in a tone that sounded a lot like 'wah, wah, wah'.

Grabbing the remote control, Alex quickly turned the set off and tossed the clicker aside. "Shut the fuck up and tell me what you two are doing here."

"Wow," Cam taunted. "You really are a mess. Shut the fuck up and a question all in the same sentence? Which shall it be? The shut-up part, or the what-the-hell-are-we-doing-here part?"

Drae snickered and flipped the finger. "You know exactly why we're here. You might have the highest IQ between the three of us dude, but you're a fucking nightmare when left to your own devices. Did you really think my wife was going to sit back and let you handle what's maybe the most important situation of your entire life without us?"

Holy God. Was his chest tightening like he was going to cry? Turning away quickly before his brothers could catch the riot of emotions he couldn't keep off his face, Alex struggled to clear his throat. Keeping his back turned he choked out, "Your wife is a smart-ass."

"That she is," Drae agreed. "And for some bizarre reason she thought you might need our help, so here we are. Was she wrong?"

No, she wasn't wrong at all but finding a way to say that and keeping his dignity were two separate things.

Cam picked up an impressive looking presentation in a glossy folder that Alex had been reviewing from another of the symposium's participants.

"A.I. and the Police Force of Tomorrow? Please tell me you haven't just spent a week listening to a bunch of shit that could have come from a *Terminator* script."

There was a snappy retort stuck on the tip of his tongue but discussing the pros and cons of artificial intelligence was not why they were here.

Folding like a cheap tent in a wind storm, Alex slumped into a big wing chair and groaned. "Honestly—I haven't heard but a sentence here or there all week long. This whole thing," he mumbled with a wave of his hand, "was nothing but a cover story for why I was in D.C. There could be plans for building the perfect bomb in those materials, and I wouldn't have noticed. Or cared for that matter."

"Yep," drawled Cam. "That's what we figured. But have no fear Big Daddy," he said good-naturedly. "We've got you covered."

What the hell did that mean, Alex wondered. Next thing he knew, Cam pulled a stack of papers from who the fuck knows where and started lining them up on the coffee table.

"Okay gentlemen. Enough fucking around. Time to get down to business. We've got pregnant wives," he reminded everyone, "and I for one want to get this shit resolved in a hurry so I can get back to my lady and her bump."

"So here's the deal, man," Drae directed at Alex. "We've been doing some brainstorming and think we've come up with what your next move should be. If you're still interested in getting Meghan back, that is."

Alex's head snapped up at the mention of Meghan's name. With his senses on high alert he glanced back and forth between Cam and Drae, then at the papers on the table and felt a frisson of relief race along his nerve endings. *Oh thank fucking God for meddling brothers*, he silently prayed.

"What've you got?" he asked.

Drae looked at him, smiling like a Cheshire cat with a dozen fancy sleight of hand tricks up his sleeve and started talking a million miles an hour.

"Okay. Here it is. We've done some research and got a shit ton of information about the parents and siblings. Getting them on your side is key to any hope of moving forward. Since you were a tremendous dick and let this ridiculous situation linger on for weeks, it's given your lady love had plenty of time to sulk or do whatever it is that chicks do when their men lose their shit. Chances are, they all hate your fucking guts about now."

"Word," Cam muttered with a shake of his head.

"I've checked on the father's work schedule and it looks like he'll be at the station house all day tomorrow. Same for her brothers. At work. All day. Meghan's staying at her parents' house and as far as we can tell she doesn't go out much. Pretty much she's been hanging with her mom and ignoring your ass."

So here's what we think has to happen," Cam interjected as he took over the conversation. "You need to talk with her dad first. One Patrick O'Brien. He's a Lieutenant Detective in the Special Operations Unit. Squaring things with him is step one. You might want to consider if there is anything in particular you want to ask him."

Meeting Cam's amused gaze with confusion, Alex felt like a tool when Drae cut in.

"Dude. *Jesus.* Do we have to chew your food for you? Is there anything you need to ask her father is code for getting his permission to marry the girl?"

Alex sat back in the chair with a thud, his mouth hanging open. Marry? Marry Meghan? He was still trying to get her to talk to him, for Christ's sake. Marriage seemed beyond his wildest dreams. Still… asking for her hand was absolutely the right way to go about things. *Hmm.* Maybe his brothers were on to something.

"Alright then," Drae mumbled to Cam. "He's still breathing so I suppose that means we're on the right track.

"Then there are the brothers to deal with," Drae reminded him. "Meghan was pretty vocal about how close she is to her siblings. Chances are, you're in for an ass kicking. Don't worry though, we won't let them do any permanent damage."

Fuck man, did they have to snicker like conspiratorial girlfriends? Even though they were probably right, he had some pride left.

"And that brings us to Mom," Cam added. "She's key. We've talked about this," he said, nodding at Drae. "Nothing says I'm a dick but I love your daughter better than a piece of jewelry. Your best bet is to go in prepared to show her an engagement ring, and if that doesn't get her on your side, we don't know what will. Just remember to agree to anything Mom wants—even a long engagement if it means at the end of the day, Meghan is on a plane heading back home with you."

Wow, Alex thought. Proposing marriage, having an engagement ring, probably getting a serious ass kicking. Twenty minutes ago he was contemplating every imaginable loser scenario in the book and now look at him.

Searching his brothers' faces as they eyed him with expectant expressions, it felt like a huge weight had been lifted off his shoulders. He'd told Tori he was going to go and get Meghan and bring her back but he hadn't a clue how to make that happen. Luckily for him, Drae and Cam had walked down this odd road ahead of him and were prepared with some damn good ideas.

"Anything?" Cam asked.

Checking his watch as he ran his hand through his hair, Alex told them, "Let's go find a jewelry store."

Drae and Cam suddenly high-fived each other and bellowed, "Fucking Eh!"

Drae handed him a piece of paper with four jewelry stores listed. Pointing at the first one he said, "I'd start here. It's old school with high name recognition. Women love that shit."

"Bitches like romance," Alex muttered.

"What?" Cam barked.

Drae laughed and said, "That sounds like something my wife would say, am I right?"

Alex nodded and smiled. "Smart woman, that one. I hope you know what you've fucking got there, Lieutenant," he told Drae pointedly. "You too, Cameron."

"Do you think we'd be here trying to get your moldy ass married off if we didn't?" Cam laughed. "Time to join the party Major. Now get your shit together and let's go spend a metric crap ton of your inheritance and get Meghan the flashiest bling available."

"The second your symposium wraps up tomorrow we are wheels up and Boston bound. If everything goes according to plan we should arrive at her Dad's station by mid-afternoon. Everyone on board with that plan?" Drae asked.

After a quick head shake, Alex hurried off to get cleaned up giving Drae the perfect opportunity to pull his cellphone out and send a text to his wife.

Big Daddy Update: make the call.

MEGHAN WAS HELPING CLEAR the dinner dishes when her phone chirped. Checking the screen she saw it was Tori calling so she quickly dried her hands and scooted into the den where she could take the call in peace.

"Hi Tori. What's up?"

"Well, you are clearly," came the answer. "And thank God. I was getting worried Irish when you didn't answer your phone."

"Oh, that," Meghan replied. "Sorry. I was under the weather for a few days and my phone was on vibrate."

"Everything okay?" her friend asked with concern lacing her words.

"Yeah. More or less. I sort of fell apart at the beginning of the week. You know how it is. But I'm much better now. *Physically*." She let the emphasis in her statement hang by itself in the air.

"Aw, sweetie. Wish I were there to give you a hug. I told you everything's gonna be okay. You have to trust me on that."

"My dad thinks I should call Alex. What do you think?"

She heard Tori chuckling on the other end and wondered what the hell that was all about.

"Irish—you scared the fucking shit out of the man, and that's saying a lot."

"How?" Meghan moaned. "How could I scare someone who's been ignoring me for weeks?"

Tori's chuckle became a full-throated laugh. "Well, by not answering your phone of course silly! He finally found the balls to call you and almost jumped off the ledge when you didn't pick up or respond to his message."

"He didn't call," Meghan cried, alarmed. "I'd know if he called. Please don't tease Tori. I'm not all that together at the moment."

"Sweetie, he did call. Tuesday night. Said you didn't pick up and he was forced to leave a rambling message. You mean you didn't hear it?"

"No, I didn't hear it," she wailed as anxiety bounced off her nerves. "Fuck! Hold on. Let me check my call history."

Three taps on the phone later and she saw that he actually had called and left a voicemail.

"Oh my God, Tori," she whimpered. "What the hell is wrong with me? I checked for email once I was back in the land of the living but never thought to double-check for missed calls. And I somehow missed that little squiggly that indicated a voice mail. Fuck, fuck, *fuck*."

"Settle down Irish. It's okay. Believe me. Probably better this way, anyhow."

"How do you mean?" Meghan was pretty sure her life was flashing before her eyes. Here she'd been waiting for Alex to call yet days had gone by since he had. How could she be so stupid?

"Look. When he couldn't reach you the minute he climbed down off his high horse and decided it was time to talk—kinda knocked him down a few pegs. Which, if you think about it, is a good thing." She heard Tori snort in amusement. "Only a man and a Justice Brother would be so full of himself to imagine that he could go radio silent for weeks then expect to make everything better on the first attempt. Served him right when you didn't answer. Seriously Meghan."

"Was he mad?" Meghan sat cross-legged in an arm chair, hunched over and gripping the phone like it was a lifeline, waiting for Tori's reply.

"Mad? Are you kidding? He was practically hysterical. As in almost on the verge of tears. He thought you were purposely refusing contact. Sobered his ass up right quick, let me tell you."

"Oh my God," Meghan groaned.

"Listen up, Irish. Time to get your head on straight. I sent the guys to D.C. and just heard from the husband. I'd say you'll be hearing from that man of yours soon."

"Are you serious?"

"Yep. Indeed I am. C'mon. You know that Alex is a mess on his best day. Getting all that noise in his head to quiet down is a big undertaking but the brothers are on it, okay? Now don't start overthinking— just go with it. My suggestion—when we hang up, listen to his message. If I know him at all, and believe me I do, it's probably pretty comical."

"My God Tori. What would I do without you?"

"You'd be spinning your wheels in frustration I suppose!" She laughed. "He's coming to you Irish, just like I said he would. Oh, and for the record, it was a quick, bent over the edge of the bed spanking for having run my mouth. But oh baby, was it worth it!"

Meghan barked out a laugh and said, "That's no way to treat a pregnant woman. Even one with a big mouth."

"Are you kidding? There are times when I act like a brat just to make sure he'll pink my ass! Go and listen to the message and try not to laugh. And Meghan, I'll see you soon."

Disconnecting the call, Meghan quickly went to her voicemail and listened to Alex's message. Oh my God, he was adorable. After replaying it five times, she smiled and hugged the phone to her chest. Hearing him stammer and hesitate was priceless. If he still wanted her, she had a ton of stuff to do starting with a trip to the salon for a mani-pedi. First thing tomorrow morning she intended to take up her mother's suggestion and hit the fashion boutiques to find something that would set his hair on fire when she finally saw him face to face.

For the first time in weeks, she actually fell asleep when she hit the bed several hours later.

ALEX CHECKED HIS SUIT jacket pocket for the hundredth time to make sure the ring box was still there as his cab pulled up to the red brick building where Meghan's father worked. He'd planned out what he wanted to say to the man who pretty much held his balls in the palm of his hand. He'd be fucked six ways from Tuesday if he couldn't win him over.

It occurred to him that he'd been on a lot of missions in his time. Serious shit with deadly consequences, the sort of stuff he'd struggled with for years. But nothing he'd done before was as scary or as potentially life-altering as this meeting. The thought was immensely sobering.

Handing the driver the fare and a hefty tip, he climbed from the cab and gathered his wits about him as he stood on the sidewalk eyeing the old red bricks on the façade of the station house as he adjusted his tie, smoothed his hair. Feeling rather like Drae, he pulled on his cuffs until he was satisfied he looked the part he was playing—that of a gentleman and successful businessman with a serious purpose in mind.

Pushing open the door to the station, he stepped inside the ancient police building and swiftly headed for the desk. A serious looking policewoman with an expression that bordered on hostile eyed his approach.

"Is Detective Patrick O'Brien available?" he asked.

"Who's doing the asking?" she bit out. Clearly she had missed out on charm lessons.

This was it, he thought. *Please Lord, don't let me fuck this up.*

"Tell him Alex Marquez would like a word with him on a personal matter."

"Is that so?"" she replied with the charm of a serial killer. "Pahk yer ass over there," she nodded at some dilapidated chairs, "and I'll see if he's accepting callers."

As he took a seat Alex couldn't help but wonder how his Irish goddess had managed to avoid the heavy Boston accent that he'd been hearing from the moment the plane landed.

Looking at his watch he noted the time and wondered how long the irritating intake cop was going to have him sit there and stew before letting Detective O'Brien know he was there.

FRIDAY MORNING HAD BEEN a whirlwind for Meghan and her mother. Starting with a visit to a local salon where they each indulged in spa manicures after an enjoyable stretch in one of those cushy massage chairs while they enjoyed a delightful pedicure, they'd stopped for a restorative jolt of caffeine while they planned out their shopping strategy.

Focusing on a slew of high-end Southie boutiques, they'd visited half a dozen shops where, at her mother's insistence, Meghan tried on nearly every available white dress they could find. In the end she decided on a stunning number that reminded her of something a Jennifer Lopez type might wear. It was form fitting with cap sleeves and a low square neckline that with the right bra would put her tits on glorious display. But what made it really awesome was the silhouette created by dark green material for the back of the dress that wrapped around to frame the front, which was a soft shade of white. The contrasting colors and the way the material hugged her figure highlighted her bodacious curves. There was no way her Major wouldn't need to wipe away a bit of drool when he caught sight of her in the sexy outfit.

Next came a pair of delicious open toed, high heels with an ankle strap that made her legs look amazing. She'd indulged her mother with a pair of sophisticated L.K. Bennett heels that the saleswoman insisted were just like the shoes Duchess Kate wears. Watching her ma twirl and preen before the mirror as she admired the classy footwear was nothing short of delightful. So was the hilarious conversation between her adorable parent and the shop girls about English royalty and how nobody wore shoes or hats better.

Lingerie was next and to her astonishment, Ma had suggested an exclusive boutique that specialized in outrageously sexy underthings. Apparently her mother had a secret guilty pleasure when it came to undergarments. Knowing that Alex really, *really* liked naughty undies, she went a bit overboard and practically bought out everything the store had in her size. Didn't help that Ma was egging her on every step of the way.

Their shopping spree wouldn't be complete without indulging in two over-the-top purchases, a glorious white Hermès bag for Meghan and an outrageous Fendi for her mother. Yeah, it was a bit much, but after all, what good was having all that money if she couldn't go a little crazy at times?

They'd had a ball and while not exactly setting her credit card on fire, they had racked up quite a sum. It was well worth it though not just to spoil her mom but also to see her eyes twinkling with mischievous delight as she prodded Meghan to walk a bit on the wild side.

When Maggie O'Brien suggested in all seriousness to her only daughter that they visit an exclusive, high-end establishment that was for all intents and purposes a friggin' adult boutique specializing in sex toys and naughty accessories, Meghan abruptly pulled the plug on their shopping spree. There was no way she was browsing lube and hand-cuffs with her mother by her side. It was bad enough that she suspected her proper and well-mannered mother was a member of the Vibrator of the Month Club.

After stopping for a late lunch that she still had no appetite for, by the time they got back to the house, Meghan was exhausted. The weeks of stress and unhappiness that eventually made her sick still lingered despite knowing that Alex was finally coming to his senses.

Eventually she gave up any pretense of being productive and went off to take a nap. The last time she'd seen her mother, she was chatting with a neighbor over coffee, but two hours later, after passing the hell out and sleeping like the dead, she awoke to an empty house and what looked like a hastily scribbled note.

Meggie,

Daddy called and asked me to meet him at the station. After, we'll grab dinner. Heat up some leftovers if you're hungry

Ma

Finding herself alone wasn't such a bad thing. The shopping spree had really wiped her out, physically and emotionally. She hadn't been taking care of herself, not by a long shot, and she knew that pulling it together was a necessity.

Still, it was a bit odd—the note her mother left. She knew Maggie had a particular dislike of the station house where her father worked. Hardly a pleasant, happy environment, going there always reminded Ma of the bad people and unspeakable crimes that made up her dad's work-world. Those reminders made her anxious and worried—something the entire family tried to avoid like the plague. Nothing upset everyone's apple cart quicker than an overwrought mother.

And so she forced herself to eat something healthy instead of the ice cream and gallons of coffee that had been keeping her going for the past few weeks. She then curled up on the sofa and mindlessly watched some television. When nothing held her attention, she settled on QVC, eventually becoming engrossed with being *In the Kitchen with David* and ordering a bunch of cool things she thought would please her mother.

Hours later when she was almost dozing under a soft throw blanket with the remote control still clutched in her hand, she heard her parents come home. Sitting up, Meghan stretched and worked out some couch potato kinks just as they walked through the door.

"Hey, you two," she called out. "Have a nice dinner?"

"Prime Rib Friday at Baxter's," her mother replied drily without looking in Meghan's direction.

To say she was surprised by her normally talkative mother's seeming dismissal when she immediately headed for the stairway to the second floor bedrooms was an understatement. What the hell was that all about?

"Off to bed," Maggie called out, flying up the steps like a bat out of hell.

Meghan frowned as she took in her mother's unusual behavior. It was so unlike her. When she found her father staring at her pensively she flinched, surprised.

"Okay, Da," she griped. "What's up? And don't act like you don't know what I'm talking about. Is everything alright at the station?"

"Everything's fine, Meggie," he told her with a half smile that didn't quite reach his eyes.

She sat silently and watched while he wandered here and there around the den as he put on a good show of straightening up a room that didn't have a single thing out of place. Eventually he stopped the charade and turned to face her with a deep expression of love for his only daughter that warmed her heart.

"Any plans for the weekend?" he asked.

Okay, now she really was starting to freak out. The way he asked the question made her wonder what was going on in his head when she heard a slight hesitation in his voice. She couldn't imagine why, but it made her feel like she was being set up for an intervention.

"Yeah, actually," she answered pithily. "Was thinking about getting season tickets for the Yankees," she muttered knowing full well that her dad was a die-hard Red Sox fan.

"Mmm, sounds good," he replied.

What the hell was going on? When Patrick O'Brien didn't so much as react a whit to her statement she knew he was a thousand miles away.

"Um, I think I'll join your ma. It's been a long day. You good, daughter?"

"Yep, Dad. I'm good. See ya in the morning."

And just like that her anxiety level skyrocketed and a ball of worry settled in the pit of her stomach. Something was definitely up but she couldn't begin to imagine what.

MEGHAN AWOKE AFTER YET another restless night, courtesy of the odd behavior her parents displayed the night before. Feeling like she was trapped in a stress bubble that simply would not pop, she lingered in the shower almost draining the water heater in an effort to quiet her troubled emotions.

Having a cop for a father and surrounded as she was by her firefighter and EMT siblings, she couldn't help but worry that she was missing something or that some sort of serious situation was being kept from her.

"Damn alphas," she muttered to the silence in her bedroom. The very last thing she needed were more reminders of a certain domineering and powerful man who still had not surfaced even though Tori insisted he would.

Checking her phone yet again, hoping to see that he'd called or left a message, she was disappointed to see that Alex was still maintaining radio silence. According to the information her friend had shared, his business in Washington had wrapped up—so now the waiting game was in full swing. In all honesty, she wanted quite badly to call him and throw herself at his feet. It didn't even matter anymore about his guilt or his issues or anything for that matter. She'd take him in all his fucked-up glory if it meant being back by his side.

Not bothering to properly dry her hair, Meghan gathered her unruly curls into a messy tangle and secured it with a clip before pulling on a long sleeved tee that had seen better days and a pair of sloppy sweats with the logo of her old school on one hip. Both garments hung off her frame, a stark reminder of the weight she'd lost and her less than robust appearance.

What-fucking-ever. She didn't care. The sad truth was, she wasn't sure she'd ever be able to care about much of anything ever again.

Missing Alex had become a full-time job. One that was eating her alive from the inside out.

"Meggie. Can you come down here a moment?" she heard her mother holler from the first floor.

"I'll be right there, Ma. Just give me a minute," she answered back hastily. "Will you put the coffee pot on?"

"Not a problem," came the answer that seemed a bit more chipper and happy than the way her mother had seemed last night.

Well, thank God for that, she thought. With her own emotions in turmoil, Meghan didn't think she could handle anyone else's problems right now.

DRAE FELT A BIT like a hostage negotiator as he slid from the cab and stood on the sidewalk outside the O'Brien brownstone. Adjusting his tie and tugging on the cuffs of the tailored dress shirt he wore with his Savile Row suit, he took a deep breath and gathered his thoughts. With Victoria anxiously texting him every five minutes and Alex acting like he was about to walk the green mile, he felt the weight of everyone's future bearing down on him. As Cam's last minute back slap and gravely muttered, "Don't fuck up," played over and over in his head, he climbed the short flight of steps and silently prayed for strength.

He knocked and when Maggie O'Brien opened the door, smilingly sweetly and asked, "May I help you?" Drae recalled Alex's words the previous night describing the comely woman as a shark in sheep's clothing.

At first glance he could see where Meghan inherited her beauty. For a woman in her mid-fifties she was extraordinarily attractive with a bombshell figure reminiscent of a fifties Hollywood star—dark auburn hair showing not a bit of gray, a pleasing smile, and the same intense green eyes her daughter shared—she was quite the sight. Irish through and through, she reminded him of a young Maureen O'Hara—which was by no means a bad thing. *Jesus.* If the woman before him was any indication of how Meghan would look in thirty years, Alex was one lucky bastard.

Extending his hand he turned on the St. John charm—something his wife reassured him was sure to get results—and smiled back.

"Mrs. O'Brien? My name is Draegyn St. John. I'm a friend of Meghan's from Arizona." He thought it best to set out the facts from the start so she wouldn't have to cross-examine him. "Is she here?"

The minute his name hit her awareness, the smile changed from brilliant and welcoming to conspiratorial and mischievous.

"Well, it took you long enough," she remarked with a wry grin as she took his hand and pulled him into the house.

Only his years of surveillance training kept the relief that swept through him from showing on his face. Getting through the inevitable conversation he was about to have with Meghan was one thing. Handling the mother who had threatened Alex with bodily harm was another.

As she lead him into what at one time was probably considered the front parlor, she remarked, "Why didn't he come himself?"

Keeping to his charm offensive he smile and winked. "I don't think we're quite there yet, Mrs. O'Brien. I'm here to lay the groundwork so your daughter hopefully won't rip a certain someone's face off before he has a chance to plead his case. If I recall, she had a certain ball busting way about her."

Maggie O'Brien snorted in a not amused at all kind of way. "Yes, well that may have been true before but your Major has done quite the number on her Mr. St. John. You may be surprised by what you find."

Oh, snap. Score one for the grizzly bear Mama protecting her own. She stepped back into the foyer and yelled, "Meggie. Can you come down her a moment?"

When Meghan answered, "I'll be right there, Ma. Just give me a minute. Will you put the coffee pot on?" Drae straightened and thought, *Showtime.*

It took two or three minutes until he detected the sound of someone moving about in the hallway upstairs as all the while those knowing green eyes coolly assessed his every breath and movement. Damn.

This lady was good.

When he finally heard footsteps descending the stairs, Drae found that he was holding his breath. Didn't help that the phone he switched to silent chose that moment to vibrate. There was not a doubt in his mind that it was his spunky wife trolling for an update.

Just as Meghan's feet hit the last step her mother announced, "You've got a visitor, *mo stoirín*." When she moved aside so her daughter could find him with her searching eyes, Drae almost fell over in shock at what he saw.

Fuck. Her mother hadn't been kidding. No words could do justice to the shock that raced through him at Meghan's appearance. In a word, she looked like shit. Being used to seeing her vibrant, full of life, and always perfectly dressed, it was startling to find her barefoot, looking like a homeless person in clothing that seemed several sizes too big, hair a holy mess, and dark smudges under her normally bright eyes.

"Meghan," he choked out, forgetting to hide his reaction from his voice.

The expression on her face went from curious to gut-wrenching surprise in a nanosecond. Part of him wanted to fucking kill Alex for putting that look in her eyes.

"Draegyn," she whimpered a split second before she burst into tears and crumbled to her butt on the last step as painful sobs filled the air.

"Holy Jesus," Drae mumbled as he hurried to her side. "Don't cry honey. Your tears are gonna kill me."

Pulling her to her feet, he wrapped her in a solid embrace as she melted in his arms crying wretchedly. From the corner of his eye he saw her mother wipe away her own tears before she quietly left them alone.

What else could he do except stand there and let her cry it out? The upset he felt at her reaction to finding him in her parlor tore at his emotions. Remembering the way Alex had cold cocked him with a hearty punch to the jaw after Victoria had left him when he'd acted like an insufferable dick early in their relationship, he felt the same impulse come over him. When he got the chance, he just might repay the action with a jab of his own.

The woman shaking uncontrollably in his arms leaned away and looked at him for a second, then threw herself back into his hug, wailing, "I…I never thought I'd see you again."

Yep. He was going to smack the fucking shit out of Alex. If he didn't, Victoria would once he told her about Meghan's emotional breakdown.

Steering her into the parlor, her feet stumbling every step of the way, he tried to calm her down. "Please don't cry anymore, honey. It's not good for you."

Getting her settled on a loveseat, he grabbed a box of tissues from a table and helped dry the tears rolling down cheeks that had sunken in—a sad reminder of how much she'd suffered in the weeks since Alex had sent her packing.

As the emotional storm calmed, she grabbed onto his hand and wouldn't let go. Taking a seat beside her, Drae reached deep inside and brought his reeling emotions under control. Seeing her so distraught made him physically sick as only a man who'd come perilously close to losing the love of his own life could. When he was finished here he was going to call Victoria, profess his undying love over and over, and send her the biggest, most outrageous floral arrangement he could find. *Just because.*

"Sorry," she murmured with a sobbed hiccup. "I haven't been well and seeing you was a shock."

"No need to explain Meghan," he muttered tersely as thoughts of pounding Big Daddy into the dust flashed in his mind's eye. *Fucking asshole.*

"Is he okay?" she asked in a voice way too small for the vivacious woman he knew her to be.

Drae could only shake his head in wonder. *Go figure*, he mused. Here she was, a shadow of her former self, and all she could think of was Alex. He sighed and squeezed her hand.

"He's fine although seeing you like this makes me want to do his ass some serious harm."

"It's not his fault," she quickly tried to reassure him. "He can't help how he feels." Her voice faded to a whisper on her words.

Clenching his jaw, Drae kept his immediate disagreement with what she said to himself. She must love him very much to be so accepting of Alex's emotional failings.

"We need to talk Meghan. You up for what I have to say, honey?"

She nodded as she bit her lip, releasing his hand and sitting back. "You sound so serious Draegyn. Do I want to hear this?" she asked with a frightened little wobble in her delivery.

"Probably not. But it needs to be said and you need to hear it."

"Okay."

Fuck, man. If she bit her lip any harder she was gonna draw blood.

"FIRST OF ALL, HE wants to see you and yes, he knows I'm here. Ordinarily, I wouldn't dream of interfering in either of my brothers' lives but before you and Alex come face to face again, there's something I want to say."

"Tori told me that he…" she said before self-censoring the rest of her response and lowering her eyes so he couldn't guess at the rest of her answer.

Drae chuckled and nudged her with his shoulder. "It's alright Irish," he said using the affectionate nickname for her that his wife favored. "I'm well-aware of my wife's meddling ways."

Meghan blushed and attempted a shaky smile. "I'd have been lost without her all these weeks, Draegyn. Truly. Don't be upset with her."

"Are you fucking kidding?" he barked out laughing. "I'm in no way upset with her, honey. In fact I'm glad, and so is Alex, that she kept the lines of communication open." Shaking his head he added, "You women know how to stick together."

"So do you Justice men," she reminded him somberly.

"Point well taken. Which brings me to the purpose of this visit."

He let some silence wrap around them for a moment—each of them reluctant for what came next. Clearing his throat, he leaned over and impulsively kissed her on the forehead. When she searched his eyes to explain his unexpected action he tried to smile reassuringly.

"Here it is Meghan. In all its fucked-up glory, I need to tell you a little bit about the real Alex Marquez. Without a second's hesitation you should know that in my estimation a more honorable man has never existed. His sense of integrity and the things that ground his morals make him a man amongst men. Understand?"

Her lip quivered but she held it together and nodded at him to go on.

"When we all met, him, Cam and I—we instantly bonded. Even though we each came from distinctively different backgrounds, it was as if for each of us we could see the best in the others. Cam and I with our fucked-up families, and Alex with his picture-perfect childhood may seem like an unlikely trio but when shit gets real, I wouldn't want anyone else by my side. In the beginning we shared a boots on the ground existence. Shit kicking boots at that, the kind we were trained for. Together we dealt with ambushes, undercover assignments, body counts, getting shot at, and an epic crap ton of shit that only happens in war. None of it was pretty. All of it was fucked up. Alex came to the attention of those in power due to his insane tech background and natural leadership abilities. People respected him and counted on his calm under fire. We were all slogging through our third deployment when a maneuver near Kandahar went terribly wrong. After the team leader was wounded it was Alex who stepped up and finished what had been started. Got all of us to safety while also completing the mission. Fuck it if the goddamn brass didn't immediately promote his ass. That's how he eventually becomes a commanding officer. Believe me, he hated the promotion, hated what it meant. He'd have gladly stayed in our team, putting his life on the line in some deadly situations but that's not how shit works in the military."

Drae heard the angry emotion in his voice and dialed it back a bit. No use in scaring the shit out of her. What was done was done where that fucking war was concerned. It was his job to just tell the story and try not to rage out while doing so.

"Every minute of every day that he was in command literally chipped away at his soul. He felt every tragedy, mourned each lost life, and regretted the civilian reactions and the inevitable collateral damage. It wasn't a good time. Not for a man with Alex's moral code. But war and the drive to survive have a way of overriding all those virtuous principles. Not even Cam and I, as close as we were to the Major, knew most of the horror and shit he dealt with. When the suicide bombing happened, the one that took your fiancé's life and almost blew Alex to bits, everything changed in a heartbeat. He actually believed that had he known in advance what the enemy was up to that he could have prevented what happened. Losing control of the perimeter and being attacked from within was a cross he felt was his and his alone to bear. It's bullshit, of course, but that's Alex at his core."

He saw Meghan shudder. "It must have been horrible, Draegyn. The way you talk about the war gives me chills. Back then, I couldn't understand how David could be so blasé about all of it but hearing you explain what it was like for the men and women in harm's way, I think I understand better now."

"Here's the thing Meghan. The way Alex reacted to the anniversary was fucking inevitable. He feels those things deeply. Maybe too deeply and until you came along he was weirdly at peace with spending the rest of his days atoning for what he thought were personal failures. Being around you changed that, and we all saw it but him. Even though his rational mind now admits that he overreacted, it really doesn't change what goes on inside his head. Or his soul. You need to understand that before you make any decisions about the future. He's *always* going to struggle with it. It's who he is. Not even the way he feels about you is going to change that."

"I don't want him to change," she exclaimed. "Truly, I don't. Survivor's remorse is something I understand. Honestly, that he feels that way only makes me care for him more."

"I'm relieved to hear you say that. Cam and I, we'd lay down our lives for Alex. I'm not shitting even a little bit when I say that every day of my life I hope to be half the man he is, and I know Cam feels the same. This wasn't his first moral crisis nor will it be the last. Personally, I hope you two can work this out. You're good for him."

Fixing her with a sly grin he added, "And my wife thinks you're the tits *and* the balls so that obviously has to count."

It was good to see a small smile light up Meghan's face. In fact he would have sworn that as his sad tale was drawing to a close he thought he saw some of the green sparkle returning to her eyes.

"Do you understand what I'm trying to get at, Meghan? Can you take him on those terms, knowing that he's gonna carry that shit inside him forever?"

Tears started spilling down her cheeks again but this time she held on to her composure.

"He's everything to me Draegyn. It nearly killed me to leave but I knew he had to work it out on his own. If being with me was going to cause him pain…well, that's the thing *I* couldn't live with."

Satisfied, Drae drew her into a major bear hug.

"You have a lot of thinking to do, honey. This isn't a rehearsal. You need to be sure how you feel about all of this so you make a decision that's best for you, okay?"

"Should I call him?" she asked.

"Fuck no," he chuckled.

"But…I don't understand. Is he here? In Boston? What am I supposed to do?"

Grinning from ear to ear he laughed. "We're all here. Cam is holding Alex's fucking hand as we speak. That's how this shit goes."

Meghan threw her arms around his neck and kissed him on the cheek. "I love you guys."

"Well, good. Remember to say that to my interfering wife."

"What should I do?"

"You need to think all this through, Irish. Alex knows what's in his heart. You have to be sure of what's in yours."

"Understood," she replied.

"Call me when you're ready, and I'll tell you what happens next."

She rolled her eyes and groaned. "Really?"

"Yep." He thumbed a dark smudge under one of her eyes and mumbled, "He needs a serious ass kicking for putting you through this and that's the very reason why you have to really think this through. It's not going to be easy. Just ask Victoria and Lacey too. We're fucked up, the three of us. Happily ever after comes with a price. The moment you're one hundred percent clear on what you want, you call me, okay?"

"Thanks Draegyn. Will do."

She called him later that afternoon. "I want to see him. Hear what he has to say before I make a decision."

"Wise move," he told her as he swatted Alex's hand away when he tried to grab the phone. "Here's what you're gonna do. Head to the Four Seasons hotel and go to the front desk. Identify yourself and ask for an envelope left for you by Mr. Marquez."

"Are you friggin' kidding? An envelope? What the hell Draegyn!"

Glaring at Alex again for trying to get in on the conversation, he ended the call saying, "What the hell does my wife always say? Bitches like romance? Well, have a little faith Meghan. Ask for the envelope."

He heard her sigh heavily into the phone. "There better be romance in that envelope Mr. St. John, or I swear…."

"That, my dear, is entirely up to you," he laughed.

DRESSED TO THE NINES in her new white dress and sexy shoes, Meghan arrived at the swanky Four Seasons in a bit of a fog. Draegyn's explanation of Alex's time in Afghanistan gave her a lot to think about. She completely understood why he implored her to think it all through before she came to any decisions. Loving Alex Marquez as she did was not a guarantee of an easy future. He had demons and if she took him on, those nightmares and the emotional aftermath were going to be coming along for the ride.

After much deliberation she felt she knew what was in her heart but she needed to hear from the man himself. Needed to know what he was feeling and understand how he saw the future and if there was any place in his life for her.

After stating who she was and asking if anything had been left for her at reception, the terribly proper and uptight man behind the marble counter handed her the envelope Drae had told her to expect.

With trembling hands she peeked inside the envelope and found a room key along with a piece of hotel stationary on which Alex had scribbled, *Another message to follow.*

Meghan struggled during the elevator ride to pull it together as her heart thumped wildly in her chest. It took several tries with the room key to open the door whether from her shaking fingers or the fact that she twice inserted it the wrong way.

She'd never stayed at the Four Seasons in Boston so when the door finally swept open she gasped at the lavish charm of the magnificent Presidential Suite complete with a fireplace and a baby grand piano. Remembering their shared love of music and the many times they'd played the vintage piano at the Villa together, her heart skipped a beat.

In front of her on the table in the foyer was an open laptop next to a display of white roses with a single green rose in the center. Spying a card amongst the flowers, she bit her lips to stop them from quivering when she saw what was written. Once again in Alex's distinctive handwriting he'd scrawled, 'A green rose is the symbol of hope and optimism.' Pushing her face into the elaborate arrangement, Meghan inhaled deeply of the intoxicating scent and willed her nerves to calm.

For a second she had to grip the edge of the antique table for support as her senses and emotions overloaded. When her eyes eventually drifted to the laptop she saw a post it note on the computer that said, 'Press Enter.'

When she did, a picture appeared on the screen. The one she recalled Alex took of her and Zeus snoodling in the bed of the truck that day in the desert. Along one side of the picture were Alex's words.

For me, these past years have been about penance. Atoning for my failings, my actions, and my faults. That was what the war did to me. Living with regret became the air I breathed.
I watched Cameron and Draegyn overcome all that and find happiness. I even helped them see that the past doesn't have to devour the present, all the while cursing myself for things that can't be changed. Salvation wasn't an option for me.
And then you came along, sweet lady. Unexpected. Without judgment. A heart so open and giving, it humbled me.
In a moment of weakness, I was tested ~ and failed again. Something I'm not proud of.

But I'm just a man. Flawed, and yes, afraid. Terrified of what loving you would mean.

Now, it's your forgiveness that I seek.

Meghan~ even though I don't deserve it, you are my absolution and redemption in every way that matters.

I'm not making excuses. I've been an ass, know what I've done—know that I hurt you and let you down. Leaving that morning was unforgivable. Pushing you away was the biggest regret of my life and that's saying a lot.

If it's too late ~ I'll understand.

If there's even the slightest chance ~ go to the bedroom and open the box on the bed

P.S. Your dog misses you

Meghan's heart was beating so fast she had a hard time swallowing. Looking toward the open doors leading to the bedroom, she saw a blue box lying on the muted gold bedspread.

On feet that didn't feel like they were touching the floor, she drifted toward the box like a fragment of metal being drawn by a powerful magnet.

Alex had given her so many gifts during their time together. All of which she left behind in Arizona. This one however, felt gigantic. She knew, whatever it was, some sort of crossroads was involved.

Shaking like a leaf, she lifted the lid with trembling fingers and separated the blush colored tissue paper to find a stunning gold bracelet hung with two small hearts. On one heart the word *Mine* was engraved and the other read *Yours*. The hearts faced each other when they dangled, so the evocative words touched. Just like the words lovers whisper in the night, they were meant for just the two of them.

Underneath the bracelet was a small card. Her heart clutched as she read what he'd written.

If the hearts have no meaning, leave the bracelet, and I'll understand.

But ~ if you feel the way I do, put the bracelet on and text me the first thing that comes to mind.

Meghan was having one of those out-of-body moments that she

knew would define her life from this moment on. If she put the bracelet on, she'd be opening herself up to a future with her fucked-up, damaged Major that she knew in her soul would be no easy ride. But if she walked away, she'd be leaving her heart behind and that was something she just couldn't do.

There really wasn't a decision to make. Fate had already made it for her. Fastening the bracelet around her wrist, she felt tears welling in her eyes at how right it felt and how perfectly the two hearts lay against each other.

"Oh baby," she murmured in the silence of the empty room.

Retrieving her bag from where she'd dropped it in the foyer, she fished around for her cell phone as she walked aimlessly around the magnificent living room. Bringing up a message screen, she paused. What should she say? He asked her to text the first thing that came to mind. Taking a deep breath she typed in '*Yours*' and pressed send.

Less than five seconds later she heard a sound across the suite and spun around in time to see Alex walking through the door, his phone clutched in his hand and a look of utter astonishment on his face. In that moment she knew with absolute certainty, when all his defenses were down, that he hadn't been at all sure what her answer would be. She'd never loved him more.

Eyes locked, they made their way to the other. Meghan thought her big, hunky lover was amazing with his scraggly beard and mussed hair, when he dressed in jeans molded to his hard body that made her brain melt. But the sight of him in a tailored business suit that fit him like a second skin, clean-shaven and groomed like a damn movie star, her heart started thumping wildly again. The man was magnificent, and it was all she could do not to climb on him like a tree.

Before the titillating thought faded, she was caught completely off guard when Alex dropped to his knee at her feet. Blinking in confusion, she searched his face and then stopped breathing when he reached into his jacket pocket and pulled out a black velvet jewelry box.

In the silence of the room she actually heard the box creak open as he lifted the lid to reveal a dazzling ring with a large Asher cut diamond in a raised antique setting surrounded by emeralds.

"Meghan Elizabeth O'Brien. You are the love of my life. You've saved me in every way a man who was lost and alone could be saved.

You are more precious to me than you could possibly understand, and I will cherish and adore you every moment of our lives."

He took the ring from its cushion and gestured to her. Without hesitation, Meghan gave him her hand as a single tear made its way from the corner of her eye and drifted slowly down her cheek.

Sliding the beautiful ring onto her finger, he asked in a voice choked heavy with emotion, "Will you stand by my side from this second forward and do me the honor of being my wife?"

There were no words she could say, so she dropped to her knees and fell into his waiting arms, the warmth and promise of his embrace meaning as much as the words he'd just spoken.

With her tear-soaked face pressed into his neck, Meghan felt all the pain and confusion of the last weeks evaporate. She was back where she belonged and that was all that mattered.

"I love you, baby," she groaned in a voice that offered an eloquent glimpse into how badly she'd been hurting without him.

"Is that a yes?" he murmured. She heard the hopefulness in his voice along with a rare flash of nervousness that made her tighten her arms around him.

Pulling back to look into his eyes when she gave her answer, Meghan lost control when she saw that his cheeks were also covered in tears. With profound reverence, she placed her hands on either side of his handsome face and kissed them away.

"Of course it's a yes. How could it be any answer other than yes? Don't cry baby. I *love* you, and everything's going to be alright." She put her lips on his with all the love and promise she could gather in a kiss meant to heal.

"Oh my God, Meghan," he groaned. "I love you so much. You'll never know how sorry I am for what I put you through."

He was pressing gentle kisses all over her face and neck while she clung to him, her body pressed tight against his, just like the two hearts dangling on the bracelet.

"I'm so proud of you," she whispered.

Alex looked at her, a little shell-shocked and a lot confused. "I haven't done anything to be proud of," he grumbled, his beautiful eyes expressing soulful regret. "Especially not where you're concerned."

She poured her heart into the gaze she fixed on his face. "Oh, but you have. Finding your way through the dark is no easy thing, my love. It takes great courage to let go of the past, and I'm going to make sure you never regret it."

They kissed then, still on their knees, wrapped in one another's embrace. It was the sort of kiss that hopeless romantics dream of and write about.

Alex was at peace for the first time in his adult life that he could recall. Hearing Meghan express her love had moved him beyond words. He meant it when he told her she'd saved him. The redemption he'd been seeking all these years was right there in her arms. Just like Cameron and Draegyn before him, finding his soul through the love of another had finally sent the demons packing and laid the past to rest.

When he'd burst into the suite it had upset him greatly to see evidence of how his woman had been suffering these last weeks, making him wish Drae had punched his lights out when he came back from visiting her instead of glaring at him with reproach blazing in his eyes. He'd given Alex the dressing down of his life, shaming him with angry caustic words as he laid into him, describing in horrifying detail Meghan's loss of vibrancy and the telltale evidence of illness visible on her face. Seeing her in the flesh again, he made a silent vow to put her needs, her safety, and her wellbeing above his own from this day forward. Never again would he be selfish enough to subject her to such pain and confusion. She was far too precious, the gift she was giving by trusting him with her heart and soul marked him forever after.

Somehow they made it from their knees into the bedroom but it wasn't Alex who had gotten them there. He knew that because their progress wasn't stopped until it was his legs connecting with the bed as Meghan feverishly writhed against him. Overcome with emotion, he held her in his arms and crushed her magnificent body to his.

Taking her hand, he lifted it to his mouth and kissed her knuckles above where his ring now sat. The symbol of his possession twinkled in the sunlight filtering through the sheer panels covering the windows. Still holding her hand, which he was thrilled to feel was trembling slightly, he twirled her around so her back was facing him.

Sweeping aside her hair, he undid the button of her dress; kissed the tiny swath of skin he'd exposed, and then slowly pulled the zipper down. He made a silent vow then and there to *always* be there to unzip her so she would not only know just who she belonged to, but who worshiped her beyond measure.

When the dress was undone, he spread apart the sides and ran his fingers down the skin of her back right to the place where her ass started to flare. Pushing the sexy two-toned dress that showcased her gorgeous curves off her shoulders, Alex had to quickly swallow when it wafted to the floor and he saw sheer white panties that left little to his imagination. There was nothing about her fucking ass that he didn't adore and seeing it displayed in all its glory in the see-through silk got him hard as stone in seconds.

The plump curve of her backside was begging for his touch. Sighing with a mixture of lust and appreciation, he caressed her through the delicate silk as she stepped out of the dress and kicked it aside. She didn't waste any time spinning around on her sexy high heels with a wicked expression on her face that let him know they were totally in sync. Of course the equally sheer and just as sexy bra that made her already delicious breasts look like a dream come true only added to her naughty appeal.

Reaching for his tie, she deftly loosened it before sliding the jacket off his shoulders where it joined her dress on the floor. Alex's lips curled into a half-smile when she all but shredded his shirt in her haste to undress him.

He hated taking her outrageous shoes off, but he didn't have much choice if he didn't want to end up with the heels digging in to his flesh. Before long they were on the bed, half-naked, limbs entwined, whispering words of love between deep, wet kisses. Entangled as they were, first with him crushing her body into the mattress and then with her sprawled on top of him, his hands made quick work of her lingerie. When he'd bared her to his touch he rolled her beneath him and removed his briefs, caressing her magnificent breasts with his eyes.

Wearing nothing but his ring and the delicate gold bracelet with the two hearts, Alex made love to her with a passion that made her cry out in ecstasy. As she moaned and whimpered underneath his powerful frame, he flexed his hips and ground against her deep and slow until neither of them could take it anymore. With her legs wrapped around his waist as she clung with trembling arms to his neck, and he kissed her with all the love he had in his heart and soul, propelling them both to a staggering climax. In the aftermath, his beautiful Meghan sobbed softly in his arms, telling him with her tears and quivering body how much she adored him. After the erotic storm had passed, he cradled her on his chest and let the moment speak for itself.

Eventually, she raised her head and smiled with those sexy green eyes that didn't hide anything from him.

"I asked your father for permission to marry you," he told her. He thoroughly enjoyed the look of total shock that spread across her face. She hadn't expected that.

Alex was an old-fashioned guy at heart. Having fallen in love for the first and last time in his life, he intended to experience every facet of the journey. Manning up and asking for her hand hadn't been easy or comfortable. Patrick O'Brien had not made the request an easy one. Especially not after he threatened Alex with deadly consequences if he, God forbid, hurt his precious daughter as he had ever again. He'd felt like a gladiator fighting for his life when her brothers appeared on the scene and breathed fire in his direction while her quiet mother blew her disapproving wrath at him.

"What?" she squeaked. "When?"

He smiled and cuddled her close. "Yesterday."

"Wait, wait, wait, wait, wait," she burst out bewilderedly. "You talked to my dad? Yesterday?" She made the *yesterday* sound like someone was in danger of getting his or her ass kicked.

"Yes. And your mother and brothers too. They're a scary bunch. Deval threatened to castrate me and your mom, who I might add is in no way a lady when she's pissed, told me rather bluntly what she planned on doing with my balls if I didn't make things right with you."

"Oh my God! You're serious, I can tell. That explains why my parents acted so strange last night." Alex felt her smile when she pressed her face into his chest and giggled.

"Damn right I'm serious. I had to show your mom the ring and all but agreed to a fucking cathedral wedding, which by the way will be officiated by my Uncle Eduardo. I've already checked with him to make sure it was possible."

Meghan chuckled and snuggled against him. "Holy shit. My parents will be parish royalty once it gets out that there's a priest in the family."

"And my family, by the way, is equal parts stunned and thrilled that an Irish goddess was foolish enough to fall for my sorry ass shit. That's a direct quote from my sisters."

Her head flew up, and she looked him in the eye. "You told them even before I said yes? What if I'd walked out of here and left the bracelet and you behind?"

"Sweetheart, I loved you enough to lay it all on the line. Asking your parents and telling my family meant that no matter what happened, I was owning both my feelings and whatever your decision would be," he told her solemnly.

She trailed her fingers softly across his lips and leaned in for a quick kiss. "Then you're lucky I'm so in love with you."

He laughed and hugged her tight. "And to be clear, if you *had* walked out of here, I would have stalked that sexy ass of yours for an eternity until you eventually caved and forgave me."

"What happens now?" she purred. He loved the sound of his woman when she was contented.

"Well, there's an easy answer to that my beautiful and amazing love. I believe your mother is packing your bags as we lay here—which means had you said no she would have had to knock some sense into that head of yours—and then we are boarding the agency jet as soon as we can."

"Why?" she groaned. "Can't we just enjoy the moment?"

"No can do, *Mi hermosa esposa*," he informed her in perfectly accented Spanish. "That means my beautiful wife which is exactly what you will be in as quick a way as possible. First, you have to say yes to a dress and secondly, your sister-in-law-to-be is about to give birth any day. She has specifically asked for you to be present when the baby arrives, and I'm to tell you to bring the camera."

Alex was startled when his naked fiancée leapt off his chest and landed beside the bed in a move that would make the most graceful of jungle cats jealous. "Get your ass in gear. Major. All you needed to say was *the baby's coming*. That's something I don't intend to miss!"

He sighed dramatically and sat up, quirking an eyebrow at her. "Giving orders already, are we? Don't you have to wait for the vows first?"

She grinned at him and palmed her luscious tits. When his eyes flared with appreciation she pouted prettily and teased, "You can tie me to the bed when we get home. *If you hurry.*"

Hearing her refer to the Villa as *home* melted his heart as his barking laughter met her naughty suggestion. Sitting up he swung his legs over the side of the bed and pulled her to stand between his thighs.

"Whatever your heart desires my sexy fuck goddess. I am yours to command," he told her touching the two hearts dangling from the bracelet.

"Mine," he growled a second before his lips latched on to a pouting nipple.

"Yours," she sighed. Moments later she speared her fingers into his hair and yanked his head back. "Mine," she growled at him.

"Completely yours," he agreed.

It would be a long time after that before they actually got around to checking out of the hotel.

Epilogue

"HE'S SO BEAUTIFUL," MEGHAN cooed as she cradled Dylan Henry Cameron in her arms. The perfect combination of his mother and father, he had pale skin, soft dark hair, sweet lips, and deep blue eyes.

She wasn't sure who looked more ecstatic. Cameron, who couldn't quite get over the fact that he had a son, or Lacey who appeared to all the world like a beatific angel mother as she gazed adoringly at her infant son and devoted husband. Such rapturous joy was beautiful to witness.

Alex slapped Cam on the back and congratulated his brother with undisguised affection. Not able to forgo a playful jab, he teased the new father in a conspiratorial tone. "Just think. If Drae and Tori have a girl, it could be the start a Justice dynasty."

Draegyn laughed heartily and hugged his wife close. "Dynasty my ass! Should the newest St. John be of the female persuasion, in addition to a gun-toting father, she will have a fire breathing dragon to keep all male suitors away."

Tori chuckled and rubbed her round belly. "We'll know in a few months but either way, Family Justice is expanding. Oh, and by the way everyone, my mother is coming for a visit before it's my turn in the birthing suite so you'll all be expected to act accordingly." Turning a sweet-as-pie look on Meghan she teased, "You're up next in the baby sweepstakes, Irish."

Meghan blushed and looked quickly at her hunky fiancé. Planning a wedding was just a sideshow to what was really driving both of them. As far as she was concerned they couldn't get married quickly enough. When they'd talked of having children, Alex had made it clear that he wanted a family with her. And by that he meant *now* and not some vague time in the future. Meghan hadn't been able to concentrate on anything else ever since.

Sure, a big flashy wedding with all the bells and whistles was one of those fantasies most girls dream of but the truth was, the idea of having a baby with her husband-to-be was a thousand times more appealing. A wedding was just a moment in time—building a family was something they would share for a lifetime.

Meghan handed the sweet baby boy swaddled in a pale blue blanket to her Major and beamed with love when he eagerly cuddled his new nephew. Watching him lean down and press a soft kiss on the baby's brow melted her insides.

Lacey looked around the hospital room, sniffed and then wiped away a tear bringing Meghan and Tori quickly to her side. "My family," was all she needed to say. The poignancy of those words from someone who'd been abused and abandoned as a child filled the room with emotion. The look Cameron gave his Ponytail touched Meghan's heart.

Leave it to Tori to lighten up the mood and bring the giggles. She quickly snapped her iPhone into the dock on Lacey's nightstand and scrolled till she found what she'd been looking for. Next thing anyone knew, the sound of Sister Sledge singing "We are Family" filled the room.

As Alex cradled the first in the next generation of sons and daughters who would make their unusual family even stronger, with his brothers Cam and Drae smiling contentedly at his side, their women rocked out with glee as Tori and Meghan shimmied and danced around the room while the three sisters-in-law sang their new theme song and welcomed the future they'd dreamed of.

It should go without saying, but... *And They All Lived Happily Ever After*.

And the story doesn't end there!
Coming Soon......

FAMILY JUSTICE

Catch up with Cameron & Lacey
Draegyn & Victoria
and
Alex & Meghan
when Tori's mother, Stephanie Bennett comes for a visit

Acknowledgements

First and foremost, I want to express my undying gratitude to **Jenny Sims**, the best editor anyone could ask for. You came into my life at the perfect moment, with your mad skills, wit and encouragement and have 'hands down' changed my life.
Jenny, in case you didn't know it, you were the first.

Thanks to my talented cover designer, **Ashley Baumann**.
Her job can't be easy! It takes someone unique to read between the lines and bring a book cover vision to life. You did my Justice brothers justice!

Thank you to **Stacey Blake** ~ the best formatter on the planet.
I got choked up the first time I saw the formatted copy of Book 1.
The dog tags were an inspiration!

Special thanks to **Rebecca Bennett** and **Nicole Huffman** for jumping in and being such awesome PA's. You've been a *huge* help. It's taken an enormous, stressful weight off my shoulders knowing you're on the job so I can focus on the stories and not get all worked up about some of the pesky details.

A million butterscotch candies and more hugs and kisses than can be showered on three people in a hundred lifetimes go to my **daughter** and **grandsons**.
The best moments of my life are when they are around.
That said, I'll think twice before ever asking again, "Is it clear? Can I go now?"

~Onward~

About the Author

Suzanne Halliday writes what she knows and what she loves – sexy adult contemporary romance with strong men and spirited women. Her love of creating short stories for friends and family has developed into a passion for writing romantic fiction with a sensual edge. She finds the world of digital, self-publishing to be the perfect platform for sharing her stories and also for what she enjoys most of all – reading. When she's not on a deadline you'll find her loading up on books to devour.

Currently a wanderer, she and her family divide their time between the east and west coast, somehow always managing to get the seasons mixed up. When not digging out from snow or trying to stay cool in the desert, you can find her in the kitchen, 80's hair band music playing in the background, kids running in and out, laptop on with way too many screens open, something awesome in the oven, and a mug of hot tea clutched in one hand.

Visit her at:

Facebook https://www.facebook.com/SuzanneHallidayAuthor

Twitter@suzannehalliday

Blog http://suzannehallidayauthor.blogspot.com

Check out the Pinterest Boards for my stories
I love getting feedback from readers!
http://www.pinterest.com/halliday0383/

Printed in Great Britain
by Amazon